SEABORNE

THE LOST PRINCE

SEABORNE

BOOK ONE

THE
LOST PRINCE

MATT MYKLUSCH

EGMONT
Publishing

New York

EGMONT

We bring stories to life

First published by Egmont Publishing, 2015
443 Park Avenue South, Suite 806
New York, New York 10016

Text copyright © Matt Myklusch 2015
Map copyright © Adam F. Watkins 2015
All Rights Reserved

1 3 5 7 9 8 6 4 2

www.egmontusa.com

LIBRARY OF CONGRESS
CATALOGING-IN-PUBLICATION DATA
Myklusch, Matt.
The lost prince / Matt Myklusch.
pages cm. -- (Seaborne ; book 1)
Summary: When thirteen-year-old Dean Seaborne's latest spy mission for the Pirate King
takes him to the mythical island of Zenhala, his life changes as he fights to prove that he
is the island's long-lost prince.
ISBN 978-1-60684-525-7 (hardcover)
[1. Pirates--Fiction. 2. Princes--Fiction. 3. Spies--Fiction. 4. Islands--Fiction.] I. Title.

PZ7.M994Lo 2015
[Fic]--dc23

2014025071

ISBN 978-1-60684-525-7
eBook ISBN 978-1-60684-526-4

Printed in the United States of America

For Dean, a treasure more precious than gold

THE
GREAT STORM

BERMUDA TRIANGLE

Here there be monsters

ZENHALA

THE
GREAT STORM

Part One

HIS MAJESTY'S SECRET SERVICE

CHAPTER 1

SWIMMING WITH SHARKS

I don't suppose it would change anything if I said I was sorry...."

Dean Seaborne looked around the ship with a strained smile as rain fell hard against his shivering body. His words hung in the air like a bad joke. Gallows humor doesn't work when coming from a thirteen-year-old boy who is about to die. Dean was terrified thinking about the punishment his captain had planned for him. It wouldn't be long now, and it wouldn't be pretty. Most pirates made you walk the plank if you crossed them. Not this captain. Not One-Eyed Jack. He was a bit more creative. He also happened to be the pirate king of the Caribbean, and like it or not, that made him Dean's boss. At least, for as long as Dean was still alive.

Dean gulped as One-Eyed Jack gave him a look mean enough to make a killer squid spill its ink. He was a large, barrel-chested man with a head like a cannonball, and the battle-worn face of a bare-knuckle boxer. His black leather eye patch, bald pate, and sun-scarred skin gave him a fierce, grisly countenance that was well earned, for he was a mad combination of short temper and violent rage. His name was known throughout the Caribbean as a merciless buccaneer, and otherwise-dauntless men trembled before him—his own crew most of all.

One-Eyed Jack had been known to keelhaul men over such minor transgressions as not laughing hard enough at his jokes, or remarking that the weather was hot when he had already decided it was merely warm. Whether or not he had even told anyone how he felt about the weather was beside the point. One-Eyed Jack was not a man to be trifled with by anyone or anything.

Dean felt the tip of a dagger in his back as one of One-Eyed Jack's men nudged him toward a rusty iron cage. It was One-Eyed Jack's right-hand man, Scurvy Gill, a slender, filthy pirate with eyes in the back of his head. Gill's only job was to watch the captain's back, and nothing got by him except perhaps a bar of soap. Black water ran off his body as the falling rain washed over him, but no storm on earth could scrub his grubby hide clean. Dean stepped inside the cage and ran his hands along the bars. He was thin enough to squeeze out between them, but he wouldn't get the chance to try. Scurvy Gill pulled a red cloth out of his pocket, blew his nose with it, and offered it to Dean. "Blindfold?"

Dean's lip curled upward. "No. Thank you." If he was going to die today, he would go to his grave without Scurvy Gill's handkerchief wrapped around his head, thank you very much. The cloth smelled of rotten eggs, pickles, and very pungent mucus. Just the thought of it gave Dean the chills. He felt as though he'd dodged a musket ball when Scurvy Gill tucked the cloth back into his pocket, even as the door to Dean's cage slammed shut.

"Hoist away, lads," ordered One-Eyed Jack.

A team of pirates pulled on a thick rope, and Dean's cage rose a foot off the deck. "Whoa." Dean grabbed hold of the bars for balance as the strongest men on the ship heaved away at the line. It ran through a pulley at the end of a yardarm high above his head. The other end was tied to an eyelet at the top of his cage. One-Eyed Jack's crew hauled Dean up over the gunwale and swung him out over the waves. A piercing wind blew right through him as he hung there, trapped and helpless. It was a cold, wet morning, and charcoal-gray clouds filled the sky.

One-Eyed Jack put a hand out to catch a few raindrops. "Looks to me you've seen your last sunrise, boy. Mr. Gill, have our guests arrived?"

"Got their invitation right here, Cap'n." Scurvy Gill dumped a bucket of chum over the side. Moments later, a group of large dorsal fins swirled about in the water below. Dean's eyes went as wide as sand dollars, and his stomach tied itself into an icy knot.

He shook the bars of his cage. "Captain, please! I'm begging you, don't do this!"

One-Eyed Jack snorted out a small laugh. "You call that begging?" He spat something sticky and brown onto the deck. "You're not even trying." He nodded to his men. They let the rope slip and caught it just above the waves. Dean leapt about the cage as sharks snapped at his toes. He grabbed the bars above his head and pulled his feet up. "Help!" he cried as he held on for dear life. "Somebody, please!"

The crew of pirates laughed. One-Eyed Jack leaned out toward Dean with a hand cupped behind his ear. "What's that, Seaborne? I can't hear you all the way up here. For a second, it sounded like you were asking my crew for help!" He turned to face his men, looking very much amused. "What say you, lads? Anyone care to lend the boy a hand? Scurvy Gill, how about you?"

Scurvy Gill bit a dirty fingernail and shook his head. "Sorry, Cap'n. I'm busy."

One-Eyed Jack nodded. "Of course. Your personal hygiene comes first, I know that." He put on a mock frown and turned back toward Dean. "Sorry, son. Scurvy Gill says he's busy." He turned up his palms. "What can I say? I tried."

Dean clung to the bars as One-Eyed Jack snickered away, safe on the deck of his ship. He was having a jolly good time as the sharks poked their noses up out of the water below. Dean was angry with himself for crying out like that. He knew no one was coming to his aid. His nerves had gotten the better of him was all.

"It's your own fault you're in there, you know," said One-Eyed Jack, turning serious for a moment. "Running away after all I've given you . . . what were you thinking? Thanks to me, you had food! Shelter! Gainful employment! I would have thought that earned me some small modicum of gratitude, but no. You choose to repay me by deserting your brethren in the Black Fleet. By deserting *me*!" One-Eyed Jack touched his fingers to his chest. "You wound me, Seaborne, truly. My feelings . . . they're hurt!"

Dean grunted as he shifted his grip on the iron bars of his cage. He couldn't believe what he was hearing. First of all, One-Eyed Jack wasn't like normal people. He didn't have feelings. Second of all . . . Food? Shelter? *Gainful employment?* Was he serious? The most Dean could say for One-Eyed Jack was that he'd given him a job, and a lousy one at that. One-Eyed Jack had a fleet of ships, an army of pirates, and a vast network of spies. Dean was one of his best. Spies like him stowed away on ships and found out what they were carrying, infiltrated their ranks before raids, and even spied on One-Eyed Jack's own men from time to time, just to keep an eye on things. Sure, Dean got food and shelter, but there wasn't much beyond the unreliable protection of his fellow pirates, and a moldy slice of bread now and then.

Working as a spy in One-Eyed Jack's service was a miserable existence with a bleak future. Dean hated it. More than anything, he hated scouting ships for the pirate fleet to raid. He felt like the angel of death delivering innocent sailors into the hands of One-Eyed Jack and his men. It had been different when he was just a small child. Back then, he didn't have any choice but to go along. Now that he was thirteen years old, Dean had decided that he didn't want that life anymore. He didn't belong with One-Eyed Jack and his band of cutthroats. He was tired of being Dean Seaborne, pirate spy. He wanted something better. He wanted a new life. Now he had one coming his way, all right ... the afterlife.

"I thought you was supposed to be a smart one, Seaborne!" Scurvy Gill tapped the inside of his left forearm. "Ain't no use runnin' when yer so easy to spot."

Seaborne frowned at the mark that had been tattooed on his own left arm. Every one of One-Eyed Jack's spies had been given their own unique brand. Dean's was in the shape of three wave crests rising inside a circle. Dean kept the mark covered up most of the time, but sooner or later, someone always saw it. After he didn't report back from his last assignment, the word went out to all the other spies that he was a deserter, and One-Eyed Jack wanted him found. It was only a matter of time before he was spotted, captured, and taken to the island of St. Diogenes for punishment. Now he was back on One-Eyed Jack's ship, the *Maelstrom*, dangling in a giant lobster trap over a family of hungry sharks.

Dean's arms and legs were getting tired. He couldn't hang up there at the top of the cage forever. He shifted his grip again, muttering under his breath. "Maybe if I was as filthy as you, this mark would have gone unnoticed, Gill."

"What's that, boy?" Scurvy Gill asked.

"Nothing!"

The grime-ridden pirate scowled. "Take 'im down again!"

The pirates let go of the line, and Dean's cage dropped for a second time. He wasn't ready for it. Dean lost his grip and fell right along with the cage. He hit the bottom and tried to get up quickly, but his feet slipped through the bars and down into the water. He pulled himself up, fast as he could, just before the sharks could bite off his legs. He got a firm stance with the arch of each foot resting on the bars at the base of the cage. Seawater splashed up past his ankles, and a frenzy of sharks filled the water beneath him. Dean screamed as the cage rocked from side to side. Hundreds of ravenous teeth pressed up from below, desperate for a mouthful of flesh and bone. Before the sharks got him, Dean felt the cage rise up out of the water. The pirates on deck pulled him back up. Scurvy Gill and the rest of the men were laughing hysterically. Dean gritted his teeth. This was fun for them. Live entertainment for as long as it lasted. What could be better?

"Any last words, Seaborne?" One-Eyed Jack waved at the laughing pirate crew. "Maybe you want to ask this lot for help again?"

Dean took a deep breath. Anger wasn't going to get him

anywhere. All he could do was throw himself at the mercy of the pirate king's court. "Captain, I'm sorry I ran off. It was a mistake. I can see that now. Please, give me another chance. I'll do anything."

"Why would I want to do that?"

"Because I'm good at my job! Captain, you know I am. I'm a good spy. I eluded your men for nearly a month at sea. I can't remember anyone ever lasting that long on the run, can you?"

"Reminding me of your crimes is *not* the way back into my good graces."

"I'm sorry, sir. Truly, I am. Please, I've never let you down before, have I?"

One-Eyed Jack tilted his head to the side. "No, you haven't. That's what makes this so difficult. You had a future here, Seaborne. I was actually starting to like you."

Really? 'Cause I can't stand you. Dean bit his tongue and wiped a mixture of rain and sweat from his brow. "Like I said, Captain, it was a mistake. I just . . . I didn't understand how important it was to you that I stay a spy."

One-Eyed Jack's expression turned wild, and he straightened his back with a start. Dean got a cold feeling in the pit of his stomach. He didn't know what he'd just said, but it had clearly been the wrong thing to say.

"Important? *You?* Important?"

One-Eyed Jack drew his cutlass and stormed over toward the men holding the rope. He raised his sword high, looking to cut the line that held up Dean's cage. The crew scattered and Dean's stomach shot up to his chest as he felt the cage drop. He took a deep breath as the white water and swarming sharks raced up at him from below. Dean plummeted into the wild sea, completely submerged. Cold seawater stung his eyes as a blurry vision of sharks surrounded him. They banged against the cage's rusty iron bars, pounding it with all their might.

This is it, thought Dean. *I'm dead.* Even so, his survival instincts kicked in. He resisted the urge to scream, trying to keep his lungs filled with air as long as possible. The sharks pushed forward, and he waved his arms frantically, trying to push himself back. There were more sharks behind him, on top of him, and below him. Dean saw nothing but bubbles, churning water, and teeth. It felt like every shark in the sea was outside his cage, and all of them were starving. The biggest of the bunch, a great white, was the hungriest. Dean's heart pounded in his chest as the relentless predator bashed into the rusty iron door of his cage again and again.

The shark wedged its nose in between the bars and spread its jaws wide. As Dean's short life flashed before his eyes, he remembered the tale of an old sea dog who had once boasted that he'd survived an encounter with a great white. The old man's story was that he had punched the shark square in the nose, and it had swum off like a frightened minnow. Dean hadn't believed a word of it at the time, but at this point, anything was worth a shot. He slammed the palm of his hand into the shark's nose, hard as he could. It was an action he regretted almost immediately. The shark didn't swim away. Instead, it was as if Dean had energized the beast. Enraged, the shark redoubled its efforts to get him, pushing forward so hard that the bars of his cage began to bend. There was nowhere for Dean to go.

Just when Dean had lost all hope, his cage was hoisted out of the water. He gasped for air and crawled into a corner of the cage as it climbed higher and higher above the waves. Trembling, Dean looked down at the primal chaos below. The sharks were still circling, and the great white was thrashing about, visibly angry about its stolen meal. The cage drew level with the *Maelstrom*'s cannons, and Dean saw the crew tugging on the line. One-Eyed Jack hadn't cut it after all.

One-Eyed Jack stood with a foot on the ship's railing. He pointed the tip of his blade at Dean. "I see what the problem is now. You're getting too big for your britches. Don't be getting all high and mighty on me, boy. There's nothing important about *you*. What's important is that everyone knows there's only one way out of the pirate king's service—death. Are we clear?"

Dean nodded rapidly. "Aye aye, Captain. Yes, sir. Absolutely."

One-Eyed Jack stared Dean down for a few seconds before he finally lowered his cutlass. "Reel him in, men."

The crew pulled Dean's cage back over the deck of the ship and opened up the cage. Dean fell out face-first and collapsed with his cheek pressed against the floor. Never before had the mildew-soaked timber of the *Maelstrom* smelled so sweet.

One-Eyed Jack stayed at the railing of the ship, looking out on the horizon. "Today's your lucky day, Seaborne. I'm going to give you that second chance you were hoping for."

Once again, Dean couldn't believe his ears. He leapt to his feet. "Thank you, Captain! You won't regret this. You won't! I swear, I'll never—"

"Quiet yourself before I change my mind!"

Dean buttoned his lip.

"Make no mistake, this decision isn't born out of any affection for you. The only reason you're alive right now is because I have a task for which you happen to be ideally suited." One-Eyed Jack turned to face Dean. "I want you to look in on one of my ships. The *Reckless*. You know it?"

Dean searched his memory. "The *Reckless*... Captain Harper's ship?"

One-Eyed Jack wagged a finger at Dean. "*My* ship. They're all my ships. Remember that."

"Yes, sir. Of course, sir." Dean was being very careful not to say anything that might trigger One-Eyed Jack's infamous temper once again. For the moment, his head was off the chopping block, and he meant to keep it that way. He could scarcely believe he was back on the ship at all, but he was starting to understand why his life was spared. "Gentleman" Jim Harper was more than just the captain of the *Reckless*. He was the youngest captain in the Black Fleet—the leader of the Pirate Youth. One-Eyed Jack was right; Dean was ideally suited for this job.

Scurvy Gill came up behind Dean and put a hand on his shoulder. "The cap'n's been hearin' some rumblings about Harper lately. Last few payments from the *Reckless* have been a bit light. Word is, Gentleman Jim's holdin' out on us. Yer going to find out what's what, savvy?" Dean nodded, but Scurvy Gill wasn't finished. He leaned in close. "If ya don't come back this time, we'll do a lot worse than feed ya to the sharks, understand?"

Dean winced. Scurvy Gill's breath smelled like a dead octopus. "I understand." He pulled away from Gill's grip and turned to One-Eyed Jack. "I'll do you proud, Captain."

Scurvy Gill kicked Dean's legs out and shoved him to the deck. "Never mind that. Just do yer job."

Dean stayed down as One-Eyed Jack walked over to where he was. "Aye, Seaborne. Do your job. Get inside, gain the man's trust, and report back what you see. Quickly. You've officially used up the last of my patience. You don't want to be disappointing me again."

"No, sir."

One-Eyed Jack walked off, and Dean sat up. For once, the two of them were in total agreement. Dean definitely didn't want to disappoint him again. He had been given a second chance. There would not be a third. Dean resolved to look at things differently from here on in. It was time for him to count his blessings and resign himself to the fact that he was a pirate spy, for better or for worse. If he was very lucky, he'd live to be an old pirate spy. *This is my life*, Dean thought. *This is it.*

CHAPTER 2

BEEN CAUGHT STEALIN'

Dean studied Gentleman Jim Harper from across the crowded tavern. It wasn't hard to see how the man had gotten his name. He was a handsome rogue, sharply dressed in a spotless black frock coat and brilliant blue doublet. His mustache and goatee were neatly trimmed, and his long, auburn hair was washed clean. Gentleman Jim took more pride and care in his appearance than any pirate Dean had ever seen. Dean watched him at cards with the other pirates at his table. Gentleman Jim cut a dashing figure, but he was tougher than he appeared at first glance. His shoulders were broad, his hands were quick, and his eyes were unafraid. He had a strong presence about him. Of course he did. One-Eyed Jack would never have made the man a captain otherwise.

Dean hung back in a corner of the room. Gentleman Jim hadn't noticed him yet, and he wouldn't, either, not until Dean wanted him to. The crowded tavern was the kind of place where it was easy for someone Dean's size to get swallowed up by a crowd. It was also the kind of place Dean wasn't old enough to be in yet, but rules like that didn't apply on St. Diogenes. They did, however, apply on board Gentleman Jim's ship. His crew was made up of kids who were all within a few years of Dean's age, and their captain kept them out of establishments like this. Dean had counted on that. He needed to get himself a place on the *Reckless* if he was going to spy on its captain, and he didn't have time to go through the Pirate Youth to do it. Gentleman Jim's crew was known to be a tight-knit, territorial, and suspicious bunch. It would have taken months for Dean to work his way into their circle and build up enough trust to even get introduced to Gentleman Jim. But Dean had a plan.

The moment Dean had been waiting for arrived when the card game broke up. The pirates Gentleman Jim had been playing with got up to leave, and he was alone at last. *Time for part one.*

Dean wove his way through the crowded room and took a seat at Gentleman Jim's table. The young captain looked up at his uninvited guest and pulled the coins he'd just won a few inches closer to his side of the table. Dean leaned back and put his hands up, indicating he had no designs on Gentleman Jim's gold. "Five minutes of your time, sir. That's all I ask. It isn't much, really . . . five minutes to change your life?"

Gentleman Jim eyed Dean suspiciously for a moment, then chuckled and went back to counting his winnings. "What makes you think my life needs changing?"

"Begging your pardon, sir, but you're on St. Diogenes. There's only one man on this island who couldn't use a change of scenery."

Gentleman Jim took a swig from a pewter tankard and wiped the foam from his beard. "All right, lad. I'll grant you that."

Dean smiled. "No reasonable man could argue otherwise."

Truer words had never been spoken. St. Diogenes was One-Eyed Jack's private island. Its main port of Bartleby Bay was a dreadful place made up almost entirely of taverns and gambling halls. The dirty shacks and crumbling buildings that housed these seedy establishments were all on the verge of collapse, as were most of the pirates who frequented them. Men in town had far too much rum in their stomachs, and not a single night passed without a series of brawls, robberies, and murders. Bartleby Bay was not a safe place by any means, but it was safe from the law. Mountainous and inaccessible from the north, the island possessed a well-defended harbor that made it an ideal pirate haunt. St. Diogenes was a kingdom ruled by One-Eyed Jack.

Gentleman Jim dropped his coins into a velvet pouch and tucked it into a pocket inside his coat. Careful not to stare, Dean took note of exactly which one.

"What have you got for me, then? What's going to change my life?"

Dean hunched his shoulders and looked around guardedly. Once he was sure no one was eavesdropping, he produced a small scroll that he had tucked inside his shirt. "A map. A map and a chance for a fortune in gold."

Gentleman Jim was unimpressed. "You don't say. A map to where?"

Dean looked around again. He made a big show of shielding the map from prying eyes. "Let's just say it leads to an island in the Bermuda Triangle. A *golden* opportunity, if you get my meaning."

Gentleman Jim stroked his beard. "I do indeed. . . . How did you come by this map?"

Dean gripped the map tight, holding it as if it were the most valuable thing in the world. "You have to understand, I wasn't always the worthless street rat you see before you today, sir. I was once a deckhand on a shining ship, a golden vessel from a magic island . . . a trade ship from Zenhala." He leaned in to whisper the last part for dramatic effect.

Gentleman Jim could barely hide his amusement. "The island where gold grows on trees? Truly? You're native to the Golden Isle?"

"Born and bred, though I've not seen it for some time."

"Why not? What happened to you, lad?"

Dean put on a sad face. "My ship was attacked by pirates. I

was knocked overboard. Lost at sea for days I was, but I survived and ended up here. Still can't decide if that makes me lucky or unlucky."

"I'd say a bit of both."

"I'll admit it hasn't been easy, making it on these streets, but I won't be staying much longer. You see, I know the way home." Dean offered up the map. "From the looks of things, you're a gambling man, sir. I'll wager that where other men see risk, you see reward. Play your cards right with this hand, and the pot will be bigger than you can well imagine."

Gentleman Jim sized up Dean for a moment before he took the map from his hand. He spread it out on the table and shook his head. It was a crude, worthless plot of lines scribbled down in haste, nothing more. "This looks like you drew it."

"Aye, sir. I drew it from memory."

"What am I supposed to do with it? It's a mess."

"I can read it for you."

Gentleman Jim leaned back with a smile. "Now we come to it. That's what you want in return for this, I take it? A ride?"

"Aye, sir, a place on your ship. Nothing more. It's in your interest to take me with you. If we arrive together, you'll be hailed as a hero bringing a native son home to Ze—" Dean stopped and looked over his shoulder again. He lowered his voice. "Home to Zenhala. If you go it alone, the welcome would not be warm, I assure you."

Gentleman Jim leaned forward and rubbed his hands together. "Why do I get the feeling we'd never reach the island either way?"

"Sir?"

Gentleman Jim pushed the map back to Dean. "I know what this is, son. Either you have friends out there somewhere who would attack my ship off the coast of some godforsaken rock, or you'd rob me blind while I slept and set me adrift on the waves. Don't let the fancy clothes fool you. I'm as much a pirate as any other man in this room. I know a con when I see it."

"Sir, it's not like that. I swear on the—"

"I'll give you a bit of free advice, lad. If you're interested, that is . . ."

Dean slumped in his seat and let out a sigh. "I'm listening."

"Good. Smart boy." Gentleman Jim took on the manner of a teacher with a lesson to impart. "You moved too fast with all of this. Your delivery had its moments, but overall it was over the top. You came to *me*. That's no good. Better if you let the mark think he's figuring the game out for himself. Even better if he thinks he's figuring out something you don't want him to know. And if you're going to trade on this 'lost son of Zenhala' grift, you might as well say you're the lost prince. You do know that part of the story, don't you?"

Dean nodded. "Everyone knows that story."

"Good." Gentleman Jim leaned back and folded his arms. "Let's hear it."

Dean looked at Gentleman Jim, who was waiting patiently for him to begin. The moment had the feel of an audition. He went along and told the tale, heavy on the theatrics:

"Lots of ships have gone out looking for Zenhala over the years, but there's only one whose crew ever lived to see its shores. A pirate ship with a bloodthirsty captain and a cutthroat crew. They fought their way across the Bermuda Triangle's death-infested waters and made it all the way to the island—past sea serpents and squalls. When they got there, they stole every coin of the fabled golden harvest, but that wasn't the most valuable treasure they took away with them. The pirate captain also took a hostage to cover his escape . . . the king and queen's newborn son."

"And that's you," Gentleman Jim cut in. "From now on, you're the lost prince, and the man who brings you home will earn himself a rich reward from your father, the king. This deckhand-on-a-trade-ship business . . ." He shook his head. "It doesn't fly. Not enough there. Small bait won't ever catch a big fish, understand?"

Dean crumpled up his fraudulent map, unconvinced. "I always thought the lost prince con was a little hard to believe. It's too much, don't you think?"

"No, I don't. That's a common mistake. You *want* to offer too much. Never underestimate what the promise of gold will make a man believe. Small dreams don't have the power to move men. They have to be big. Remember that."

"Aye, sir."

"And next time, get yourself a decent map. That was terrible."

Dean nodded. "Aye, sir. Thank you, sir." He stood up, dejected.

Gentleman Jim sighed. "Don't be so hard on yourself. It wasn't all bad. Just keep at it and you'll get there. Better luck next time, eh?"

Dean nodded and stood up from the table. A barmaid passed behind him, holding a tray filled with rum and grog. Dean turned to leave and walked right into the barmaid and her overloaded tray. The drinks spilled all over the pirates at the next table.

"GAH!" A mountain of a man cried out as if he'd just been stabbed with a harpoon. He shot out of his seat, ready to do at least that much to the person responsible. "Who's the dead man who just poured a plate of drinks down my back?"

All eyes turned to Dean. He looked up, quivering, as the giant pirate peeled off his sopping-wet coat and stared him down, seething. The man towered over Dean. He was well over six feet tall and nearly three hundred pounds. His powerful muscles were tucked away beneath a thick layer of blubber, but the added bulk just made him more intimidating. He was like an ogre dressed up in a man's clothes, only stronger and perhaps more prone to fits of rage. As the barmaid cursed Dean without end, Gentleman Jim came to his defense.

"Easy now. The boy didn't mean for that to happen. It was an accident."

The massive pirate Dean had spilled the drinks on wasn't listening. He just scowled and drew back his hand.

Here it comes, thought Dean. *Time to take a hit.* It was part of the job. The way he saw it, everybody took a hit now and then.

The rum-soaked pirate backhanded Dean with a meaty paw. Dean turned so that his shoulder absorbed most of the impact, but the blow still sent him flying back into Gentleman Jim. The young captain helped him up. "You all right, lad?" Dean shook his head clear and rubbed his eyes.

"I think so."

"Good. Get out of here. Lively now!"

Dean nodded and scurried off. The enormous pirate took a step after him, but Gentleman Jim blocked his path. "All right, that's enough. Enough, I say! It's over!"

"What about my pint of—"

"I'll get you another, just calm down!" Gentleman Jim pushed the man back and reached into his coat for a gold doubloon. "I'll get you another myself. I . . ." He trailed off as he fished around in his pocket for the coin purse he'd put there a moment ago. He couldn't find it. He checked his other pockets with a puzzled look on his face. It was gone. "I could have sworn I—" Dean was almost at the door when Gentleman Jim realized what had happened. From across the room, the pair locked eyes. Dean shrugged apologetically, held up the red velvet coin purse, and darted out the door.

CHAPTER 3

THE PIRATE YOUTH

D ean had barely gotten across the street when Gentleman Jim dashed out after him. He pointed at Dean and shouted at the top of his lungs.

"That boy's got our loot! After him!"

A ragtag gang of boys loitering nearby looked up in alarm. Dean knew they were Gentleman Jim's crew, the Pirate Youth. With their messy hair and ripped-up clothing, they looked just like Dean, only tougher. They had a little more meat on their bones, and a slightly larger chip on their collective shoulder. They looked angry as they sprang to their feet. Dean took off running, and the group chased after him. He ran down the street, leading them through a crowded maze of ramshackle sheds and squalid hovels. He chose terrain that prevented them from ganging up on him, and it was a good thing too, for with each passing block, their numbers grew. Before Dean knew it, the Pirate Youth outnumbered him twenty to one.

Dean took them down narrow paths that ran through condemned buildings and burned-out inns. There was no shortage of such structures in Bartleby Bay. A first-time visitor to the town would have found it to be in a terrible state of disrepair, but the truth was it had never been in a state of "repair" to begin with. The buildings in town were crooked and bent, its dirt roads cleaner than most feet that walked them. As always, the town was noisy and alive with action, which worked in Dean's favor. The pirates of St. Diogenes were a dangerous and unpredictable bunch. As he ran, Dean knocked into as many of them as he could, hoping his pursuers would be slowed down by the pointless squabbles that would erupt in his wake. Sure enough, men were soon cursing, arguing, and outright fighting in the street. Gentleman Jim's boys were caught up in the scrum, and Dean broke for the relative safety of Fort Diogenes.

The fort was an old, broken-down military base that was barely still standing. It had been erected long ago under the orders of whatever king or queen had ruled the island at the time. Over the years, St. Diogenes and the port of Bartleby Bay had been conquered and reconquered with such frequency that it was hard to keep track of who was in charge from day to day. It wasn't until after a hurricane destroyed the fort and much of the island that One-Eyed Jack decided to settle there. After that, the island finally knew stability, for the people who lived there knew *exactly* who was in charge. One-Eyed Jack's continued presence on St. Diogenes was a testament to his power and a constant reminder of who truly ruled the waters of the Caribbean.

Dean bounded up the smooth stone slab that ran to the entrance of the fort. Long ago, heavy iron cannons had been rolled up ramps like this one. Dean had stashed his secret weapon near the top of the slope. It was a contraption he'd built himself, using clay wheels he had stolen off a pushcart down on the docks, and a broken plank of wood that he'd pulled off a cabinet. Dean crossed the threshold of the fort and found the wheelboard right where he'd left it. Board in hand, Dean sprinted across the main courtyard, leaping over rubble from the crumbling walls all around. The lookout tower was still standing, and Dean raced up the spiral staircase to the turret. Once he arrived, he took a moment to catch his breath. He waited for the crew of the *Reckless* to reach him. On one side, he looked out on the cliffs of the island. Waves were breaking against the rocky edge of St. Diogenes, hundreds of feet below the tower window. On the other side was only the ruined interior of the fort. A debris-strewn square was filled with rocks, weeds, and useless old artillery. A wide stone staircase on the far side of the plaza led to the storage areas in the basement. Another staircase on that level led outside. From there, a final set of rickety wooden steps hugged the cliffs, winding down to the water below. That's where Dean was going. The only things standing in his way were twenty young pirates and Gentleman Jim Harper. They gathered beneath the tower, out of breath and looking more than a little annoyed. The largest boy in the group threw a rock up at Dean. He ducked for cover, and it bounced off the edge of the window, knocking out a good chunk of the wall.

"That could have taken my head off!"

The young pirate held up another rock. He was a tall, muscular lad with the body of a man and the face of a boy. His dirty blond hair was pulled back behind a bandanna, and Dean got a good look at his eyes. This kid meant business. "If I have to come up there after you, I promise you the next one won't miss. Now, get down here before I—"

"Ronan." Gentleman Jim said, putting a hand on the boy's shoulder. "That's enough. It's over." Ronan and the rest of the mob settled down as their captain called out to Dean. "There's nowhere else for you to go, lad. You had a good run, but it ends here. Don't make it end badly. Come down freely, return what you stole, and I promise you won't be hurt."

"Much," added a weasel-faced pirate in the crowd.

Gentleman Jim gave the boy a hard stare. "Rook." He spoke to him with less patience than he had Ronan, saying his name as if it meant "shut up." The boy was beanpole thin with arms like broomsticks, and dirty enough to be Scurvy Gill's protégé. He frowned, but he followed the implied order and held his tongue. Gentleman Jim reached a hand toward Dean and motioned for him to come down. "Turn yourself in, and no one will harm you. You have my word."

Dean planted his feet. "The word of a pirate? What's that worth?"

"You'd be surprised. There's more than one kind of pirate."

Dean let out a terse laugh. "News to me." He nodded and withdrew into the tower. A moment later, he came flying out the window with the wheelboard under his feet, and one hand on the deck. The wheels hit the edge of the fort's outer wall, and Dean kicked hard, taking flight over the crowd below. He touched down in the square, rolling fast, and carved a serpentine path through the Pirate Youth, staying low and out of reach.

"That's it! Take him!" Gentleman Jim shouted as Dean flew by him, making hard, grinding turns.

"I don't think so," Dean said. He rolled across the square, jumped over a cannon, and kept going. One of the young pirates chasing him ran right into it. Dean glided along, skating the stone floor toward the edge of the courtyard. It looked like he was headed for a dead end, but the interior base of the fort's walls had a small incline he could use. He rode up hard and put a hand down to swing the board around in a violent, sweeping motion. While the pirates chasing him were still on their way up, Dean came back down without losing any speed. Back on the flat surface of the plaza, he cut back and forth, changing direction faster than his pursuers could anticipate. He flew over the smooth flagstones of the fort, and Gentleman Jim's crew ran into one another trying to grab him. Dean made them look like they had lead boots strapped on their feet. They couldn't lay a hand on him, and he was just getting warmed up.

The tower directly across from the one Dean had jumped out of had toppled over and split in half years ago. Dean faked out three different pirates on his way toward it, and rode up its smooth interior surface like a surfer on a wave. Gentleman Jim's boys chased him up there, but when he reached the top, Dean put a hand down once again and swung his legs out to come back at them in a sharp cutback turn. Before they knew it, he was headed straight for them. Again, he stayed low. He kept his knees bent and his arms in, fingertips grazing the stone as he zigzagged his way down the ramp. The pirates fell over each other trying to catch Dean, but he was already gone. He fired back into the square and made for the staircase in the far corner. He was almost home free.

When he reached the stairway to the basement, the shifty-looking pirate called Rook was standing on the top step. Dean didn't slow down. It was a game of chicken, and Dean wasn't turning. Just before they collided, Rook took a step back and lost his balance. As he tumbled down the stairs, Dean kicked hard and flipped the board up to the stone railing. He sledded down the staircase banister to the first landing, jumped over Rook, and hit the fort's lower level, wheels rolling. He shot down a dark hallway, taking the wheelboard as far as he could. When he hit the cobblestones and overgrown weeds at the edge of the fort, he picked up the board and ran for the cliffside exit.

Dean charged down the steps on foot. He could have skated down, but he figured he had shown off enough already. If he didn't slow down, the Pirate Youth would never catch him. He looked up to see where they were. What he saw was a big kid looking down on him, the one with the rocks, whom Gentleman Jim had called Ronan. Dean slowed his pace. That guy wasn't going to catch him. He was big, sure, but he wasn't fast. Dean just hoped he wouldn't throw any more rocks at him. As it turned out, Ronan threw something much heavier. Dean's eyes went wide as Ronan put a hand on top of the wall and swung his legs over the side.

"You've got to be kidding me."

Ronan jumped clear of the fort and barreled straight toward Dean. Against all reason and common sense, Dean froze, standing there like a target someone had dropped a bomb on, which wasn't far from the truth. Ronan landed right on top of Dean, hitting him like a pyramid of cannonballs.

The decrepit old staircase buckled under the force of Ronan's impact. Rotten wood splintered at every anchor point. The landing steadied for the briefest of moments, then dropped out beneath Dean and Ronan's feet. It was at least a hundred-foot drop to the shallow water and jagged rocks below. It would have been a watery grave for them both, but Ronan wrapped an arm around a portion of the banister that was still intact, and Dean grabbed on to his legs. "Hang on!" Ronan shouted. He was strong enough to pull them both up onto the steps, where they crawled to the nearest sturdy landing and collapsed.

"You don't . . . get away that easy," Ronan said, breathing heavily.

"Easy! Are you crazy?" Dean laid his head down and let out a pained groan. *What does it take to impress these people?* Everything hurt, but that was all right. Dean closed his eyes and waited for the others to come down. It was all part of the plan.

CHAPTER 4

Sign Aboard, Matey

Ronan and his mates dragged Dean back to the fort and threw him into an empty storage locker. Gentleman Jim was inside waiting for Dean when he tumbled in the door. "Give us a moment." Gentleman Jim ordered. Everyone left the room except Ronan. He handed over Dean's wheelboard and stood with his muscular frame blocking the room's only exit. The pirate captain looked the board over, inspecting both sides. He spun one of the wheels with his hand. "Quite a show you put on out there."

Dean sat up with his back against the wall. "You want lessons? Maybe I can show your boys how to ride. Just takes a little practice."

Gentleman Jim gave Dean a thin smile and set the board aside.

"I meant back in the tavern. Not many people can pull the wool over my eyes like you did. You must have thought it was funny, all the advice I was giving you. . . . 'Let the mark think he's figuring out the game for himself. Even better if he thinks he's figuring out something you don't want him to know.'" Gentleman Jim shook his head. "You knew your scam with the map to Zenhala was too obvious. You counted on it. Once you'd set me at ease, you engineered that scuffle and lifted my coin purse in the confusion. It really was well done."

Ronan grunted. "Not well enough."

Dean shrugged. "I didn't count on your generosity. You buying that pirate a drink wasn't part of the plan. Not typical behavior for a man in your line of work."

"I'm not your typical man. What about you? What line of work are you in?"

"There's no mystery to me. I'm just a poor boy trying to get by on the streets of Bartleby Bay. I do what I have to in order to survive. I make no apologies for that."

"Nor should you. But, if survival's all you want out of life, I can't help you. On the other hand, if you want to truly live . . . then maybe we can talk. First things first. I believe you have something that belongs to me?"

Dean went into his pocket and reluctantly pulled out the stolen coin purse.

Gentleman Jim took a seat on a rock and counted out the coins, making sure it was all there. It added up to quite a tidy sum. "More than you expected, eh? It's all I have in the world, but it isn't mine to keep. This is the pirate king's tribute. You mentioned him when you sat down at my table. I assume you know what he's capable of?"

"Aye." Dean nodded. *Only too well.*

"He gets a piece of all the loot plundered in these waters, every month. One-Eyed Jack gets his money or heads roll, no exceptions." Gentleman Jim held up the coin purse. "If you had stolen this, you would have stolen from him. Your life would have been worth less than a peg leg made out of sea sponge. You're lucky we caught you."

"I think you're the lucky one."

"Luck's got nothing to do with it," Ronan said.

"Now, now, Ronan. He's not wrong. It would have meant my head if he got away with this." Gentleman Jim tucked the pouch away in a pocket that closed with a button. "Yours too, perhaps. Who knows where you all would have ended up without me to look out for you?"

"Nowhere good. What are we going to do with him, Captain?"

Gentleman Jim rubbed his beard. "That's really up to him. He's a clever thief, this one. My question is, can he be an honest thief?"

Dean turned Gentleman Jim's words over in his head. He had just hoped to impress him enough to get offered a place on his ship. The conversation appeared to be headed in that direction, but there was apparently more to it than that. Gentleman Jim was a riddle Dean had yet to figure out.

"An honest thief . . . What does that mean?"

"Well, for starters, it means you never steal a man's last dollar, or stab a friend in the back. Think we can trust you that far?"

Dean shrugged. "I've never done either of those things." That was true, but mainly because Dean rarely stole anything himself. His job as a spy was to set things up so that other pirates could steal them. As for stabbing his friends in the back, Dean didn't have any friends to stab. His job got in the way of that. He was always alone, always on the move, and always pretending to be someone else. It wasn't the best recipe for building strong and lasting relationships.

Gentleman Jim looked over his shoulder. "What do you think, Ronan?"

"I don't know, Captain. He stole from you—from all of us. I don't trust him. Besides, we don't even know if he can sail the sea without losing his lunch."

"Sail?" Dean asked. "Sail where? What are you talking about?"

"Back in the tavern, you said you wanted a place on my ship. Did you mean that?"

Dean did his best to look surprised. In reality, he was relieved. "Are you serious?"

"Always."

Dean paused for a moment. He didn't want to appear overeager. He had to stay in character and play his part to the end. "I don't get it. I steal your gold, and instead of taking it out of my hide, you offer me a place on your ship. Why?"

"Like I said, you impressed me back there. Also, I think I can help you."

"Help me?" Dean squinted at Gentleman Jim. "What do you care what happens to me?"

"I've got a bad habit of taking in strays and other lost causes. Used to be one myself." Gentleman Jim paused. "I don't know, maybe I'm wrong about you. Could be your life's filled with promise and you don't need my help. Is that it? Are things really going that well for you?"

Dean looked down at his shoes. Taking stock of his life always had a negative effect on his mood. He had heard it said that the ocean made all things possible. That the world was filled with wonders, and a man could set sail with one life and come home with another. In Dean's experience, nothing could have been further from the truth.

"No, sir. The way things are headed, I'm not going anywhere at all."

As long as Dean could remember, he'd been part of One-Eyed Jack's crew, trapped in the service of the pirate king. He had been raised by pirates, which was a lot like being raised by no one. That was what Dean's life had in it. Nothing and no one. That was all he'd ever have. His course was firmly plotted, never to change.

"Only one man on this island couldn't benefit from a change of scenery," Gentleman Jim reminded Dean. "Be honest with me. What have you got to lose?"

Dean felt a pang of guilt. His plan had worked. He was in. The real question was, what did Gentleman Jim have to lose? The answer was probably everything.

Dean shook his head. "I don't know. A complete stranger who wants to help me? Sounds too good to be true."

"It's not. Before you decide, you should know this offer comes with a warning. If you sign aboard my ship, you're enlisting in the pirate king's Black Fleet, just like me, Ronan, and every other pirate out there, regardless of age. Once you're in, you're in for life. There's no way out, save a trip to the great beyond. Do you understand what I'm saying?"

Dean nodded. He understood all right. Not only was his name already in the pirate king's book, but he had almost made that trip in the belly of a shark. "I understand."

"If you want in, you better be sure. Now or never, lad. I won't ask again."

Dean thought it over a little more, got on his feet, and stood up straight. "You don't have to. I'm in."

"You're sure?"

"I'm sure."

Gentleman Jim clapped his hands. "Good, then it's settled. What's your name?"

"Dean Seaborne."

Gentleman Jim shook Dean's hand. "Welcome to the *Reckless*, Dean Seaborne. I'm Jim Harper, better known as Gentleman Jim. Captain Harper to you. You've met my first mate, Ronan MacGuire." Dean offered his hand to Ronan, but the first mate folded his arms and looked away.

Dean withdrew his hand with a shrug. "I guess if I'm going to be an honest thief, I'd better get started. These are yours, Ronan. You, uh . . . dropped them." Dean pulled a handful of coins from his pocket and held them out in an open palm.

Ronan looked down at Dean's hand in disbelief and pulled out his own pockets. Sure enough, they were empty. "Why you little—give me those!"

Gentleman Jim laughed as Ronan snatched the coins out of Dean's hand and counted them twice for good measure. "You mean you actually had the nerve to pick his pocket on the way in here? After he caught you?"

Dean turned up his palms. "I couldn't help myself."

"Hah! You'll fit right in, Seaborne. Let's go introduce you to your shipmates." Gentleman Jim led the way outside. Dean went to follow him out, but Ronan blocked the door with his arm and stared at him, looking like a volcano ready to blow.

"It was nothing personal, Ronan. What do you say? No hard feelings?"

Ronan shook his head. "Don't get too comfortable here, Seaborne. There's something about you. . . . I don't know what it is yet, but I can tell you don't belong. You're not one of us. Don't go thinking you are."

Dean grimaced and pushed his way outside. Ronan had him pegged from the jump. He was right. Dean *didn't* belong. It was the story of his life. Dean didn't belong with One-Eyed Jack and the Black Fleet, and he never got to stay anywhere else long enough to belong there, either. He had no real home. No real mates. He spent all his time on the go, hopping from one foot to the next . . . from one *lie* to the next. This Ronan was a sharp one, but Dean wasn't worried. This was just a job like any other. He wasn't there to make friends, and he wasn't staying long enough to make enemies. As soon as he found out why Gentleman Jim's payments were coming up short, he would jump ship and be nothing but a memory.

Outside, Gentleman Jim had gathered up the crew. "On your toes now, mateys! I've got an announcement. We set sail with the evening tide, and when we shove off, it'll be with a new point man. You know him as the boy who just made a monkey out of all of you, riding around here on a plank of wood with wheels. Who knows? Maybe he can teach you a thing or two. His name is Dean Seaborne, and he's one of us now. Let's give him a real Pirate Youth welcome, eh?"

The crew stared at Dean in absolute silence. The only sound came from the gulls flying overhead and the waves breaking against the cliffs. Dean's new shipmates looked at him as though they wanted to break him in half.

Gentleman Jim clapped a hand on Dean's back. "That's a real Pirate Youth welcome, all right. Don't worry, lad. It takes time. They'll warm up to you."

Dean shook his head. *Not likely.* "What happens now, Captain? What does that mean, a new point man?"

"It means we're gonna throw you to the sharks and see if you can swim. Think you can manage it?"

Dean's lips formed a crooked smile. "Believe it or not, that's how I ended up here in the first place."

PART TWO

HONOR AMONG THIEVES

CHAPTER 5

SEABORNE ADVENTURES

It turned out Gentleman Jim was only partly kidding. As the wind pulled Dean across the water on a short wooden board, sharks were the least of his concerns. He struggled to see where he was going. The shining glow of the Caribbean's crystal water had been stolen by the night sky and a thick fog no man's eyes could pierce. Dean sliced blindly through the murky haze. Leather straps held his feet in place, and in his hands he held a small crossbar with long lines tied at each end. The lines ran up to a miniature sail that pulled him along faster than any ship could go—faster than any fish, for that matter! His new shipmates in the Pirate Youth had called the contraption a kiteboard. No one had taught Dean how to ride it, but his wheelboard experience had helped him pick it up rather quickly. Under different circumstances, he would have actually found kiteboarding to be great fun, even if he did feel as if his arms got ripped of their sockets every time the wind changed direction.

Dean rode up over swells of seawater like ramps, launching himself into the air. Once he was airborne, the sail lifted him even farther. The wind pulled him twenty, sometimes thirty feet up into the sky and just as far across the water. He twisted and turned as he went. When he wasn't sailing high above the ocean, he was skidding across its face like a fisherman who had hooked a whale but was too stubborn to let go of his line.

All the while Dean raced across the waves, spinning and thrashing, he paid close attention to a length of rope that trailed behind him. The rope was hooked onto a harness on his waist that tethered him to the *Reckless*. He was careful not to run out of line as he flipped from wave to wave. The fog was thicker than paint, but with a little persistence, he spotted the soft glow of lanterns advancing through the mist. Ringing bells told him a ship was up ahead. Dean turned his sail into the wind and came about, heading for a large square-rigged merchant vessel christened the *Santa Clara*.

He sped toward the ship, caught a wave, and jumped. A strong updraft carried him high into the air, and he let the wind carry him as far as it could. When he finally began his descent, he waited until the last possible moment and then let go of his sail, which flew off and disappeared into the fog. Dean continued to fall, faster now, bearing down on the *Santa Clara* and its unsuspecting crew. He pulled his legs up to clear the ship's gunwale as he closed in and just barely made it over the side. He touched down with a thud, and his board skidded across the deck's wooden planes with rapid bumps. Sailors' heads spun around from every direction as they let out shouts of shock, alarm, and general confusion. Dean sprang up onto the quarterdeck, snatching a cutlass from the side of a slow-footed seaman as he ran. Quick as lightning, he unhooked the thick rope tied to his harness and lashed it around the mainmast, thus connecting the *Santa Clara* to the *Reckless*. Once he was certain his knot wouldn't come undone, he started reeling in the slack.

"Who the devil are you?" a voice called out. Dean raised his eyes toward the stern end of the quarterdeck, where a man stood in a cabin door. He wore a bright red coat with fine gold trim, and buttons made of polished brass. Oily black hair fell down around his shoulders in tight curls. He had a thin mustache and the air of a man who thought a great deal of himself. Judging by his formal dress and general tone of righteous indignation, Dean concluded he was the ship's captain. "Well? Speak, boy!" the captain demanded.

Dean put up a finger, instructing the man to wait as he hauled in the rope that tied the two ships together. The captain stood dumbfounded as the boy went on with his work. Rope piled up at Dean's feet until at last he pulled and the line did not give. He gave it two good tugs to signal his mates, and dropped the line on the deck. "There." He clapped his hands together and turned to face the simmering captain. "You, sir. You asked me a question just now. I'm afraid I wasn't paying attention. What was it you wanted to know?"

The captain scowled at Dean. "I want this boy in irons. Now."

Two able-bodied sailors stepped forward to take hold of Dean. They were tough, weather-beaten men with leathery hides and fists the size of horseshoe crabs. Dean grabbed the cutlass he'd stolen as he came on board and cut through the air like a swashbuckler. "I give you fair warning. Any man who lays a hand on me will leave it at my feet."

The two sailors paused a moment, then shared a laugh at Dean's expense. They drew out their own blades and closed in on him. Dean stood his ground, waiting until they came close enough to strike. Once they did, he chose the man on the right and lunged forward with his sword, pushing him back. The sailor on the left swung his blade at Dean, but he ducked beneath its edge with time to spare. The sword sailed harmlessly over his head and lodged itself firmly in the mast. As the man tried to pry it loose, Dean delivered a kick to his stomach that knocked the man clean off the quarterdeck. Dean spun and pulled the sword free himself, then turned back toward his other attacker. Swinging both swords, Dean cut a wide swash through the air as he went at the man. The sailor backpedaled and tripped on the tangled line Dean had just pulled on board. He fell hard on his backside, and Dean pressed his advantage.

"Do you yield?" The tip of his cutlass was dangerously close to the man's throat.

The sailor nodded several times and scurried back like a frightened rat. Dean smiled as he shrank away. The man had taken him for an easy mark. Dean was nothing of the sort. You don't last very long as a pirate spy if you can't hold your own in a fight.

"What's the meaning of this?" the captain demanded. "Who do you think you are, boy?"

Dean cleared his throat and recited the lines that Ronan had made him memorize. "My name is not important. What is important is the message I carry. As of this moment, your ship and its cargo are at the mercy of the pirate Gentleman Jim Harper. You might not believe it, but today is your lucky day. Gentleman Jim will gladly give quarter to any and all who lay down their arms and surrender. You can run up a white flag now, or wait until Gentleman Jim gets here, but it's faster and more civilized if you surrender before he arrives. My captain is a busy man, and he appreciates your cooperation. I can assure you he will treat you every bit as well as you treat him."

The ship's captain stared at Dean in silence, thunderstruck

by the boy's proclamation. After a few quiet moments, a smile formed on the captain's lips and he burst out laughing. His crew took the outburst as permission to do the same and roared with laughter as well.

"Surrender? To a pint-size pirate?"

"Been too long in the sun, I'll wager!"

"At his captain's mercy, he says! Where is he, then?"

Dean shook his head as the rowdy seamen mocked him. He had expected his youth and boyish looks to get in the way of the message he was sent to deliver. With a head full of short black hair, bright blue eyes, and a full set of teeth, he was hardly Blackbeard the pirate. He appealed to the *Santa Clara*'s captain directly.

"I know it's hard to accept, sir. No man wants to surrender his command, but please, be reasonable. Are you really going to send all these men to their deaths just to satisfy your own selfish pride?"

The captain's smile faded into a sneer, and his laughter into a growl. He drew a pistol on Dean. "Mind your tongue, boy. You're on *my* ship. I don't take that kind of talk from my men, and I'll be tarred if I'll take it from a whelp like you. What makes you think I won't shoot you dead and toss your body to Davy Jones right now?"

Dean held out his arms. It wasn't the first time he'd had a pistol pointed in his direction. He knew full well their accuracy was terrible except at very close range. "Go ahead and shoot. I wager you'll be lucky to hit the ocean if you try. More likely you'll hit one of your own men. But that's not why you won't fire on me."

The captain cocked his pistol. "Why won't I, then?"

Dean glanced down at his feet. The whole time he and the captain had been talking, the line he'd tied to the mast was slowly being drawn out by someone in the fog who was tugging on the other end. What was once a twisted heap of rope was now pulled nearly taut. Dean smiled and stuck to the script. "You won't shoot because my captain would take that as a personal insult. The offer of quarter would be withdrawn, and my shipmates would cut every throat on this ship, down to the very last man. You see, Gentleman Jim commands a ghost ship, crewed by one hundred of the blackest souls that ever sailed the sea. Stole them right out from under the devil's nose, he did. They're so grateful, they do whatever he says, and it's them who are coming for you now."

Dean locked eyes with the captain and didn't blink. The sailors on deck swallowed hard as the rope continued to stretch out before him. A strong gust of wind swept the fog from the deck, and moonlight bathed the *Santa Clara* in an eerie glow. Murmurs ran from bow to stern like an army of mice. Half the ship's crew appeared anxious to know what was pulling on the other end of the rope. The other half looked afraid to find out. All of them seemed to regret laughing in the face of death when Dean seemed so certain it was coming to call.

"If it's blood you're after, Captain, you'll have it. But you'd be wise to save your powder for my shipmates. I didn't come here alone."

As the last few yards of line went over the side, the tune of a pirate shantey drifted in. All hands on deck, the captain included, stood on guard as they looked around, trying to find the spot from whence it came. A moment later, the *Reckless*—a large, three-masted, well-armed galleon flying the Jolly Roger—emerged from the fog. It was a nightmarish vision. Half of the Pirate Youth stood at the edge of the ship wearing face paint and skull masks. They each held a torch in one hand, a cutlass in the other, and shouted demonic battle cries. The other half flew in from above, riding more kiteboard rigs. They descended upon the *Santa Clara* like shrieking harpies, and the crew on deck ran for cover. Dean saw Gentleman Jim at the center of it all with his sword held high in the air. He gave the order to attack, and Dean's ghostly shipmates came over the side like a giant wave crashing to the shore.

CHAPTER 6

THE GENTLEMAN'S CODE

The *Santa Clara*'s captain dropped his pistol and ran. His men did the same, throwing down their swords before the first "ghost" came aboard. Dean watched the Pirate Youth overwhelm the ship, working fast to round up its crew and bind every man on deck with strong ropes and tight knots. The battle was over before it began, and well before anyone realized they had just surrendered to a ship full of children.

Gentleman Jim came aboard last, moving with no greater urgency than a man strolling down a beach at sunset. He walked up a gangplank to join Dean on the quarterdeck as his crew secured the ship. Back on the *Reckless*, a team of young pirates turned a massive capstan to haul in the rest of Dean's line, singing as they worked to pull the two ships together. Gentleman Jim clapped a hand on Dean's back and gave a hearty laugh. "Beautiful! They all but wrapped her up and tied her with a bow, didn't they?"

Dean shook his head in admiration. "I have to hand it to you, Captain. This is as good a con as I've ever seen. This lot bought it hook, line, and sinker."

"Thanks to you. Give yourself some credit, lad. It all starts with the right setup. You did well—especially for a first timer. Fine work."

Dean basked in the glow of Gentleman Jim's praise. He wasn't used to that kind of encouragement. It was true, he deserved some credit for spooking the ship's captain and crew, but as far as he was concerned, the real work had been done by the Pirate Youth. They were professionals through and through. Dean watched as they went about their business, taking control of the *Santa Clara* in an orderly, bloodless fashion. He liked the way Gentleman Jim did things. It was smart. What was the point of executing brutal raids and innocent sailors when you could simply trick a ship's captain into giving up without a fight? Dean could see why Gentleman Jim was known to inspire strong loyalty from his crew. Under his command, they not only filled their pockets with gold but had a much better chance of living long enough to spend it. Dean was happy to have played his part in the production well, and lamented the fact that he was there only as part of a larger charade. He could have fit in nicely with the Pirate Youth had they met under different circumstances. It would have been a good life, being part of this crew. But who was he kidding? One-Eyed Jack would never have allowed it. Dean was a spy. That was what One-Eyed Jack wanted for him, and if he was spying on Gentleman Jim, it meant his days were numbered anyway.

Gentleman Jim approached the captain of the *Santa Clara*. Standing eye to eye, the two men did not seem all that different. Gentleman Jim took his hat off to the *Santa Clara*'s captain as Ronan relieved the man of his sword and pistol.

"I officially accept your surrender, Captain . . . ?" Gentleman Jim paused and motioned for his counterpart to offer his name.

"Cordoba."

"Captain Cordoba. You chose wisely, sir. No cargo is worth dying for."

"Don't patronize me, you pirate scum." Cordoba struggled to get at Gentleman Jim, but Ronan and two other pirates held him fast. "Coward! What kind of a man hides behind children like this?"

"What kind of a man *surrenders* to children? Really, Captain, I thought you Spaniards were made of sterner stuff."

Cordoba flew into a rage, rattling off an endless string of rapid-fire insults. At least Dean assumed they were insults. He couldn't say for sure since he didn't speak Spanish, but judging from the way Cordoba was frothing at the mouth, it was a safe bet.

"Please, let's not be uncouth, Captain Cordoba. We're partners now, you and I. The least we can do is speak to each other in a civil tone."

"Partners? What the devil are you talking about?"

Gentleman Jim smiled. "It's simple. Your pride is going to help keep our secret. After all, you're not going to tell anyone you were robbed by children, are you? I doubt that very highly. No, if I have the measure of you down squarely, you'll swear it was a whole fleet of savage buccaneers, or perhaps even a real ghost ship that struck you. Men like you make it possible for my crew to run our scheme over and over again with impunity. I appreciate your help, sir. You have my thanks."

Dean watched Cordoba's face twist into a mask of pure hatred, probably because he knew every word that had just been said was true. Gentleman Jim laughed. "I love the Spanish. Such a proud people."

Captain Cordoba spat on Gentleman Jim's lapel, and Ronan punched him in the jaw with the speed and fury of a typhoon wind. Cordoba staggered back in shock.

"It seems you need a lesson in manners," Gentleman Jim said. He calmly took a handkerchief from Cordoba's pocket, used it to wipe off his lapel, and tucked the soiled square of cloth back where he found it. "First mate, have you the sock?"

Ronan snickered. "Aye, Captain."

Dean turned up his nose as Ronan pulled a putrid black sock

from his back pocket. He could smell it from ten paces away. The sock smelled even worse than Scurvy Gill's handkerchief, if such a thing were possible.

"What is that?" Cordoba asked, gagging as the sock's hateful aroma punched its way into his nostrils. The filthy length of cloth looked like it could stand up all on its own.

"What does it look like?" Gentleman Jim replied. "It's a sock taken off the dirtiest pirate I ever had the misfortune of sailing with. Now, if there are no further questions?" He gave a nod to Ronan, who stuffed the sock into Cordoba's mouth and tied it in place with a bandanna. Cordoba's eyes watered, and he let out muffled cries of anguish and outrage. Gentleman Jim rolled his eyes. "Captain, if you don't have anything of value to add to the conversation, I'm going to have to ask you to please be quiet." Ronan and the rest of the Pirate Youth laughed. "Take him away!" The crew of the *Reckless* carried Cordoba off, and Gentleman Jim flashed a rogue's smile. "Now then, lads. Let's get a look at our loot."

"You heard the captain!" Ronan bellowed. "Get your hides to the hold and haul up your treasure!"

A cargo hatch on the main deck flew open. "Already done that!" said the mangy, spindle-legged boy named Rook. He came up from below, leading a pack of young pirates toting crates, which they dropped on the deck with a thud. Rook took no part in the heavy lifting but, rather, concerned himself with a group of missionaries who had followed him and the others out. Their leader, a white-haired old man with a kind face, tugged at Rook's elbow, pleading with him to leave their cargo be. Rook pushed the frail clergyman down without a second thought. "Plenty more where that come from, there is."

Rook seemed quite pleased with the day's haul, but Dean saw a problem straightaway. The crates were marked with crosses and looked quite hefty. If missionaries had ever traveled with this much gold, it was the first he'd heard of it. Dean watched Gentleman Jim and Ronan trade wary looks. There was a good chance this raid had been all for naught.

Ronan jumped down from the quarterdeck. "Somebody help that man up," he said, pointing to the old missionary. He slapped the top of a crate with an open palm. "Pry them open, boys. Let's have a look inside."

Dean leapt down to the main deck and helped the elderly minister back on his feet. He then grabbed a pry bar and lent a hand with the crates. Just as he had suspected, there was no treasure inside. Instead, the boxes were filled with dried meats, rice, and grain.

Gentleman Jim's eyes narrowed. He gripped the railing of the quarterdeck hard enough to leave thumbprints in the finish. "What is this? This ship was meant to be carrying Spanish gold!"

"Gold?" The old missionary limped forward. "No, sir. Our mission booked passage on this ship to aid the hurricane victims of San Petit. Our only cargo is food, medicine, and the good Lord's word."

"No gold?" Gentleman Jim leaned forward as his men pried open the other crates. "None?"

Dean inspected each box thoroughly. There was always a chance that the old preacher was a fraud hiding gold bars beneath his Bibles, but it wasn't very likely. The man's soft blue eyes twinkled with less guile than a baby dove's. Dean turned to face his new captain with empty hands. "I'm afraid not, sir. Just food and supplies."

The missionary stepped in front of the crates, shielding them with his body. "Have mercy, Captain. Let us pass. If not for our sake, then do it for your own! What will you say on the day of your judgment if you steal from women and children barely clinging to life? How will you explain leaving countless innocents to waste away and die? Please, sir, if you won't think of them, think of yourself. Think of your soul!"

The impassioned plea hung in the air, heavier than ten cannonballs. "Blast it all," Ronan muttered.

Gentleman Jim shook his head. "Rook, seal up these crates and stow them with the others down below. We're leaving."

Rook's head shot up. "What?"

Dean spun around as well. "We're leaving?"

"Bless you, sir! Bless you!" cried the old missionary, clasping his hands together.

"But, Cap'n! You can't!" Rook sputtered.

"We came here for gold, Rook, not the food of starving children." Gentleman Jim turned back toward the *Reckless* without touching so much as a single grain of rice. Dean couldn't believe his eyes.

Rook grabbed the captain's shoulder and pulled him back. "In case you hadn't noticed, sir, we're not far from starvin' ourselves. We're down to hardtack and leather, we are!"

Gentleman Jim stopped short and stared at Rook's hand on his shoulder. Rook withdrew the offending appendage, but the expression on his face remained angry and defiant.

"How long have you been part of my crew, Rook?"

Rook grunted. "Eighteen months."

"Eighteen months and you still don't understand the way things work. Or is it that you just don't want to? I'm tired of your insubordination. I didn't ask for your opinion, and I don't care to hear it expressed again. I'm a generous man, so I'll allow you to survive this one final lapse of judgment." He held up a finger. "One. Don't mistake my good nature for weakness or I *will* make an example of you. Get to work."

Rook planted his feet. It looked to Dean like he might actually challenge Gentleman Jim, as foolish as that would have been. Dean didn't do anything. He kept his mouth shut and watched the action unfold, just as a good spy should. Ronan got in between his captain and the insubordinate crewman, just as a good first mate should. "You hard of hearing? Your captain gave you an order, you pox-faced bilge rat! What're you doing still standing there?"

Rook pointed at the missionaries. "If I wanted to do charity work, I would've joined up with their lot. We can't afford to turn our backs on any kind of loot. Not after the month we've had. The pirate king expects a real tribute this time, not more excuses."

"The pirate king will get his due," Gentleman Jim said. "He always does. Are you suggesting I pay him with crates of rice and grain?"

"Either that or the ship that carries 'em!"

Gentleman Jim shook his head. "I'm not that kind of pirate. My crew steals from people who can afford it, people who deserve it, and if we're lucky, both. That's the Gentleman's Code."

And that's why it doesn't pay to get attached, thought Dean. His mission was now complete. Gentleman Jim's fate was sealed. In less than a day, Dean had rooted out the reason the last few payments from the *Reckless* had been light. Gentleman Jim wasn't skimming off the top, he was leaving money on the table. Not quite the damnable offense that One-Eyed Jack had suspected him to be guilty of, but that hardly mattered. Either way, he was costing One-Eyed Jack money, and would pay dearly for it once Dean made his report. Dean felt sick. He suddenly remembered why he hated his job enough to run away.

"Gentleman's Code?" Rook cackled. "Not that kind of pirate?

Beggin' yer pardon, Cap'n, but there's only *one* kind of pirate."

Gentleman Jim's cutlass flashed from his side. Its edge came to rest against Rook's jugular. "I respectfully disagree. There's all kinds. . . . There's the kind that follow orders, the kind that swim home, and the kind that have their throats cut. Which one are you?" Rook shuddered and pulled his neck back from Gentleman Jim's steel as far as he could.

"I'd say he's the kind who'll button his lip if he wants to live," Dean called out, surprising himself. The logical part of his brain had told him not to get involved with matters that didn't concern him, but he couldn't help it. Mutinous pirates were like an infection that had to be stamped out immediately, and the fact of the matter was, Dean liked Gentleman Jim. Even so, speaking up in his defense was an odd gesture considering what he was about to do to the man. If only there was some way to warn him without getting in dutch with One-Eyed Jack again.

Rook looked around for allies among the crew of the *Reckless*. He found there were none to be had, and held his tongue at last. Gentleman Jim stared him down with hard eyes. "If you want to find yourself another ship in the Black Fleet, you're welcome to do so. In fact, I highly recommend that course of action. But right now you're part of *my* crew. I'm the captain here, not you. As long as that's the case, you will obey my orders, or you will regret it for the rest of your short, miserable life. Is that understood?"

Rook's eyes turned to slits. "Aye, Cap'n." He looked like he would have rather eaten worm-ridden hardtack than fall in line with Gentleman Jim's orders, but with a sword at his throat, he was inclined to do little else.

The confrontation ended without any bloodshed. Rook did as he was told. He sealed up the crates and helped put them back where they belonged. Once that was done, the Pirate Youth shut up the missionaries in Cordoba's quarters and tied up the rest of his crew. As the boys took their leave of the *Santa Clara*, Dean tapped Ronan's shoulder. "This is probably a stupid question, but does One-Eyed Jack know anything about this Gentleman's Code we keep?"

"You're right, Seaborne. That is a stupid question."

Dean looked at Ronan. "You don't think it might be a problem one day?"

Ronan called to one of his mates and jerked a thumb in Dean's direction. "Listen to this one. He takes point on a single busted raid and suddenly he's an expert on looting ships."

"That's not what I meant, and you know it. You're truthfully not worried what could happen if he found out?"

"Relax, will you? We've been working this way for years. Years. Unless you plan on ratting us out the next time you and One-Eyed Jack have tea, I think we'll be fine doing things our way."

Ronan grabbed a line and swung back to the *Reckless*.

Once his boots hit the deck, he threw the rope back so Dean could follow.

Ronan had no way of knowing the truth of his words. "You'll be fine, all right," Dean muttered as he took hold of the line. He wouldn't be having tea with One-Eyed Jack, but the two of them would definitely be talking, and the conversation would spell the end of Gentleman Jim and the Pirate Youth. Dean wished he could do something for them, but he wasn't sure he had the stomach to try. He was already on One-Eyed Jack's bad side. He had to follow orders. He had no choice.

Dean swung back to the *Reckless* with the rest of the Pirate Youth. Once everyone was back on board, Gentleman Jim cut the line that tied the two ships together. He gave the *Santa Clara* a mighty shove with his boot, and they were off. As the *Reckless* sailed away, Dean could tell its captain wasn't happy about going home empty-handed, but that was the least of his problems. The ship had only just pulled away from the *Santa Clara* when Dean heard its cannons sound. The crew on deck ran to the railing as Cordoba opened fire. Gentleman Jim rubbed his beard, grumbling. "Well, that's gratitude for you."

A cannonball pounded the hull of the *Reckless*, and the ship began to list. The shift in balance was slight at first, but when Dean felt it happen so fast, he knew the damage was bad. He ran to the side to get a look. Sure enough, the shot had torn a gaping hole in the boat. "We're taking on water!" he shouted as the deck angled down further. Another cannonball hit its mark, and the *Reckless* shook so much that Dean had to grab hold of the rigging to keep from flying away. He climbed back onto the deck, but knew he wouldn't be staying very long once he got there. None of them would, not with an ocean of water pouring into the lower decks.

"Looks like we're all the kind of pirates that swim home now!" Rook called out from across the ship.

Dean didn't know whether to feel sad or relieved as he watched the horizon tilt. He hated to say it, but Rook was right. The *Reckless* had begun its final journey, straight to the bottom of the sea.

CHAPTER 7

THE WRECK OF
THE RECKLESS

M an the lifeboats!" Gentleman Jim yelled. "Abandon ship!"
Dean blinked. *Already?* Most pirate captains he knew
waited until they were safely off the boat and rowing hard for
shore before they gave that order. Gentleman Jim apparently felt
his crew deserved more than the standard pirate code of "every
man for himself."

"Ronan! Get the boys off the ship and get us ready for a long
journey. No one gets left behind, you hear? No one!"

"Aye aye!" Ronan shouted back. Dean was taken aback by the
code of honor that was enforced on board the *Reckless*. It took a
special kind of madness to try to be a pirate and a good man at

the same time, but somehow Gentleman Jim pulled it off. That said, his noble heart wasn't doing him any favors. His ship was sinking fast, and if the crew was to survive, there was much to do and not a moment to lose. Dean had seen ships even larger than the *Reckless* vanish forever beneath the waves in just over fifteen minutes. He and the rest of the Pirate Youth ran about the ship readying launches, gathering provisions, and throwing any object that would float over the side.

There were far more people than lifeboats, which meant that anything that would keep a person dry and out of the water could not be allowed to go down with the ship. Hatches were broken off at the hinges and thrown overboard. The door to the captain's cabin came next, followed by his table, which was stubborn as an oyster that refused to part with its pearl. Its legs had been bolted to the deck to keep it from sliding about, so the boys had to chop them off with hatchets and carry the tabletop out by itself.

Stripping down the ship was the kind of job that wasn't easy under normal conditions, and even harder while under attack. Captain Cordoba was relentless in his campaign to sink the *Reckless*. He fired his cannons in broadsides, sending walls of shot at the doomed pirate ship. Most of the cannonballs missed their mark, but when they hit, they tore through wood like parchment, and splinters filled the air with flying needles. Gentleman Jim's crew raced across the deck of the *Reckless*, ducking, dodging, and shielding their eyes as they tried to save everything that wasn't nailed down.

Amidst the chaos, Dean grabbed a handle on the main cargo hatch and called for help opening it. What he got was a quarrelsome pair of twin pirates named Kane and Marko. They helped lift open the hatch, and Dean pointed at the freshwater stores kept down below. "If we want to drink something other than salt water once this ship goes down, we'd best get those barrels out fast. Let's go!"

"Right," Kane said, tapping his brother on the shoulder. "You go down with him and hand up the barrels. I'll stay up here and take 'em from you one by one."

Marko scrunched up his face. "Why am I the one going down there? You get below and hand 'em up to me."

"I'm not going down there! What if something happens and I end up stuck under a barrel? The ship's sinking, you know."

"I know the ship's sinking! I suppose it's all right if I get stuck under a barrel?"

Marko shoved Kane, and Kane shoved him back. Dean got in between them before a fight broke out. "We don't have time for this! One of you has to go. I don't care who. I'm not strong enough to bring them up myself."

Marko presented Kane to Dean. "He's the stronger one. He should go down."

"Me? Stronger?" Kane shook his head. "I don't think so. You punched me in the eye a fortnight ago and it still smarts! Look here, see the bruise? It's yet to fade!"

"Blow me down!" Ronan thundered, coming up behind the twins and grabbing each of them by the collar. "What is this? Rook's skulduggery contagious? Get down there before I chain you both to the rudder!" He pushed Kane and Marko through the open hatch. "Haul up those provisions! First the water, then the food. Now!"

The pirates hit the lower deck hard and scrambled to their feet, ready to do their part at last. "Thanks," Dean said to Ronan.

Ronan shook him off. "I didn't do it for you. Without that water, we're dead."

Dean shrugged. "Whatever the reason, it doesn't matter. You two! Here!" Dean slid a gangplank down through the hatch for the twins to roll the barrels up on. He stood ready to receive the first one when a chain shot struck the ship. Two large cannonballs strung together with iron chains wrapped around the mainmast and pulled it down.

"Look out below!" Gentleman Jim yelled as the mast toppled over. Kane and Marko covered their heads and ran. Wooden spars from the sails stabbed into the deck as they fell. Lines snapped and shot back like whips. Almost everyone on the ship's upper deck jumped overboard as the mainmast crashed down. It lay across the deck like a fallen giant, and several young pirates were pinned beneath the sails that came down with it. Dean went to cut them free, but Cordoba's last cannonball hit the broken mast first. It spun around the splintered base and swept across the deck like the hand of a vengeful god, taking out everything in its path. It was headed right for Dean and Ronan when Gentleman Jim came out of nowhere and shoved them out of harm's way. They tumbled down through the main cargo hatch to join Kane and Marko.

Dean landed on his feet and turned around just in time to see the mast deal the captain a crippling blow. He watched from below as Gentleman Jim's body took flight.

"CAPTAIN!" Ronan cried.

Dean sprang up and poked his head out of the hatch. Gentleman Jim was nowhere to be seen. Most of the crew was gone too. The swinging mast had all but cleared the deck. Dean pulled himself up out of the hatch and ran to look over the side. Half the crew was in the water and swimming for their lives. Gentleman Jim was floating facedown, bobbing along like a piece of driftwood. Ronan dove in after him before Dean even had a chance to point him out. He reached the captain quickly and turned him onto his back, supporting him about the neck and shoulders. Ronan looked around for a piece of floating wreckage to grab hold of before they both drowned.

Dean spied a pirate rowing alone in one of the lifeboats that had come off the *Reckless*. "You there! Turn around! The captain's been injured!"

The pirate turned his head, but he didn't turn the boat. Dean's heart sank when he saw it was Rook steering the lifeboat.

"Seaborne!" Ronan called out. "I'll take care of the captain! You take whatever you can and get off that ship!" He turned and yelled to Rook. "Ahoy! Toss me a line, you lice-infested sea bass!"

Rook held up a length of rope and grinned a slimy grin. Dean figured there was about as much chance of Rook sprouting angel's wings and flying off to heaven as there was of him lifting a finger to help Gentleman Jim. Luckily, Rook's hand was forced when a few more boys climbed into the tiny boat and he was no longer alone. Bowing under pressure from his shipmates, he threw out the line.

Without the captain, the evacuation devolved into chaos. Dean called for Kane and Marko, but they had jumped ship with the rest of the crew. He was left alone on board with all the food and water.

"Perfect," Dean grunted as he watched the freshwater stores roll around below. They needed those provisions, but he couldn't bring them up alone. With the bow of the *Reckless* already dipping below the waves, the ship's angle was too steep and unforgiving to merit even an attempt. Raising each barrel took two men when the ship was level.

"Think," Dean told himself. He paced the ship, racking his brain for a solution as the front end of the *Reckless* sank deeper and deeper below the waves. Meanwhile, the stern end of the ship rose higher and higher out of the water. Dean went to the side and grabbed on to the gunwale for balance. That was when he looked over the railing and saw a hole in the ship's hull two decks down. Dean snapped his fingers. "That's it!" He grabbed a hatchet and jumped back down through the main cargo hatch. If he couldn't bring the cargo up, he'd roll it out instead.

Dean ran to the ship's store of rations and went to work pushing the food and water across the floor. It should have been an impossible task for a boy his size, but as the ship continued to sink, the floor's incline increased. With a little help from gravity, he was able to roll all the barrels down through a hatch that led to the ship's middle deck. Once that was done, he jumped down after them and ran to the opening in the wall he'd spotted from up above. Moonlight poured in through the ship's wounded hull, which was preferable to seawater, but Dean was not seeing *enough* light. The hole was only slightly larger than the cannonball that had created it. Dean had to make it bigger if he meant to get the barrels out that way.

He swung his hatchet into the planks of wood surrounding the hole. He pried boards loose and kicked them out as the *Reckless* sank. Packs of rats scurried under his legs and out through the break in the wall as he hacked away. "Brilliant," he said, grumbling.

"Just brilliant. Staying on board a ship when even the rats know it's time to leave!"

He gave the wall one final blow as the last wave of rats ran by him. The hole was now wide enough for the barrels to easily pass through. On the lower deck, gravity now worked against Dean. He had to move the barrels uphill to get them off the ship, but thanks to his work with the hatchet, the hull was wide open. Bracing his back against the wall and pushing with his legs, Dean sent the rations out over the side, one after the other. His shipmates outside cheered him, but he took little notice. At this point, it no longer mattered if the Pirate Youth accepted him as one of their own. With or without a ship, Gentleman Jim was going down. Dean's report would see to that. The Pirate Youth's days were done. All that mattered now was getting off the *Reckless* before it was too late. Dean knew he couldn't get all the barrels out, but he vowed to save as much food and water as he possibly could. It was either that or pray for rain, and maybe even turn cannibal out on the open sea. He found neither alternative appealing. The very idea kept him going back for more barrels.

He finally had to stop when the bow of the *Reckless* became completely submerged. The stern climbed up high into the air, and the ship rose to an angle that was hard for Dean to move across. The slope of the incline was so steep and the floor so slippery that he struggled to negotiate the deck. He threw out a few coiled piles of rope to tie the barrels together and prepared to take his leave.

"Godspeed, old girl." Dean patted the ship's hull. "You held out as long as you could."

The *Reckless* groaned in reply. Dean froze in place. Was the ship talking to him? Dean realized his mistake when he saw the straight beams of the hull begin to curve. He drew in a sharp breath as the wooden frame of the *Reckless* strained against gravity and bent, right at its center— right where he was standing. The stern was rising too high. The ship was approaching a vertical orientation and buckling under its own weight.

Wood splintered and broke all around him. The floor, the wall, the ceiling . . . everything was torn asunder as the ship split in half. It was the loudest sound Dean had ever heard at sea, louder than a thousand cannons. He shielded his eyes as the deck cracked and fell away beneath him. He fell right along with the broken pieces of the ship. The ocean wrapped itself around him, and the currents sucked him down deep.

CHAPTER 8

GOING UNDER

In the water, Dean got tangled in rope lines from the sails and rigging. He tried to kick them off, but that only served to make matters worse. Ropes tightened around Dean's limbs like octopus tentacles as the sinking ship pulled him down, refusing to let go. The water grew colder and darker with each passing second. Dean's mind flashed back to the harrowing minute he had spent underwater with the sharks. That was nothing compared to this. As painful as being eaten alive would have been, it would have at least been over quickly. Drowning on board the *Reckless* would take time. Dean didn't want to die like that. He didn't want to die, period. Thoughts spun around his head like the wheel of a ship with no helmsman there to steady it. He thrashed about like a fish caught in a net until finally he realized brute force wasn't going to get him anywhere. He gathered up his wits, along with the hatchet he'd nearly forgotten, and cut himself free. By then, he didn't know which end was up, but he followed the bubbles and swam for the stars. His lungs felt ready to burst.

A few moments later, Dean broke through to the surface and breathed deep, grateful breaths.

"Here!" Ronan yelled, pulling him out of the water and into the boat. Barrels of food and water floated all around them. The crew was scattered across the waves, fighting to stay on top of the rations.

"Did everyone get off?" Dean asked.

"Aye." Ronan nodded. "Now that you're here. You took your time, Seaborne. That was either the bravest thing I've ever seen, or the craziest."

Dean settled into the lifeboat, breathing heavily. "Probably a bit of both." He looked at the wounded captain, then out at the wreck of the *Reckless*. "Don't worry, it won't happen again."

Ronan watched the ship slip away. "No, I suppose it won't, at that." He patted Dean on the back. "You did right by us here, swabbie. Good job."

Dean leaned out of Ronan's reach. "I didn't do it for you. We're dead without those provisions, remember?"

Ronan laughed. "Don't kid yourself. We're dead either way. We already didn't have enough gold to give One-Eyed Jack a proper tribute. That was bad enough, but now we've lost his ship as well! The only good news is the ocean will kill us long before he gets a chance."

Dean grimaced. "I take it the captain didn't name you first mate for your optimism."

"Look me in the eye and tell me I'm wrong. We're a few days from shore in any direction. We'll never make land just bobbing along the waves, and any ship willing to rescue the likes of us will probably be filled with men who want to see us hanged. What do you think is going to happen out here?"

Dean nodded gloomily as the waves lapped against the tiny boat. Something in the water caught his eye. "I don't know. You never can tell what the tide will bring in." Out of nowhere, the handheld sail Dean had discarded earlier when approaching the *Santa Clara* drifted up. He snatched it out of the water. More sails could be seen floating among the wreckage. With the means to catch the wind, land didn't seem so impossibly far off anymore.

"Look at that," Ronan said. "First bit of luck we've had on this run. I'll take that as a good omen. Lord knows we could use one."

More than you know, thought Dean, feeling guilty again. He rolled up the sail and stowed it next to the sleeping captain. "We'd best get to work."

Over the next few hours, the former crew of the *Reckless* used the rope lines Dean had salvaged to tie up anything that would float. Dean's efforts to save the barrels and rigging proved to be the difference between life and death as the Pirate Youth fashioned together a giant wooden mound. It was an impressive construct, more island than raft, and large enough to fit the full crew of fifty pirates. Granted, nearly half of them had to hang off the side and float along, but that was better than being left behind.

They spent the next few days floating around the Caribbean and trying to reach the nearest island. Dean and a few others used the miniature sails to catch the wind and pull the raft forward, while Ronan organized the crew and assigned tasks to keep them focused on the positive work of staying alive. He did an able job filling in for the captain, who was still passed out in a lifeboat tied to the raft. Ronan had done all he could to make Gentleman Jim comfortable. A satchel was placed beneath his head for a pillow, and a few swatches of fabric were propped up over his body to keep him in the shade. He woke up only for a few feverish, delirious moments at a time. Those moments passed as quickly as they came, and all hands on deck were thankful for it. Odds did not favor the captain living to see the shore. Odds didn't favor anyone on board. Floating on barrels filled with water, salted meats, and pickled vegetables had given the crew a boost to start their journey, but water and supplies were running low even before the *Reckless* went down. It was only a matter of time before morale started to crack.

The Pirate Youth drank no water on their first day. On the days that followed, rations were kept to sips. Even the captain got his, though he drank last and took the least. Ronan would bring a small amount to Gentleman Jim and pour it in his mouth. By the second day, Dean could see that Rook considered this a waste of water, but it took him until the third night to do anything about it.

Dean was up late manning one of the sails when he saw Rook creep past his sleeping shipmates. Dean would have paid Rook no mind if he had just walked across the raft normally, but the focused effort he made to be quiet seemed suspicious. Everything about Rook seemed suspicious, the object he had concealed in his right hand most of all. Rook stopped at the edge of the raft and picked up the rope tied to Gentleman Jim's launch. He pulled the line tight and crouched down before it. A dagger twinkled in the moonlight. Dean drew in a sharp breath. *He means to cut him loose.*

Thinking fast, Dean let out the sail and jumped into the air. The wind carried him across the raft in a flash. "Avast!"

Rook whirled around with his knife drawn, but he wasn't ready for Dean flying through the air at such a speed. Dean threw his feet into Rook's chest and knocked him back into the ocean. Ronan woke up when he heard the splash. "What just happened?"

Dean let go of one end of the sail and landed next to Ronan. "Not much. Rook offered to give up his place on the raft, that's all."

"What? Man overboard!"

"No, you don't understand," Dean said, picking up Rook's knife. "He tried to cut the captain's line."

Ronan's eyes lit up with rage. "Rook, you double-crossing cur."

A wave splashed Rook in the face, and he choked down a mouthful of salt water. "The cap'n's dead! We'll all die of thirst if you keep wastin' our water on 'im!"

Rook tried to climb back onto the raft, but Ronan stepped on his fingers. "The only water that's been wasted here are the drops you drank. But, if it's water you're after, you've got all you can stand down there. Take as much as you like. That's where you'll be spending the rest of this trip, however long or short it might be."

Rook gave Dean a look that would have disarmed a swordfish. Then he tied a loose rope around his wrist, in case he ever lost his grip on the raft, and snarled at Dean and Ronan. "This ain't over. Yer gonna wish you never met me, the both of ya!"

"I already wish that," said Dean, meaning every word. This job had completely gone to wreck. He'd broken all the rules of spy craft—the same rules that had kept him alive all these years. Don't get attached to people. Don't get involved in matters that don't concern you. Don't linger long enough to make enemies. He felt Ronan's hand on his shoulder.

"Thanks for that, Seaborne. I think I might have misjudged you."

Dean shook his head. "Don't thank me yet. We're still a long way from home."

Ronan laughed. "Where's that? I don't know about you, but my home's lying in pieces on the ocean floor. There's no home for the likes of us. At this point, our only hope lies in getting rescued by the right ship."

"Thanks, Ronan. You always know just what to say."

Time passed, food ran out, and the boys languished beneath the hot Caribbean sun. When the water ran dry, as sooner or later it had to do, the crew faded fast. Dean held out as long as he could, but eventually he succumbed to the heat just like everyone else.

CHAPTER 9

DRIFTERS AND GRIFTERS

When Dean opened his eyes, he found himself in a much better place than the one where he had last closed them. In fact, he had somehow ended up in a better place than he'd ever been before.

Saved? I don't believe it. We're saved!

His vision was fuzzy, and it took a moment for the room to come into focus. Moonlight shined through the stained-glass window behind him, and oil lamps lit the room with a soft amber glow. When his eyes finally made their peace with the light, Dean wasn't entirely sure if he could trust them. He was in bed, resting comfortably. He was safe, warm, and above all, dry. His first thought was that he was either dreaming or dead.

Dean propped himself up in the bed, resting on his elbows. The bed was heavily laden with soft pillows and made up with clean sheets. As he pressed at the cushions beneath him, he realized someone had changed him into clean clothes as well. He felt the fine, smooth cuff of his sleeve. It was the kind of fabric One-Eyed Jack's men took off trade ships during raids. He was on board a ship, and it looked as though he'd been given the captain's cabin. Why? How long had he been there? Where were the others?

Dean's throat felt dry and scratchy. His questions would have to wait. Right now, he needed one thing and one thing only.

"Water?" asked a voice.

Dean's head snapped around. His hands shot out. He hadn't noticed the man beside the bed before. He hardly noticed him now. Dean saw only that the man was holding a tall glass of water. Dean swallowed it all down in a single gulp, then spit up at least half, choking through a violent fit of coughs.

"Slowly," the man said, patting Dean on the back. He refilled the glass from a pitcher on a table next to the bed, this time only to the halfway mark. He passed it back to Dean. "Just sip it to begin."

Dean nodded, feeling foolish. He knew a person in his condition had to take it slow with his first sip of water, but he couldn't stop himself. He was so thirsty. Acting with a clearer head the second time around, he finished the short glass, kept it down, and drank another full one.

"Thank you," Dean said, clearing his throat. "I'm in your debt, sir."

The man waved a finger back and forth. "No. It is my honor to help you in your hour of need. More than you could possibly imagine."

Dean squinted at the man and turned the odd reply over in his brain. An honor? To help *him*? The man who had given him the water was old, but hale and hearty. His stark white hair and full beard made him look wise and worldly instead of withered. He had the tough leathery skin of a lifelong sailor but the build and bearing of a man whose life had not been long at all.

"You are no doubt wondering who I am," the man said.

"I'm wondering why I'm in here all by myself. Where are the others? I can't be the only survivor. Am I?"

"Your mates are all safe on board this ship."

Dean breathed a sigh of relief. It was odd, but he felt real concern for Gentleman Jim and his crew. *Why?* He wasn't one of them. The fact was he hardly even knew them, but the feelings were there just the same.

"I believe introductions are in order." The old man stood up and took a formal bow. "My name is Verrick. You are a guest on board my ship, the *Tideturner*. Please, if you would be so kind as to tell me whom I have the honor of addressing?"

Dean furrowed his brow. Twice, Verrick had said it was an honor to have him on board. That was strange enough all by itself, but it was stranger still now that the man had made it clear he didn't know who Dean was. "They call me Seaborne. Dean Seaborne."

Verrick raised an eyebrow. "Seaborne, you say? But that's the name reserved for . . . "—Verrick motioned with his hands, searching for the right words—"for *fatherless* children."

Dean nodded. "I take it you thought I was someone else?" His lips formed an apologetic smile. "Sorry to disappoint you. I was wondering why you were so honored to play host to a sea-born orphan." He motioned to the bed and his fine sleepwear. "In such style too."

"It's true, then? You have no family to speak of?"

Dean shook his head. "None but my shipmates."

"Where are you from?"

Dean's eyes narrowed. This Verrick certainly asked a lot of questions. "I don't claim to be from anywhere. I know where I live and where I've been, but no more than that. My only home is the ocean blue."

Verrick stared at Dean, deep in thought. "I don't believe it."

Sensing his time in the lap of luxury was nearing an end, Dean threw back the covers. He started to climb out of bed, but Verrick motioned for him to stay put.

"The wreck of your ship. Your mates tell me pirates had a hand in that."

Dean nodded. "That's true enough." And so it was.

"Pirates," Verrick said with gravel in his voice. "Scum of the sea. Their wretched lot has played an even greater part in your life than you realize, I'll wager."

Dean tilted his head to one side. *Another odd comment.* Something was off about Verrick. He could feel it. "Sir, you still haven't told me why I'm in here all alone. At first I just assumed I'd taken the longest to recover, but I can't help but think there's something else going on."

Verrick pointed at Dean. "You're a clever one. It's no wonder you've survived this long."

Dean studied Verrick. "Why do I get the feeling you're not talking about surviving out on the waves with the rest of the crew?"

Verrick smiled. "Because I'm not." He sat down across from Dean and leaned in toward him. "Tell me, Dean, what do you know about Zenhala?"

"Zenhala?" Dean smirked. "Are you serious? "What has that got to do with why I'm here?"

"Everything. I take it you've heard of the island?"

"Every sailor worth his salt has heard of Zenhala."

"Good, that will save us time. Less to explain."

Dean shook his head. "There's nothing to explain. The Golden Isle's a myth."

"Many sailors would disagree with you."

"Desperate men and fools."

Verrick shrugged. "Some perhaps. But please, indulge me.

What about the traders of Zenhala? Surely, you must know of them too...."

Dean nodded, playing along. He knew everything there was to know about Zenhalan folklore. He wouldn't have used it in the grift he ran on Gentleman Jim otherwise. "The traders are like the leprechauns of the Caribbean. They go out into the world once every year to exchange the golden harvest for goods and supplies. If you're lucky enough to come across one of their ships, you keep it in your sights and follow it back to the Golden Isle. If you can keep up, that is."

"Easier said than done, is it?"

"They say the traders of Zenhala move through market towns like ghosts and sail across the ocean with skills that shame Lord Neptune himself."

"Really?" Verrick smiled. "They say all that?"

"That and more."

Verrick tugged at his beard with a modest grin. "Well, that's the real trouble with legends, isn't it? They get all blown out of proportion. One has to be careful not to let that kind of talk go to his head. Pride is a sin, you know."

Dean looked at Verrick. "That's what this is, then? You want me to believe you're a trader of Zenhala?"

"You don't believe in the Golden Isle? Not even a little?"

"Sir, I may be a child in your eyes, but that doesn't mean I believe in fairy tales. There is no Zenhala. It's a legend, nothing more."

"Believe it or not, I love to hear people say that. That brand of skepticism has kept my island safe for hundreds of years."

"And yet, here you are, telling me your secret. A boy you dragged out of the ocean and hardly know. I appreciate your help, Captain Verrick, but I don't know what you hope to gain spinning this tale for me."

"More than you can possibly imagine." Verrick slid his chair close to Dean's bedside and lowered his voice. "You see, I'm not a trader of Zenhala. Not anymore. For the last thirteen years, I have been a seeker. A seeker for the lost prince."

"The lost prince?" Dean had to laugh. A few days earlier, he had been selling Gentleman Jim practically the same story. "Save your breath, Captain. I've heard this one as well."

"You haven't heard it from me." Verrick took Dean by the hand. "Thirteen years ago, a pirate captain fought his way across the Triangle's treacherous waters and made it all the way to Zenhala. He stole every coin of the island's golden harvest and more—much more. The loathsome knave killed my queen and took her infant son hostage. He set sail with Zenhala's greatest treasure, swearing to throw the boy overboard if we pursued him. My king's hands were tied. It killed him to do it, but he couldn't risk the life of his only son. He let the man go."

"And the prince is still out there," Dean interrupted. "I told you, I know this story. I know all the stories." He tried to pull his hand back, but Verrick wouldn't let go.

"The story isn't finished. I and others like me have been looking for that boy ever since, but now the search is over. At long last, the prince has been found. This mark you bear is proof." Verrick turned Dean's wrist over and exposed the small tattoo on his inner arm. "Three wave crests rising in a circle. It's the mark of the Royal House of Aquos, Lord of Zenhala."

Dean was struck dumb by Verrick's claim. It took him a moment to formulate a reply. "I don't understand. You think I'm the—"

"You're my prince. And it is my great honor to be the one who brings you home."

Dean squinted hard at Verrick. He'd heard twenty versions of this story if he'd heard a single one. The tale of the lost prince was popular among bandits who traded in Zenhala's legend. Many a crooked man had posed as the guardian of a child he'd claimed to be the lost prince, and begged shipowners to take them home. The gullible fools who were taken in by this scheme were led into ambushes and robbed of their cargo, their ships, and in some cases, their very lives. Verrick's take was different. A grifter trying to convince a penniless boy that *he* was the prince? Where was the profit in that? Dean was certain that Verrick was engineering some kind of scheme, but for the life of him, he couldn't figure out the angle.

Dean felt at the small tattoo One-Eyed Jack's men had branded him with years ago. "You're mistaken, sir. I got this mark when I was purchased at a young age by a wealthy shipowner." That was Dean's standard cover story to explain the mark on his arm.

"And where is that wealthy shipowner now?"

Dean looked away. "Killed by pirates." As far as Dean knew, that was the truth. He had never been given any reason to doubt it. His earliest memories were all on board the *Maelstrom*, being yelled at by One-Eyed Jack. He had been taken in a raid at an early age and shanghaied into his service. Dean had grown up spying for One-Eyed Jack; that was all he'd ever known. He'd die spying for him too, one way or the other.

"You've been plagued by pirates since birth, haven't you, Your Grace?"

"Don't call me that. I'm no prince."

"How old are you?"

"Thirteen."

"There, you see? You're the correct age, and you've already admitted that you're an orphan with no real knowledge of his origins. You misspoke before when you assumed I was expecting someone else. If anything, you've proven yourself to be exactly whom I've been looking for."

Verrick pressed a coin into Dean's hand. Dean held it up to the lantern and saw that it had been minted with the same sigil that was tattooed on his arm. He was shaken by the sight of the coin's imprint. Its presentation was a powerful move on Verrick's part. He had played his hand well, but Dean knew a con when he saw one. It would take more than a single piece of gold to buy his trust.

"This doesn't prove anything. This mark on my arm is common. Everyone from slavers to spice traders has flown a flag with this symbol."

Verrick took back the coin. "That is by design. My people have worked very hard to place that mark throughout the seven seas. Thanks to our efforts, it has been used at one time or another by nearly every kind of sailor. When we fly that flag, we can claim to be anyone we wish. Surely you can understand why we need to employ such deception."

Dean nodded. If there was one thing he understood, it was deception. On that score, he and Verrick seemed to be cut from the same cloth. The old man had an answer for everything, just like most professional thieves. Dean racked his brain, trying to figure out what he was up to. All he could figure was that Verrick intended to kidnap him and ransom him back to his family. That had to be why he had casually inquired about his father, then the "wealthy shipowner's" current whereabouts. He was using Zenhalan folklore as a means to separate Dean from the others, just as Dean had used it to separate Gentleman Jim from his wallet. If only Verrick knew how little he stood to profit from his ruse. There wasn't a man alive who would part with a pocketful of sand to broker Dean's safe return. Dean was determined to be long gone before Verrick found out he was wasting his time. He rubbed his head and winced. "Sir, this is a lot to take in. I need to think . . . I need to think about—"

Dean tried to get up and feigned exhaustion, nearly falling out of bed. Verrick caught him before he hit the ground.

"You're still delirious from the heat, my lord. You need to rest." Verrick helped Dean back into bed. "I'll not be losing you now, not when we're so close to restoring Zenhala to glory."

Dean lay back down and did his best to look weak and weary. In his current state, it required very little acting. "Where are we? Are we going to Zenhala now?"

"Not yet. The ship is docking at Bartleby Bay to unload your crew and restock on supplies."

Dean sat up with a start. "Bartleby Bay? On St. Diogenes?"

Verrick took Dean's reaction in stride. "It *was* the closest island."

"It's also a notorious pirate haven."

Verrick patted Dean's shoulder. "Don't worry. You'll soon leave these pirates behind, once and for all. Sleep well, my prince. We sail for Zenhala with the morning tide."

As soon as Verrick closed the door behind him, Dean sat up. "Not with me you won't." He flipped the gold coin across his knuckles and held it up to the lantern once more. Lifting it from Verrick's pocket had been a simple matter. Now it was time for a closer look. Dean brought the coin up to his teeth and bit down.

Sure enough, it was solid gold. He couldn't believe it. This Verrick must have really thought he was worth something to go through such trouble. Dean knew better. One-Eyed Jack had always been there to remind him he was worth less than a torn sail.

The *Tideturner* dropped anchor off the coast of St. Diogenes. Dean heard the Pirate Youth talking as they were led off the ship, and he searched his cabin for a way to join them. The footsteps he heard outside his door told him that the window was the only option. He spun it open and nearly jumped out of his skin when he saw Ronan on the other side. He was hanging on to a rope with his feet pressed up against the stern.

"Ronan!"

"Quiet! You want the whole blasted ship to know I'm outside your window?"

Dean put his hands up. "Sorry," he said in a normal speaking voice. Ronan winced and put a finger to his lips. "Sorry!" Dean said again, this time in a whisper.

"Never mind that now. Are you all right? What did they want with you?"

Dean shook his head. "You wouldn't believe me if I told you."

"Tell me later, then. Right now, we've got to get you out of there. There's treachery afoot."

Dean gripped the windowsill. "What is it? Has something happened?"

Ronan nodded. "It's the captain. Verrick's men said they got everybody off the raft, but Gentleman Jim's not aboard."

"Not on board? Where is he?"

"I was hoping to find him in here with you. Have you seen him?"

"No."

Ronan hung his head and sighed. "Could be the raft came undone while we were out . . . could be they're lying and they've got him stowed somewhere else. I'm going to find out. The ship's going down to a skeleton crew as they go ashore. They're just leaving a few guards behind, there outside your door." Ronan dropped down the rest of the line into the water and reached out a hand. "Come on, now. Won't get a better chance than this."

"I can't believe you came back for me."

"Captain's orders, remember? No one gets left behind." Dean took Ronan's hand and climbed into the window frame. "Besides, somebody has to go square things with One-Eyed Jack."

Dean let go of Ronan and stepped back. "Square things with One-Eyed Jack? What are you talking about?"

"Don't tell me you already forgot we lost our ship."

"I haven't forgotten anything. What are you saying? You want *me* to go see One-Eyed Jack?"

"I know it's a tall order, but I wouldn't ask if I didn't think you could handle it. You just have to buy us some time."

"I can't speak for the *Reckless*." Dean shook his head. "I'm the wrong guy for the job. The really wrong guy. You have to trust me on that."

"I do trust you, and you're the only guy left. I already sent the rest of the crew off."

"What about you?"

"I'm staying to look for Gentleman Jim. I know I said I didn't trust you before, but after watching you get the water off the ship, and the way you saved the captain—"

"You were right not to trust me! Ronan, I'm not who you think I am. I'm one of the pirate king's spies."

Ronan froze in place. His eye twitched. "What?"

"I'm sorry, but it's true. I wish it weren't. He sent me to find out why Gentleman Jim's payments came up short these last few months. If I go see him, he's going to want to know about the Gentleman's Code."

Ronan gritted his teeth. "You two-faced—you'd do that? Rat us out to One-Eyed Jack?"

"I don't want to! I've got no choice in the matter. He owns me. He owns all of us!"

Ronan raised a fist to pound the hull of the ship. He stopped himself just before he hit it, mindful of the noise it would make and the attention it would draw. He took a deep breath and looked at Dean with fire in his eyes.

"You're going to fix this, Seaborne. I don't know how, but

you're going to make it right. Gentleman Jim got hurt saving your skin. Yours and mine, remember that. You owe the captain your life, and if you don't make good on that debt, I'm gonna come collect. We don't owe One-Eyed Jack anything until the end of the month, understand? You're going to ask him to lend us a ship so we can go get the loot he's due."

"Lend us a ship? Are you crazy? He'll kill me just for asking!"

"Good! At least that'll be one less thing for me to do." Ronan gripped the rope and started climbing up toward the deck. "Start swimming, Seaborne. It's a long way back to shore."

Dean leaned out the window and watched Ronan climb out of sight.

"Not long enough."

All things considered, his conversation with Ronan had gone better than he expected. When Dean saw Ronan make a fist, he thought for sure he'd be losing some teeth. He took a final look around his cabin, safe in the knowledge that he'd never again experience such luxury. Part of him wanted to stay, but that would have been folly. Verrick's scheme could only be another problem he didn't need. When someone locks you in a room and lies about why they put you there, you don't stick around. You break out, first chance you get. Dean took the gold coin out of his pocket and stared at it, thinking about Verrick's story. "Prince Seaborne." He laughed. "If only it were true."

CHAPTER 10

BY ORDER OF THE KING

Dean felt bad about ruining the fine clothes that Verrick had given him, but it couldn't be helped. He crept into the water and swam hard against the current for the better part of an hour. Fortunately (or unfortunately, the way Dean looked at it), he didn't have to make it all the way to shore. He only had to reach a small, rocky inlet called Dead Man's Cove. The cove was aptly named, for it was the place where One-Eyed Jack's ship, the *Maelstrom*, was moored. As Dean approached, One-Eyed Jack's flag loomed large in the moonlight—a one-eyed skull resting over two crossed swords with a crown above its head. Many years had passed since One-Eyed Jack had personally gone on any raids, but there wasn't a soul at sea who didn't still fear his version of the

Jolly Roger. Dean was no exception to that rule. He grabbed hold of a rope ladder that hung off the side of the ship and rested a few moments, fearful they might be his last.

Eventually, Dean found the will to pull himself out of the water. He climbed up the side of the ship without any idea what to say or do when he next saw One-Eyed Jack. The only thing he knew for sure was that he would not be asking him for another ship, no matter what Ronan had said. That was just crazy. Dean half expected to be killed just for delivering the bad news about the *Reckless*. He wasn't about to waltz into the lion's den and start twisting its tail. That was a good way to get your head bitten off.

As Dean went up the ladder, feelings of dread and guilt grew stronger with each passing rung. It was true, Gentleman Jim had gotten hurt while saving his life, but those scales had been balanced when Dean saved him from Rook. They were even, whether Ronan saw it that way or not. Dean had to worry about himself now. He wasn't part of the Pirate Youth. He was a spy. If he was very lucky, he'd live to be an old spy. That was it.

He reached the top deck and climbed aboard. A scar-faced pirate stepped forward with a lantern in one hand and a pistol in the other. "Who goes there?"

Dean stepped into the light and held up the mark on his arm. "Dean Seaborne, to see the pirate king. He's expecting me."

"Seaborne? He's been looking for you, boy!"

"I just said that."

The pirate holstered his pistol and grabbed Dean by the arm. He dragged him across the deck as if he hadn't come aboard of his own free will. Dean struggled to keep up. *Right. I'll be lucky to spend my life trapped with these idiots.*

The scar-faced pirate pushed Dean toward a heavy black door. It groaned as it opened, and he heard One-Eyed Jack's voice on the other side.

"How many blasted lumps of sugar did you put in this? One or two?"

One-Eyed Jack sat at the captain's table, angrily quizzing a hapless pirate about a cup of tea. He was dressed in a nightshirt, looking half-asleep and completely homicidal. As always, Scurvy Gill stood behind his left shoulder, looking like he'd just crawled out of a coal mine.

"Speak up, you spineless wretch! How many?" One-Eyed Jack asked again.

The pirate, a large thuggish man called Lunk, swallowed hard. He had a broken nose and a dim look about him. Dean could tell he was afraid to speak. Lunk was both out of place and out of his depth pouring One-Eyed Jack's tea. "I think I put in . . . one sugar?"

"You think? You don't sound very certain."

Lunk thought a moment. "Two. It was two, I'm sure. Two sugars."

One-Eyed Jack frowned and let the cup slip from his grip.

It dangled from his index finger, spilling everywhere. "Mr. Gill? Left foot."

Scurvy Gill stepped forward and threw a knife. Lunk cried out as the blade lodged square in his boot. One-Eyed Jack stood up and threw his empty cup at his head for good measure. "Don't you even *think* about pulling that knife out until you've brought me another cup of tea! And this time, you'd do well to remember that it's one sugar! ONE! Now, get out of here before I lose my temper! Away with you!"

Lunk hobbled off, whimpering. The scar-faced pirate who had brought Dean in hurried out after him. Dean tried to slip away as well. The captain was in a mood. It was no good dealing with him when he was in a mood. Unfortunately, Scurvy Gill had already spotted Dean.

"Not so fast, Seaborne. Sit yerself down." He pushed out a chair, using the toe of his boot, leaving a greasy black mark on the seat. Scurvy Gill was still the dirtiest pirate Dean had ever met. The crew had a running bet as to when his last bath was, and as far as Dean knew, no one had ever guessed less than thirteen months.

Dean crossed the room to the chair and gulped as he took a seat at the captain's table. One-Eyed Jack picked up the empty saucer that had come with his teacup and held it aloft. "A simple cup of tea. Really, is that too much to ask?"

Scurvy Gill scratched an ugly rash on his neck. "Not too much at all, Cap'n."

One-Eyed Jack tossed the saucer away carelessly. It shattered on the floor. "I can't even trust these pikers to get that much right." He grunted and turned his eye on Dean. "Then we have you, Seaborne. What am I going to do with you? Gentleman Jim came back with some pathetic tributes these last few months, but at least before you joined his crew, he always came back. What did you do out there?"

"Me?" Dean touched his hands to his chest. "Nothing! What makes you think I did anything?"

"You must've done something. You wouldn't have run off again otherwise."

Dean shook his head. "I wasn't running. I came here on my own tonight. I came to make my report."

Scurvy Gill snorted. "Yer late. We already got a report."

"Aye, that we did. A ship lost, its captain dead, and the boy I sent to spy on him is nowhere to be found. I warned you not to disappoint me again, Seaborne. Do I look happy to you?"

"No, sir."

One-Eyed Jack waved a hand. "Mr. Gill, cut his throat."

Dean shook in his seat. One-Eyed Jack was going to kill him before he even got a chance to speak! He got up too fast and stumbled backward over his chair. He would have been dead meat, but Scurvy Gill reached for a knife that wasn't there.

"Bah! My blade's still lodged in that cretin's foot."

"So? You have another."

"Cap'n, it's me killin' blade."

One-Eyed Jack sighed and looked up at the ceiling. "Fine! When he comes back, then." He hollered at the door, "What the devil's taking so long?"

Dean stuck his head out the cabin door to get a look. Down at the other end of the ship, he saw Lunk hobbling along, spilling tea and leaking blood with every step he took. Dean had to talk fast or not at all.

"Captain, I wasn't running, honest! There's a good reason I didn't come back with the others. I can expl—" Dean stopped himself. "Wait a minute. Who told you Gentleman Jim's dead?"

"I did," Rook said, stepping forth out of the shadows. "Didn't know you was a spy, Seaborne. Looks like I did yer job for ya this time. Already told the cap'n everything there is to know."

Dean gritted his teeth, finally putting all the puzzle pieces together. "I'll bet you did. The rumblings One-Eyed Jack heard about Gentleman Jim . . . they came from you, didn't they? You told him about the Gentleman's Code."

"It's true, then!" One-Eyed Jack cut in. "Rook tells me Gentleman Jim walked away from filthy-rich targets time and again. Ships he could have raided for loot to pay me with, and he just let them be. You saw him do this?"

Dean felt a lump in his throat. He'd only known Gentleman Jim a day, but he mourned him just the same. The man deserved better. "If he's dead, what does it matter?"

One-Eyed Jack leaned forward. "If?"

"No, he's dead all right," Rook said, grinning ear to ear. "Lost at sea, the good cap'n was. So sad."

Scurvy Gill shrugged. "No great loss. Serves 'im right for stealin' me lucky sock."

Rook laughed, and something inside Dean snapped. He stood up and gave him a shove. "Wipe that smile off your face, you dog! If he was lost, we both know it's 'cause you cut him loose!"

"I'll cut *you* loose, ya little runt!" Rook tackled Dean. Dean wrapped his arms around him and pulled him down to the floor as he fell. The two boys were the same age, but Rook's scrawny arms packed no punch. Dean pinned Rook to the deck and swung away until the door opened up behind him. Poor knife-footed Lunk shuffled in and tripped over Rook's outstretched legs.

Tea spilled everywhere. Again.

"My tea!" One-Eyed Jack threw his hands up. "Of all the bloody—Enough! Both of you! Get up!"

Scurvy Gill separated Dean and Rook, then sat them both down across from One-Eyed Jack. "Now, look what ya did," Rook said to Dean. "Spilled the cap'n's tea—"

"Shut up, Rook!" One-Eyed Jack bellowed. "Seaborne! What do you mean *if* Gentleman Jim was lost? If he's not dead, where is he?"

Dean straightened his shirt and rubbed a sore spot on his back where Rook had punched him. "Ronan's looking for him now. He thinks the men who rescued us have him."

"The men who rescued you? What would a bunch of Good Samaritans want with Gentleman Jim?"

Dean shook his head. "They weren't Good Samaritans. They were grifters. Tried to tell me they were traders from Zenhala, they did."

"Traders from Zenhala!" Rook said. "That's a laugh."

But One-Eyed Jack was not laughing. His one good eye lit up, and he leaned across the table toward Dean. When he spoke, his voice was as soft as a whisper. "They told you *what*?"

"Wait a minute, no. Not traders. That wasn't it." Dean snapped his fingers. "Seekers! Seekers for the lost prince. They tried to convince me that I was the lost prince of Zenhala. Locked me up separate from the others. I had to swim back to get away. That's why I was late getting here."

One-Eyed Jack and Scurvy Gill traded cautious looks.

"They told ya that you was a prince?" asked Scurvy Gill. "Why would they do that?" He shook his head. "Don't figure."

The conversation's change in tone was not lost on Dean. Scurvy Gill was trying to poke holes in his story, but One-Eyed Jack was listening to him now. The mere mention of Zenhala had hooked his attention. It was just like Gentleman Jim had told him back in the tavern. Never underestimate what the promise of gold will make a man believe. "It was just a trick to get me to go quietly," Dean said, trying not to be too obvious about pushing

One-Eyed Jack's buttons. "My guess is they wanted to ransom me back to whatever wealthy relatives they think I've got. Their captain really tried to sell me on his story. Gave me his cabin . . . even put me in these clothes. Said we'd sail for Zenhala with the morning tide. I saw right through it, of course. Especially when he said they were coming here."

"Here? The ship's here?" One-Eyed Jack gripped the edge of the table, barely able to contain his excitement.

Dean nodded. "It's anchored off the coast of the island."

Rook was incredulous. "Cap'n, yer not believin' any a this!"

One-Eyed Jack backhanded Rook. "I said shut up, you!"

Dean smiled. "It's no lie, sir. I've got proof." Dean produced the gold coin that he had taken off Verrick. He slapped it down on the captain's table and pulled up his sleeve to reveal the identical brand on his arm. "There it is, the mark of the noble house of Aquos. Same as me, the lost prince." Dean winked and took a mock bow. Now that he had One-Eyed Jack's attention, an idea crept into his brain. "It's just a thought, but the Pirate Youth could easily take that ship for you and replace the *Reckless*. Who knows? There might even be enough gold on board for a proper tribute. There's still time for them to square things with you."

One-Eyed Jack picked up the coin and gripped it tight. Scurvy Gill leaned over to whisper in his ear. The two of them exchanged a few quiet words before One-Eyed Jack finally rose to speak.

"A proper tribute. What do you suppose that is, Seaborne? Normally, I take a share of each ship's monthly plunder. With the *Reckless* gone, there's no way to know how big that share should be."

Dean shrugged. "You could take everything. It's not like anyone's going to complain. They'll all be happy just to save their skins."

"You're very quick to distance yourself from your shipmates, I see. What about you, Seaborne?"

"Me?"

One-Eyed Jack held up the gold coin. "It's going to take more than this to make me whole. When the *Reckless* went down, its captain owed me money, and if he's gone, that debt falls to his crew. You were part of that crew, were you not?"

Dean scrunched up his face. "Captain?"

"You're not off the hook yet, Seaborne. Not by a long shot. I'm making you personally responsible for Gentleman Jim's tribute *and* the loss of the *Reckless*."

Dean's heart stopped dead. "Captain, you can't mean that! I wasn't part of the crew. I was there spying for you!"

"You have until the end of the month to make good on your debt. One week."

"One week! That's impossible!"

One-Eyed Jack nodded. "You're probably right. I'd say only your new friends, the traders of Zenhala, can help you now."

Dean squinted at One-Eyed Jack. "The traders? You don't honestly think those men were telling the truth."

"You'd better hope they were. But I don't want to think, I want to know. And you're going to find out for me. If they are truly from Zenhala? If they can lead you back to the Golden Isle?" One-Eyed Jack rubbed his hands together like a starving man sizing up a prize bird. "In that event, you're to signal me at once, understand?"

Dean's eyes swept the room. He felt dizzy. "Signal you? How?"

One-Eyed Jack clapped his hands and called out, "Sisto!" A large green parrot flew in through a porthole and landed on his shoulder. He motioned to the bird. "You'll send my bird back with directions. He'll find me, wherever I am. Any other questions?"

Dean felt a whirlpool churning in his stomach. "Why are you doing this? Why me?"

One-Eyed Jack grinned with a mouth full of brown and black teeth. "Isn't that obvious? You're the one that they want. You're the prince."

Dean leaned on the arm of his chair for support. So much for Gentleman Jim's philosophy of offering the mark "too much." What had he done? Zenhala was a myth. He couldn't find what didn't exist. He'd never be able to pay One-Eyed Jack what he wanted. Dean felt the room wobbling all around him.

One-Eyed Jack frowned. "What's that face for, you ungrateful blighter? You said you wanted to square things. This is a golden opportunity I'm offering. If you can find Zenhala, you'll settle more than your debt. Deliver me the golden orchard, and we'll truly be square. You can go your own way. You can be free."

Dean blinked. The room stopped moving, and his senses turned razor sharp. "Free?" He couldn't believe his ears. Dean had been press-ganged into One-Eyed Jack's service since before he could walk. Just the outside chance of freedom made him want to believe Zenhala was real. He didn't dare get his hopes up high enough for that, but the prize was worth the risk—any risk. "Did you say *free*?"

One-Eyed Jack offered Sisto to Dean. "As a bird."

Dean stood up and reached for the parrot, but stopped himself halfway. "Wait, no. Not just me. If I find Zenhala, all the Pirate Youth go free. No one gets left behind. No one but Rook."

One-Eyed Jack stroked the back of Sisto's neck as he overhauled Dean's words. "Making demands, are we, Seaborne?"

"No, sir. Just a humble request."

One-Eyed Jack nodded. "So be it. Gentleman Jim was the only one who ever wanted those half-pints anyway."

Dean took Sisto onto his arm, and Rook threw up his hands. "I don't believe this."

Scurvy Gill slapped Rook on the back of the head. "Believe it, Rook. You're goin' with 'im."

Dean straightened his back. "I'm not going anywhere with that snake. I don't trust him."

One-Eyed Jack laughed. "Don't waste your time arguing with me. Rook's coming along to keep you honest. Or rather, to keep you *dishonest*. Too much of Gentleman Jim's virtue has rubbed off on you already, I can tell. You don't have that problem, do you, Rook?"

Rook laughed. "No. Not I."

"I thought not. It's settled. You have one week and not a day more, Seaborne. You've always been a smart one. Now's not the time to be changing that. We both know there's not a place on earth that I can't get to you, so just do your job and get out of there. If I don't hear from you . . . if I even think for a single fleeting moment that you're going to run? I'll come after you with every ship I've got."

Dean nodded. "I know you will."

"Good." One-Eyed Jack glanced out the window. "The sun's almost up. Get some proper clothes on and get on your way." One-Eyed Jack had a sneer on his face. "Your loyal subjects are waiting."

PART THREE

ZENHALA

CHAPTER 11

ANCHORS AWEIGH

An hour later, Dean and Rook rowed out to meet the *Tideturner* at sea. They made it to the ship by sunrise. Dean's brow dripped with sweat as they closed in on the boat. *What did I get myself into this time?* he wondered. Dean still wasn't sure what manner of ship the *Tideturner* was, or what to make of Verrick and his crew. The ship was a Bermuda rigged sloop. Bermuda. As in the Bermuda Triangle. Dean might have hoped that Verrick's story was real if he didn't know sloops so well. The slender, single-masted vessel was a favorite of Caribbean pirates because its quick speed and low lines made it difficult to hit with cannon fire. That knowledge gave Dean pause, but he had to admit, such attributes would have proved equally valuable to the traders of Zenhala, if they existed. Dean climbed aboard with Rook at his back and Sisto on his shoulder, not knowing what to believe. When his feet hit the deck, he saw Ronan tied to the mast, being questioned by Verrick.

"I'll ask you again, for the last time. My patience is wearing thin. Where is my prince?"

Ronan struggled against his ropes to no avail. "I told you, I don't know what you're talking about. Where's Captain Harper?" he demanded.

"Neptune's beard, you're thick!" Verrick threw his hands up and turned away. "We've been through this time and again. I've not seen your captain. I wish I had! All hands were brought on board when we saved your crew. If your captain was lost at sea, he's got my sympathy, but my concern is for the living. Now the lost prince is suddenly lost once more, and he left you in his place. Where did he go and why?"

Dean paid close attention. It was telling that Verrick was so anxious to find him and continued to refer to him as a prince.

"I don't know any prince!" Ronan shouted. "How many times do I have to tell you that?"

"You know who I mean. The boy. He was part of your crew!"

"We're all boys in my crew. Who are you talking about?"

Dean stepped out into the open. "Me, Ronan. He means me."

Ronan leaned forward, squinting. "Seaborne?"

Verrick closed his eyes and gently exhaled. "The prince!"

exclaimed several members of his crew. They rushed to Dean's side, greatly relieved. The parrot flapped its wings and squawked in Dean's ear as the sailors crowded around him. Dean turned his head and tried to act like it didn't bother him. The truth was, he hated the way One-Eyed Jack's filthy bird felt on his shoulder. Its talons felt like the pirate king's own fingers digging into his skin.

Dean motioned to Ronan. "Let him go, please. If he gave you any trouble, it was only out of concern for our captain." He locked eyes with Ronan and shook his head. "I'm sorry, Ronan. You won't be finding Gentleman Jim on board."

Ronan blinked. "But he has to be on board."

Rook's lips twisted up in a wicked grin. "Take my word fer it. The briny deep be home to Gentleman Jim now."

Ronan's eyes welled up with tears. Dean balled up his fist. He wanted to knock that smile off Rook's ugly face, but it wasn't the time or place. Over at the mast, Verrick's men cut Ronan loose. He stumbled forth in a daze, crushed by the apparent loss of his captain.

"Sire, you gave us a terrible fright," Verrick told Dean. "You can't imagine . . . for us to have been searching for you so long, only to lose you again the moment we found you." Verrick shivered from head to toe. "Where did you go? Why did you leave?"

Dean smiled. "Come now, Captain. You didn't expect me to swallow a story like yours in one bite, did you?" Dean pointed to the island in the distance. "Bartleby Bay has a reputation. I followed your crew ashore to make certain you weren't pirates yourselves."

Verrick nodded. "Fair enough. I trust you saw nothing to confirm your suspicions?"

Dean shook his head. "I wouldn't have come back otherwise. But this journey still goes against every sane instinct I have. A body would have to be mad to set sail with you."

"You can't mean that."

"Charting a course for Zenhala? I do indeed. But!" Dean raised a finger. He was trying hard to make it seem like he'd come to this decision on his own. "The way I see it, you only live once. So I'm going to do it anyway."

Verrick laughed and clasped his hands together. "You can't imagine how relieved I am to hear you say that. Your kingdom will rejoice in your return." The captain of the *Tideturner* looked to his men. "It's time, lads! Time at last! Your faith has been rewarded. Our years of sacrifice are nearly at an end. Ready a launch for the prince's mates. They'll be going back to the island forthwith."

"Belay that order!" Dean called out. "They're coming with us, Captain."

Ronan joined Rook and Dean, rubbing his wrists. His skin was red where the ropes had bound him. "What's all this about? Where are we going?"

"Your Grace!" Verrick said before Dean could reply. "We can't take outsiders back to the island. It's against the law."

"The law? I thought you said I was the prince."

"Yes. Of course, but—"

"Well? Don't I make the laws?"

Verrick hesitated. He was clearly uncomfortable with the position Dean was putting him in. "It's not that simple."

"It never is. I haven't survived this long by being simple. You said as much yourself. I'm not going anywhere without protection."

Verrick put on a wounded look. "You've no need of protection here. Any man on this ship would gladly give his life for you, myself included."

"So you say. I might be willing to take a chance and trust you, but I don't know you. Not like I do Ronan and Rook. We go together or not at all. That's my final word on the matter."

Verrick rubbed his beard, grumbling. "And the bird? He comes too, I take it?"

"Sisto? He's my closest friend," Dean lied. "I can't leave him behind." Dean fed the bird a cracker and placed him in a cage that he and Rook had brought on board. Sisto snapped at Dean's fingers as he shut the door.

"Very well," Verrick said at last. "Set a course for the Bermuda Triangle, men. We're going home. All of us." The crew hoisted the anchor and loosed the sails. Verrick took the helm, and the three young pirates had a moment alone to talk.

"What the devil is going on here?" Ronan whispered. "You're a prince now?"

Dean nodded toward Verrick. "As far as he knows, yes."

Ronan leaned in closer to Dean. "What do you think you're doing? We can't sail off with these men. We have to square things with One-Eyed Jack."

"I already did that. He gave us a chance to make things right."

"He did?"

Dean shrugged. "In his own way, yes. All we have to do is cover the loss of the *Reckless* and pay the monthly tribute."

Ronan bit his lip. "Did he give us any more time?"

"No," Rook replied. "Payment's due by week's end."

Ronan's eyes went wide. "Is he mad?" He looked at Dean, who confirmed the deadline, and One-Eyed Jack's madness, with a casual nod. "How are we going to get that much loot in a single week? And why do you look so calm? What are we doing with these men? Where are we going?"

Dean took a breath. He could hardly believe what he was about to say:

"Zenhala."

Ronan did a double take at Dean. "*Zenhala?*" He looked at Verrick and his men as they prepared to set sail. "You can't be serious."

"I'm dead serious, Ronan. One-Eyed Jack said if we can deliver the gold of Zenhala, we're out of his pocket for good. You, me, and the rest of the Pirate Youth. The whole lot of us—free. How's that strike you?"

Ronan looked at Dean like a fool who didn't know the port side from the starboard. "You told One-Eyed Jack that we were going to bring him back the golden harvest of Zenhala? You call that a chance to make things right?"

"Unless you've got a better idea."

Ronan bit his lip and turned his back on Dean. He looked up at the heavens and shook his head in disbelief. "I do have one idea." Ronan spun around and punched Dean square in the nose. "How's *that* strike you?"

It took three of Verrick's men to separate Ronan and Dean. Rook cackled with glee as the two of them went at each other. He did nothing to interfere. When the fight was over, Verrick didn't know if he should tie Ronan back to the mast or throw him overboard. "Are you sure you want this one with us, Your Grace? It doesn't bode well that you should need protection from your protection."

Dean massaged his aching nose. It hurt, but it wasn't broken. "We're fine," he told Verrick. "Just a little disagreement between friends. Isn't that right, Ronan?"

Ronan snorted as Verrick's men held him fast. "Aye, Captain. Friends to the end."

Verrick put his hands on his hips and shook his head. "If this is how you are among friends, I'd hate to meet your enemies."

Dean let out a nervous laugh. "You can say that again."

• • •

The *Tideturner* sailed all day and through the night. The next morning, Dean woke up with the sun and found that most of Verrick's men were still asleep. A full day's journey into the Bermuda Triangle, and all hands on deck were snoring loud and resting easy. So far, no one on board had given Dean any reason to believe they were the con men that he first took them to be. *Could they really be from Zenhala? Do they really think I'm their prince?* Dean spotted Ronan at the bow of the ship, whittling away at a small piece of wood. He joined him there and looked out on the horizon in silence. Not a word had passed between them since their fight the previous morning. The tension was as thick as the fog clouds up ahead. Dean wanted to clear the air before they went any further.

"Look what I found below deck," Dean said, holding up a kiteboard and sail from the *Santa Clara* raid. "They must have brought it on board with the rest of us."

Ronan barely looked up from his woodwork. "Lucky. You can use that to jump ship when it's time to cut your losses here."

Dean grimaced and set down the kiteboarding rig. "You're not going to make this easy, are you? I know you're hurting right now, Ronan. You loved Gentleman Jim like a brother; any fool can see that. The man made a lasting impression on me in a day, so I can't imagine what you're feeling after sailing with him for years. But whatever's gone before . . . however we got started . . . we're in this together now. We've got to have a truce between us. You've got to trust me and follow my lead. This is what I do. We've got a chance here, but not if I can't count on you to do your part."

Ronan's knife slipped and he nicked his thumb. He cursed and threw the whittled cross he was working on to the waves. "Let me tell you what you can count on. You see those mists up ahead? They mark the center of the Bermuda Triangle. I've only come this far one other time. That's where this journey's going to end. Finding Zenhala is no plan for settling our debt with One-Eyed Jack. It's suicide. The Golden Isle's a myth, and we're all going to die chasing it."

"I see you remain as hopeful as ever."

"Make jokes if you like, but you'd share my optimism if you'd ever sailed these waters before."

"Look, I thought this was crazy at first too, but now I'm not so sure. Think about it. Would these men sail this far into the Triangle if they weren't really after the island? Would One-Eyed Jack let us go after Zenhala if he didn't think we might find it?" Dean pointed to the impenetrable fog up ahead. "What if the Golden Isle's really out there somewhere waiting for us?"

Ronan scoffed at Dean. "There's nothing out there but a watery grave. One-Eyed Jack's obsessed with Zenhala, Seaborne. He only sent us here because he's too scared to go himself. I was with him the last time he went looking. It didn't end well."

Dean's eyebrows shot up. "You sailed with One-Eyed Jack?"

Ronan nodded. "Nine years ago, I sailed with him. On board the *Maelstrom*. I was there for his final expedition."

"What happened?"

"Something I'll never forget. I was just over six years old when I joined his crew. A lowly cabin boy no one ever spoke to unless they needed someone to yell at, that was me."

"Sounds familiar," Dean said.

"Not likely. I lived through more foul weather than you can imagine, all of it right here." Ronan shivered, as if someone had just walked over his grave.

Dean looked around. The fog clouds ahead were as dark as smoke from a fire, but other than that, conditions were dead calm. "The ocean seems gentle enough this morning."

Ronan wagged a finger at Dean. "There's always a storm raging somewhere in the Triangle. Believe me, I know. Not a day went by that One-Eyed Jack didn't have us out here in the thick of it, scouring these waters for the Golden Isle. How is it you don't know that about him? One of his own spies?"

Dean scratched his head. Seven years had passed since One-Eyed Jack had sent him out on his first spy mission, stowing away on board a gold-laden trade ship. In all that time, One-Eyed Jack had never left St. Diogenes, but anything before that, Dean was too young to remember. "What made him stop looking?"

"The worst storm any of us ever saw stopped him. Dead in his tracks." Ronan pointed ahead. "It was out there, right where you and I are headed now. The weather was unnaturally cold. The clouds were black curtains drawn across the sky, and the wind scraped against our faces like frozen chunks of coral. Rain stabbed down like nails, and the waves . . ." Ronan shuddered. "Huge swells rose high above the ship and crashed down on us over and over again. I had to tie a line around my waist just to keep from getting washed away, but not One-Eyed Jack. He stood rooted to the spot like the trunk of a tree as the ship pitched up and down, nearly flipping us over."

Dean shrugged. "Doesn't sound like the storm got the better of him."

"It wasn't only the storm. We hit something out there. Or should I say, something hit us." Ronan took a deep breath. He eyed the mists up ahead with grim trepidation. "I've never spoken of this to anyone. Not ever. I didn't get a good look at first. I only caught a glimpse. A flash of lightning lit up the sky, and a tall winding shadow cast itself over the sails. I spun around to see what it was, but I was too slow. The light was already gone. A moment later, something big and heavy slapped against the boat like a whip. Decking splintered and a cannon flew through the air. Jim Harper pushed me out of the way as a hundred pounds of iron flew by, just missing me. He was saving me even then."

Dean looked out at the fast-approaching mist. "What hit the ship, Ronan?"

"It was hard to make out in the darkness, but I know what

I saw. There was no doubting its giant size and twisting shape. When the lightning flashed again, I got a good look. Big as a whale and twice as long. Its snakelike body rose up out of the water in arcs as it looped around us. Armored scales covered its hide like shields, and waves of sharp fins ran down its back like swords. That thing moved faster than anything its size had a right to. One minute I spotted its head on the port side, and then in the blink of an eye, I saw it again on the starboard. It was half the size of the ship, and it roared loud enough to drown out the storm."

Dean searched Ronan's face for a sign that he was playing with him. Instead, Ronan's eyes burned with haunted intensity. His hands gripped the handle of his knife hard enough to turn his knuckles white. He wasn't making this up.

"What happened next?"

Ronan shook his head with a sigh. "Nothing, or I wouldn't be here to tell the tale. The beast dove back down beneath the waves, and we never saw it again. But One-Eyed Jack was useless from that point on. He stood at the helm with his mouth open, just staring into the ocean. Jim waved his hands in front of his face but couldn't reach him. We would have died out there if he hadn't taken control of the ship. To pay him back, One-Eyed Jack made him a captain at the age of twenty. I joined his crew that day, and have sailed beside him ever since. But that's over now." Ronan shook his head mournfully. "I swore I'd never come back to this place, no matter what. Seems the years have made a liar out of me."

"Yer a liar, all right," Rook called out. Dean and Ronan turned their eyes up to find their unsavory comrade perched high in the rigging. "Don't pay no mind to that rubbish, Seaborne. Ain't nothin' to it but barnacles and bilgewater. There's no such thing as sea serpents."

"Actually, you'd be surprised what manner of beasts are lurking out there," Verrick said, coming up behind the boys. Dean turned around and saw the captain had changed into a formal dress uniform. He looked like a naval officer, but his colors belonged to no fleet Dean knew of. "It's true," Verrick continued. "All manner of terrible creatures prowl these waters. They weather storms you wouldn't believe for most of the year, but not to worry. They're out of season at the moment."

"Out of season?" Ronan asked.

"Aye. For one month out of every twelve, the storms around our island clear up. The sea serpents sleep a deep slumber, and the compass points north just as it should. This is the month when the traders ship out the golden harvest. It ends this week, when the moon is full."

Dean looked at Ronan. "Lot going on this week, you might say."

Verrick smiled broadly as the *Tideturner* entered the mist. "There'll be a lot going on this very morning. We're nearly there."

The ship passed through the murky vapors and emerged from the fog a few moments later, to be greeted by clear skies and gentle waves. The only creatures in sight were the dolphins splashing about off the starboard bow. "What did I tell you?" Verrick said. "Out of season." He patted Ronan on the back and continued making his rounds, checking up on the ship and his crew.

Ronan stared out at the sparkling blue water, dumbstruck. He couldn't believe the ocean wasn't churning about, black as tar. Dean put a foot up on the bowsprit and looked out on the waves with hope. "Just admit it's possible, Ronan. It's possible the island's out there."

Ronan scoffed at Dean's buoyant attitude. "You sound like every other swab who got himself drowned chasing golden trees."

"Maybe so. But I've got my sights set on bigger things than gold."

"And what might that be, pray tell? You think you're going to end up a prince and call a castle your home?" Ronan had a good laugh at Dean's expense. "If that's what you're after, you're a bigger fool than I thought."

Dean took a moment to reflect on Ronan's dream scenario. That's all it was. A dream. It would have been nice to have a home and actually belong somewhere for a change, but Dean hadn't set his sights quite that high. He stepped back down to Ronan's level. "You know better than that, Ronan. I'm not a fool any more than I am a prince. And I'm not a saint, either. I'm here to get free.

Mark my words, I'll do whatever it takes to make that happen."

Before Ronan could say anything in reply, Rook jumped down to the deck and wedged himself between them. "Look there!" He pointed out across the horizon. "Is that what I think it is?"

Ronan cast his eyes out across the waves and froze when he saw it. "Blow me down and pick me up," he said, pulling his bandanna from his brow.

"Let me have a look!" Dean pushed Ronan and Rook out of his way and searched the sea. His heart sped up as a tiny island came into view, far off in the distance. "I don't believe it."

"Don't ya?" Rook asked, elbowing Dean in the side. "Whatever it takes, Seaborne . . . that's what you said. Yer gonna get the chance to prove it."

CHAPTER 12

THE RETURN

Gather 'round, lads! Gather 'round. I've been waiting thirteen years to fly these colors."

Verrick took out a bright blue flag and held it for all to see. A mighty cheer rose up from the crew, and Verrick tossed the flag to the nearest sailor. Dean watched as a man with bushy blond sideburns snatched it from the air and scampered up the mast, light as a feather.

"Is that the flag of Zenhala?" Ronan asked as the man raised the banner high above the sails. It was a striking shade of blue, emblazoned with the same mark that was branded on Dean's arm.

"It's not a flag at all," Verrick said. "It's Zenhala's Royal Standard, hoisted only to note the presence of a monarch."

Ronan came up behind Dean. "That's you, don't forget." He gave a mock bow. "Your Majesty."

A horn sounded in the distance, startling Dean. Its clarion call rang out far and wide, cutting across the waves in every direction. Dean leaned out over the gunwale and put a hand to his ear. It was coming from the island. He heard the horn sound again, and something else besides. People cheering . . . for him. A whole island full of people were making their voices heard.

Dean ran a hand through his hair. "I don't believe this."

Verrick laughed out loud. "You keep saying that. Can I ask what it was you expected to find?"

Dean looked up at Verrick. "I don't think I expected anything. I merely hoped."

Verrick's smile could not be contained. "That makes two of us, Your Grace. Today, at last, my hopes have been fulfilled."

Verrick bowed his head and returned to the helm. Dean stayed at the railing to marvel at the view. Rook and Ronan stood on either side of him as the *Tideturner* flew across the sparkling water. The ocean around Zenhala was bluer than anything Dean had ever seen. Vivid shades of deep turquoise water contrasted with radiant shallow patches where the sea all but glowed. Alternating streaks of brilliant blue liquid surrounded the island like a seascape painted by an artist. Indeed, the whole island looked like something out of a painting. Lush green mountains with majestic waterfalls rose up behind pristine beaches covered with sand like crushed ivory. There was a rocky harbor with a stone-built dock, and the buildings of the port town were cast in a vibrant array of pastel colors. Bright, happy houses were packed in tight on the bayside rocks and scattered across the face of the large mountains to their north. The kingdom had a thriving population, and in the center of it all, an opulent white palace sat high atop a hill. There was no doubting it now. The Golden Isle of Zenhala was not only real. It was breathtaking.

"It's like nothing I've ever seen before," Dean said. "It looks like paradise."

Rook raised an eyebrow. "Who's to say it ain't?"

Ronan snickered. "Don't get your hopes up, Rook. They won't be letting the likes of you into paradise."

Rook reached over Dean to give Ronan a shove. "You self-righteous toerag. I'll make you eat them words!"

Ronan shoved Rook back. "Don't you put your hands on me again. You'll get them back with fingers missing next time."

"Enough!" Dean said, pushing them both apart. "Are you two *trying* to sabotage us?" Dean looked around the ship. Ronan and Rook's quarrel had drawn the attention of the crew. Again. "Unbelievable, the pair of you! We're this close to our goal, and still you can't control yourselves!" Dean spat on the deck. They were going to arouse suspicion if they kept fighting like this. As the only member of the group with any experience as a spy, it was up to him to set Ronan and Rook straight. He pulled them in close and spoke firmly. "This petty squabbling ends now, understand? This is no vacation we're on. It's business and we have parts to play. Get in character. We're all close friends here, savvy? I just found out I'm a prince. Heir to the greatest fortune in all the Caribbean. You two half-wits are here to protect me like the good friends you are. You're not here to meddle with each other, or with me." Dean leaned in close to Ronan. "Can you remember that?"

Ronan pouted. He was older than Dean and didn't seem to appreciate being bossed around by him, but it was obvious to all that Dean was the expert here. At least when it came to spying. "What do you know about how friends treat each other?"

"I'll fake it," Dean shot back. He poked Ronan in the chest. "If you want to bring One-Eyed Jack back the golden harvest, you'll do the same. Got it?"

Sufficiently chastened, Dean's partners in crime each gave a cursory nod and backed away. Dean took a deep breath, wondering if the two of them had the chops to pull this off. He wasn't worried about himself. All he ever did was fake who he was, so he was used to this sort of thing. Ronan and Rook were new to the spy game, and they were getting thrown into the deep end on their first time out. The very deep end. As the ship pulled into the port of Zenhala, Dean realized that the magnitude of this mission dwarfed all his past experience. A crowd had gathered at the edge of the dock. People who had been swimming on the beach, fishing in boats, or riding over waves on long wooden boards had all stopped what they were doing to watch the *Tideturner* come in. One pretty young surf rider caught Dean's eye as she passed. She stared up at him a little too long and nearly crashed into a fisherman's skiff. Dean hoped she was all right. The waters around the ship were filling up fast. Even up on the ship, Dean started to feel claustrophobic. It wasn't just the number of people that irked him, it was the level of adoration they poured his way. They were paddling out to meet the boat, excited beyond belief. People waved at Dean and embraced each other, bobbing up and down with tears in their eyes. Everyone was thrilled just to get a look at him. It was as if their wildest dreams had all come true.

Verrick motioned for Dean to join him at the wheel of the ship. "I told you the people would rejoice."

"You spoke the truth," said Dean. The frenzied display of affection boggled his mind. "This is crazy. They don't even know me."

"They know that you're their prince." Verrick pointed to the Royal Standard. "That's all they need to know."

Verrick took the boat in, and Dean looked down at the teeming masses that had assembled on the dock. The crew tied off the ship, and half the men on board jumped out to make way for the landing party. Dean's presence on the ship made it a royal party, which meant precautions had to be taken. Verrick's men formed a human barricade as the people of Zenhala stood on their tiptoes trying to get a look at Dean and reach out for the chance to touch him. The walk from the ship was a dizzying experience for Dean. He tugged at his collar. Never before had he impersonated anyone of such stature. Never had he drawn such attention to himself on a mission. A horse-drawn carriage with gilded trimmings pulled up to the end of the dock. Dean knew it could have only one destination. That's when another "never before" occurred to him. He had never before pretended to be someone's long-lost son.

"The carriage will take us to the palace," Verrick explained. "I'm sure you'd like to spend a few moments with your subjects here, but we haven't the time to spare. There are people who mustn't be kept waiting."

Dean gulped. "The king?" The more he thought about it, the more he dreaded what came next. Some things never changed. For all his skill as a spy, he had one glaring weakness—a conscience. He didn't relish the thought of conning a teary-eyed father into thinking he had his son back. Not when he was there only to take his money and run.

Verrick adopted a somber tone. "I'm afraid your father was gone as well. They say he died of a broken heart, soon after your mother was lost."

Dean stopped walking and leaned on Verrick's arm for support. He made the requisite show of emotion, looking sad and disappointed, but in his heart he was overcome with relief. "Who are we meeting, then? Who rules the kingdom?"

"The lord regent Waverland Kray. For the last ten years, he has been the steward of Zenhala and protector of the throne. He has served the kingdom well, awaiting your glorious return."

"Is he a good man, this Kray?" Ronan piped up behind Dean, hustling to keep pace with the group as they moved through the crowd.

Verrick seemed surprised by the question. "Lord Kray is as noble as the day is long."

"Is that long enough? The sun sets every day too, if I'm not mistaken."

Verrick's eyes narrowed. "What are you driving at?"

"I'm just saying"—Ronan waved toward the picturesque port town and stately mountains above—"it's a fair kingdom you have here. For more than a decade, this lord regent's been a king in all but the name. What if he doesn't want to give up the throne to my good friend here?" Ronan took Dean by the shoulder and gave him a hearty shake. Dean winced at the strength of Ronan's grip, but he appreciated his insight. He was showing his worth nicely after all that knuckleheaded bickering with Rook. Dean knew Ronan was a sharp one. He just had to keep his temper in check.

They reached the carriage at the end of the dock. Verrick's men opened the door, but Dean stopped short of going in. "Well? What about it, Captain Verrick? Is Lord Kray going to be glad to see me?"

Verrick's only reply was to shake his head, laughing.

Dean scrunched up his face. "What's so funny?"

"My apologies, Your Grace, but you are questioning the honor of *Waverland Kray*." Verrick shook his head with a smile. "If you only knew . . ."

"Knew what?"

Verrick held open the carriage door and bid Dean enter. "The fact is, Lord Kray will be happier to see you than even these fine people here."

Dean looked around at the joyous crowd. "Happier than these people?" He shrugged and climbed into the carriage as the people clamored to get one last look at him. "Why is that?"

Verrick waited for Ronan and Rook to enter the carriage, then took a seat next to the driver. "Because it means he's going to be the father of a queen one day. His daughter is Waverly Kray. Your future wife."

CHAPTER 13

BLUE BLOOD

The driver got the horses going, and Dean stuck his head out of the carriage window. "I'm sorry, did you say *wife?*"

Verrick turned around and smiled brightly. "I did!"

Dean watched the trees fly by as the carriage sped down the road. He was at a loss. "How is it that you're just telling me this now? I'm getting married?"

Verrick answered with a wry smile. "Not today." He raised an eyebrow. "At least, I don't think so."

Dean was not in a joking mood. "Verrick . . ."

"Don't worry, Your Grace. Royal weddings take time to plan. The two of you should have at least a week to get to know each other before you take your vows."

Dean's jaw dropped. "A week?"

"Watch your head, Your Grace."

Dean ducked back into the carriage, narrowly avoiding a low-hanging tree branch. Ronan and Rook were inside laughing at him. "Seaborne, you dog," said Ronan. "I had no idea you were such a ladies' man."

"Aye, congratulations to the groom," Rook added, with the tip of an imaginary cap. Sisto squawked in his cage. Even the bird was mocking him.

"Very funny," Dean muttered as the carriage drove on. "He's not serious. He can't be." Dean sat back and folded his arms. "He'd better not be."

They rode out of town following a path that overlooked the white-sand beaches of the bay on one side and the bustling marina on the other. The road wound up a hill and into the forest, which was alive with color, and not only because of the flowers that seemed to bloom on every tree. Bloodred monkeys with bright yellow eyes swung from branch to branch and sat together eating exotic fruits that Dean had never seen before. White birds with iridescent feathers flew out to glide through the air on glimmering wings. The island was a tropical dream, civilized yet unspoiled. The village below and the mountainside homes they passed on the road were all well built and kept with care. Flowers bloomed in every window, and smiling faces appeared from every door. It was the exact opposite of everything Dean had known growing up on St. Diogenes. The garbage-filled back alleys and rickety, rat-infested shacks of his youth seemed a million miles away. Dean had never dreamed a place like this could exist.

"Look there," Ronan said, pointing at a golden bird the size of a raven. It landed on a nearby branch and spread out its twinkling feathers.

Rook stuck his head out the window to get a closer look, just as a crimson monkey threw away the core of a purple apple. The fruit hit Rook square in the eye. He cursed and drew his head back in. "I hate bloody monkeys."

"Hah!" Ronan laughed. "Even so. Not every day a body claps eyes on something like that."

The carriage rounded a corner, and the royal palace came into view.

"Or that," said Dean.

Ronan, Rook, and Dean jockeyed for position at the windows to get a look at the castle. It was the most spectacular sight that any of them had ever seen. The palace looked like something out of a dream, standing over two hundred feet tall and crafted entirely of marble and white stone. The massive fortress was blinding in both its beauty and its chalk-white hue. The sun's rays reflected off its stark walls with an unrelenting glare, and that light was added to by six towers tipped with golden spires. Ornate buttresses braced the walls. Stately turrets covered every corner, and intricate embellishments graced each window. The rear of the fort was set against a mountain with a waterfall running down its face, and the front of the palace was shielded by a strong wall and imposing gatehouse. Water from the falls flowed freely through gaps at the base of the wall that were adorned with decorative fountainheads. As the carriage approached, Dean watched the drawbridge open wide and felt his stomach tighten up.

People on the road were cheering as he rode toward the palace. News traveled quickly in Zenhala. The Royal Standard had told the lookouts on land that the lost prince had returned, and the horns they blew had told everyone within earshot. From there, word of mouth had spread faster than the plague, running all the way up to the castle where Dean's future father-in-law the regent lived. Dean frowned. An arranged marriage with some spoiled princess-to-be was a complication he didn't need. Not with a couple of hotheads like Ronan and Rook to contend with as well. Dean leaned over to speak with his accomplices, who were both struck dumb by the castle. "You two just batten down your hatches in there and let me do the talking. This is a big stage we're about to step out on, you hear? Don't let it throw you. We just have to get through today. We meet the regent, get settled, and get word to One-Eyed Jack. With any luck, we'll be gone in two days' time, free to go our separate ways."

Dean's little pep talk was as much for his own benefit as it was for Ronan and Rook's. Ronan smirked. "Before your wedding? Surely not. You'll break that poor girl's heart."

Dean didn't crack a smile. "You're probably right." He didn't want anything to do with the regent's daughter. The girl had probably dreamed all her life of the day the lost prince would return. Dean was going to disappoint her in every possible way. It was probably better if they never met. If it were up to him, they never would.

The carriage passed through the main gate and pulled up to the front entrance of the castle. Verrick jumped down and threw open the doors of the brougham. "Here we are, Your Grace. The Aqualine Palace, your family's ancestral home."

Dean stepped out first, followed by Ronan and Rook. The three of them paused to take in the view, marveling at the immaculate palace. It was even more magnificent up close, seeming impossibly tall and elaborate. Only one feature was lacking in Dean's estimation. The courtyard before the main castle door was filled with decorative fountains, and none of them seemed to be working. They lined the perimeter of the plaza with ornamental figureheads of every size. The largest fountain was especially grand. A golden sculpture, depicting a team of winged horses, had been erected over an empty basin in the center of the courtyard. Dry spouts at the base of each steed's pedestal cried out for water, but there was none to be found. Not for any of the fountains.

Rook scratched his head. "Fer a place called the Aqualine Palace, these fountains seem a bit parched, eh?"

Verrick smiled. "Only for now."

The captain turned away and led the group up the castle steps. Dean hung back and snapped his fingers at Rook. "What'd I just tell you about talking?"

Rook scowled. "I don't take orders from you, Seaborne."

Ronan bumped Rook as he passed him on the stairs. "Say it a little louder, Rook. I don't think the palace guards heard you."

Dean looked up as the castle doors swung open. The soldiers posted outside them snapped to attention as he approached. Their gaze was fixed straight ahead, but Dean caught them trying to steal a glance at him with their peripheral vision. They were excited. Dean gave them a shaky nod, trying to come off a bit overwhelmed. He always took care to project the emotions that an honest person would feel had they been in his shoes. It was part of being a good spy, but in this case it was also the truth. Everything was happening so fast. Dean told himself to keep it together and press on.

He entered the palace and looked around the main entry hall. The castle interior was as white as its exterior, but with a touch of added flair. Decorative columns placed throughout the chamber ran up to the ceiling and held a golden dome in place. Colorful depictions of Zenhalan wildlife were inlaid in the floors. In the center of the room was a red marble statue of a woman holding a baby. It was the focal point of yet another dry fountain. Dean approached the sculpture with keen interest.

"The queen?" he asked Verrick.

Verrick nodded. "Built in remembrance of her. And you." He gestured toward an arch on the other side of the chamber. "Through here, sire."

Dean, Rook, and Ronan followed Verrick through the castle, studying its curious décor as they went. The walls of most corridors were made of mammoth sheets of glass that ran from the floor to the ceiling. The vast chambers behind the thick glass panes housed schools of tropical fish swimming in shallow pools of water. As Verrick addressed the guards outside the throne room doors, Dean took in the frescoes painted on the walls of the royal antechamber. There were four of them, depicting the stages of Zenhala's golden harvest. The first mural was of farmers planting seeds as a violent storm raged off in the distance. The second painting showed workers pulling handfuls of gold out of full-grown trees. The third mural portrayed a scene on the docks; crates of gold were loaded onto ships as the traders set sail under perfect conditions. The fourth and final mural was a painting of the traders returning to port with a bounty of food and livestock as the storm winds chased them home.

"Looks like we've come to the right place," Dean said. "Remember, let me—"

"Let you do the talking," Ronan said. "We know."

The guards opened the doors, and Dean took a deep breath. The curtain was up. If everything went according to plan, this would be his final performance. *The role of a lifetime*, Dean thought.

The idea brought him comfort as Verrick led the way into the immense throne hall. Its ceiling was at least two stories tall, with long blue banners hanging down everywhere. A deep blue carpet ran across the room to the throne, where a man dressed all in white was talking to the regent. The man's back was to the door, but as Dean got closer, he was able to make out what he was saying. "I must urge you to proceed with caution, Lord Kray. The timing here is suspect. I find it rather convenient that the prince should return now, just as you're about to be rewarded for your many years of service."

"I can assure you there was nothing convenient about our journey here," Verrick called out. "Or the last thirteen years at sea, for that matter."

The man in white spun around, embarrassed. He had jet-black hair that was pulled back into a short ponytail, with a gray streak in front. His thin mustache and pointy beard reminded Dean of the way people drew the devil in cartoons, but he was wearing the wrong color for that. The man was dressed in a stark white tunic and matching pants, with a cape that hung to his waist. A golden medal pinned on his breast was the only touch of color on his pallid uniform.

Upon seeing Dean, the men and women of the court bowed their heads and bent their knees. It was a strange, uncomfortable moment for Dean, but it was one that would pass quickly. The man in white did not kneel. "On your feet, lords and ladies," he said. "Members of the royal guard . . . at ease." He looked to Dean. "Forgive me, young sir. I mean you no disrespect. I just happen to be a more watchful man than most." He shook his head at the members of the court as they got up off their knees. "Someone here has to be. The cheers outside our castle walls notwithstanding, proof of your lineage has not been confirmed. You understand, I'm sure."

"Arjent Ralian." Verrick bristled. "I would not bring him before the regent if I were not satisfied that he was the—"

"His identity has not been established by anyone other than an overzealous sea captain," the man in white said, cutting Verrick off. "And I'll thank you to address me as Lord Ralian, sir."

Verrick glared at the man in white. Lord Ralian was the first person Dean had met on the island who wasn't happy to see him.

"Don't look at me like that, Captain Verrick. It's my duty to be suspicious. I have been charged with protecting this kingdom, have I not?"

"You have," a strong voice called out. "And we thank you for your devotion, but I have been charged with protecting the throne until such time as the broken line of Aquos is restored. If that day has come, then it has come." The lord regent stood up and the room quieted down. Dean was impressed. Waverland Kray might not have been born a king, but he certainly looked the part. True blood royalty or not, he had a king's bearing. The regent had a large frame and an imposing figure. A hearty beard covered his chin, and thick brown hair covered his head. The only feature missing from his royal veneer was a crown. Instead, the regent wore a gold chain with three large medallions over a formal green dress coat. He placed a hand on Verrick's shoulder. "Captain, is it true? Can it be true?"

"I believe so, my lord." Verrick stepped aside to reveal Dean. "Lord Regent Kray, it is my honor to present Dean Seaborne. The lost prince of Zenhala and heir to the golden throne."

Dean took a deep breath as Kray looked him up and down. It was quite a moment for Dean. His royal debut. The regent didn't seem convinced. Perhaps his advisor, Lord Ralian, had already succeeded in planting a seed of doubt in his mind. Or perhaps it was something more. Namely, a desire for Dean not to be the rightful heir to the throne he had just been sitting on so comfortably.

Ronan nudged Dean from behind, silently imploring him to say something. Dean realized he was falling down on the job of "doing all the talking" and bowed his head. "It's an honor to meet you, Lord Regent. Captain Verrick tells me that in my absence, you have ruled my kingdom with honor. I'm in your debt."

Kray rubbed his beard. "Your kingdom, is it? This is the house of Aquos, Dean Seaborne. How did you come by that name, if you don't mind my asking?"

"How does anyone come by a name, sir? It was given to me. Where I come from, Seaborne is the surname that all children of unknown origins get saddled with."

"Where you come from," Lord Kray repeated suspiciously.

"He never knew his family," Verrick said. "He is the correct age."

"And the mark?" Ralian asked. "Does he bear the mark?"

Dean rolled up his sleeve to reveal the brand on his left arm. Three wave crests rising in a circle. It was the same sigil that adorned countless banners hanging throughout the room. Kray took Dean by the hand and looked over the mark.

"So it would appear," Kray said. He dropped Dean's hand. It was not exactly a ringing endorsement of his claim to the throne. The regent turned his attention to Ronan, Rook, and Sisto. "Who's this you have with you?"

"These are my friends," Dean lied. "I wouldn't go anywhere without them."

"I see. Did you convince them that you're a prince too, or only Captain Verrick?"

"Actually, Captain Verrick convinced me. I never believed in this place until I met him. If you asked me a week ago, I would have told you Zenhala was a myth."

"And now here you are. An uncanny turn of events, wouldn't you say?"

"Almost impossible to believe," Ralian agreed.

"Is there a problem?" Dean asked.

"That depends," Kray replied. He looked as if he could hardly believe it himself. "I'm curious. What did you think was going to happen here today? Did you think that I would just step aside? Offer you my place on the throne? Place the crown upon your head as you came in the door?"

Dean straightened his back and looked the regent square in the eye. "If you want the truth, I didn't know what was going to happen today, Lord Kray. I didn't come here with any expectations. The only thing I knew for sure was that it couldn't be worse than staying where I was."

The regent returned Dean's steely gaze. "Is that so?"

"It is, indeed."

Kray lifted Dean's arm by the wrist and examined his brand once again. "Time will tell." He let go of Dean's wrist and opened his arms. "Welcome to Zenhala, Dean Seaborne, for I shall call you by that name until your royal lineage is proven. You and your friends will stay here as my guests until that is done. I hope you do not find my manner inhospitable, but my minister of defense is correct. We cannot rush to judgment in a matter such as this. In one week's time, the great storm will return and seal us all on this island for another year. Once that happens, we will test the veracity of your claim to the throne, and prove it beyond any shadow of a doubt. Until then, the lost prince remains lost in my eyes. Unless you think you can convince me otherwise."

"No, sir. Your words are the soul of wisdom." Dean smiled broadly. He tried to take the regent's wariness about him in stride, but it was just for show. Underneath it all, his mind was spinning like a whirlpool. "Forgive me, Lord Kray, but I do have one question. Why wait until we're all trapped here on the island? Not that one could ever feel *trapped* in such a place as this, of course . . ." He chuckled with nervous laughter. "I'm just curious. . . . Why wait for the storm?"

"Tradition," said Kray with a smile. "I expect you saw the castle's many fountains and fish tanks on your way in?"

Dean nodded. "I did. They seemed to be lacking water."

"Quite lacking, but only for now. The great storm drives seawater through the tunnels below this castle, filling the aquariums and powering our fountains in a grand display. When the water flows, we will cut into the mark on your arm and let a single drop of your blood fall into the palace fountainhead. If you're truly born of the Royal House of Aquos, the ink that stains your skin will have been taken from the flowers of our golden trees. It will also be potent enough to turn all the waters of the Aqualine Palace a rich, brilliant blue."

Dean's eyebrows went up as high as they could go. "To prove my blue blood . . . Won't that be a sight?" He turned back to look at Ronan and Rook. They seemed to be masking the same worried thoughts beneath their smiles.

"That ceremony has preceded every coronation on this island for hundreds of years. It's a sight that everyone here, including my daughter, has longed to see for quite some time," Kray said. A side door opened and an entourage of young maidens filed in. "Aha.

Here she comes now. I trust that Verrick has already told you that when the prince comes into his crown, my daughter, Waverly, has been promised as his queen?"

Dean started to sweat as the girls entered the room. "He did, Lord Kray. And I'm eager to meet her, but—"

"Lord Kray," Ralian interrupted. "Again, I must advise you to follow a conservative path in this matter."

Verrick cleared his throat. "I wasn't aware your duties as minister of defense extended to matrimonial affairs, Lord Ralian."

Ralian scowled at Verrick. "They do when the groom has his eyes on the golden throne."

"Believe it or not, I'm inclined to agree with Lord Ralian," Dean interjected.

"What?" Verrick asked.

Dean put up his hands. "I just want to put my best foot forward. Don't you all think it would be better to introduce us after I've had a chance to prove that I'm the prince? It's not that I don't want to meet your daughter, Lord Kray. I do. I just don't want to meet her if I can't tell her who I really . . . am. . . ."

Dean's words trailed off as Waverly made her entrance. It was no use trying to avoid the encounter now that she was in the room, and the point was moot anyway, as Dean realized he had already met the regent's daughter. In a manner of speaking. Waverly Kray was the surf-riding girl that Dean had locked eyes with on his way into port. The same one who had nearly crashed into a fishing boat.

CHAPTER 14

THE RULES OF ENGAGEMENT

Y ou!" Dean said as Waverly stepped to her father's side.
The regent's eyebrows knotted up with confusion. His daughter's eyes widened in alarm. "I'm sorry, do you two know each other?" asked Lord Ralian.

Waverly Kray gasped. "Lord Ralian! Of course not. How could we?"

"We don't," Dean blurted, anxious to avoid the appearance of impropriety. "I don't *know* her. I simply noticed her surfing when I arrived this morning. That's all."

"Waverly," scolded Lord Kray. "Is this true?"

Waverly flushed. "Certainly not, Father! I've been in the palace all morning."

"But—" Dean began. He halted his speech when he saw the look in Waverly's eyes. There was a message there. It was subtle, but she was shaking him off. Asking him to drop it. "Forgive me," Dean said, trying to recover. "The fault is mine, I . . . was mistaken. But I'm not mistaken when I say that you, my lady, are clearly Zenhala's greatest treasure."

The regent's expression relaxed, and Waverly looked away, smiling. Her cheeks took on a rosy tint. "Thank you, Your Grace. I am honored to meet you."

Dean bowed. "The honor is mine." And so it was, for Dean knew he was no prince. Waverly Kray, on the other hand, was a true lady. She carried herself with dignity, poise, and effortless beauty. Her hair was brown like her father's, but it was longer and had been turned a shade lighter by the sun. Her skin had been touched by those same rays and turned a rich, golden bronze. Waverly's perfect tan enhanced all her lovely features, her green eyes most of all. They sparkled like emerald starbursts washed up on the shore. Dean was caught off guard by the way they hypnotized him, but there was more to Waverly than just her pretty face. No one would have ever guessed, seeing her standing in the throne room, dressed in an elegant gown, that she had been cutting across the waves on a surfboard less than an hour ago. Apparently, no one knew about it except the two of them.

The regent kissed his daughter on the cheek and sat back down on the throne. "I'm pleased you could find the time to join us, my dear."

"I'm sorry, Father. I had to make myself presentable for the prince." Waverly curtsied before Dean. "My apologies for making you wait."

Lord Ralian flapped his cape loudly. "We actually don't know if he's the prince yet, Lady Kray. You don't have to curtsy before him, nor should you address him as Your Grace."

"Oh? What shall I call him, then?"

"Dean Seaborne. That's all we know for sure. Captain Verrick's the one who believes him to be the prince."

"Before the week is out, you'll believe it too," said Verrick.

"We live in hope," said the regent. "Dean Seaborne, I present to you my daughter, the lady Kray. If you truly are who you claim to be, then the two of you were betrothed long ago in an agreement between myself and your late father. Every prince must one day grow to be a king, and every king must have his queen."

Ralian sidled up to Kray's ear. "I beg your pardon, my lord, but the matter is not so simple as that."

"What is it *now*?" Verrick asked.

Ralian sighed impatiently. "Have you been at sea so long, Captain Verrick, that you've forgotten about the trials?"

A sudden realization took the wind out of Verrick's sails. Dean worried what that meant for him. "What trials?" he asked.

Ralian put on a condescending grin. "Ah, yes. You know nothing about our customs. And yet you've come here to rule us. What a wonderful contradiction you are." Ralian shook his head. "Fear not, I shall educate you. Here in Zenhala, we have three rites of passage—shall we say trials of manhood?—that are something of a tradition. Every highborn son who thinks himself worthy must pass at least one trial to inherit his father's titles. Had you grown up on the island, you would have gone through them all by now, but your situation being what it is, they still need to be completed."

"All three?" Waverly asked.

"That is the custom for the prince," Ralian insisted.

Verrick made his case to the regent. "Lord Kray, no. You must intervene. It would be grossly irresponsible to risk harming the prince now that he has finally been returned to us."

"Harming the prince?" Dean cut in. "What do you mean? Harming me how? What are these trials?"

Ralian eyed Dean with contempt. "Your courage must be tested by the snapdragon. Your seamanship must be proven in a race down the Bad Falls. The strength of your mind must be measured in the labyrinth below this castle." He huffed and turned to the regent. "If he is the prince, it would be grossly irresponsible for us not to preserve the honored traditions of this island. He's not prepared to take the throne as he is. He doesn't even know his own culture. Lord Kray, your daughter deserves to be courted by a true lord of Zenhala. The people of this kingdom deserve a prince who is worthy of the throne, do they not?"

"But the danger involved . . ." Verrick said. "Lives are spent in preparation of each trial. He's had no training. None!"

Ralian folded his arms. "I'm sorry. On this point, there can be no argument."

Dean didn't like what he was hearing. Nothing about these trials sounded good. The one with the snapdragon was particularly worrisome. Dean didn't know what that was, and he had no interest in finding out. All eyes turned to the regent as they waited for him to decide the matter. Lord Kray stroked his beard, deep in thought. After a few moments, he gave a heavy sigh and looked at Verrick with apologetic eyes. "I'm afraid Lord Ralian is correct. I am no happier about this than you are, Captain. It's not a circumstance any one of us would wish for, but that's been true of this affair since it first began thirteen years ago. I swore to protect this throne, and that includes making certain that only those who are worthy sit upon it. The trials must go forward."

Verrick looked at the floor and gave a resigned nod.

"However, given Dean's lack of readiness—a situation he finds himself in through no fault of his own—we will take measures to safeguard his life. Lord Ralian. Your sons have proven themselves champions in each trial, have they not?"

Ralian puffed up his chest. "All three boys, my lord. We accept nothing less in my family."

"Good. We will proceed with your sons serving as Seaborne's seconds to help him complete each test."

Dean expected Lord Ralian to protest, but instead the man's face lit up. "A splendid idea, Lord Kray. I never would have thought of that." He smiled at Dean. "It will be an honor and a privilege."

Dean grimaced. Ralian's happiness struck him as cause for concern. This job grew more complex with each passing minute. He hid his concern behind a smile. "If I knew there were going to be so many tests, I would have studied harder," Dean joked.

Lord Kray shifted in his seat. "I'm afraid you won't be laughing when you face the trials, but they are hurdles you must clear. They have deep meaning for us, and for you as well. If you are who you claim to be, that is. They're the price of your crown. Will you pay it?"

Dean squared himself up and lifted his chin. If he couldn't convince these people that he was their prince, this job was over before it began. "I'll pay any price to claim that which is rightfully mine, including your daughter's hand in marriage."

Dean flashed a smile at Waverly. She didn't return it. He was playing the gallant young lord and hoping to impress her with bold, confident talk. It didn't work. Dean couldn't be sure, but it looked like she just rolled her eyes at him.

Dean's promise seemed to have the opposite effect on the regent. "Well said," he declared. "I hope you live up to those words. We'll soon find out. We need to move quickly if we want to stay ahead of the storm. For now, make yourself at home. You've had a long journey. Rest. The trials will begin tomorrow. Lord Ralian, can I trust you to see to the details?"

Ralian stood at attention before the regent, with a hand pressed to his heart. "You can always trust me, Lord Kray."

Dean frowned as Ralian bowed down with an exaggerated motion, holding out the hem of his cape. He never trusted anyone who talked like that, and as far as he was concerned, people wearing capes were automatically suspect. Of course, that didn't place Lord Ralian in any kind of rare company. Growing up among pirates had made Dean suspicious of almost everybody. Something told him that before he left this island, he'd be grateful for that fact.

CHAPTER 15

SPIES LIKE US

Royal stewards showed Dean, Ronan, and Rook to their quarters and left them alone. They were given a lavish state apartment in the castle's west wing all to themselves. It was big enough to fit half the Pirate Youth with room to spare, and helped Dean forget his looming trials for the moment. He walked from room to room, marveling at the wealth and splendor of it all. There were three bedrooms, a large drawing room, two small parlors, and a study. Once again, Dean found himself envying the life of a prince. A few days earlier, he had believed Verrick's cabin on board the *Tideturner* to be the height of luxury. Now he was the guest of honor in a suite of rooms fit for a king. That's what he was supposed to be, after all. A future king. Dean couldn't believe how far he'd come, even if he was there under false pretenses. "I could get used to this," he said with a smile.

Rook slammed Sisto's cage down on a nearby table, causing the bird to squawk loudly. "Whaddaya think yer doing, Seaborne?"

Dean turned around. "What are you talking about, Rook?"

"Back there, in the throne room. You didn't ask 'em about the orchard!"

Dean rolled his eyes. "Of course I didn't ask them about the orchard. What do you take me for?"

Rook grabbed Dean's arm. "I took ya to be the pirate king's top spy! What do you mean, 'of course not'? Did you forget why we're here?"

"Hands off, Rook!" Dean pulled his arm away. "I know what I'm doing. You're the one who's out of his depth. I purposely didn't mention the orchard because I'm not the prince here yet. I'm not going to come in here asking these people where they keep their gold. That's what a thief would do."

"Don't give me that," Rook sneered. "You coulda worked it in if ya tried. You was just too busy makin' eyes at the regent's daughter."

"I was not."

"You were, and I don't like it."

"Why's that? Jealous?"

"Of what? Yer not a prince! They'll find that out when One-Eyed Jack gets here." Rook went to Sisto's cage and slid up the door. "Check that desk for ink and paper. We'll send the bird out with a note tellin' how to get here."

Ronan swooped in and shut the birdcage door. "Not so fast." He stepped in front of Sisto's cage, muscling Rook out of the way. "One-Eyed Jack sent us here to find the golden orchard. So far, I haven't seen it."

Rook tried his best to get past Ronan, but it was no use. "Get off it. The gold's here somewhere. We'll find it."

"I didn't realize it was so easy," Dean said. "Weren't you just yelling at me for not asking the regent where it was?"

Rook made a face at Dean. "We'll find out where it is when our mates sack the island. One-Eyed Jack has ways of gettin' information outta people."

"I don't want any part of that," Ronan said. "We're not that kind of pirates. Gentleman Jim taught us better."

Rook let out a groan. "Not this again. You'll follow that man right into the grave, ya will. What did his way of doin' things ever get 'im besides lost at sea?"

Ronan got right in Rook's face. Eyeball to eyeball. "You don't talk about Gentleman Jim, Rook. Not ever. And if I find out you had something to do with what happened to him, you'll pay for it. Like you wouldn't believe. Understand?"

Rook stood his ground and stared right back at Ronan. "The only way you'd find out somethin' like that would be if I was dumb enough to confess, which I ain't. So I s'pose that's that, ain't it?"

Ronan clenched his fist. Another fight was brewing. Dean wasn't going to stop this one. They were behind closed doors, which meant Rook was fair game. "We'll see," Ronan said, but he never threw a punch. Instead, he locked Sisto's cage and put the key around his neck.

"What are you doing?" Dean asked.

"Gentleman Jim might be gone, but we're still his crew. That means we steal from people who can afford it, people who deserve it, or both."

Rook held out his arms and motioned to the luxurious apartment. "Are you daft? Look around! This lot can afford it."

"Find me the golden orchard and we'll know for sure," Ronan said. "Until then, that bird stays in his cage. We're going to honor the Gentleman's Code. I don't expect a scoundrel like you, or a spy like Seaborne, to understand, but it's what we're going to do, just the same." Ronan tucked the key inside his collar and puffed out his chest. "Either of you got a problem with that?"

Dean studied Ronan's unwavering gaze, then looked over at Rook, who had taken off his belt and wrapped it around his fist. "C'mon, Seaborne. He can take us one at a time but not the two of us together. Let's get that key."

Dean leaned back in his chair and put his hands behind his head. "Sorry, Rook. I'm with Ronan on this one."

"What?" Rook and Ronan both asked at the same time.

Dean smiled. "We're going to keep to the code."

"What for?" Rook stomped his feet like a child throwing a tantrum. "Gentleman Jim wasn't even your cap'n, Seaborne."

"He was for long enough. Besides, I'm not getting One-Eyed Jack worked up about this place until I see its treasure with my own eyes. We're here for the golden harvest. I'm not calling One-Eyed Jack in until I know it's here."

"I don't like it." Rook shook his head. "Not one bit. One-Eyed Jack said if we find the island to signal him at once. Yer changin' the plan."

"Then I'm changing it," Dean said. "You don't have to like it."

Rook looked at Dean as if he didn't know what to make of him. Then a realization struck him. "Oh, I see what this is. Now yer the one who's stallin'. You wanna stay here and play house with that mincy little lady, don't ya? What do you think, yer gonna marry the regent's daughter? Live happily ever after?"

"That's not it at all."

"The devil it ain't. What happened to 'meetin' the regent, gettin' settled, and gettin' word to One-Eyed Jack'?"

Dean shifted uncomfortably in his seat. "We're not settled yet, are we?"

Rook balked at Dean's explanation. It was such a weak excuse, there was hardly any point making it.

"We're as settled as we're ever gonna be, Prince Charmin'. Don't forget, that smile of yers . . . yer fancy words . . . it's all just a mask hidin' who ya really are—a pirate spy. We're all spies now, and we need to call our friends in before they find us out."

Ronan covered Rook's mouth and slammed him into the wall. "One-Eyed Jack's no friend of mine, you wretch. And no one's going to find us out if you can stand to keep your mouth shut."

Dean got up and stood next to Ronan. "I think we all understand each other now. You're not in charge here, Rook. What's more, if you can't shut your mouth, he'll shut it for you. Are we clear?"

For a second there, Dean thought he saw Ronan smile. He wondered if the truce he'd hoped for was forming around a mutual dislike of Rook. It was hard to tell. The smile vanished as quickly as it came. Rook's expression was easier to read. He looked daggers at Dean and Ronan before finally nodding in agreement. Ronan let him go.

"This is how it's going to work," Dean announced. "If we're going to find what we came here for, we need a distraction to cover us while we look. That's me. You both saw the people out there. These are my people. At least they seem pretty happy to think so. Everyone wants to see what I'm doing . . . where I'm going . . . they can't get enough of me. That's good. These trials they're setting up should occupy everyone long enough for you two to find the orchard. Once that's done, we'll signal One-Eyed Jack and get out of here. Agreed?"

"Agreed," Ronan said. "*If* we find the orchard."

Rook straightened his clothes and stepped away, giving a cursory nod. He wasn't happy about the plan, but he'd go along with it. He didn't have any other choice. "We don't have forever to wait. The storm comes back in one week. After that, we're stuck here, and everyone's gonna learn the hard truth about their precious lost prince."

"Glad to see you were paying attention," Dean said. "I guess we better start looking."

PART FOUR

TRAPPED IN
PARADISE

CHAPTER 16

MASKS

Finding the golden orchard proved easier said than done. One look out his bedroom window was all Dean needed to see that the small island was big enough to hide the fields of gold rather well. Either that, or its people were simply smart enough not to plant them out in the open like fools. Dean didn't know why he had thought things might be otherwise. Hiding the orchard was the only sensible thing to do. If the legends were to be believed, Zenhala had been burned once already by pirates who came to steal its harvest. At this point, Dean was out of reasons not to believe the legends. He had found the Golden Isle, but the hunt for the Caribbean's most storied treasure had just begun.

Dean, Ronan, and Rook spent their first day in Zenhala

touring the palace and quietly checking things out. They started small, trying to keep a low profile as they scouted the island, but it was clear that more than a casual stroll around the castle would be required. They climbed every tower and looked out in every direction, hoping to get a sense of where to begin. From the highest points of the Aqualine Palace, they could see far and wide, but they could see only what was in plain sight. The mountains behind the castle blocked their view of half the island. What was on the other side? A waterfall ran out from a forested valley between two green peaks. What was in there? Anything? There was only one way to find out. The three boys agreed that Ronan and Rook would strike out at first light and start the search. Meanwhile, Dean would occupy himself, and the locals, with whatever Zenhalan trials of manhood they threw his way.

Verrick stopped by that evening to give Dean the details of each trial, none of which made him feel any better about rushing into tests that people usually spent their whole lives training for. But Dean's life had been another kind of training. Years as a spy had taught him to adapt to any situation. *I've been through worse than this*, he told himself. *If the pampered lordlings of this island can pass these trials, so can I.* It was settled. There was no point fretting over it. Everyone had a part to play, and Dean's role was that of the diversion. Even so, he went to bed that night wondering what in the world he was doing.

His situation had become so implausible that he would have

never believed it if it weren't happening to him. It wasn't just that he'd ended up a guest in a mythic palace. He was also on the cusp of earning his freedom from One-Eyed Jack's Black Fleet. All he had to do was send out Sisto with a note, and he'd be out of One-Eyed Jack's pocket forever. This job should have been ending, not beginning. So why had he agreed to wait on getting word to One-Eyed Jack? He tried to tell himself it was because of what Ronan had said. They were honoring the fallen captain's code. The captain he had known for a grand total of one day.

Who am I kidding?

Yes, Dean had liked the way Gentleman Jim did things. And, yes, it was true that he didn't want One-Eyed Jack's men to raid Zenhala and torture innocents until they gave up their treasure. Dean had brought that fate down on unsuspecting souls many times before, and had hated himself for it each time. How many ships had he doomed by telling One-Eyed Jack what cargo they carried and where they meant to go? Dean had long ago lost count. He wasn't proud of his body of work as a spy, but he had done what he had to do in order to survive. Now, if he did it just one more time, he would finally have the chance to *live*. But, when the moment came, he had hesitated and chosen Ronan's way over Rook's. He took the harder, more uncertain path. Why? His conscience was real enough, but that didn't tell the whole story. He liked Ronan more than Rook. That was a factor too, but not a deciding one. It wasn't as if they were friends. Dean didn't have any friends. But he wanted one, and if Dean was honest with himself, he wanted more than that. Deep down he knew that Rook was right about him. Part of Dean was stalling because of Waverly Kray.

It made absolutely no sense whatsoever. Dean didn't know her. He would never know her. That was how these things worked. He didn't stay anywhere long enough to make friends, and he always left before he had the chance to make enemies. Following that rule had kept him alive. It didn't matter that it wasn't much of a life, or that he'd already broken that rule on board the *Reckless*. Dean had no future with the lady Kray and he knew it. He was a pirate, and here in Zenhala, they hated pirates more than anyone. It was just as Rook had said; the Dean Seaborne she smiled at wasn't him. It was a mask he hid his true face behind, and the only way for him to take it off for good was to betray the trust of Waverly and her people. Like it or not, that was what he did. That was who he was. Dean had to leave Zenhala before the storm returned and everyone discovered he was a fraud. The best he could do was to see that they remembered him as a fraud who cost them gold instead of blood. He resolved to focus on the task at hand and find the orchard. Nothing else mattered.

The life of a prince, he thought as he tried to fall asleep. Royals got everything handed to them on a silver platter. Never in his life had Dean even dared to dream about a girl like Waverly. His conversation with her in the throne room had been the first time he'd ever spoken to a girl his own age. Dean had never before had the opportunity. Not on any ship at sea, and certainly not in Bartleby Bay. Men kept their daughters hidden away in places like that. Dean couldn't keep his mind off of Waverly. He was excited to see her again the next day and, at the same time, worried that he wouldn't know what to say when he did. It seemed his life had prepared him for any situation except this one. Dean forced himself to focus on the task at hand. He already had one impossible goal to shoot for—freedom. Life on his own terms was hard enough to imagine, let alone life with someone else. It couldn't happen. Not as long as he worked for One-Eyed Jack. Guys like him didn't get the girl, the gold, or the glory. Such things weren't possible. And yet, here he was, on the verge of having one impossible dream come true. . . . Was there a chance for more? A chance to have it all?

No. He was dreaming.

It wasn't long before he was literally dreaming. Dean had been given a large four-poster bed with a mattress so soft he swore it had to be stuffed with tufts of cloud, but still he tossed and turned. Somewhere around midnight, Dean rolled over, blinked his eyes open, and drew focus on a shadowy figure dressed in black. Half of his brain was still asleep as the masked man stood over him and raised a hand high in the air. A knife caught the glint of the moonlight, and Dean drew in a sharp breath as the dagger flew.

It didn't fly down at him. It sailed backward through the air, and the killer with it. Someone had yanked the carpet out from under his feet.

"I had a feeling someone might pay us a visit tonight," Ronan said, tossing the carpet aside.

Dean sprang up, his senses rocketing to fully awake and alert status. The killer rolled with his fall and came to rest in a three-point stance. There was a tense moment with Dean standing on the bed, Ronan a few feet off, and the killer crouched low on the ground. "Rook?" Dean asked. He was the first person Dean thought of when he wondered who might be under that mask. Rook had plenty of reasons to want him dead, and Dean knew that when it came to killing someone in their sleep, he was a brave soul indeed. The killer said nothing. They'd figure out who he was later. Right now, the knife lay between the three of them, waiting to be used.

The assassin went for his knife. Dean went for the assassin and wrapped him up before he got his hands on the blade. Ronan picked up a chair and went to swing it, but at the last moment, the killer spun Dean around. Ronan smashed the chair on his back instead.

"Whoops."

Ronan dropped the broken remains of the chair as Dean crumbled to the floor. The killer shoved a palm into Ronan's nose and kicked him in the chest. Dean got up on all fours and shook like a dog drying out his fur. His head hurt terribly and his back hurt worse, but he was still thinking straight and could see better in the dark now that his eyes had adjusted. He grabbed a splintered chair leg and jammed the pointy end into the assassin's ribs.

The villain cried out in pain. He swung the knife around, catching Dean in the mouth with the butt of the handle. Dean fell. The killer staggered a step and clutched his side.

Dean spit blood. "Ronan, take him! Now!"

But the killer was already at the window. Ronan got a hand on him, but the man was too fast. He slipped away, losing only his mask in the process. Before anyone saw his face, he let go, sliding down the wall on a rope. Halfway down, he cut the line and dropped the rest of the way to a balcony below. From there, he was lost to the shadows.

Dean and Ronan leaned out the window, looking down and breathing heavily. They traded weary looks, silently agreeing that it was pointless to pursue. After a few moments, they drew themselves back inside and slid down to sit on the floor with their backs against the wall. It was as quiet as the grave in the royal apartment. Loud snoring in the next room broke the silence. Ronan got up and threw open Rook's door. Sure enough, he was in his bed, fast asleep. The two boys grumbled at their useless comrade.

"I thought it was him coming after me," Dean said.

"Funny how neither one of us thought to call him for help," Ronan replied. "We should have had him sleep in your bed. The killer might have done us a favor."

"I need to speak to the regent about this. Tonight. I'm the prince. I should have guards. Security, protection."

Ronan shook his head. "If the regent wanted to protect you, he would have sent guards." He tossed Dean the killer's black mask. "Instead, he sent him."

Dean did a double take at Ronan. "You think this was Kray?"

"I don't trust him. Think about it. A whole week to wait before this royal blood test of theirs? Three dangerous trials between now and then? He's stalling. Forget giving you his daughter; Kray's not giving up the crown."

Dean chewed on that a moment. He wasn't sold on Ronan's theory. "I don't know. Kray seemed like an honest man to me."

"So? You seem like an honest man, and you're a liar through and through."

Dean smirked. Ronan had probably meant it as an insult, but there was no arguing the truth of his words.

"You don't have to take my word for it," Ronan said. "When I was looking around today, I made a few inquiries. So many people were happy you'd been found, I wondered what they would have done if you weren't. Turns out, after thirteen long years, they were ready to give up looking. The honorable Lord Kray was due to get his crown this very week. When the storm returned, they were going to make him king. No longer the regent, but a real king. You still think he's your friend?"

Dean held up the mask and gripped it tight. It seemed he wasn't the only one on this island who was hiding his true face. "I don't have any friends."

"We have to be more careful. I'd start sleeping with one eye open if I were you."

"I don't think I'll be getting any sleep at all tonight. You go ahead, though. You deserve it. I'll take the next watch."

Ronan didn't need to be told twice. It had been a long day, and a much longer night confirming his suspicions about their host. He patted Dean's shoulder and got up to go to bed.

"Hey, Ronan," Dean called out before he disappeared into his room. "You make a pretty good spy. Thanks for saving my life."

Ronan nodded. "Sorry I hit you with that chair."

Dean rubbed his sore head. "It's all right. Everyone takes a hit now and then." Ronan retired to his room and closed his door. Dean wiped his mouth and winced. His fingers were covered with blood. The cut on his lip was painful and messy, just like everything else in his life had been lately. "The life of a prince," he said, this time with a bitter laugh. It was time to stop the bleeding.

CHAPTER 17

SURVIVAL OF THE FITTEST

What happened to your face?" Verrick asked.

Dean touched his lip as if he was noticing for the first time that it was swollen. He was surprised that Verrick had taken so long to mention it.

"This? Nothing. I slipped on the stairs this morning."

Verrick took a moment with that. "You slipped on the stairs?"

"I was lucky. Could have been worse."

Verrick studied Dean as they walked along a clean-swept gravel path on their way to a rocky inlet near the edge of the island. A detachment of royal guards marched ahead of them, with another unit on hand to guard their rear. "Forgive me, Your

Grace, but are you sure this didn't have anything to do with the broken chair I saw in your quarters this morning?"

"It was an accident, Verrick, that's all. And please, enough of this 'Your Grace' business. Call me Dean."

Verrick gave a reluctant nod as he escorted Dean to the first trial. "Of course, Your Gra—" The captain stopped himself. "That is, *Dean*. I simply feared you and your mates might have been at it again."

Dean forced out a laugh. "We don't fight all the time."

"Of course not."

"Sometimes we sleep."

Verrick smiled, but the joke was wasted on him. The point he was making would not be so easily sidetracked. "I must confess to being confused by these friends of yours. If you brought them here for protection, why are they off sightseeing without you this morning?"

Dean sighed. "You have a lot of questions today."

"I don't mean to pry."

"It's all right," Dean said, but really it wasn't. Verrick was someone who *wanted* to believe Dean was the prince. If he was put off by Ronan and Rook's absence, others were sure to be as well. Dean kicked himself for not realizing this was suspect. It was exactly the scrutiny he couldn't afford. Not everyone shared Verrick's enthusiasm for his claim to the throne.

They came up on a ridge that overlooked the ocean. A large

crowd had assembled, with hundreds of people packed in on top of rocks that ran all the way out to the water. Tall banners with wave-crest sigils flapped in the wind. Dean scanned the crowd and noticed someone missing.

"I see my friends aren't the only people who aren't here. Where's the regent? Isn't he coming?"

Verrick looked slightly embarrassed. "I'm afraid another matter required Lord Kray's attention this morning."

Dean nodded. *I'll bet. Probably the same matter that jumped out my window last night.*

"But he asked for you to dine with him this evening. And also that Lady Kray come escort you to the trial."

"Lady Kray's coming?"

Verrick noted the change in Dean's tone. "Is that a problem?"

"Of course not. It's just . . . I don't know. Maybe. I'm not ready to see her yet." Verrick's face told Dean he didn't understand. "Verrick, I grew up on dirty ships sailing out of filthy port towns. I don't know how to talk to a lady. What am I supposed to say to her?"

Verrick smiled. "Just be yourself."

Dean let out a small grunt. *Right. That's the last thing I can be.*

They rounded a corner and found Waverly there, waiting. Dean couldn't believe it, but once again, he fell under the spell of her eyes. He lost his thoughts and found it hard to concentrate on anything but the way the dawn made the wispy ends of her hair light up with sunshine. As he approached her, any ideas about what he wanted to say vanished from his mind. He kept it simple. "Good morning, my lady."

"Good morning." She smiled.

They stood atop a flight of stone steps that led down to the water's edge. Waverly glanced at Dean's elbow, then up at his eyes. She was waiting for something, but what it was, Dean couldn't guess. Verrick bent down toward his ear. "The stairs are slick with ocean spray. You may wish to offer the lady your arm."

Dean shot his arm out, elbowing Waverly in the side. "Sorry. Are you all right?"

"It's fine," Waverly assured him. She rested her fingers on his arm, and they descended the staircase together. Verrick trailed a few steps behind them as they went. Multitudes of onlookers stood perched on the rocks that bordered the staircase on either side. They stared at Dean in awe and whispered to each other as he passed:

"Look at him, he has no idea."

"Is he really going to do it? He hasn't trained."

"Of course he's going to do it, he's the prince!"

Dean swallowed hard as their murmurs gnawed at his ears. No one there was cheering as they had yesterday. He had never seen such a large gathering stay so quiet. He wished they would make some noise, if only to take the pressure off of him. Dean was usually content to have a quiet moment alone, but he found he abhorred silence with Waverly. He felt he should say something and that every second he let pass without a word reflected negatively on him. He wanted to talk, but when he tried to speak, every word he knew filled his mouth at once. It was all he could do to keep them from spilling out at the same time.

"Why did you lie?" he asked Waverly. Hardly the gem he had meant to open with.

Waverly looked at Dean as if he were something she needed to scrape off the bottom of her shoe. "Excuse me?"

Dean kicked himself, but once the words were out there, they were out there. He leaned in toward Waverly and spoke softly so Verrick couldn't hear. "In the throne room yesterday. You told your father you were in the palace all morning. We both know that isn't true."

Waverly relaxed her frown and put on a trickster's grin. "Yes, I suppose we do."

"So you were the girl I saw surfing."

"You know I was."

"Why pretend otherwise?"

Waverly chuckled. "You have a lot to learn about palace life. My father doesn't think surf-riding befits a lady of my station. I hope you're not too shocked by my behavior."

Now it was Dean's turn to laugh. "My lady, it would take more than the sight of you surfing to shock me." Waverly's hand left Dean's arm. The look on her face brought his snickering to a halt.

He was saying and doing everything wrong. "I'm sorry, I don't mean to laugh. I am shocked actually, just not by you. Or at least not *just* by you. Everything about this place is a shock. You're right. I've never had any experience with royal life. I lived my life out on the waves, far, far away from anything like this."

"Really." Waverly twirled her hair with her finger. "You'll have to tell me more about that later. Assuming you survive the trial."

"Yes, the trial." Dean frowned. They had reached the bottom of the staircase. "For a moment, I nearly forgot why we came here today."

"This passage ends at a small sheltered bay where you and I will part ways. There's a cave on the windward side of the island that can be accessed from the water. That's where you're going."

Dean nodded. "To face the snapdragon. Is there a reason I have to start with the most dangerous of these three trials?"

"They're all dangerous," Verrick called out. He trotted down the steps to join Dean and Waverly at the bottom. "This one comes first because if you aren't strong enough to face the snapdragon, there's no point in wasting time with the other two trials."

"And if the snapdragon eats me, there'll be no need."

"It's just a small sea serpent," Verrick said.

"Oh, yes," said Waverly. "It's an absolute pussycat."

Dean felt like he had a jellyfish swimming in his stomach. "This isn't some game to see if I'm brave enough to enter the cave, is it? This sea serpent . . . it's a real thing?"

Verrick nodded. "The snapdragon is very real. It's lived on this island since the time of our ancestors."

"Wonderful." Dean shook his head. "What is this trial supposed to prove other than the fact that I'm crazy enough to swim with sea serpents?"

"It proves many things," Verrick said. "Bravery, for one. Fighting prowess another. It proves self-restraint and mercy as well. The presence of mind required to defend yourself without killing your opponent is no small thing. The snapdragon is an ancient wonder of Zenhala. Its death would be just as tragic as that of any young lord sent to face it. Present company excluded, of course."

"You don't seem too worried," Dean said to Verrick.

"He's not the one going in there," Waverly said.

Verrick put a hand on Dean's shoulder. "You just need to last three minutes in the cave. After that, the trial judge will drop a rope down through the top of the chamber. Climb to safety and you've passed the test. Simple as that."

"Right. Simple." Dean took a few deep breaths, trying to mentally prepare himself. "All right, fine. How hard could this be? Every noble son on the island has to do it, right?"

Waverly shook her head. "Actually, no one does this trial. Junter Ralian was the first to try since before I was born."

Dean squinted at Waverly. "What are you talking about?"

"All Zenhalan nobles must pass *one* of the three challenges,"

Verrick explained. "They get to pick their trial, but Junter had no choice. The eldest son of House Ralian always faces the snapdragon. It's a tradition with their family. Junter trained all his life to prepare. As a king's son, you must conquer all three challenges, but you've had no training. That's why Waverly's father, the regent, has seen fit to grant you seconds."

Dean snorted. "Yes, to protect me. How thoughtful of him. I still haven't met this Junter. How did he survive his three minutes with the snapdragon?"

"You'll have to ask him." Verrick guided Dean around the corner. The waterfront came into view along with more spectators. The waves were filled with people in boats, and a throng of men and women crowded the pier at the end of the staircase. Standing in front of the congregation were four people dressed in white. It was Arjent Ralian and his three sons. "There they are," said Verrick. "Junter, Jin, and Jarret."

The tallest of the Ralian boys was a bulky, muscular lad. He was bigger than Ronan, with a head shaped like a square and a vacant look on his face. His short black hair was combed forward toward his forehead. The second-tallest of Lord Ralian's sons was closer to Dean's size. He had an athletic frame, shoulder-length hair, and a cocky, mischievous grin. The third brother was the smallest of them all, in both inches and pounds. He had a slight build with almost no meat on his bones. His hair was pulled back into a ponytail like his father's.

"Please tell me Junter's the big one," said Dean.

Waverly nodded. "He is."

"He's not the smartest of the three, but he is by far the strongest," Verrick told Dean quietly. "You'll be glad to have him with you."

Dean grunted. He wouldn't be glad about facing the snapdragon with ten Junters by his side.

The contingent of guards entered the crowd and cleared the way to a wooden deck where Waverly and Verrick could watch Dean's trial. Two guards remained on the path to take Dean the rest of the way. Dean deposited Waverly on the steps of the viewing platform and rejoined his military escort. "Wish me luck," he said.

Waverly looked sad. She paused at the base of the steps and spoke in a voice that was just above a whisper. "You don't have to do this, you know."

"Your father said I did."

"He said you had to if you want to win the crown and marry me."

"Is there another option?"

Waverly looked at Dean with genuine concern in her big green eyes. "There'd be no shame in walking away. Whatever you might think, you're not ready for this. You can't be. I'd hate to see anything bad happen to you."

Dean took a step back. He wondered if Waverly was trying to warn him about something other than the trial. Did she know her father tried to have him killed a few hours ago? Maybe she was trying to save his life by getting him to abandon his royal aspirations. Then again, maybe she just didn't want to marry him. Getting him to quit was the easiest way to break off the engagement, short of his death. If that was her worry, she had nothing to fear whether he lived or died. A royal wedding was the only scenario less likely than his quitting this job halfway through. "I'm touched by your concern, Lady Kray, but I have to do this. I've never been one to show my stern to a challenge. If I turned my back on this one, I'd regret it for the rest of my days. More than you can ever imagine."

Waverly smiled at Dean. He let her take his words as a compliment. She didn't realize what he really meant. What he was truly after.

"You're very brave," she told him.

Dean smiled. "It's been nice talking with you. I enjoyed this."

"Good luck, Dean Seaborne."

Dean threw a wink at Waverly as he took leave of her. "Thanks."

I'm going to need it.

CHAPTER 18

SNAPDRAGON GROTTO

Junter Ralian shook Dean's hand with a mumbled grunt when they were introduced. He had a firm grip that all but crushed Dean's hand, but he didn't say sorry. That word didn't appear to be in his vocabulary. Dean suspected the same was true of many other words as well. One look at Junter told Dean he was a fighter, not a thinker. He said nothing as the trial judge, an ancient little man with a thin, stringy beard, went over the rules of the challenge one more time. He didn't say much more as they rowed out to the snapdragon's den in a small two-man boat.

The one positive about the situation that Dean could figure was that half the kingdom had turned out to see him take on his first trial. Just as he had hoped, that would make it easier for Ronan and Rook to search for the golden orchard. With any luck, he'd live long enough to see how they fared. As he and Junter skirted the coast of the island, Dean was left to ponder the nature of the beast in silence. Junter offered neither advice nor reassurances. His expression was blank as he pulled back on the oars, effortlessly rowing the boat all by himself. He didn't look the least bit scared, but Dean supposed he had reason to be confident. Junter was the biggest young man he had ever seen. If Dean didn't know any better, he would have sworn the oldest Ralian boy was a full-grown adult.

"How old are you?" Dean asked him.

Junter reset the oars and heaved against the waves. "Seventeen."

Seventeen, Dean thought. *Almost a man.* Junter was two years older than Ronan, but three times his size. "And you've done this before?"

"I have."

Dean waited a moment for Junter to elaborate, but he never did. He left it at that, answering the question exactly as it was asked, offering up nothing more. Dean stared at him from across the boat. "Well? If you've got any suggestions for dealing with the snapdragon, don't be shy about it. Let's hear them."

Junter gave an uninterested shrug and grunted as he worked. "Stay away from its mouth. Don't die."

Dean's appreciation for his muscle-bound partner was waning fast. "That's very helpful, Junter. Thank you. I'm glad you're here."

Oblivious to Dean's sarcasm, Junter gave an ignorant, happy smile as they crossed over to Zenhala's windward side. The elements were harsher in that section of the island, and the shift in weather conditions was immediate. The sky turned overcast, a light rain fell, and the sea grew rougher. Dean scanned the countryside for a glimpse of the orchard, but saw nothing. Vegetation was sparse, and there was no jungle or beach. Just the foot of Zenhala's largest mountain terminating in steep cliffs and rocky crags. Jagged, spiky outcroppings rose up from the sea like spikes, blockading the island from large ships. Dean and Junter's tiny boat wove its way between the natural stone barricades until they reached a tiny crack in the island's rock face. It was as if a stone shard had been removed from the mountain, just big enough to grant them passage, but only if the ocean cooperated. The water was choppy. Waves broke hard against the cavern's exterior, hiding the opening, then revealing it again. There wasn't much room to pass through. If the tide had been a foot higher, the door to the cave would have been completely submerged. As it was, they could barely hope to fit. The prow of the ship hit hard against the top of the entrance as the waves knocked the boat around inside the stone gap.

Junter looked at Dean. "Ready?"

Dean held tight to the sides of the boat. "Why wouldn't I be? You've prepared me expertly."

Junter ignored the comment. "Lie down," he said as the

whitecaps rocked them back and forth. There was a rope anchored to a steel eyelet above the narrow crevice. He grabbed hold of it, and timed the ship's rise and fall with the waves. Junter pulled hard on the rope when the tide was on a downswing, and dropped to his back as the current shot them into the snapdragon's den.

Dean held his breath as they slid through a short tunnel, racing from darkness into light. Once they entered the cave, Dean had to rub his eyes and look again to make sure he wasn't imagining things. The water in the Snapdragon Grotto was calm and glowed with supernatural luminescence. The entire cave was flooded with brilliant blue light. Dean's mouth fell open as he marveled at the hidden wonder. The cavern was a wide basin thirty feet across, with a dome-shaped roof thirty feet high. The waves had carved it into the mountain over thousands of years, using vivid, glimmering water that simply had to be enchanted. Its fluorescent radiance put sparkling blue sapphires to shame, and made the water outside seem unclean by comparison. Dean cupped his hand and let the water run through his fingers.

"What is this? Magic?"

Junter rowed up to the wall of the cave. There was a stone ledge on one side of the basin that was big enough to stand on. He climbed out of the boat and cleared his nostrils with a mighty blow, emptying the contents of his nose into the water in a way that made Dean think of Scurvy Gill.

"What?" he asked Dean, as if he had just done the most civilized thing in the world.

"Nothing. You just remind me of someone is all."

Junter wiped his nose with his sleeve. "It's not magic. The water out there's the same as the water in here. It's just the sunlight reflecting through the sea."

Dean looked around. "Reflected from where? The cave's completely closed off."

Junter pointed back at the opening they had just come in through. "Right there." Dean joined Junter on the ledge and looked over at the blinding white light beyond the break in the wall. He didn't see how it could have caused the glimmering effect inside the cave. "There's another opening too, somewhere else in here," Junter continued. "Somewhere below the waterline, or so the scholars say. You'd have to go swimming to find it, which I don't recommend."

Junter kicked the boat into the center of the pool and took a pack off his back. He reached inside the bag and took out a long heavy chain, all bunched up together. He loosened his grip on the links, and an iron ball the size of a grapefruit hit the stone floor with a heavy clang. He tossed Dean the bag. "You'll want to arm yourself." Dean took the bag with pleasure, but he was less than thrilled by what he found inside. He pulled out a net and two wooden sticks strung together with black rope.

"What's this supposed to be?"

"That's something the traders brought back from the Far East, years ago. My father's weapons master called them nunchakus."

Dean gave the sticks a try and spun the nunchakus around. He nearly clocked himself in the head. "What am I supposed to do with this? Why isn't there a cutlass or another one of those?"

Junter held up his ball and chain. "You ever use one of these?"

"Let me guess, you swing it around and hit things on the head. Seems simple enough to me."

Junter shook his head. "A weapon like this needs a practiced hand. The snapdragon is a Zenhalan treasure. It's hundreds of years old. If you kill it, you fail."

"What if it kills me? What then?"

"That's what I'm here for."

"What's that?"

Junter busied himself checking the links on his weapon. "To make sure it doesn't."

Dean sized up his dim-witted partner, feeling a little uneasy. He hadn't met the other Ralian brothers yet, but it was clear that Verrick had been right about Junter not being the smart one. "Let's hope you're a better fighter than you are a conversationalist."

"What'd you call me?"

There was a noise at the top of the cave, and Dean looked up to see a hatch being pulled open. "Never mind."

Light poured in from above, causing the water's mystic blue

color to fade. Dean shielded his eyes and saw the trial judge poke his head in. "Sons of Zenhala, I salute you!" he called out. "Your bravery is unmatched just for setting foot in this cave. Should you emerge unharmed, your noble hearts will be proven beyond contestation. This is your last chance to turn back. Shall we proceed?"

Junter spit on the ground and rattled his chain. "Get on with it, old man."

Dean was surprised at Junter's lack of respect for his elders. He looked at his own pathetic weapons. He was as ready as he could hope to be. "Aye, sir. Proceed."

The trial judge nodded and withdrew. Through the opening at the roof of the cave, Dean watched him stand and raise a conch shell to his lips. Its booming call was loud enough to wake the dead, and Dean knew it would soon bring the snapdragon. He held tight to his weapons, despite his lack of faith in them. The trial judge disappeared from sight as the rooftop hatch was moved back into place, and Dean took a breath. *Three minutes, starting now.*

"He's not going to watch?" asked Dean.

Junter shook his head. "They're afraid the creature might snap at them."

Dean looked at the ceiling. He hadn't expected that the snapdragon would be able to reach that high. "Captain Verrick said the snapdragon was small."

"It is. For a sea serpent."

Dean's mouth went dry. The water stirred. Junter lifted his chin toward the shifting current, his eyes on full alert. "There. You see it?"

Dean's eyes darted around the cave. "No. Where?"

Something swooped around the edge of the water, and the empty boat spun away from the ledge. It settled in the center of the pool. Junter spun his ball and chain in slow circles, getting ready to fight. The beast came around again, and followed the same path. This time, a row of sharp dorsal fins broke the surface of the water as it passed. The creature's back was visible only for a moment before it dove out of sight. Junter shifted his weight to his toes and swung his ball and chain fast enough to make it hum.

"It's coming."

Dean's heart sped up. The water in front of him swirled ominously, a thin veil that hid but would not hold back the creature below. He searched the cavern for defensive positions. More ledges like the one he was standing on lined the walls, high and low. Some were bigger than others, some longer, and some shorter. If Dean had to move, and he would most certainly have to move, he would use them to stay out of the water. The snapdragon was coming. Dean couldn't see it yet, but he knew it was there. It circled the pool faster and faster, making the boat he had come in on spin like a carousel.

The snapdragon shot straight up out of the water and changed direction in the blink of an eye, bearing down on the rowboat and punching straight through it. Dean had hardly gotten a look at the beast before it vanished beneath the waves once again. Splintered wood floated around the pool, left behind like a vicious calling card. Dean looked at Junter with wide eyes, but the Ralian boy paid him no attention. His eyes were on the pool. "Here it comes!"

The snapdragon sprang up again and arched its neck like a cobra ready to strike. It stared down the two boys and growled. Dean froze at the sight of it. Its curving, snakelike body was long and thick like the trunk of a palm tree. Only a portion of it was out of the water, and Dean put the beast at ten feet long with another twenty feet below. It made a chittering, clicking sound as it bared three rows of sharp teeth and looked back and forth between Dean and Junter. No doubt it was trying to decide which one of them would make a tastier treat. Its eyes were a mix of gold and dark bronze. Thick white drool hung down from its jaws like clam chowder. Its tough blue-green hide shaded to lime on its belly, and its back was covered with sharp, irregular-shaped fins. They grew along its twisting spine like razors, clumped together in random patches with large gaps between their spiky clusters.

Junter swung the ball and chain around in a wide loop, putting some distance between himself and the snapdragon. "Hello again, ugly. Remember me?"

The creature hissed at Junter and craned its neck away, turning toward the other side of the ledge, where Dean was standing. Dean looked at the wooden sticks he had in one hand and the net he had in the other. He might as well have brought the snapdragon flowers. Dean swung the nunchakus back and forth, but he didn't know how to use them. It was a good thing Junter was there.

That thought lasted Dean all of two seconds, as Junter swung the iron ball forward in a wide looping arc that the snapdragon dodged easily. The beast darted at Junter's feet, and when he jumped back, the iron ball spun out, pounding Dean in the stomach. So much for Junter's practiced hand.

All the air left Dean's body in an instant. He thought he was going to throw up. Dean dropped to the ground as Junter ran and jumped onto another ledge along the cavern wall. The snapdragon nipped at his heels, then turned back toward Dean, who was still sprawled on his stomach. "Seaborne, move!" Dean heard Junter shouting, but the voice sounded miles away. Somehow, he found the strength to roll out of the path of the snapdragon's diving teeth. The bite snagged his shoulder and tore his shirt, but not his flesh. The near miss gave Dean a shot of adrenaline that got him up as the sea serpent hit the waves and came back around for another attack. It reared its ugly head and paused again, this time focusing solely on Dean. Junter had the ball and chain spinning in front of him like a shield. Dean had nothing. One hand was clutching his stomach and the other was empty. His weapons were on the ground, five feet away. They might as well have been on the other side of the ocean. The nunchakus and net hadn't proved very useful, but Dean was far from ready to give up on them. He felt naked without them. He ran forward and snatched his weapons as the snapdragon launched itself at him. He just barely got them off the ground and back out of range in time. Dean sprinted across the stone platform and jumped, landing on another ledge. The snapdragon was right behind him. Dean swung the nunchakus at its face, and the creature ripped them clean out of his hands. It crushed them in its jaws like toothpicks and shrieked out an earsplitting howl.

Dean kept moving. He ran and jumped up, climbing onto another platform on the wall. *This is insane!* he thought. *What am I doing? No way is this worth it.* He looked around. There was nowhere to go. His back was literally against the wall. Dean had no idea how much time had passed so far, but he knew it wasn't enough. The snapdragon gnashed its teeth and dove at him again. He dodged to the left, and the creature's face hit the wall behind him. Dean lost his balance and fell, landing on a wider ledge below, closer to the water. The snapdragon was entirely focused on him. Junter had his iron ball spinning in a wide orbit, pinning Dean and the sea serpent on the opposite side of the cave.

"What are you doing, Junter? Help me!"

Junter swung the ball and chain at the snapdragon and missed. It hit the ledge above Dean. Rock fragments rained down on his head and neck.

"Watch it!"

"Sorry! I'm not used to being in here with anyone else."

"Well, you ARE here with someone else! Me! Be careful with that thing!"

The snapdragon spun around on Junter to strike him, but he used the ball and chain to fend off its attack. Once again, the creature shifted its focus to Dean.

"You need to come around to this side," Junter said. "Get behind me!"

It was a nice idea. Junter had been very effective in using his weapon to keep the snapdragon at bay, but he wasn't giving Dean any opening to get in behind its protective rotation. "How am I supposed to do that if you won't let me pass?"

"If I stop swinging the ball, that thing will tear me apart before I get it going again. You have to time your jump just right. You can do it!"

Dean gritted his teeth. *Some help this guy turned out to be.* He put his head down and ran along the wall toward Junter's side of the chamber. The snapdragon dove headfirst into the water and threw its tail out, swatting Dean like an insect. He went flying and nearly fell into the water, but he held on, got up, and timed a perfect leap across the cave to get past Junter's swirling weapon.

Dean stood up and felt the breeze from the spinning ball and chain's vortex cool his back. He had made it to the protected side of the cave, and that wasn't all he'd done. The conch shell horn blew again, and the stone slab hatch on the roof opened up. The trial judge threw a line down. Dean had made it! It had been the worst three minutes of his life, but all things considered, the time passed quickly. He had made it through. Dean smiled up at Junter, even though his oversize comrade had proved to be more of a hindrance than anything else. "Time to go?"

Junter nodded. "It's time, all right." He gave the iron ball one last good swing to push the snapdragon back, and let go of the chain as it looped back around toward Dean. The ball hit the wall well above Dean's head, but as it fell, the chain flew out and wrapped itself around his left foot. Dean was hooked. The iron ball bounced off the wall and into the water. The snapdragon pounced on it, and the pull of the chain took Dean right off his feet. Before he even knew what was happening, he was under the waves—in the water with the snapdragon. Dean swam furiously for the surface with the iron ball weighing him down. He got a breath of air, and one last look at Junter as he jumped off the ledge and grabbed the trial judge's rope.

The weight of the chain dragged Dean under again, and from his squiggly, undulating point of view, he watched as his bulky second left the cave first. The light from the world outside vanished as they closed him in. Just like that, they had given up on him. He was trapped. Dead in the water with a chain around his leg and a hungry sea serpent ready to eat him. He looked around, frantic. The water was clear, but he didn't see anything. He reached for the chain on his leg, desperate to unhook it, when a pack of bony thorn spikes opened up his side. The sea serpent had brushed by him, using its razor-sharp fins to cut his ribs. It hurt like the devil, and the cuts were numerous, but not deep. The snapdragon was toying with him.

Dean ignored the pain in his side and reached for his leg again. He got himself free, and managed to hang on to the net Junter had given him, not that he expected it to do him any good. The snapdragon swam by again, and the current shoved Dean aside. He was off balance and disoriented, but he grabbed hold of Junter's ball and chain as he flailed about in the water. The sea serpent came at him once more, and Dean had just enough time to stuff the chain into its mouth before it bit him. He crammed a handful of iron links into the creature's gaping maw and pushed himself away. The snapdragon shook its head back and forth as it choked on the chain, but it spit out the links and whipped its tail into Dean's midsection. This time, there would be no ignoring the pain. Dean coughed out all the air he was holding in. It was over. He needed to breathe immediately, but he wouldn't live long enough to die from a lack of oxygen. The creature was coming back. As it closed in on him, only one thought came to mind. Something an old sea dog had once told him. It hadn't been much help the last time he tried it, but anything was worth a shot.

As the snapdragon swam up to eat him, Dean punched it square in the nose. It was his drop-dead last chance, and he got in a good shot, right above the snapdragon's top row of teeth.

Miraculously, the creature's whole body quivered, and it stopped dead in place. A shiver ran through the serpent's body from head to toe, and its eyes rolled around in its head like cannonballs on the deck of a ship.

Dean blinked twice at the motionless beast. *Glory be, it worked!*

He didn't know how long it would last, but the odds were, not long. He had just a few seconds left to follow Junter's only worthwhile piece of advice. "Stay away from its mouth. Don't die." Dean figured the best way to do that was to get somewhere the creature's teeth couldn't reach, like the back of its neck. He still had the net in his hand. He wrapped it around the creature's back and hooked it over a crooked dorsal fin. He gave the net a tug. It was secure. He climbed onto the snapdragon's back and held on tight. *This better work.*

A few seconds later, the snapdragon bucked. It was no longer paralyzed. It was able to move again, and move it did. It shot up out of the water and tried to flip Dean off its back. It roared. It howled. And when it couldn't shake Dean, it dove back under the water and tried to throw him off. The snapdragon spun around under the water, trying to rid itself of its pesky rider. Dean's lungs were fit to burst, but he didn't let go. The snapdragon tried to bite him, but it couldn't reach him where he was. No matter how hard it tried, it couldn't lose him. Failing in those attempts, it swam rapidly at the wall of the cave. Dean thought it meant to throw him hard against the stones and crush him under its weight, but just as he braced for impact, they passed through the wall. Dean opened his eyes. They had gone through the cave's other opening. The one Junter had said was under the water somewhere.

The creature surfaced in the water outside the cave, with Dean riding its back like a bucking bronco. The light outside was intense, but Dean had never been so happy to see the sun. He breathed deep and held on tight. Images of the outside world raced in and out of his vision as he held on to the rampaging sea serpent. He saw the people who had come to watch his trial. They were all leaving. A dejected procession of Zenhalans who had understandably assumed the snapdragon had eaten Dean for breakfast. The beast shrieked with righteous fury as it snapped at Dean and tried to shake him off. The people heard and came running back. Once again, they cheered for Dean. He paid them no attention. He had to focus on the task at hand. If he let go, the snapdragon would surely devour him. Dean held on. Up and down the snapdragon went, taking him on a mad ride. It was furious. It was wild. It was . . . beaten.

Just when Dean thought he could take no more, the snap-dragon settled into the water, breathed deeply, and swam gently along the surface. Dean unclenched his body and rode its back as if it were an old sea turtle. He was astonished as the snapdragon turned around and looked at him. It was tired, and submitted to Dean for all the world to see. Dean nudged it with his knee and pointed to a chain of rocks he could follow back to shore.

"How about over there," he said. Miraculously, the snapdragon did as he commanded. There was now an understanding of sorts between Dean and the snakelike beast. It swam on, taking Dean exactly where he wanted to go. After Dean had dismounted, the snapdragon paused a moment with him before it left. Dean reached down and patted its head.

"Thanks for not killing me."

The snapdragon let out a weary warble, and swam away. Dean watched it disappear from sight, then stood up and looked at the crowd of people all around him. It took him a second to realize they were waiting for him to say something. Too tired for that, he raised his arms high in the air, victorious in battle. That was statement enough. The people shook the island with their cheers. They lauded him like a conquering warrior, which wasn't far from the truth. All he'd had to do was survive the snapdragon, but he'd done a sight more than that. He'd done the impossible, and bent it to his will. He'd tamed the beast. Across the water, Dean saw Junter standing with the trial judge, looking sour. His brothers were laughing at him. Waverly, for her part, seemed to be stunned by what he'd accomplished. Dean smiled. Maybe this stunt had been worth it after all. It was too early to tell. Dean only knew one thing for sure. Ronan and Rook had to find the orchard fast. He couldn't take much more of this.

CHAPTER 19

ALL THAT GLITTERS

"What do you mean you didn't find anything?" Dean said. "You had all day!"

"Ease off a point there, Seaborne." Ronan took a bite out of a piece of fruit that looked like an apple except its skin was a bold shade of purple and its insides bright yellow. "It takes time to look for something without looking like you're looking. What'd you expect? You said yourself these things take time."

Dean stared out the royal apartment window into the setting sun. He could hardly stand to look at Ronan and Rook. "That doesn't mean we have time to waste. I turn every head on this island for an entire day, nearly losing my own in the process, and you two come back here empty-handed. What'd *you* expect? That I'd be happy?"

Ronan patted a sack filled with more of the same fruit he was eating. "I wouldn't say we came back empty-handed exactly. I found a grove filled with these purple lovelies, and Rook"— Ronan motioned toward the tub in the next room, where Rook was nursing dozens of scratches and bite marks all over his body—"Rook found out the local wildlife is a touch aggressive." He made no effort to hide his delight at Rook's discomfort.

"Hardy-har-har," Rook said, no doubt taking his first bath in a year. "Next time, maybe you'll take the jungle and I'll search the fields. Mark me, those red monkeys wasn't just aggressive. They was pure evil!"

"Don't speak to me of monkeys," Dean snapped. "I wrestled a sea serpent today."

"Oh, go on."

"It's true!"

"I heard it was a small sea serpent," Ronan said, unimpressed.

"If you ever have the opportunity to see for yourself, you'll find a small sea serpent is still plenty big. Not that the pair of you could find anything. You didn't turn up so much as a clue."

Ronan took another bite of the fruit he'd been enjoying. "Ask me, you're the one who's clueless. Dining with the lord regent tonight? You've got it bad, haven't you, Seaborne?"

"What are you talking about?"

Ronan looked at Rook. "What am I talking about, he says. As if it isn't plain as day."

"Aye," Rook said as he got out of the tub and covered himself with a robe. "She's a fair lass, Seaborne. She ain't worth dyin' over."

Dean left the window. "I'm not going to dinner because of her. And if Lord Kray wants to poison my food, he can do it any time. He doesn't have to wait until I'm sharing his table."

Ronan tossed Dean a shiny purple apple. "He can't poison you at all if you stick to eating what I fresh-picked."

Dean caught the fruit and threw it back at Ronan. "If he wants to kill me, he doesn't have to lift a finger. The way these trials are going, I'll be dead by tomorrow night."

"And who set you on that path but Kray? You're crazy to take up another invite from him. You don't belong at some fancy dinner. You're out of your depth."

Dean checked his appearance in the mirror and combed his hair with his hand. "You're probably right. But you haven't left me much choice, have you? Someone has to get the information you two failed to come up with today."

"I'm telling you, don't go," Ronan said. "Come up with some excuse, tell him you're tired from your trial, but don't do this."

Dean went to the door. "Not only am I going, but I'm coming back with a lead on the orchard, and no bones about it. Try to stay out of trouble while I'm gone, will you?"

And with that, Dean left. He didn't quite storm out of the room, but he didn't leave with a smile on his face either. His foul mood was partly due to the way the day had gone, but it had been added to by what Ronan and Rook had said about Waverly. What bothered him most was the fact that they were right. She was clouding his judgment, and he knew it. He just didn't care to admit it, and worse than that, he didn't care to stop it, either. Dinner with the regent was an unnecessary risk, but he was taking it just the same. If Dean were honest with himself, it was only for the chance to see her.

He met the Krays outside in an open-air dining room. Their table was on a terrace at the end of a long narrow footbridge. He walked across, stepping on bright blue flower petals that were strewn about the path as he went. Dean approached the table, and the regent rose to greet him with open arms.

"Seaborne! Dean Seaborne, tamer of wild snapdragons. Come! Join us. We've been waiting for you." Lord Kray put his hands on Dean's shoulders and gave him a healthy shake. The regent was in fine spirits this evening. "I'm sorry I couldn't be there this morning. State affairs prevented me, and for once I was grateful, so concerned was I for your safety. But I see now there was nothing to worry about. Not a highborn son in the history of this island has ever done what you did today! What's your secret, lad? How did you do it?"

Dean chose his words carefully. The regent was brimming

with enthusiasm, but Dean saw the true question being asked beneath his friendly overtures: *How are you still alive?*

"I just followed my second's advice," Dean told the regent. That was true enough, even if Junter himself was worse than useless. "Thank you for sending him to help me."

"Yes, Junter. I'll have to tell his father you said that. Lord Ralian was rather upset with his son for leaving you behind."

"As well he should be," Waverly said. "Junter should be ashamed of himself. He was downright cowardly. When only he emerged, I was certain you were dead."

"For a moment, Lady Kray, I was too."

"Come. Sit," said the regent. He directed Dean to a seat at the banquet table. "You must tell us all about it."

Dean took the chair positioned at the regent's right hand. Waverly sat on her father's left, just across from him. "Actually, I was hoping we might discuss tomorrow's trial. After today, I think I need to prepare myself a little more thoroughly."

"Tomorrow's trial is the test of seamanship. You grew up at sea, didn't you?" The regent waved his hand. "Racing down the Bad Falls should be a mere trifle for a lad with your experience."

"Even so, you can't blame me for being curious. I'm a stranger here. Tell me more about the Bad Falls."

Waverly pointed out over the terrace. "The peak behind this castle is Mount Skytop. It has three waterfalls, each one larger than the last. You have to ride them on your way down the mountain. It's not that difficult." She turned up her palms. "You'll have a kayak. Just hold on tight."

Dean nodded. They were giving him only the basics. He knew that much already. "I don't understand. How can we have a test of seamanship if we don't head out to sea? There has to be more to this."

"Wild animals live along the river," Waverly said.

"But nothing so fierce as the snapdragon," her father added.

"The last waterfall is almost two hundred feet," Waverly continued.

"But you don't have to go over it," her father cut in.

"You don't?" Dean asked.

"Not if you know the way around," the regent said. "And you'll have Jin Ralian there to guide you. He's the finest sailor in Zenhala. The second trial is simply less dangerous than the first. Most young lords choose this one. You have nothing to fear."

Dean grimaced. The regent's efforts to downplay the dangers ahead left him unconvinced. After the fiasco with Junter, he was worried how much help Jin would offer him. He wanted to pursue the matter further, but there was no point. Lord Kray and Waverly were too eager to hear the details of his early-morning brush with death. They would not be dissuaded, so while trying hard to sound modest, Dean provided his hosts with a faithful account of his time in the Snapdragon Grotto. As much as he could get out, anyway. Waverly kept interrupting him with questions, and the regent kept imploring him to sample the island's local produce.

Even before he sat down, Dean could tell this meal would be unlike any he had ever had before. Dinner had yet to be served, and the table was already overflowing with food. There was a long platter filled with the purple apples Ronan was so fond of, as well as several other types of fruit Dean had never seen before. There was an endless supply of bread, cheese, and butter. Far more than the three of them could hope to finish, especially if they meant to eat a full plate of food afterward.

At a nearby table, Dean spotted a large glass cylinder filled with clean, chilled water. He could tell its temperature was cool by the little droplets that beaded up on the outside of the glass. He wondered what well it had been drawn from that it had come so clear, and how the palace staff had managed to keep it so cold. Everything looked wonderful, but he couldn't take for granted that it was all safe to eat. As Dean told his story, he watched his hosts, careful not to take from any tray that Waverly or her father had not eaten from first. He saw danger on every plate and inside every glass. He wondered if he had made a grave mistake in coming. Servants poured wine for the regent, and tea flavored with cuts of fruit for Dean and Waverly. He accidentally dropped his goblet on purpose as he took it, just in case the cup itself was laced with poison. "I'm sorry, how clumsy of me." He rose and helped himself to an empty chalice from the table with the water tank. One couldn't be too careful at a dinner like this.

"Where was I?" Dean asked, getting back to his story.

"Riding the snapdragon," Waverly said. "Father, you should have been there. It was amazing."

"I can imagine."

"I still can't believe you did that," said Waverly. "I never would have dared such a thing."

"You do yourself a disservice, talking like that." Dean said, thinking about the way she cut over the waves on her surfboard. "Never? I find that hard to believe."

Waverly smiled back at Dean. "It's true. I can't imagine doing anything like that."

"Of course not," Dean replied.

He liked sharing a secret with Waverly. In a day that was already filled with excitement, this unspoken agreement between the two of them excited him most of all.

The moment did not go unnoticed. Dean and Waverly seemed more amused with each other than their words warranted, and the regent picked up on it. He cleared his throat. "You still haven't said how you managed to tame the snapdragon. Please, do tell us."

Dean shrugged. "There's not much to tell, I'm afraid. It all happened so fast. I saw an opportunity and took it before it went away, that's all. In moments like that, you just act. You do what you have to survive, no more. That's how I grew up. It's all I've ever known."

"If you don't mind, I'd like to hear more about how you grew up," said the regent.

"Yes, what did you do before you came here?" Waverly asked. "Where are you from?"

"Nowhere worth mentioning. That's the truth." It was the truth too. *Or at least as much as I can safely tell.* Dean wanted to tell Waverly everything about himself, but he couldn't tell her who he really was. Why he was here. He could, however, tell her what made him who he was. That way, when this was all over and he was long gone, she might at least understand why things had to be this way. "I grew up on the waves more than anywhere else. I learned to sail by stowing away on ships, and did whatever I could to earn a meal each day and a quiet corner to fall asleep in each night. Unfortunately, no matter what direction the winds took me, I never got very far. Somehow, I always ended up right back where I started. It's like I was anchored in place. There was always something holding me back."

"I know how you feel," Waverly said.

Dean looked up. "Really?"

"Waverly Kray." The regent set down his chalice with a thud. "That kind of talk is not appropriate."

"Oh, Father, I'm just making conversation," she said, waving him off. "And I'm sorry, but it happens to be true. You might as well know it now," she told Dean. "Here in the palace, your life is not your own either. Mine has been planned out and put on hold since the day I was born. I've been waiting, you see. For you."

"That is an honor and a privilege," said the regent.

"And my duty as well, but that hasn't made the waiting any easier. But now that he's finally here, my life can go on as planned." Waverly took a long sip of her tea. "Just as I've always dreamed it would." The queen-to-be eyeballed her father in a way that made Dean uncomfortable. She didn't look very happy.

"I think I know how you feel," Dean said. "All my days, I've lived by someone else's rules. Waiting for my life to begin, wondering if it ever would. It hasn't been easy for me either, but now that I'm here . . . I feel like I might finally get the chance to be captain of my own ship. To be free. I've never felt free a day in my life, but I will soon."

Waverly's lips formed a sad smile. "I wouldn't be so sure about that."

Dean wasn't thirsty, but he took a drink anyway so he wouldn't have to reply. He didn't know what to say. He couldn't say what he really meant—that he'd be free from One-Eyed Jack once he delivered the gold of Zenhala. He couldn't share his past with Waverly, even if he felt they both wanted the same things for their future.

"I think what our guest is trying to say is that he'll be free from the life he knew," said the regent. "Free from hunger and fear. Here in the palace we have soft beds, clean clothes, full bellies. . . . This is a blessed life."

"It is for some," Waverly said. "You know what they say," she told Dean. "All that glitters isn't gold."

"That will do, Waverly." The regent stared at his daughter, lecturing her with his eyes before he turned to address Dean. "This island isn't perfect. I don't mean to say that it is. We have had our share of hardships, just like any other place in the world, but we see them through. I daresay we've withstood worse than you can well imagine. In the old country, before our people came to this island, they were constantly under siege for their golden trees. Those were dark times, but our ancestors found this lost, magical island and ushered in an age of prosperity. With the exception of one terrible day thirteen years ago, the people of Zenhala have been always safe here. With the right man leading the way, we always will be."

"I don't understand," Dean said. "The old country? Are the Zenhalan people not native to this island?"

"No. It was discovered ages ago by Captain Verrick's great ancestor. He set out to find this place when it became clear we could no longer defend our ancient lands. He was chasing legends, searching for a long-forgotten island we might call home. Back then, the island had no name. Only a bearing in the Bermuda Triangle. The sea serpents that prowl these waters, the yearlong storm . . . those things turned others away, but they attracted him. He knew this place was the perfect haven for us to grow our gold in secret, if he could only find it. With his mastery of the sea and a bit of good fortune on his side, he made land and planted our flag. We've been here ever since."

"He must have been a great sailor to weather the yearlong storm."

The regent shook his head. "No ship weathers the great storm. Not when it reaches full strength. He came at the right time. That part was luck, both good and bad. It was easy enough to get his ship in, but he had to wait a whole year to get himself out. Moving our kingdom to this island was a long process. It took us many years to understand the weather patterns of the Triangle."

A sailor at heart, Dean was fascinated by the secrets of the Bermuda Triangle. "How is it that no one else has figured out which month the storm breaks? I'm surprised people don't realize the traders go out at the same time, year after year."

"But they don't go out at the same time, year after year. There is no one safe month on the calendar when the great storm breaks. Tides turn. The weather shifts. Our ancestors"—the regent motioned to himself and Waverly—"the Krays of old, studied the stars to predict it." The regent pointed out over the terrace to a watchtower on a bluff overlooking the ocean. Its roof was a golden dome with a giant spyglass sticking out of it, aimed at the sky. "We employ their methods to this day, charting the heavens, mapping the weather, and planting our harvest accordingly."

"Mapping the weather?" Dean got up from the table, went to the terrace, and looked at the watchtower. "Does it work?"

"Of course it works. Our island relies on the gold trade for everything. The Watchers have just finished charting next year's storm."

"Incredible. I should very much like to see that."

"You will," Lord Kray replied. "And if you think that's something, wait until you see the orchard."

Dean closed his eyes. *Finally!* He was starting to think they were never going to mention that.

"The golden orchard, yes of course," he said, casual as he could manage. Dean put a hand to his brow and scanned the countryside. "Where is it planted?"

"You can't see it from the terrace," Waverly said.

"Is it far away? Perhaps we could take a tour after dinner if there's time."

"There's plenty of time," said the regent. "At least there will be. Once you finish your trials."

Dean tried not to show his disappointment as he returned to the table. "Of course. Forgive me. I'm getting ahead of myself."

"Not to worry. This will all be over soon enough."

Dean nodded. *That's what I'm afraid of.*

Lord Kray looked at Dean. "You seem overwhelmed. I understand. I'm sorry to put you through this, unprepared as you are. It isn't fair, I know, but it's a great responsibility that awaits you, and we must do all that we can to make you ready. Looking back, even I was not ready to watch over this kingdom thirteen years ago. Fate forced my hand back then, just as it forces yours today. Just know that I hope you succeed. You seem a good lad, and I hope with all my heart that it's you who takes the throne and my daughter's hand in marriage. Too long has this island been without its sovereign. The people cry out for their king. They deserve a king." Lord Kray raised his glass toward Dean. "I'm starting to think they might finally get one. To you, Dean Seaborne. To the future and a new golden age."

The regent's speech took Dean by surprise. It had been delivered with such earnest fluidity, and did not sound like the words of a man bent on holding on to power at any cost. Dean raised his goblet and returned the toast. "To the future."

As Dean, Waverly, and her father drank, dinner was served. The entrée was a cut of fish so big that, if had they been on a ship, four sailors would have shared it. It smelled better than any food Dean had ever been served, but his burgeoning faith in his host was tested when he realized exactly what was on his plate.

"Lord Kray, is this puffer fish?"

The regent nodded. "Very good! I didn't think you'd recognize it. 'Tis a Zenhalan delicacy. Upon my word, when prepared correctly, the puffer fish is the most delicious thing you'll ever eat."

"And when prepared incorrectly, the last. Puffer fish are poisonous, are they not?"

The regent wagged a finger. "Not in the royal chef's hands. It has to be cut just right, but don't worry. Puffer fish are his specialty. He knows precisely what to do."

Dean wiped his mouth with a napkin. "I'm sure he does."

He looked down at his plate and saw the trap the regent had laid for him. He was a crafty one, Lord Kray was. The way he had flattered Dean, getting him to drop his guard just before serving him the deadliest fish in all the sea. *How did a double-dealer like this ever raise a girl like Waverly?* He resolved not to be taken in by the regent this way again.

"Before we begin, I'd like to offer another toast," Dean said. He stood up, discreetly sliding his plate out over the table's edge as he rose. "Your words have inspired me, Lord Kray. I shall play the hand fate has dealt me to the end. The people of this island have waited long enough. They deserve a good and decent king, and I will give them that. Here and now, I pledge to pass any test you put before me and win the golden throne." He turned to Waverly. "And when I am king, my lady, I promise to never again leave this island." He raised his glass. "To life finally beginning."

"Bravo!" said the regent, as if nothing in the world would make him happier. He stood and clinked goblets with Dean. Waverly remained seated and did not drink. Dean had meant to get under her father's skin with his toast, but it seemed that she was the only one he'd managed to upset.

"Darling, what's wrong?" asked the regent. "Are you all right?"

Waverly put a hand on her stomach and shook her head.

"Father, I'm suddenly not feeling very hungry. I wonder if you might excuse me?"

"I hope you're not leaving us," Dean said.

"I'm sorry," she said, her tone sharp and final. "I need to go lie down." Her father reached a hand out to her, but Waverly pulled back, making more apologies as she hurried away from the table.

Dean watched her go with a sheepish look on his face, wondering if it was something he had said. He absentmindedly set his drink down on the edge of his plate, and the weight of the goblet flipped his puffer fish onto the floor. He made no excuses for his clumsiness this time around.

"Hmm," said Lord Kray as his servants swooped in to clean up the mess. "I'm surprised to find the boy who tamed the snapdragon so awkward."

Dean sighed as Waverly sped across the footbridge. "I suppose I'm just a fish out of water." Dean then eyed the watchtower in the distance.

He'd be heading back to sea soon enough.

CHAPTER 20

THE VIEW FROM MOUNT SKYTOP

The next morning, Dean found himself as far from the sea as he could possibly get. He had hiked up Zenhala's highest mountain alongside much of the island's nobility, followed closely by every man, woman, and child in the kingdom. That's what it felt like. Dean looked back on the legion of people who had followed him up the trail. By that point, every soul on the island had heard tales of his fearless bout with the snapdragon. The crowd from his first trial had grown, checked only by the mountain's steep terrain. Dean's second trial was about to begin.

The trial judge led the way, helped along by a tall walking stick and Captain Verrick's right arm. Dean was right behind them with Ronan and Rook at his side and Jin Ralian at his back. After a long trek up the mountain, the trial judge halted the group's climb on the banks of a fast, narrow stream. The old man took a moment to catch his breath, and the crowd waited patiently for him to recover. Dean hopped up on a rocky crag to take in the view from Mount Skytop. At this elevation, he meant to keep a sharp lookout for the orchard. Ronan and Rook did the same, but no one spotted any golden trees. Dean's mind drifted downstream toward the watchtower.

As the venerable old trial judge huffed and wheezed, the three boys moved away from the rest of the people who had scaled the mountain to see Dean off. "There it is," Dean whispered to Ronan and Rook, pointing at the tower in the distance.

When Dean had returned from dinner the night before, they had chided him for not coming back with information on the orchard as he'd promised. It was only after Dean told them what he'd learned about the island's storm cycle that Ronan and Rook agreed the evening had not been wasted.

"As soon as the trial begins, you two make your move on the watchtower. You'll need to get yourselves in position to slip away beforehand, so pick a spot now."

"Done," Ronan said, all business. As Dean continued to distract the local populace, their job would be to find out when the storm was expected to break next, just in case. It was an insurance policy of sorts. They couldn't afford to go back to One-Eyed Jack empty-handed. If they were forced to bring him something other than treasure, the Golden Isle's bearings and the dates of its next shipment would be the next best thing.

One hoped.

"The regent said the Watchers had just finished their work, but if the tower's not empty, you'll have to think on your feet. Just don't ask too many questions in there."

"How many is too many?" Ronan asked.

"One is too many."

"One?" Rook asked. "What are we s'posed to do, then?"

"Make observations," Dean said. "Let them talk. Your best bet is to go in marveling at the work the Watchers do. It doesn't matter what you say as long as you flatter them. One of the first things I learned in this business is people love talking about themselves. Give them a chance to boast and they never shut up."

"What are you all looking at?" Jin Ralian called out, approaching the trio.

Dean, Rook, and Ronan spun around to face him. "Nothing!" they all said at once.

Their sudden, simultaneous turn froze Jin in his tracks. "Forgive me, Your Grace," he said, aware of his intrusion and possibly a little suspicious. "I don't mean to interrupt, but it's time for us to brave the rapids."

"Your Grace?" Dean repeated, surprised to hear the words

come out of Jin's mouth. "Your father said it was too soon to address me like that. I figured you would share his opinion."

"I did," Jin replied. "But that was before the snapdragon." He motioned to the river. "Shall we?"

"Aye." Dean jumped down from the rocks. "That's what we're here for."

He walked with Jin to the water's edge, with Rook and Ronan in tow. "Can I offer you a word of advice?" Jin asked him.

"Advice? Please do." Dean was surprised. After his experience with Junter, he wasn't expecting much help from Jin.

"I imagine that after riding the snapdragon yesterday, the idea of going out on this river doesn't faze you one bit. Is that fair to say?"

Dean scrunched up his face. "I wouldn't say I'm completely unfazed, but . . . yes, I've been led to believe the worst is behind me."

Jin shook his head. "Underestimating today's trial would be a mistake. The river is wild, the falls are treacherous, and there are predators everywhere. You'll want to stay close to me out there."

Dean nodded. "Fair enough. I hope you'll make it easier than your brother did."

"The regent told my father you had only good things to say about Junter's service."

"I was being polite."

Jin grimaced. "No need for that. Junter's performance yesterday was an embarrassment. He disappointed my father and brought shame to my family. Rest assured, I will not fail as he did."

"Good man," Dean said. He studied Jin, trying to get a read on him. He was more talkative than his brother and said all the right things, but what he left unsaid rattled Dean. He wouldn't fail in *what*? Jin seemed concerned with defending his family's honor, but Dean couldn't be sure about his intentions. At this point, everyone was suspect.

The boys joined Verrick and the trial judge on the riverbank. Dean looked around. "I see the regent is missing again."

Verrick spoke up. "He and Lady Kray are waiting at the palace, where the Bad Falls end."

"Is that what ya call 'em?" Rook pointed downstream at a small drop before the river bend. "Don't seem all that bad to me."

The trial judge smiled. "This is just the start of the course. Three mighty waterfalls stand between the peak of Mount Skytop and the palace. Each one is larger than the one before it, and each stretch of river is rougher than the last. You will see," he told Dean. "No true lord of Zenhala harbors any fear of the ocean. If you mean to rule this island, you must show us you can hold together in the harshest of storms. Therefore, you will be tested under the worst conditions we have available: the raging rapids of the Bad Falls. Young Jin will be your guide. You will face this challenge together. You must be bold, you must be capable, and above all, you must be quick." He held up a small hourglass filled with fine golden sand. "The regent holds an identical hourglass at the foot of the mountain. If you fail to reach the palace before the last grain falls, you fail the trial. If that happens, you will not be king no matter what color your blood proves to be."

The judge's aides dragged two kayaks into the water and held them tight, lest the current carry them off. Jin waded out toward the boats.

Dean looked downstream, wondering if the golden orchard was somewhere down the river. He followed after Jin and climbed into the boat. "What say you, Ronan? Not too late to join the party."

Ronan laughed. "I like the view up here just fine, thank you." He reached into his satchel and took out Dean's kiteboard and mini sail, which he had folded up neatly and tied with a string. "Just in case."

Dean took the board and sail and stowed them inside his kayak. He got in and took up a double-sided paddle. "I'll see you at the bottom."

Ronan shook his hand. "Good luck."

Dean shoved off, and the judge blew the ceremonial conch horn, marking the start of the trial. As Ronan and Rook disappeared into the crowd, he turned his attention to the river. The Zenhalan test of seamanship was under way.

CHAPTER 21

BRAVING THE RAPIDS

Dean had never rowed a kayak before, but he had seen natives use them to row out and meet ships off the coast of tropical islands. The technique was easy enough to pick up, and he had Jin's example to follow. He wasn't worried. People cheered from land as the river carried Dean and Jin over the small waterfall that Ronan had made light of earlier. Unafraid, Dean went first, taking a big stroke with his paddle as he approached the lip of the falls. The drop was only few feet, but it felt like more when he landed. His last push with the paddle had propelled him out over the falls, and the boat hit the water flat, magnifying its impact. A lightning bolt of pain struck Dean's spine, and the force of landing nearly broke his paddle across his body. "Ouch," he said as the current shot him forward.

Jin let out a whoop as he splashed down behind Dean, his landing smooth and graceful. He quickly caught up with Dean, laughing all the way. "All right, there?" he asked.

Dean twisted around, working a kink out of his back. "I'll be fine."

"Of course you will. You did well! You're a natural."

"Thank you." Dean leaned into his shoulder to wipe water from his face without taking a hand off his paddle. He didn't feel like a natural. If anything, he felt he'd underestimated the river, but before he had a chance to say so, Jin was paddling ahead and out of sight.

"Paddle!" Jin shouted. "This is the gentle part of the river. We need to move if you want to beat the clock and pass this trial."

Dean nodded and dug deep, paddling hard to keep pace with Jin. The river bounced him around, but he kept himself upright, getting the hang of it as he went. It wasn't all that hard. The trick was to take alternating strokes, paddling on either side of the kayak to keep going straight ahead. Starboard, port, starboard, port, starboard, port. Dean established a rhythm, doubling up a stroke here and there to steer clear of rocks or duck under a low-hanging tree branch. People all along the river called out raucous huzzahs as he rowed past them. Their excitement was infectious.

Dean had to admit, it was a fun ride even if it was a little rough. He caught up to Jin as the river picked up speed. The water was choppy, but he had sailed in worse. *This isn't so bad. I can do this,* thought Dean. Just then, the roar of rushing water filled his ears.

"Jin!" he called out. "The falls . . . How big are they?"

"The first is thirty feet. We can go over that one. The others we'll avoid if there's time."

"If there's time? How about we make time?"

"That's the plan. We run a longer course that way, but we'll make our way down in one piece."

"I like the sound of that. No way around the first waterfall, then?"

"Afraid not. We have to stay the course."

Dean scanned the waters up ahead. He didn't trust Jin, but he needed him to get down the river. The five-foot drop at the start of the course had hit him like a cannonball in the back. A thirty-foot waterfall sounded horrible, and the ones that followed were out of the question. Especially the last one. The two-hundred-footer at the end would turn him into a bag of broken bones.

Dean's loyal subjects cheered him on. Their cries did little to boost his spirits. The crush of falling water drowned out any noise they made. Dean's fervent hope was that it drowned nothing else. As the falls approached, he tensed up. Jin urged him on. "You can do this!" he shouted, pulling up alongside Dean. "I'll go first this time. Watch me! Do as I do."

"Watch you how? I'll be right behind you!"

"Then listen! When you reach the falls, steer clear of the rocks on the right. Aim for the center! The drop is more gradual there, carved out by the water. If you go over too steep an edge, you'll flip your boat on the way down. You don't want that." Dean shook his head. No, he didn't want that. "And don't paddle off the lip of the falls! You'll shoot yourself out past the water and land flat again. Last time it hurt. Do it here and you'll break your back."

Dean nodded. "Don't break my back. Got it!"

"Keep your paddle in the water when you go over the side, but don't row. Keep yourself connected to the current. Once you go off the edge, hold the paddle along the boat like you're getting reading for a roll, understand?"

Water splashed into Dean's face. "What's a roll?"

"And brace yourself! Tuck your head in your arm. For God's sake, protect your head!" The falls came into view, loud and terrible. "This is it!" Jin shouted. "Ready?"

Dean's heart shrunk. "No!"

"Here we go! Don't worry. The river does all the work; you're just along for the ride!"

And with that, Jin was gone. He raced ahead to get in position at the mouth of the falls. Dean watched as he held his paddle in the water on approach, and then in a wink, he was gone. Alone, Dean turned as white as the water of the rapids. The confidence he had felt at the start of the course deserted him. The falls were too big. They were coming too fast. He wasn't ready for this by half, but there was nothing he could do. The relentless current sped up and the waters grew more turbulent. Dean reminded himself that the river's heavy flow was a blessing. Its cascading torrents of white water would dig out a deep basin below the falls. There would be no rocks waiting to greet him when he landed. All he had to do was to bring the kayak down and keep going. "Nothing to it," he told himself, trying to sound convincing. "Just go with the flow."

He came up on the falls with his paddle in the water, just as Jin had said, and kept it there just as Jin had done. Past that point, he had seen none of Jin's trip over the falls. When Dean reached the edge and saw the drop, it surprised him. The waterfall was not a flume running down a ravine like the last one had been, but an arc of water shooting out into the open air. Dean slid into the liquid onslaught with a scream and fell, as if riding a bridge of water down to the river below. The kayak went vertical, and Dean lost his mind, followed quickly by his paddle. He didn't drop it. He threw it away and ducked down in his kayak, wrapping his head in his arms as he plummeted through the air. The nose of his kayak pointed straight down, and when it hit the water, Dean was thrown forward, back, and then upside down. Each blow punished his body, sinking him deeper below the water. The deluge forced him under and kept him there as the kayak submerged completely. It surfaced with its topside down and Dean's head underwater. He pulled his head out of his tuck position and took in a mouthful of river. He choked on it as the falls pounded down from above. Disoriented, Dean didn't know what to do next or which way was up. Then he remembered something Jin had said: "Like you're getting ready for a roll." The words stuck in his head, a question that had gone unanswered.

What the devil was a roll? Suddenly, it struck him.

Roll!

Dean grabbed the port side of the boat and pulled hard to starboard, rolling the kayak up and setting himself aright. He gasped and air filled his lungs. He was alive! He had won no points for style with such an ugly trip down the waterfall, but that meant less than nothing. All that mattered was that he'd made it. The hard part was over, and thanks to Jin's advice, he had made it through. His suspicions about his guide seemed unjustified.

Dean hunched over in a painful fit of coughing. He blinked his eyes clear, trying to get his bearings. He didn't see Jin or anyone else. The merry line of onlookers that had followed him up the mountain had ended at the edge of the falls. Dean watched them shrink from sight as the river carried him down and away through a dark forest glade. The jungle grew thick and the shadows grew long with vines hanging down from above.

"I don't believe it," Dean heard Jin say. "You made it."

"Jin? Where are you?" Dean twisted around, searching for his second. He found him paddling in from the river's edge. "I lost my paddle," he added helplessly.

"Did you? Here, take mine."

Jin lifted his paddle out of the water and swung it like a sword. It struck Dean like a cannonball to the brow. His head snapped back. He slumped over his kayak, reeling in pain and shock.

Dean moaned and tried to get up, but he couldn't move. He tasted blood as it dripped down his face. A red line ran across the hull of his kayak, and the splashing water washed it away. Dean watched the process repeat, over and over. He didn't get knocked out, but he was struck dumb, to be sure. Woozy and drifting, he felt Jin steering his boat, guiding him toward . . . something. What was going on? When his head stopped hurting long enough to hold a thought, he looked up to see that he and Jin were parting ways. His second was on the opposite side of the river, paddling off. Before he left, Jin turned and saw the clarity in Dean's eyes. "Oh, good, you're back. I was afraid we wouldn't get to say good-bye."

Dean rubbed his aching head, still a bit groggy. "What is this? What are you doing?"

"Isn't it obvious? You're such a natural, I thought you were ready to take the fast way down. Without me. How does that sound?"

The river split in two and a heavy current carried Dean toward the sound of more rushing water. Without a paddle, he had no way to change course. He was trapped. "I should have known. The regent doesn't quit, does he?"

"The regent?" Jin laughed derisively. "If you think I'm doing all this for the regent, you're dumber than my brother. How he failed to feed you to the snapdragon, I'll never know. Blind luck, I suppose."

Dean blinked. "What?"

"That's the trouble with luck," Jin said. "It runs out. Farewell, my prince!"

Jin barked out a smug laugh and departed safely at the fork in the river. Dean was left to brave the rapids alone. Abandoned by his traitorous guide, he didn't waste time swearing revenge on Jin. Dean set his sights dead ahead and went to work looking for a way out of the mess he was in. He had to get his feet back on solid ground, but how? He couldn't fight the current with his hands. Without a paddle, just staying in the boat was a challenge. The river charged ahead like a team of wild horses, bucking hard as if angered by Dean's attempt to ride it. He couldn't steer and he couldn't use the kiteboard to escape, either. The thick jungle canopy didn't allow for enough wind to give him lift.

The next waterfall loomed large and deadly. It was louder than the last one and, at this point, unavoidable. Dean took a deep breath as he drifted toward it. With no paddle to make use of, he stuck his hand in the river as the current sucked him in. The last thing he saw before a barrage of water enveloped him was a drop of at least seventy-five feet down. Dean hugged the hull of the kayak as the rushing water engulfed his body, certain that his boat and bones would soon be crushed into matchwood.

His descent was like tumbling through the riptide of a wave, and at the same time, so much worse. Dean felt as if the great Lord Neptune had taken all seven of his seas and poured them down upon his head at once. The force was incredible. It flooded his ears, eyes, and nose. Dean thought it would never stop. When he reached the bottom, he didn't even know it. He felt as though a fist made of water had pulverized his body, and now he was inside that fist, spinning in endless dizzy circles.

The spinning did end, eventually. The water pouring down from the falls pushed him out and away from the rocks they ran off. Dean found himself drifting slowly away, alive and whole. He felt at his chest and flexed his fingers, confirming that everything was still in working order. It was a miracle. The water was calm in the pool at the foot of the falls. He had a few moments before the current swept him away again. He could make it to the river's edge. He was nearly there!

"Ha!" Dean shouted. "I'd like to see the look on your face now, Jin Ralian!" Instead, Dean saw a blue tiger with orange stripes prowling around the riverbank. "Okay, maybe not," Dean said, reversing his course and pushing away as fast as he could. The tiger showed its teeth and growled at Dean as he made a hasty retreat. Several more blue tigers stalked the river's edge in the places where it was safe enough to swim, and by the time they were gone, it no longer mattered. Dean scowled as the kayak picked up speed again and the current pulled him back down the river. "Nothing so fierce as the snapdragon," he muttered. That was what the regent had said. "So much for that!" Dean watched the garish blue cats shrink from sight as the third and final waterfall drew near.

Time was running out. The massive two-hundred-foot behemoth falls next to the palace would be Dean's final fall in more ways than one. He was desperate to find something—anything—that might save his skin, when suddenly the trees thinned out and the forest opened up. Dean grabbed the kiteboard and unwrapped the sail, flapping it open in a single motion. Seconds later, he had traded his kayak for the board and was out of the water, being pulled by the wind to the falls. "Thank you, Ronan!" he shouted as he took to the air, riding up over rocks and splashing downstream. A strong wind carried him down the river. He rode the current right up to the falls and over the edge. The kayak flew out unmanned and was lost in the water. Dean breezed down safely, gliding peacefully beneath the kiteboard sail.

A large crowd had gathered at the base of the falls outside the Aqualine Palace. Everyone was looking the wrong way. They all expected him to paddle in on his kayak by way of a stream that ran around the falls. As he descended, Dean searched the crowd for Waverly. The regent was there, as Verrick had promised, but he was alone. When he turned and saw Dean floating down over the massive waterfall, his eyes went wide. One by one, the other people saw too, and as a wave of recognition washed over the crowd, their exultation shook the castle walls. Once again, Dean had not only survived the trial, he had conquered it in spectacular fashion.

A reveling sea of people rushed to greet Dean as he landed, crowding the water's edge. Of everyone present, Lord Kray cheered the loudest. He even waded out to meet Dean, dressed in all his noble finery. The regent showered Dean with exuberant praise. "Amazing! Simply amazing! You finished the course with half an hourglass to spare! Over the great fall no less!"

"Where is Jin?" a voice called out. "Where's my son?"

Dean looked and saw Arjent Ralian standing with Junter and Jarret. They were the only people not applauding. "That's a good question," Dean said.

As if on cue, Jin paddled into sight. He was rowing across the same stretch of river that everyone had expected to see Dean arrive on. The look on his face suggested disbelief and wonder. Dean could tell he was terrified. *As well he should be.*

"You're alive?" Jin said meekly.

Dean crossed to Jin and greeted him like a brother. "Of course I'm alive! You worry too much." He turned to the regent. "Jin insisted on taking the long way down. Some people have no sense of adventure. More is expected from a prince." Dean helped Jin out of the water and put his arm around him as though they were mates.

"I don't understand," Jin said.

"Neither did I. Until now." Dean patted Jin on the shoulder and gripped his side in the same place he had stabbed the failed assassin two nights earlier. "I learned a great deal from this one." Dean smiled as Jin winced in pain. "A great deal indeed."

CHAPTER 22

EYES ON THE PRIZE

"W e shouldn't be here," Rook groused.

"Where's that?" asked Dean. "Here on this island or here hiding in these bushes?"

"Take yer pick," Rook said. "We oughta be lootin' this rock with a fleet of pirates, not sneakin' around like—"

"Spies?" Dean cut in. "That's what we are, in case you forgot." Night had fallen and the three boys were watching the watchtower, waiting for it to empty out.

"The time for spyin's come and gone," Rook said. "I'm a pirate. Ask me, it's high time we got back to piratin'. Why don't we send the bird out and tell One-Eyed Jack where we are? He'll turn this island upside down and shake its gold from every tree branch and pocket. We don't have to be wastin' our time like this."

"Stow that talk," Ronan told Rook. "I told you I'm not going to see One-Eyed Jack lay waste to this island. It's not going to happen. Not by my hand."

"Nor mine," said Dean. "You want to call in One-Eyed Jack, you should've done a better job of finding the orchard."

"It's been two days and we haven't found a single golden leaf," Rook said. "Let alone a whole orchard! For all we know, there isn't any gold left to find. It's probably all been harvested and sent out with the traders. We're running out of time, and we wasted all day today trying to get into that blasted watchtower."

Ronan took umbrage at that. "We didn't waste anything. I got us into that tower."

"So? We didn't find anything."

"We found out how the Watchers do their job."

"We didn't find out nothin' worth *nothin'*," Rook spat. "We don't know where the orchard is or when the storm is gonna break next. If we're not careful, we'll end up completely empty-handed."

"That's why we're here tonight," Dean said. "Insurance."

His plan was to sneak into the watchtower and find out when the traders would ship out with next year's harvest. If Dean and the others got that information to One-Eyed Jack, he could be ready with the whole Black Fleet when they did. A king's ransom, his for the taking. He'd have to wait a little while for it, but that was better than nothing. If worse came to worse and the golden orchard couldn't be found, Dean could at least give him that much.

"Insurance," Rook said, mocking Dean. "One-Eyed Jack wants his gold now, not some poker chip he can't cash in till next year."

"We'll get him gold," Dean said. "There has to be something here worth stealing. We just have to think smaller. Find trees bearing gold that didn't bloom in time for the trade ships. We'll give One-Eyed Jack Zenhala's bearing, the great storm's timetable, and whatever gold we can find. That ought to be enough. That ought to hold up our end of the bargain." He nudged Ronan. "Right?"

Ronan gave a nod that was lacking in confidence. "It *should*."

They both looked at Rook to see what he thought. Rook smirked as if they were signing their own death warrants. "You better hope so. It's yer funeral, if it don't. Yers anyway, MacGuire. Seaborne won't be leavin' this island alive. We know that much."

"That'll do, Rook," Ronan growled.

"I'm not sayin' nothin' he ain't already figured out hisself," Rook countered. "There's been a knife at his throat since we first got here." He turned to Dean and jerked a thumb in Ronan's direction. "This one I understand. He's all wrapped up in Gentleman Jim's idiot code, but you . . . why're you so soft on these people who're all tryin' to kill ya?"

"They're not *all* trying to kill me," Dean said.

Rook shrugged. "Only takes one. I'm just lookin' out fer ya here. No one else is. Not yer mate Ronan, and not yer pretty little lady, either."

"Leave her out of this."

"Hah!" Rook cackled. "That's what I told ya to do, remember? But you wouldn't listen. A boy like you's got no business with a girl like that. I'll wager she knows it too. Ain't stopped her daddy from tryin' to kill ya, has she?"

Dean frowned. "No."

But Dean wasn't so sure Waverly's father wanted him dead. Not anymore. Back on the river, Jin had said he wasn't working for the regent. Whether Jin was the regent's man or not, he wasn't likely to admit it, but Rook's taunting stuck in Dean's craw just the same. He had sworn not to be taken in by Lord Kray again, but despite everything that had happened, Dean still found it hard to see the man as a killer. He just didn't get that feeling about him. Dean had known bad men in his day. Bad men were all he'd ever known. Waverly's father didn't fit the bill.

Unfortunately, he couldn't take the chance of being wrong. He couldn't go to the regent with the Ralians' treachery. Not when it was still possible that he was the one behind it. He couldn't tell Waverly what Jin and Junter had done, either. She'd want to tell her father, and then Dean would have the same problem all over again. Dean did trust Verrick. He could tell him what was happening, but Verrick would cause such an uproar that the regent might be forced to call off Dean's last trial. He couldn't have that. Dean knew the trial was a death trap, but it didn't change the fact that he needed it to distract the islanders while Ronan and Rook searched for the orchard. Dean was trapped, same as always. The only course he could plot was none at all.

Dean sensed that Ronan could see the wheels turning in his head. Ronan patted his shoulder. "You're in a bad spot, Seaborne. I know it. I do. If it means anything to you, you've got my respect for seeing this thing through."

"A lotta good that'll do 'im when he ends up dead in a ditch," Rook said. "When you're layin' there, just remember you did it to yerself. Yer the one that wanted to be a prince and make time with the regent's daughter."

"I told you to leave her out of it," Dean warned.

"Livin' in a dream world, you are. That's what ya get. A target on yer back, front, port side, and starboard." Rook laughed. "They're comin' at ya from all angles, mate."

"I'm not your mate, Rook."

"Not my prince, neither," Rook said through gritted teeth. He gave Dean's head a shove.

Dean lunged for Rook.

The two boys grappled with each other in the brush until Ronan broke them up. "Belay that!" he rasped in a hoarse, angry whisper. "Both of you, stop it! We're here to do a job, not meddle with each other. Your words, Seaborne, remember? Now, look down there."

He pointed over the bushes. Lights were going out in the watchtower windows. Dean and Rook hushed up. A few moments later, the last two Watchers left the building and locked up for the night. Dean remained silent even after they disappeared down the mountain trail. He was upset with himself for letting Rook get to him. That shouldn't have happened. He had to do a better job of staying cool.

"You all right?" asked Ronan.

Dean shook his head. "This isn't how I work. I'm used to keeping a low profile. This job . . . everything about it has been wrong from the start."

"It's a new experience for me too," Ronan said. "What do you say we just keep our eyes on the prize?"

"Eyes on the prize," Dean repeated. He got up and started off toward the watchtower. "No bones about it."

CHAPTER 23

ALL ALONG THE WATCHTOWER

The watchtower stood alone on a promontory overlooking the ocean. It was a squat, blocky structure that, due to its position on the peak, had seemed taller from afar. A wooden staircase wrapped around the mountain all the way up to the main entrance, which had been left unguarded. It was an easy enough thing for Dean to pick the lock on the front door and slip inside. Ronan and Rook hurried after him. They waited until they were safely inside the tower before they lit their lanterns, just in case anyone was watching.

The tower's lower levels were a chaotic mess. Cluttered desks were covered with journals, calendars, and bits of scrap paper that had been scrawled with illegible handwriting. Everywhere Dean looked he saw books—sturdy new ones and brittle ancient tomes written in a dozen different languages. They were jammed into shelves, piled high on tables, and stacked up in corners on the floor. There were pieces of wind gauges and weather vanes at workstations. Star charts were spread out on drafting tables and marked with quizzical notations. Dean spied a roll of parchment that took up an entire wall and couldn't help but feel intimidated by it. The paper was littered with symbols he didn't recognize, and equations he couldn't understand. Everything about the place reeked of wisdom beyond his ken.

"I'm starting to see why they don't post guards at the door," Dean said. "How could anyone but the Watchers make sense of this?"

Ronan lit a lantern by the stairs and motioned for Dean and Rook to follow him up. "Not to worry. This is just the science behind their machine. We don't need to understand how it works. It's enough for us to know that it does. Up we go now. Step lively."

When Dean got upstairs, he found it sparse, clean, and empty. At first glance, it was the exact opposite of the floor below. There was nothing but a white stone pedestal in the center of the room, with an iron brace around it. Upon closer examination, Dean saw that both the pedestal and the brace ran up through a wooden platform overhead, where a complex network of gears and hydraulic pistons split off to line the bottom of the decking above. Dean whistled.

"Impressed?" Ronan was already climbing a ladder up to the next level. "That's nothing. Wait until you get a load of this up here."

Dean followed Ronan up to the observatory level, where he came face-to-face with the largest spyglass he'd ever seen. It was five times the size of a cannon, perched high atop a wide steel shaft. A spiral staircase twisted up toward a seat that had been planted at the base of the telescope, and the shaft holding up the entire apparatus was connected to the web of gears beneath the floorboards. There were handles, levers, and cranks aplenty to adjust its position. Rook shifted a few. "Don't play with those," Dean said, swatting his hand away. "Ronan, you really understand how to use this thing?"

Rook shook his head no.

Ronan heaved on a line that ran through a series of pulleys on the wall. "I understand enough."

Each hard tug of rope opened a hatch in the tower's dome roof a little wider. After Ronan finished sliding the roof open, he pushed a big red button. Pumps in glass tubes pressed down, water bubbled, and pistons fired. Dean heard the sound of compressed air being released as the steel shaft extended, stopping only after the end of the spyglass had been raised up out of the tower.

"Amazing," Dean marveled.

"That it is," Ronan said. "The Watchers spend all year maintaining and calibrating this contraption. Apparently, it can only predict the storm's next break now, before the winds pick back up. They get one shot at this and that's it, so they have to make sure their tools are precise."

"How do they know?" Dean asked. "How'd they figure all this out?"

"You're asking me?" Ronan replied. "I don't know how they cracked this nut, but they've been doing it since before we were born." He pointed up at the night sky. "You line up Orion's belt in the sights of that spyglass, and it'll tell you when next year's storm will die down."

"Orion's belt?" Rook said. "What're you talkin' about?"

Ronan sighed. "Weren't you paying attention in here today? Orion's belt! How long have you been a sailor, and you don't know your stars?"

Rook scowled. "How long you been a pirate, and you don't know how to . . ." He trailed off, trying to come up with something clever.

"Don't think too hard, Rook," Dean said. "You'll hurt yourself." He put a hand on Ronan's back and lowered his voice. "Ronan, this contraption is beyond the likes of us."

Ronan shook his head. "The Watchers told me how they do it. It's not as hard as it looks."

"They just volunteered all this today?" Dean asked. It sounded too good to be true.

"It was just like you said. Once I buttered them up, I couldn't shut them up. Half the time, I didn't understand what they were talking about, but what I did catch was simple enough. The answers we want are written in the stars."

Dean shook his head in wonder. "This I have to see." He started up the spiral staircase that led to the spyglass. "Rook, you keep an eye out that window. Let us know if you see any trouble coming our way. Ronan, can you work these levers by yourself?"

Ronan spit into his palms and rubbed his hands together. "Aye."

"All right," Dean said, climbing into the red velvet chair beneath the spyglass. "Let's get a look at the weather."

Dean settled into his seat and got his bearings. The end of the spyglass was there for him to look into, and below that, a console filled with confusing controls. There were sliding switches, knobs, and a calendar readout made up of three wheels. There was one wheel for months, one for days, and one for years. Dean looked through the spyglass and saw three circular targets he could adjust. He twisted a few knobs on the console, and the date wheels scrolled as the targets moved. The readout would reveal the storm date to him once the targets clicked into place along Orion's belt.

"Do you see it?" Ronan called out. "The constellation?"

Dean looked again. "I think so. Rotate me clockwise, toward

you." Ronan cranked a gear, and the spyglass swiveled. The years clicked forward on the readout as he moved. "All right, stop!" Orion the Hunter came into view. Dean fiddled with the controls, but the scope's markers couldn't reach the stars in his belt. "No good! Angle me up a point, Ronan."

Ronan tried a few more levers until he found one that tilted Dean's chair back and the spyglass skyward. Months scrolled by on the console as he moved Dean into position. Dean focused the lens, but his sights were still off. Ronan had moved him too far. It took some doing, but with a little back and forth, Dean and Ronan got the spyglass in place before either one of them lost patience with the other. From there, Dean could make the final adjustments himself. He leaned forward to line up the targets with the stars. A few more minutes and he would have it.

"How we doing up there, Seaborne?" asked Ronan.

"Quiet!" Rook called out from his perch at the window. "Someone's comin'."

Dean's head shot up. "How much time do I have?"

"Not much. They're on the stairs outside the tower."

"They're on the stairs and you're just telling me now? What are you doing over there?"

"The best I can!" Rook called back. "I'm lookin'. I didn't see 'em before now!"

"How many are there?" Ronan asked.

"Just one. Can't tell who it is."

"I knew this was going too smoothly," Dean muttered. "Why should anything we do here come easy?" He swallowed hard and turned back to his work. There would be time to yell at Rook later. Right now, he had to focus. The console before him was an endless array of knobs and dials. Sweat beaded up on his brow as he tried them all, fine-tuning the spyglass's sights, but the mutinous little targets refused to go where he wanted. Dates on the calendar wheel ticked up and down as Dean worked. Downstairs, he heard the tower doors open.

"Hurry up, Seaborne," Rook said.

"Before they get here, you mean? Brilliant, Rook. Thank you." Dean bit his lip and kept twisting knobs, turning dials, and sliding switches. Eventually, he found the right ones, and the targets did as he asked. The three gold rings in the spyglass fell over the stars in Orion's belt. The numbers in the date box clicked into place. He had it.

Dean sat back and stared at the date of next year's harvest, committing it to memory. It was ten months away. Not quite a year, but still a long time to wait. One-Eyed Jack had never been known for that kind of patience, but if there was ever a treasure worth waiting for, this was it. Dean sprang from his seat and sped down the spiral staircase.

"Do you have it?" Ronan asked, his voice just above a whisper.

Dean nodded and jumped down to the platform. Ronan and Rook doused their lights and followed him below, taking cover behind the spyglass's massive stone pedestal. They could hear someone in the offices downstairs. "Who is it?" Dean asked Rook. "A Watcher? A guard?"

Rook shook his head. "I don't know."

Dean frowned. The three of them stared at the door in silence. When it opened, the face behind it belonged to the last person Dean expected to see.

"Hello?" Waverly Kray called out, holding a candle. "Is somebody there?"

CHAPTER 24

LIVING ON THE EDGE

D ean, Ronan, and Rook huddled together behind the stone column. It was so quiet in the tower that a small shuffle of feet, a sniffle, or a breath was all it would take to give them away. They kept still and quiet as Waverly climbed the ladder to the platform above without noticing them. After she passed, Ronan and Rook crept toward the door, but Dean held back. Ronan stopped and looked at Dean. He motioned with his hands, silently asking what he was waiting for. "You go on ahead," Dean whispered. "I want to see what she's up to."

Ronan rolled his eyes. "I'll bet you do. Forget her, Seaborne. Come on."

"I'm serious, Ronan. Aren't you curious what she's doing here?"

"Not enough to get caught sneaking around this place."

"I won't. Trust me."

Ronan shook his head. "I hope you know what you're doing."
He followed Rook downstairs and vanished in the shadows of the
stairwell. Dean waited until he heard Waverly's footsteps leave
the platform, then followed her up.

He peeked over the edge of the deck and looked around. The
tiny, flickering flame of her candle made her easy to spot. Waverly
had not gone to the spyglass but to a staircase on the wall instead.
Dean watched as she went all the way up to the open hatch in
the dome.

What is she doing?

She climbed through the portal and went outside. Dean raced
up the steps after her and slowed his pace as he neared the top.
He tiptoed the rest of the way to the wall and looked outside.
Waverly was standing on the ledge overlooking the water. Dean
watched as she took off her robe, tied a weight around it, and
threw it into the darkness. She wore a formfitting one-piece suit
as she stepped up to the precipice and took a deep breath. Dean's
heart leapt into his throat. She was way too close to the edge.

Is she going to jump?

"Be careful!" Dean rushed out and grabbed her wrist before
she fell.

Waverly screamed a bloodcurdling cry that felt like a knife in
Dean's ears. She almost lost her footing as she pulled herself free

of his grip. In trying to save her, Dean had almost scared Waverly to death. "You!" she said, after she realized who had grabbed her. "What are you doing here?"

"Saving you! What are you doing here?"

"Jumping!" She backed away from the ledge in a hurry. "You nearly killed me!"

"No, I didn't." Dean was confused. "Nearly killed you? You just said you were going to jump!"

"Into the water!" Waverly clarified. "Where else would I go?" Dean said nothing. "It's called cliff diving, we're just not on a cliff. It takes concentration. You nearly knocked me off the roof. I would have fallen to my death."

Waverly's green eyes burned with anger. Dean felt like a fool.

"I see. In that case, I'm sorry. Carry on."

"Carry on!" Waverly repeated, indignant. "Thank you very much, Your Grace. How lucky for me that you were here to save me!"

"I was only trying to help. I didn't mean to—"

"How long have you been here? What are you doing up here?"

"Where? Up here?" Dean sputtered out words, stalling. "I . . . wanted to see the watchtower. Your father made it sound so intriguing, I couldn't resist."

"My father." Waverly looked up at the stars. "What would he have said if I'd died doing this? It would have made him right all along." She shook her head. "I would never have forgiven you."

Dean scratched his head. "You'd have been dead. So there'd be no forgiveness to be had either way. But I am sorry, and I'm glad you're just here for a little diversion, even if it is a touch"—Dean searched for the right word—"insane."

Waverly gave Dean a playful look. "Says the boy who wrestles sea serpents and flies off waterfalls."

"Heard about that, did you?"

"I did."

Dean smiled. "I looked for you at the trial today. Where were you?"

Waverly's anger was faded. "I'm here now. Care to join me? There are two ways off this tower. The safe way." Waverly pointed back inside. "And the fun way." She pointed out to sea.

Dean looked down at the ocean, nearly one hundred feet below. It dawned on him what Waverly was asking. "You're joking. I'm not following you down there."

Waverly looked disappointed. "Suit yourself."

Before Dean could say another word, she turned and sprang off the roof with a light graceful step. He gasped as she executed a perfect swan dive, holding her form all the way down. *She's mad. That's all there is to it. She's crazy.* Waverly sliced into the water with the tiniest hint of a splash. In the moonlight, he could see her waving him down. Dean took another look at the water.

"I must be crazy too."

He backed up a few steps and ran full speed ahead toward the ledge. He didn't dive like Waverly. He just leapt out as far as he could, trying to clear the rocks the tower was built over. He was scared of the fall, but he jumped anyway.

When he hit the water, it hurt.

"Ow."

"Not bad," Waverly laughed as she swam for the shore. "No points for style, but high marks for bravery. Not bad at all."

"I'm glad you approve." Dean grunted. "I doubt your father would."

Waverly stepped onto the beach and found the robe she had thrown down. "There are a lot of things my father doesn't approve of. Too many, in fact."

Dean got out of the water and looked up at the watchtower. "In this case, I might have to agree with him. I don't understand. Surfing's one thing, but why do this?"

"Why did you do it?"

Dean shrugged. "You dared me to."

"That's right. And you don't show your stern to a challenge. Do you?"

"Not usually."

"Neither do I. Was it fun?"

Dean struck a pose with his hand on his chin like a man deep in thought. "I'm not sure yet. I think so." He thought a little more. "Yes. Yes, it was," he added with a smile.

Waverly laughed. "Good. Enjoy it while you can. You'll have to give up this kind of fun when you're king. Your life is too valuable. That's what they'll say. My father never lets me do anything for that exact reason."

"That's because you're his daughter. It's different with me. He's perfectly happy to risk my life."

Waverly's smiled faded. "That isn't fair. The trials are island tradition. It's not his fault you've been thrown into them this way."

Dean nodded. "Maybe not." He still wasn't sure about the regent, but even if he was trying to kill him, the man was still her father. She didn't know what he was up to. She couldn't have known, and she couldn't be blamed for missing it, either. How could she see her father as a killer? Even Dean had a hard time seeing it. "I don't mean to insult your father. I'm sorry if I offended you last night at dinner too, but I have to admit I don't know what I said wrong. I thought the evening was going fine until you ran out."

"It *was* going fine. I thought you understood me, but then you said—" Waverly turned away and shook her head.

"What did I say? Whatever I said, forget it. You might as well. I was only saying what I thought I was supposed to say. That's all I ever say to anyone."

Waverly squinted at Dean. "You don't speak your mind?"

"No," Dean laughed. "Hardly ever. I can't do that. Not with you. I don't know how to speak to a"—he was going to say *girl* but stopped himself—"to a lady."

"Ugh," Waverly scoffed. "Don't say that. It's not me."

"Of course it is."

"No. It isn't. I don't want a sheltered life at court with royal galas and fancy gowns. I want to go out there and see the world as you have. I've been stuck on this island all my life. Now that you're here, it seems I always will be. Queens don't get to have adventures, no matter how much they might wish for them." She looked at Dean. "You know, I considered running away when you came back?"

Dean was taken aback at Waverly's admission. "I had no idea."

"It's true. Did I manage to shock you this time?" Her eyes were welling up. She wiped them clean before any tears escaped. "You must think I'm ridiculous. Especially growing up the way you did."

Dean shook his head. "I don't think you're ridiculous."

"Yes, you do. You must. You think I'm a spoiled little rich girl."

"No, I don't. And you don't have anything to worry about, Waverly." Dean hesitated. "Between you and me, everyone here believes I'm the lost prince far more than I do."

Now it was Waverly's turn to be surprised. "You don't believe it?"

Dean pursed his lips. "Let's just say I'd be very surprised if my blood turned the palace water blue."

"But last night you said—"

"What was expected of me."

"Do you always do what people expect you to do?"

"I try to go my own way. It never works out."

"At least you're being honest."

"That's me. Honest to a fault."

Waverly turned up her palms. "I suppose it's of little consequence. It doesn't matter what we believe. For better or worse, truth always comes out in the end."

"I'm not usually around for that."

Waverly gave Dean a puzzled look. He could tell she wanted to ask what he meant, but she didn't. For his part, he wanted to tell her, but couldn't. He could feel Waverly opening up to him, and he didn't like lying to her, but he couldn't bring himself to tell her the truth. He could only trust her with part of it.

"I'll tell you a secret if you like, Waverly. I don't want to sit on a throne in the Aqualine Palace all my life either. I know what it's like to be stuck somewhere, unable to leave. My life is out there on the waves. You and I both want the same thing—freedom to live life on our own terms."

"If that's the case, you should leave this place now, just in case you're wrong. Royal life is a gilded cage. Kings have to stay with their kingdoms."

"Not always," Dean said, remembering One-Eyed Jack's promise to come after him. "Believe me, there's more than one kind of king."

CHAPTER 25

THE THIRD SECOND

The next morning, Dean got up early and went looking for a palace guard. "Excuse me. Can I trouble you for a favor?" he asked the first one he came across.

The guard snapped to attention. "Your Grace! Of course. Anything. Anything at all."

Dean smiled. He had expected such an answer, but it was still nice to hear the words spoken out loud. "It's nothing too important," he told the man. "I've just decided not to use Jarret Ralian as my second in today's trial. Someone should probably tell him."

The guard was clearly taken aback, but he didn't say so. It

wasn't his place to question princes. "It shall be done at once, Your Grace. I'll see to it personally."

"Very good." Dean waved his hand, already taking his leave. "Thank you."

As he turned away, he enjoyed the guard's stunned reaction. Dean wished he could be there to see Jarret Ralian's expression when he heard the news. The little twerp was probably plotting to kill him right now. Dean wasn't about to give him that chance. Not after the first two trials. *Fool me once, shame on you. Fool me twice, shame on me. Fool me three times . . . I'd have to be a bloody moron.*

It was Dean's final day on the island. The great storm was fast approaching. It was time for his last trial and last chance to find the orchard. If Dean's crew came up dry this time, that was it. They had to cut their losses and run. At least, now that he knew when the next harvest shipped out, Dean had a backup plan. The plan wasn't perfect, but it delivered the gold in a manner he could live with. It squared with his moral compass. The way Dean saw it, if Zenhala had gold to trade, it had gold to spare. He could live with One-Eyed Jack raiding their boats. The question was, would One-Eyed Jack let him? Dean much preferred to deliver the treasure by week's end, as he'd been ordered to do. He still held out hope that the orchard could be found.

While Rook was roaming the island and searching for golden

trees, Dean and Ronan were deep in a cavern underneath the palace. Unfortunately, no large crowds accompanied the trial this time. Just a small retinue from the regent's court. Waverly and her father were both present, as were Verrick and the trial judge. Arjent Ralian was there too, along with all three of his sons. Dean was surprised they dared to show their faces around him. He gave the Ralians credit for nerve, if nothing else.

The cave was dark and wet, lit only by lanterns that the small assembly from the palace carried with them. Seawater poured in from outside, ankle deep and still in some areas, waist high and thrashing in others. The trial judge stood on an outcropping of stone and presented Arjent Ralian. "Before we begin, I am told Lord Ralian wishes to make a statement."

Ronan elbowed Dean. "Bet I know what this is about."

"Yes," Arjent began, giving Ronan a stern eye. "If it is not too late, I'm hoping your friend will come to his senses and employ Jarret's services as his second. Though it has never been this island's custom to accommodate the prince in such a manner, the sons of House Ralian have answered the call. My children have placed their lives on the line enduring their trials a second time, and serving the would-be prince admirably. Not that he shows any gratitude. Instead, he insults my son, declining his valiant offer to reenter the labyrinth on his behalf. He doesn't even tell him to his face. He sends a palace guard to deliver his message!"

Lord Ralian looked upon Dean with contempt. "Despite all of that, even now, Jarret stands ready to face this challenge with you, Dean Seaborne. If you ask it of him."

Dean fought the urge to applaud. In his view, a performance like that deserved nothing less than a standing ovation. Arjent Ralian had done a wonderful job of feigning outrage. His son Jarret was equally talented. All through his father's speech, he stared at Dean, pretending not to know why he had been rebuffed. Dean recognized the act for what it was. The mask of a practiced liar, taking care to display the emotions that an honest person would feel. He knew that trick well, and saw something of himself in Jarret. The two boys were the same age exactly, but both of them were older than their years. Like Dean, Jarret's handsome features were young and innocent, but he had the deep eyes of an old soul. Dean liked to think the similarities ended there.

"I'm sorry, but my decision is final," Dean stated.

"This is most unwise," said Lord Kray. "I allowed these trials to go forward on the condition that you would have seconds to assist you. Thus far, you've exceeded our greatest expectations, but the tunnels beneath the palace are perilous. I cannot allow you to risk your life in this fashion."

"You think Jarret can make the maze less perilous?" Ronan asked.

"The trial is only given when the aqueducts are empty," the

regent replied. "Jarret navigated the labyrinth in record time, just this month. Right now, no one knows these tunnels better than he does."

"Lord Kray speaks the truth," said Verrick. "You can't go in there alone."

Dean patted Ronan's shoulder. "I'm not going in alone. I'm taking Ronan."

"Him?" Arjent Ralian was incredulous. "A *commoner?*"

Ronan puffed up his chest. "Is that a problem?"

The trial judge cleared his throat. "These trials are intended for those of noble birth only. I mean you no offense, my son, but I doubt you are equal to the task that stands before you."

Ronan grinned a crooked grin. "My blood might not be as pure as that of the lost prince here, but I know a thing or two about a thing or two. What exactly are you testing for here?"

"Intelligence for one, judgment another . . . the ability to keep a clear head under pressure comes into play as well. This trial is a journey through the subterranean labyrinth of the Aqualine Palace. The tunnels that channel ocean water through the castle are mostly empty during the great storm's hiatus. You must find their center, directly below the throne room." The judge turned to address Dean directly. "Do that, and you will earn your place on the golden seat within."

"What do you mean the tunnels are *mostly* empty?" Dean asked. "They flood? No one said anything about that."

"Didn't they?" Jarret Ralian said, speaking up for the first time. "These tunnels channel seawater through the Aqualine Palace. Obviously, at high tide, the ocean floods them. Look around you. All this water has to go somewhere."

Dean watched the ocean crash against the cavern walls, with no small amount of angst. The thought of drowning in a dark maze beneath the palace did not sit well with him.

"Water levels down here tend to rise as the great storm approaches," Verrick explained, picking up on Dean's trepidation. "This test is typically given at the beginning of harvest season to give the runners ample time to navigate the labyrinth. People have been known to get stuck in there for weeks. Some never come out."

"Jarret did it in less than an hour," Arjent Ralian proudly proclaimed. "But if you insist on doing things your way, so be it. I see now that I was too hasty with you. Such resolve is an admirable quality. It will serve you well as king . . . if you survive."

"Don't worry, not all the tunnels flood," Jarret assured Dean. "Just make sure you're not in the wrong place when the ocean comes in. That's all."

The trial judge rested a concerned hand on Dean's shoulder. "You'll have nothing but a lamp to light your way and a stick of chalk to mark your passage. Jarret is very bright. Are you sure you won't lean on his experience to guide you?"

"I'm sure," Dean answered. "And we're wasting time. Especially if I'm going to break his record."

Jarret laughed out loud. His father gave out a disgruntled "humph."

Waverly, who had been quiet up to this point, stepped forward to offer Dean a canvas bag, tied up tight at the top. "If your mind's truly made up, you'd better take this. Just in case."

"What is it?"

"Food and water. Verrick did not exaggerate. People have been lost in there for days or more. You'll be glad you took it with you."

Dean held up his lantern and a piece of chalk. "I have everything I need right here. Don't worry. I'll be standing in the throne room by lunchtime."

Waverly thrust the bag on him. "*I insist you take it.* I brought it here for you."

Dean was taken aback by Waverly's forcefulness. He looked at her with puzzled eyes. Ronan leaned into Dean and nudged him. "Just take the blasted food, Seaborne. Time's wasting."

Waverly gave Dean a look that said *Listen to your friend*, and he realized there was no reason not to. "Forgive me, my lady," he said, taking the bag from her hands. "Thank you for thinking of me. I'm in your debt."

Waverly smiled. "That's more like it. Make sure you have a drink before you get started."

"Can we go now, Your Grace?" Ronan asked, placing added emphasis on Dean's false title.

Dean nodded. "Aye, let's get moving. Where is the entrance to the tunnels?" The trial judge pointed the way, and Dean started up the incline. Ronan followed after him, but when he passed Jarret Ralian, he tripped and tumbled down a ravine. Ronan came up soaking wet and writhing in pain.

"Ronan!" Dean slid down to him. Verrick and the Ralians followed.

"He tripped me!" Ronan shouted, his finger pointed squarely at Jarret.

The Ralian boy put his hands up. "An accident, I assure you! Here, let me help you."

"Don't touch me!" Ronan said, pushing him off.

Verrick and Dean stepped in to help Ronan up. "Talk to me, Ronan," said Dean. "Are you all right?"

Ronan nodded. "I twisted my ankle, that's all. I'll be fine." When Dean let Ronan go, it was plain to see the opposite was true. He shuffled forward, limping badly and wincing with every step. He could barely walk.

Verrick shook his head. "That ankle needs to be wrapped and bound tight."

"What's this?" asked Jarret. "Could it be that I am needed after all?"

"No," Dean said. He looked at Ronan, but they both knew he couldn't go. Traipsing through underground tunnels was out of the question in his condition.

"I'm afraid there's no one else," said Jarret.

"I'll go alone, then," Dean said. "You did."

"You're not me. You'll drown in there."

"With or without you?"

"How dare you!" Arjent Ralian shouted.

"I'll go," said Waverly.

"What?" the entire party exclaimed, Dean included. All eyes turned to her as Dean's insult to Jarret was upstaged by something even more scandalous—a woman facing the trials of manhood.

"I'll go," Waverly said again. "Why not?" she asked, the question directed at her father more than anyone. "If I'm to rule beside him one day, shouldn't I have to earn my place as well?"

"Absolutely not," said the regent. "I forbid it!"

"It's not your decision, Father."

"I am the lord regent of this island, young lady!"

"But you don't get to choose who he takes as his second." Waverly turned to the trial judge. "Isn't that right, sir?"

Everyone looked at the judge. The regent's eyes burned with such fury that Dean thought the old man would melt under his gaze. The judge withstood Lord Kray's glowering as he contemplated the matter in silence. After a long moment, he sighed with resignation. "I'm afraid Lady Kray is correct. The decision belongs to the boy who would be king. The first second has been declined, his replacement incapacitated. . . . If he were to bestow the honor on a third person and that person were to accept?" The judge shook his head. "None of us can force him to choose otherwise."

"Waverly, please. This is no place for you," her father pleaded. "You know as well as I, you don't like places like this."

"It's not up to me, Father. It's up to him."

The eyes of the group turned once more, this time to Dean. It fell to him to decide the matter. The regent glared at Dean, simmering but silent. He shook his head slowly, warning him not to put his daughter in harm's way. Dean looked right past him to Waverly. "You're sure you don't mind being my third choice?"

Waverly folded her arms. "As long as you don't refuse me."

Dean smiled. He looked over at Jarret, who was visibly frustrated and foiled. He looked at Ronan, who gave him a go-ahead nod. Dean could practically read his thoughts. Anything was better than a partner who was trying to kill you—even a girl. But Ronan didn't know Waverly as he did. Dean reached out a hand to her. "My lady. How could anyone refuse you?"

CHAPTER 26

THE LABYRINTH

A re you okay?" Dean asked.

"I'm fine."

"You don't look fine."

"I'm fine."

Dean put his hands up and backed off a step. He wouldn't push things any further, but Waverly did not look fine, no matter what she said. She looked upset. Her trademark bravado and vigorous spirit had faded shortly after they entered the caves. The fearless young woman he had come to know had vanished, to be replaced by a timid girl who jumped at shadows as she inched forward cautiously with her lantern. Dean couldn't figure it out. The tunnels were by no means hospitable, but they were not as bad as he had expected. They were narrow, winding, and dark, to be sure, but the lanterns he and Waverly carried lit their path well enough. The caves were damp and smelled of mildew, but the seawater that charged through them all year long had smoothed out the stone passageways and flushed out the rats and other vermin. The two of them could proceed without fear of running into the kind of critters most people were scared of. Or so Dean thought. A crab skittered across the path, causing Waverly to scream and jump back.

"It's just a crab," Dean said, steadying her. "Are you okay?"

Waverly shuddered and let out a deep breath. "I will be. It's nothing. I just don't like it in here, that's all."

"Right," Dean said, wondering if he had made a mistake in choosing her as his second.

"Don't look at me like that."

"I'm just surprised. You're like a cat on hot bricks. I've seen you surf giant waves and jump off cliffs, but in here—"

"In here it's different. Those are things you do outside. I like to be outside. I don't like tight places." Waverly looked around, loathing her environment. "Underground. In the dark."

Dean nodded. "So your father said. But if that's the case, why did you volunteer to come in with me?"

"I didn't want to, but you were so insistent on not using Jarret as your second. Why were you so dead set against him, anyway?"

Dean couldn't give Waverly an honest answer. If he told her

the Ralians had been trying to kill him, he'd have to answer the next logical question: Why hadn't he told anyone about it?

"I don't trust him," Dean said. "Call it a hunch."

Waverly shrugged. "Can't say I blame you. I've never liked him either." Dean grinned. They even disliked the same people. Waverly was the best. She led the way forward as the mouth of the cave opened up to a wide underground chamber. Inside, she took a deep satisfied breath and stretched her body from head to toe. "There. Much better."

Dean waved his lantern around the cavernous hollow. "That depends on how you look at it." Six different tunnels split off from the chamber they were in. The labyrinth had begun in earnest. "I don't suppose you have any idea which way to go?"

"None whatsoever."

Dean grimaced. "I didn't think so." He took out the piece of chalk that the trial judge had given him. "Might as well try our luck. We'll mark the tunnels we take at each fork in the road, noting the order we take them. That way, if the trail leads us back in a loop, we'll be able to tell." Dean picked a tunnel at random and wrote a large number 1 on the wall.

Waverly shook her head. "I'm not trusting my life to luck. Open the bag I gave you. Take out the water bottle."

"We'd be wise to save the water."

"If there was water in the bottle, I'd agree with you. But there isn't."

"What?"

"See for yourself."

Puzzled, Dean dug into the bag Waverly had insisted he take. Inside he found two loaves of bread, two apples, and one glass water bottle without any water in it. Dean uncorked the bottle and took out the scroll she had tucked inside. A message in a bottle. "Is this what I think it is?" He smoothed the parchment out against a stone and examined it in the light of the lantern.

"If you think it's a map of the labyrinth, then yes. It is."

Dean felt as though his entire body had been filled with sunshine. "Waverly, I could kiss you right now. Where did you get this?"

Waverly smiled. "The first lords of Aquos mapped these tunnels before they built the palace. Their bravery inspired this trial."

"But how did you come to hold a copy?"

"I have a knack for getting into places I shouldn't," Waverly said with a wink. "In truth, I got the idea from Jarret Ralian. You don't really think he beat the maze in less than an hour on his own, do you?"

"I should have known he had some kind of hornswoggle up his sleeve."

"And now, so do we. I hope you're not above cheating to win."

Dean laughed. "Not today. When did you get this?"

"This morning. Right after I heard you refused Jarret's help.

Someone had to make sure the tides didn't beat you to the throne room."

Dean was shocked at Waverly's boldness. "I can't believe you gave this to me in front of everyone. You know, if I got stuck down here, you would get your wish. You wouldn't have to marry the prince."

Waverly nodded. "I considered that."

"Did you really?"

"Yes, but then I realized something."

"You couldn't bear the thought of anything happening to me?"

"No." Waverly grinned. "That even if I didn't marry you, I'd still have to marry. Most likely, my father would have matched me with one of the Ralian brothers." She made a face as if she had just drunk spoiled milk. "They are the second-richest family in the kingdom, after all. Noble marriages are just business transactions. A means to an end."

"Is that right?" Dean said, finally seeing the true face of his enemy. "So if I was out of the way, and one of the Ralian brothers married you, he'd inherit the throne from your father once they made him king. Wouldn't he?"

Waverly nodded. "Quite the prize, aren't I?"

"Yes, you are." As a new piece of the puzzle fell into place, Dean saw the big picture at last. It wasn't the regent who'd been trying to kill him. It was the Ralians. It had been only the Ralians all along. Dean wished Waverly had said something about them earlier. He might have figured it out sooner. Then a better thought popped into his head. "You wanted me to win. You chose me over them."

"I wanted you to live. The women of this island have been saving your life since the day you were born. This is no time to break tradition." Waverly smiled and checked the map. "This way." She took Dean's chalk and marked the cavern wall as she entered the correct tunnel. It was not the one Dean had picked.

With the map in hand, Dean and Waverly navigated the labyrinth with little difficulty. For the most part. The greatest obstacle they encountered early on was water in places where the tides had pushed the ocean up into the caves. Some of the downward-sloping tunnels had failed to drain back out when high tide receded, which slowed and nearly halted their progress. Dean slipped and fell while walking through one of the watery channels. He shot his arms up as he went under the water, managing to keep the map dry, but dousing the light of his lantern. After his fall, he and Waverly walked the path with greater care so as not to make the same mistake. If her lantern were lost, all hope would be lost as well. The pitch-black meandering caverns offered no light except what travelers brought in with them. Without it, they were as good as dead.

From that point on, Dean and Waverly moved more slowly and huddled close together, sharing her lamp's light. The deeper they went into the labyrinth, the smaller the tunnels became.

Working in greater darkness did little to increase Waverly's fondness of such tight spaces, and the road grew harder to travel. In some cases, they had to climb straight up, bracing their backs against narrow passageways and pushing with their feet. Up they went. On they went, holding tight to the blazing-hot oil lamp and contraband map as if their lives depended on it. Which they did.

As they neared the end of the maze, Dean found the continued presence of residual tidewater vexing. "The water flooded all the way up here? How do people get lost in these tunnels for weeks? I've yet to find one we wouldn't drown in at high tide."

Waverly shook her head. "That's why no one runs the maze this close to the storm. It's too dangerous. Jarret took no chances and did it the first day of our harvest." She looked around and shook from head to toe. "I really . . . I don't like it in here, Dean. We need to get out."

Dean looked at Waverly. It was hard to tell in the lantern's amber light, but she looked pale, her lips somewhat purple. He'd seen those symptoms before out at sea. Some people took ill on the waves after being cooped up belowdecks too long. They had to get outside and would go up above in a squall if it meant they could get a breath of fresh air and a clean look at the sky. People with that affliction could be unpredictable and downright dangerous to themselves and others. That was something Dean and Waverly could not afford at the moment. "We're almost there," he reassured Waverly, holding up the map. "Look here, it's just a short way. Come on." He took her by the hand and led her forward. "Don't think about the tunnel. Focus on something else. Tell me, what did you mean when you said Zenhalan women have been saving my life since I was born?" he asked. Dean's goal was to keep her talking. To keep her with him.

"I mean . . . if you're the prince. The queen, your mother, she gave her life for you. She cut out a pirate's eye before letting him take you. I suppose she didn't save you completely, but she tried. And you did live."

Dean looked at Waverly. "She cut his eye out? Truly?"

"Of course. Don't you know the story?"

Dean paused a moment, thinking about a certain one-eyed pirate who was known to be obsessed with Zenhala. "I've heard a hundred stories about this island. The one about the pirate losing his eye . . . that's true?"

"It is," Waverly said, sounding more like herself. "But what am I saying? You don't think you're the prince."

"That's right. I don't."

Waverly studied Dean a moment. "Is it my imagination or do you sound less certain than you did last night?"

"I think the caves are affecting your hearing."

"I don't know. You've surprised everyone else here. Why not yourself?"

Dean thought about it. He was the right age. His arm bore the right mark. Also, he had never known his parents and had been the property of a one-eyed pirate since birth. Alone, each point meant nothing, but together . . . Was it possible that he really was the prince of legend? *No. Of course not.* He couldn't afford to pin his hopes on crazy dreams. They were sure to fall apart on him. He had to hold on to what he knew for sure. *Stick to the plan. Stay the course. Leave while you still can.*

"Come on. We're in the home stretch now," he said, tapping the map with his finger. "The exit lies a mere fifty feet away." Dean took Waverly by the hand and led her around a corner. They stopped short when they saw the flooded tunnel. "Or not."

The way forward ran downhill and was filled with black water. That was bad enough, but to make matters worse, the tunnel angled straight down at the far wall and ran beneath an overhanging rock formation. To get to the other side, Dean and Waverly had to leave their light behind and completely submerge. If they wanted out of the labyrinth, they had to swim for it.

"Are we sure this is it?" Waverly asked.

Dean checked the map. "It had better be. Getting here was hard enough, and there's no time to turn back now."

"That's not exactly what I want to hear."

"This is it," Dean said. "We know it is. Look." He waded into the water and jumped in when he reached the drop-off point. He dove down and swam around, blindly feeling at the rock walls with his hands. "There's room to swim," he said when he came back up. "We're almost there."

"Is it dark?" Waverly asked.

Dean climbed out of the water. Of course it was dark. "There's no other way to the throne room. We have to do this." He reached out a hand to Waverly. "I'll be right there with you."

Waverly nodded reluctantly and set the map and lantern down on a dry stone ledge. She took Dean's hand and followed him into the deep water. "Oh, this is cold."

"You go first. That way, I can keep my eyes on you."

"Okay."

"Take your time. We'll go when you're ready."

Waverly took a moment to steel her nerves and dove under the water. Dean swam after her. It was dark without the lantern and beyond scary to be swimming blind in a tunnel that, for all he knew, could be a thousand feet long. But the map had gotten them this far, and he had to trust it. What choice did he have? He felt the walls with his hands as he swam. He could see nothing. A family of fish swam by, startling him, and Dean knew they had the same effect on Waverly, for she was right behind them. He tried to stop her as she passed him, but she pushed him off, kicking wildly and swimming back the way she came. Dean couldn't call after her underwater. All he could do was follow her back to the beginning of the flooded passage.

By the time Dean surfaced, Waverly had already gotten out of the water. She was sitting at the end of the tunnel, shaking, with her arms wrapped around her knees. "I can't do it. It's too far. It goes on forever."

"It doesn't go on forever. It's fifty feet. Maybe a touch less. We were almost there."

"I'm not going back in there. I can't."

Dean got out and sat down next to her. "Of course you can." She was chilled to the bone, as was he. He put an arm around her, which helped a little bit. He didn't want to cause her any additional panic. "Take your time. We'll try again when you're ready."

"I said I'm not going back in there!" Waverly said, shoving Dean off.

Dean leaned back. "Wow. I guess we finally found something you're afraid of."

"I'm not afraid!" Waverly snapped. Then she sighed, realizing how ridiculous she sounded. "Fine. So what if I am?"

Dean snapped his fingers. "Exactly. So what? That's the way to get around fear. You just have to realize you don't have a choice. When you want something, you go after it, no matter what. You want to live, don't you?"

"Yes."

"Then we have to get down that tunnel. It's not as if we can stay here forever. You didn't pack enough bread, and even if you did, the tide will come by nightfall. The choice is drown here or drown in there. But at least in there you have a shot." He stood up and held out his hand. "Please. You have to try."

Waverly looked up at Dean, then down at the water. "I'm not going first."

"No. That was a mistake. We'll do it together this time."

"You won't leave me?"

Dean knelt down in front of Waverly. "I wouldn't have made it this far without you." He took her hand in his. "I'm not leaving you for anything. If we drown in there, we drown side by side. That's the deal."

Waverly gave a slight chuckle. "How can I pass up an offer like that?"

"Just remember, you volunteered for this."

Waverly and Dean got up, and in they went, back into the long dark tunnel. The water was just as cold and black as it had been the first time. Holding each other's hand, they swam slower than before, but this time, they swam forward and kept going. The course was twisting and uncertain, but they didn't stop. To Dean, the tunnel felt longer than fifty feet. It felt more like a hundred, but as they neared the end, a faint light began to grow. They pushed themselves toward that light with all the strength they had, pulling each other along until they reached the end of the tunnel. They broke through the water at the same time, gasping for air. The water was shallow enough for them to stand. Between great heaving breaths, they reached for each other and embraced.

"Thank the stars," Dean said.

"Thank *you*," Waverly replied.

Dean shook his head. "We did it together."

"And I never want to do it again."

"Agreed!"

They were in another large underground chamber, this one right below the throne room. Up at the roof, Dean saw glass tubes that led to fountains in the great hall above, ready to be filled by furious, churning seawater. Light pouring in from overhead illuminated a spiral staircase in the center of the room, which wound up to a door in the ceiling. A round marble slab with a triple wave crest was carved into its underside. Waverly directed Dean's attention to it. "Go. Pound on that door and all the nobles in Zenhala will hail you as the heir of Aquos." Dean started up the stairs, and Waverly grabbed his wrist. "You can count me among them. The blood test tomorrow is a formality now. No one but the true prince could ever accomplish all that you have done."

Dean didn't know what to say.

He led Waverly up the steps and banged on the door in the ceiling. A crowd of cheering nobles could be heard on the other side. For the first time since he'd set foot on Zenhala, Dean wondered if he might be deserving of their praise.

CHAPTER 27

LAST DANCE

That night, a feast celebrating Dean's successful completion of the trials was held in the Aqualine Palace. Ronan wanted to leave before the party started. He wanted off the island as soon as possible, before the storm hit. Rook's final attempt to locate the orchard had been fruitless, and there was no point in staying any longer. It was time for the three of them to head back and take their chances with One-Eyed Jack.

Or maybe just two of them would go.

Ronan and Dean might have suspended hostilities with Rook during their time on Zenhala, but neither of them had forgotten his treacherous nature. Dean worried what Rook would do when the three of them stood before One-Eyed Jack once again. He couldn't be trusted to hold his tongue when One-Eyed Jack asked why his parrot was never sent back with directions. But if Rook weren't there, Dean and Ronan could make up any story they wanted.

That was how it had to be.

They would leave Rook behind to get sealed in by the storm, and send out Sisto right before they left. By the time the parrot reached St. Diogenes, and One-Eyed Jack started sailing, it would be too late to get ahead of the storm, but he would see that they had sent the bird. He just had no way of knowing *when* they had sent him. Dean would give One-Eyed Jack the dates of next year's harvest, and a map to the island. Without Rook there to muck things up, it could work. He could still get out of One-Eyed Jack's pocket if everything went according to plan.

Unfortunately, that meant Rook would be left on Zenhala, free to tell everyone all about Dean. Rook would drag his name through the mud, which was exactly where it belonged, but Waverly would hear everything. Who he was. What he was really doing on the island. He'd never get the chance to explain himself. As the time to leave drew closer and closer, Dean found he liked the plan less and less. He found himself looking for reasons to put off leaving. The party was as good an excuse as any.

"Ronan, we can't leave before the feast. I'm the guest of honor. They'll know something's wrong if I don't show up. We have to make an appearance. Don't worry, we can leave halfway through."

Ronan looked skeptical. "I'm sure you've slipped out of tighter spots than this."

"Come on," Dean pleaded. "We can ditch Rook at the party and make our escape before anyone knows we're gone. As long as people see him, they'll assume we're somewhere nearby. It's perfect. Besides, when's the next time someone's going to hold a feast in my honor? I can't miss this."

"There it is," Ronan said. "That's what I'm worried about."

"What?"

"You don't want to give up the good life. You want to keep playing prince and take your princess to the ball."

"Wrong," Dean said. "That's wrong. I'll have you know Waverly doesn't even like dances. She's not like that. She likes surfing, cliff diving, and that sort of thing. She loves the ocean like I do."

"Really? Maybe you should ask her to come with you, then."

"Do you think she would?"

Ronan glared at Dean. He was being sarcastic. Dean felt like an idiot. The words had slipped out before he could stop them.

"Look," Ronan began, taking pity on Dean, "you want to have one last dance with your lady friend, fine. We'll go."

Dean's face lit up.

"But don't get it into your fool head anything's gonna come of it. We leave this place tonight, you hear?"

Dean clapped his hands. "Ronan, you're a prince."

"Belay that!" Ronan shot back. "I've had my fill of princes."

"Fair enough." Dean laughed and ushered Ronan limping out the door. "Let's go find Rook."

The party was a grand affair, held in the palace throne room. Ronan might have had his fill of princes, but the nobles of Zenhala took a different view. By then, the prevailing wisdom at court was that Dean had to be the prince, and the lords and ladies of the kingdom feted him lavishly. There was music, food, and a great deal of merriment. In the minds of all the guests, only the lost prince could have conquered each trial in the spectacular fashion that Dean had managed. Everyone was delighted to see him. He was congratulated by everyone he met, just as Waverly said he would be. Dean left Rook and Ronan at a large buffet table and walked the room, trying to find her. He was going to miss Waverly. Life in the palace would be hard to give up too. When he left the lap of luxury this time, he knew it would be for good. Dean tried to console himself with the fact that he never belonged there to begin with.

Dean walked around the room, stopping in front of the Golden Throne. He looked at the brand on his arm.

Unless I do belong . . .

For the second time that day, Dean wondered if it could all be true. He had passed the trials, sure enough, but he attributed that to a little bit of skill and a whole lot of luck. The trials were not proof of royal lineage, regardless of what the guests at the party thought. The royal blood test—that was the only one that mattered, and that was a different story. Staying to take that test and waiting until the storm sealed him in was a risk he couldn't take. What would happen if he stayed and his blood wasn't blue? Would they make him leave? A year down the road, when the storm broke, would he be sent out into the world to try and explain to One-Eyed Jack where he'd been all this time?

Or worse, maybe they'd let him stay, but without the crown. He wouldn't be the prince. He wouldn't have Waverly. He might have to stand by and watch as she was wed to one of Arjent Ralian's sons. The idea was too horrible to think about.

"There he is, the man of the hour!" someone called out. It was Jarret Ralian. He strode up, wearing a grin that Dean wanted to plow his knuckles into.

Speak of the devil.

"Congratulations on beating my record in the tunnels. A mighty feat, even if it did take two of you to do it." He snatched two goblets from a passing server's tray and handed one to Dean. Jarret clinked the cups together and drained his dry. Dean didn't drink a drop. "What's your secret, Dean Seaborne?"

Dean set his glass down untouched. "I cheat. Usually does the trick, wouldn't you agree?"

Jarret looked amused. "Yes, I would, but I'm not talking about the trial. I couldn't care less about that. I'm wondering what your *secret* is."

Dean's eyes narrowed. "What are you talking about?"

"Please, let's be frank. It took you long enough to figure things out, but surely by now you've realized why my family wants you dead."

Dean nodded. He had indeed. "You want Waverly."

"It's not Waverly. It's what comes with her." Jarret indicated the Golden Throne. "My father challenged the three of us to kill you during your trials and make it look like an accident. Whoever succeeded would be the one he put forth to marry Waverly Kray in your place."

Dean regarded Jarret like a tiger that could pounce at any moment. "Why are you telling me this?"

"Because if you wanted to turn us in, you would have done so by now. I'm curious. What tipped you off? Was it the first time Jin tried to kill you or the second?"

"Junter tried too," Dean said.

Jarret shook his head and made a clicking sound. "He didn't try very hard." He leaned toward Dean and put a hand to his mouth. "Just between you and me, my brothers aren't very bright.

Jin's got a sailor's knot where his brain should be, and I'm fairly certain Junter has a third bicep between his ears."

"Ah," Dean said. "You're the smart one. Is that it?"

"Smarter than you."

"If that's true, why did you lose?"

"I haven't lost anything. You see, I know something these people don't." Jarret reached out and put his arm around Dean. "You're not the lost prince," he whispered.

Dean removed Jarret's arm as if it were a piece of seaweed that had washed up on his shoulder.

"When you first got here, I was afraid you might be the genuine article. My father was convinced, but I had my suspicions. They were confirmed when you didn't say anything about Jin's second attempt on your life. Honestly! He didn't even try to hide what he was doing that time. You knew beyond a shadow of a doubt it was him, and still you said nothing." Jarret's eyes flitted about the room and eventually settled on Rook, who could be seen stalking the edge of the dance floor, stuffing his mouth with shrimp. "That got me thinking. . . . If Dean Seaborne will keep quiet about something like that, what terrible secret must *he* be hiding? I'll find out. I might have missed my chance to drown you in the tunnels, but we aren't finished, you and I. You'll never sit on the golden throne. That belongs to me."

A footman at the door announced Waverly's arrival. She

entered with grace and beauty, a priceless treasure in more ways than one.

"So will she," Jarret said, picking up Dean's untouched goblet. "Enjoy your party. It's almost over."

Dean stood there simmering as he watched Jarret leave. The way he paused in the center of the floor to offer Waverly a respectful bow boiled his blood. The little hellion was right. If they stayed here, she might actually end up with him.

He had to do something.

Dean crossed the floor to Waverly. "Was that Jarret I saw you talking to? What did he want? Was he bitter that you and I broke his record? I hope he was."

Dean took Waverly by the hand and led her back to the door, away from everyone. "Forget him. I have to ask you something. Something important."

"What is it?" Judging from the look on Waverly's face, she could tell it was something that was weighing heavily on Dean.

He shook his head. "Not here. We have to go somewhere first."

"Where?"

Dean looked around to make sure no one else was listening. "The orchard," he said, his voice just above a whisper.

At first, Waverly thought he was joking. When she realized he was serious, she gasped. "The orchard? Why?"

Dean took a breath. There was no turning back now. "Because

I'm not the prince, Waverly. I can't be. All these people here tonight are wrong about me. They'll find that out soon enough. So will you."

"No, Dean. You don't know that. You're just scared."

"That I am. With good reason."

"What reason? You already conquered the trials."

"Tomorrow's test is the only one that matters. I'll take on any challenge, but I can't change the color of my blood. You'll see. Tomorrow, you'll see. I'm telling you the truth."

"I don't understand. What does this have to do with the golden orchard?"

"I can explain everything, but it has to be there. I want to see it. I need to see it. Please, will you take me?"

Dean looked deep into Waverly's eyes, silently pleading with her. She looked back, conflicted and confused. After what felt like an eternity, she closed her eyes and nodded. "Meet me outside the main gate in ten minutes."

CHAPTER 28

Forbidden Fruit

Ronan limped over to Dean after Waverly left. "All right, then? Satisfied? Can we go now?"

Dean shook his head. "Not yet. There's one last thing I have to do first."

"And what's that?"

"I'm going to ask her to come with us."

Ronan shook. He grabbed Dean's arm so hard he nearly broke it. "Seaborne! I wasn't serious when I told you—"

"She's taking me to the orchard, Ronan."

Ronan relaxed his grip. "What?"

"You heard me. She's taking me tonight. If she'll go that far with me, who knows? Maybe she'll be willing to go a little farther."

Ronan raised an eyebrow and tilted his head to the side. That changed things. "Fine. Go and see the orchard. Ask her, if you have to ask her, but get back here fast. We leave here tonight no matter what she says, understand?"

Dean nodded. "She's going to say yes. I'll meet you back in our rooms as soon as I can."

"Meet me on the docks. I'll have a ship ready. We don't have all night."

"We'll be there."

Dean left Ronan at the party. On his way out, he saw Jarret Ralian talking to Rook in a corner of the room. No good would come of that conversation, Dean knew that much. He hurried out, hoping the orchard wasn't too far off.

Ten minutes later, Dean was waiting in the shadows of the main gate, watching for Waverly. The tower bells began to chime, and Dean's body tensed up. Twelve bells rang out, tolling midnight. There was no sign of her. Dean was starting to worry when a hand grabbed his shoulder.

He jumped. And he screamed. Loudly.

"Shhh!" Waverly said, putting a finger to her lips and trying to keep a straight face. "Put this on." She handed Dean a bunched-up ball of fabric.

"What's this?"

"A cloak."

Dean examined the garment. "One of yours?"

"Yes, one of mine."

He looked at the cloak again, then back up at Waverly. "You couldn't have gotten something else?"

"What's the problem?"

Dean held up the frilly, pink cloak with two fingers, as if it might infect him. "Not very manly, is it?"

"That's the idea. If you or I get recognized, it will delay us at best and derail us at worst. You need to disguise yourself."

"Fine," Dean said, grumbling as he pulled the cloak's hood over his head.

"Do you want to see the orchard or don't you?"

"I said I'd wear it!"

Waverly let out an exasperated sigh. "Men. Let's go."

They set off on foot. "How far is it?"

"Not far."

They left the palace behind, following an eastern road around the mountains. Dean expected Waverly to ask him what this was all about as they went, but to her credit, she didn't press him for any more details. The lights of town faded into darkness as they hiked into the woods and out into the province. Moving at a brisk pace, they passed run-down homes and shaky huts along the way. Dean eyed them with strange interest. Life beyond the mountains was far less wealthy and comfortable than what he had seen on the island so far.

The road twisted through the woods, and Dean saw light

beyond the trees at the edge of the forest. He heard music and voices too. Waverly flipped up the hood on her cloak. "Keep your head down as we pass through the village. Remember, we're not supposed to be here."

"Right." Dean nodded and covered up as they rounded the bend into the village up ahead. What he saw there shocked him. The poor hamlet was almost unworthy of the name. The place was a disparate collection of lean-tos, sheds, and tumbledown shanties that called up memories of Bartleby Bay. The only difference was, the Zenhalan village was less crowded and its people less unhappy. Dean and Waverly were hardly dressed to blend in. Dressed in palace clothes, they stood in stark contrast to the shabby attire of the villagers, but the people hardly noticed. They were in the middle of some kind of celebration and barely registered Dean and Waverly's presence. As they moved through town, Dean saw people smoking pipes outside their hovels and drinking from clay cups around numerous bonfires. Music from a small three-man band was playing, and people were dancing, young and old. It was late, but the children were all up. Everyone looked thin. Sickly. Malnourished. Dean wondered why he hadn't seen these people before, and what they could possibly have to be so happy about.

"What are they celebrating?" he asked Waverly. "Do you know?"

"You," she replied. "They celebrate you. Just like back at court, everyone assumes you're the prince now that you've passed all the trials. When the storm returns tomorrow, they expect you'll prove it."

Dean said nothing. *When the storm returns tomorrow, I'll be gone.*

He couldn't understand why the fate of the prince meant so much to the people here. He had grown up in the service of a king (of sorts) and harbored no such love or loyalty for the man. Granted, One-Eyed Jack had done nothing to deserve either, but the people Dean had just seen, poverty-stricken and dressed in rags . . . what did they care if their long-lost prince came home to live a pampered life in his palace?

Dean and Waverly pressed on until the village lights shrank from sight on the road behind them. Eventually, they came upon a stream, and Waverly stopped. She pointed to a vineyard that grew beside an out-of-service mill. Dean looked around but saw precious little. The old mill's wheel was not turning. The water levels in the stream were too low to reach it, and the giant wheel hung in place like a ship in dry dock. There was nothing else in sight for miles.

"What is it?" Dean asked.

"We're here."

"I don't see anything."

"Exactly."

Waverly headed for the mill, and Dean followed. They didn't get within ten feet of the river before a door swung open. Two men wearing armor came out with their hands upon their swords. "Who goes there?" the first man called.

Waverly raised a hand, signaling Dean to stop. "Lady Waverly Kray," she announced. "And the lost prince, Dean Seaborne, soon to be your king."

The guards relaxed their posture when they realized they were dealing with royalty. They were shocked to see Waverly, and starstruck by Dean. "Lady Kray. Your Grace! 'Tis an honor. What brings you here at this late hour?"

"My father's bidding," Waverly told them. "The prince expressed a desire to see the orchard, and my father ordered that we grant his wish at once. May we pass?"

The guards were silent for a moment. Waverly's explanation was clearly a bit of a head scratcher for them. "Your father sent you here, in the middle of the night?"

"Despite our protests, I assure you," Waverly said. "I'm afraid when the subject of the orchard came up at tonight's feast, our prince was unable to hide his curiosity. So taken was he with the notion of the orchard that my father declared he must see it this very night. We tried to argue, but my father just laughed. He said this would surely be his last opportunity to give the prince an order. Father was in quite a jovial mood this evening, if you understand my meaning." She raised a hand to her lips and threw her head back as if drinking from an imaginary goblet. "Now, if you gentlemen would be so kind as to open the gates?"

The two guards looked at each other, mulling the matter over. It was an unorthodox request but one made by their current leader's daughter in the presence of their future king. In the end, that was enough. "Yes, my lady. At once." They lowered their heads toward Dean. "Your Grace."

When the guards disappeared back inside the mill, Dean nudged Waverly. "When did you become such a good liar?"

Waverly shrugged. "If I didn't know how to bend the truth every now and then, I'd never have any fun. I prefer to look at it as unconventional thinking."

Dean smiled. Waverly had stolen a map to help him cheat on his last trial. She was there with him lying on his behalf and sneaking him into the orchard. The two of them had so much in common. Dean felt certain he was doing the right thing.

"Watch this." Waverly nodded toward the old mill's door, hanging crooked on a worn hinge. Inside, Dean heard the sound of a large switch being thrown and the clicking noise of turning gears. Outside, he watched the mill's waterwheel lower steadily into the stream. It snapped into place and began to turn.

Dean breathed in sharply as the vineyard rose up out of the ground. At first, it seemed impossible, but he soon realized the vines were growing over a massive iron trellis, and the river's power had been harnessed to raise it. The two sides flipped up like the lids of a box, revealing Zenhala's priceless treasure inside.

Of all the sights Dean had seen since first setting foot on

the island, this was the most spectacular. It might have been the greatest thing he'd ever seen in his entire life. He drifted toward the edge of the orchard as if lost in a dream. The field was roughly two hundred feet long, a hundred feet wide, and filled with trees planted in neat rows. The trees were not overly large. Each one was no taller than the average man, and their trunks were no wider than Dean's legs. As expected, their branches were mostly empty, but what remained on their limbs twinkled in the moonlight, to Dean's eternal pleasure.

"Extraordinary," Dean said, his voice barely a whisper. He hesitated before entering. "Can I?"

"Of course." Waverly motioned him forward. "Go."

Dean walked through the orchard, marveling at what he found. The trees inside were already bearing fresh, new fruit. Baby buds grew on the branches like round golden apples. Most were no bigger than musket balls, but that was big enough. Flowers on the trees bloomed in a wide range of colors. There were blue trees, white trees, red, pink, and purple. They were gorgeous. "How many are there?" Dean asked.

"The orchard has exactly one hundred trees. All the noble families own trees here. That's how they all became noble in our country's first days. The trees bloom in different colors representing the houses that own them."

Dean felt a thick, blue flower petal with his fingers. "Half the trees are blue."

"Representing the House of Aquos. Your house." Waverly reached up and tore a dead leaf away from a fresh golden bud. "The Aquos family trees are not just the most numerous but also the heartiest in the orchard. They produce enough gold to feed half the kingdom and still keep your house the richest in the land."

"I've never seen anything like this."

"No one has. No one who isn't born of the island, at least. That's why I agreed to bring you here. You see, I *do* believe you're the prince. I have a feeling about you, Dean. I don't think you know yourself as well as you claim to."

"That's where you're wrong," Dean said. "I know myself all too well."

"Tell me, then. Why are we here? What is it you wanted to ask me?"

Dean looked around at the orchard. He was ecstatic. The legends were true. Without question, he could rob this place with a clean conscience. The real crime would be passing up such a once-in-a-lifetime opportunity. Dean was looking at enough gold to tide One-Eyed Jack over until next year's shipment. That plus the details of the Bermuda Triangle's storm cycle would guarantee his freedom. The only question was whether or not Waverly would come with him.

He was about to ask her when he noticed something strange about the trees. Not counting the blue trees, which took up half the orchard, every other color seemed to bloom in equal measure. "Waverly, how it is that the Ralians are the second-richest family in Zenhala? They don't seem to have that many more trees than anyone else."

Waverly frowned. "No. The Ralians are just very protective of their fortune."

Dean chewed on that a moment. "Protective or stingy?"

"Selfish and greedy is more like it. The noble families all provide for the people on their land. The Ralians keep the majority for themselves and share very little with their people. The village we passed on the way here was one of theirs."

Dean remembered the village full of people living in squalor, and the temperature inside his stomach plummeted. He got a bad feeling, the same one that had struck him on board the *Santa Clara* when he realized they were about to steal food that was meant for hungry children. "Are there more towns like that?"

Waverly nodded. "Dozens. Unfortunately, even the more generous houses can only afford to do so much. Very few crops thrive on the island except the trees you see here. That should be enough, and for many years it was. Zenhala used to be a land of plenty, but ever since you were taken, only half the Aquos family gold goes to feed the people. Half the ships that sail with the island's harvest sell it for goods and supplies. The others search for you, and the gold they carry goes to fund their year at sea."

"What are you saying? That village back there was so poor because of—" The revelation hit Dean like an arrow to the chest. "That's why the people here are all so happy to see me. If I'm the prince, it means they don't have to go hungry anymore."

"It's one of the reasons the people are happy to see you. But yes, in those villages, surely the greatest reason. Now all our ships will bring back food each year instead of just half of them."

Dean's hands went to his head. Suddenly, nothing on the island was what it seemed. He couldn't believe it, and he couldn't very well ask Waverly to run away with him now. "Why didn't anyone tell me it was like this out here? All I've seen is the riches of the palace. When I think of the feast I just left . . . How does something like that go on when people are starving?"

"Tonight was special just for you," Waverly explained. "We have not had cause to celebrate like that in some time, nor the means to do so to such excess. But it's going to be different now that you're back. I wanted to tell you about the villages earlier, but I couldn't. It was my father's decision. He feared you might blame yourself for the hardships your people have endured in your absence." Waverly put a hand on Dean's shoulder. "I can see now he was right, but you have to know it's not your fault. You haven't done anything wrong. The pirates are the ones to blame here, not you."

Dean pulled himself back, away from Waverly's hand. "This was a mistake. We shouldn't have come here."

"Dean, wait," Waverly pleaded. "Talk to me. You said you have something to ask me."

"I can't. I have to get back to the palace. Now."

"No one blames you for what happened. No one."

"Maybe not," Dean said, already heading back to the road.

But the week's not over yet.

PART FIVE

INTO THE STORM

CHAPTER 29

THINGS FALL APART

The sun was coming up by the time Dean returned to the royal apartments. He found Ronan pacing the floor, looking like a volcano whose eruption was imminent. Dean drifted into the room and shut the door. He slumped down in a chair and said nothing. His lack of any explanation pushed Ronan past his boiling point. He shook his fist, eager to punch something or, more accurately, someone. "WHAT HAPPENED TO YOU LAST NIGHT?" he exploded on Dean.

Dean stiffened his face, ready to take his medicine if it came to that. He didn't know where to begin.

"WELL?" Ronan demanded.

Dean shrugged. "I was out walking."

"Out walking," Ronan repeated. "FOR FIVE HOURS?"

Ronan's voice shook the walls. Dean massaged the bridge of his nose and yawned. "I was walking and thinking."

Ronan turned away with a growl. "Walking and thinking," he spat. "Let me guess. You asked her to come with us and she said no. Broke your little heart, did she? What did you expect? I told you it would end this way. I waited for you on the docks half the night. I nearly left without you!"

"You should have."

"I think Rook already did! I don't know where he is. You left me all alone, in the dark. I thought we were partners."

Dean shook his head. "Not anymore. I have to tell her the truth, Ronan. I'm going to do it today."

Dean couldn't have spun Ronan around any faster if he'd tried. "What?" Ronan straightened up with a start. He shot a hand to his temple as if his brain needed help processing the idea. "Hang on, what? The truth about us? What are you talking about?"

"It's over, Ronan." Dean's voice was weary. He was staring straight ahead in a daze. "We're done here. I saw the golden orchard last night. Waverly showed me."

Ronan closed his eyes and shook his head, his anger replaced by confusion. "Seaborne, you're not making sense. Back up and start at the beginning. Tell me what happened."

Dean did exactly that. He told Ronan what he had learned about how the island worked. He told him about Zenhala's poorer subjects and who provided for them. He told him what would happen if the golden harvest was stolen. "Having gold to trade doesn't mean there's gold to spare. They need it to feed whole towns of hungry people." To his credit, Ronan understood perfectly. The look on his face told Dean what he already knew. The golden orchard was off-limits. They weren't that kind of pirates.

"We can't let One-Eyed Jack sack the island," Ronan said.

"No. Not after seeing that village. I won't let him. I have to tell Waverly the truth before it's too late. It's the only way."

Ronan scoffed at Dean's proclamation. "The way to do what? Land yourself in a cell? Slow down. Let me think." Ronan walked to the window, gingerly testing his sore ankle step by step. When he got there, he leaned against the sill and exhaled mightily. "All right. This isn't as bad as you think." He turned around to look at Dean. "You don't have to tell anyone your secret. So what if you're not the prince? You never said you were. They came to you with that. You just did as they asked and jumped through their hoops. If you take their blood test today and fail, it's a disappointment, but they can't hang you for getting their hopes up. You haven't stolen anything but their hearts." He wagged a finger at Dean. "No one has to know you're a pirate."

"What about Rook? For all we know, he's already gone. You said so yourself. He'll get word about this place to One-Eyed Jack, and when the storm breaks, the pirate king will have a whole month to loot the island. This only works if we come clean. At least then, people here can protect themselves."

Ronan opened his mouth and shut it again without saying anything. He tried to find fault with Dean's logic, but came up dry. Ronan slumped into a chair by the window. "Rook." He said the name like a curse word. "Should've killed him when we had the chance."

Dean smiled grimly. "Doesn't exactly square with the Gentleman's Code, does it?"

"What if we run like we planned?" asked Ronan. "We can still leave here today. Right now, before the storm hits."

Dean shook his head. "I can't leave. First of all, One-Eyed Jack will follow me to the ends of the earth. I know he will. Second, everyone here thinks I'm the prince. They believe it now. We can't steal from these people, but we can't bolt out of here either. Lord Kray's a good man . . . an honorable man. Now that he's met me, all bets are off. He won't take the throne if I disappear. He'll keep sending out trade ships to find me. And they'll keep coming back with half-measure harvests when the people here need more. I've been thinking all night, but there's no way around it. If I want to help these people, I have to tell the truth."

Ronan sighed and leaned his head back. "They hate pirates here, Dean. With good reason. They'll lock you in a tower and throw away the key when they find out what you are."

"What if I tell them myself? If I can warn them in time, maybe they'll show me some mercy."

Ronan shrugged. "You going to stick your neck out on a maybe?"

Dean rubbed the back of his neck, an appendage he had grown quite attached to over the years. "You can still run, Ronan. You don't have to get stuck here with me."

Ronan tapped his ankle. "Wouldn't get very far, would I? I'm lucky I can walk without a crutch right now." He shook his head. "Best belay that talk. You remember Gentleman Jim's orders as well as I do. No one gets left behind. We're in this together."

Dean nodded. "Hand in glove." He was about to get up and shake Ronan's hand when he heard a muffled cry coming from Rook's room. He and Ronan exchanged puzzled looks, and got up to investigate. When they entered the room, Rook's bed was empty. "Where is he?" Dean asked.

They heard the cry again.

"That came from the closet." Ronan opened the door and found a person tied up inside. He was bound and gagged with a hood over his head.

"Rook?" Dean pulled off the hood, but it wasn't Rook underneath. It was Jarret Ralian.

"What the devil?" Ronan sputtered.

"The devil is right. Something's very wrong here."

"You think?" Before Dean or Ronan could untie Jarret and ask how he got there, they were interrupted by a forceful pounding at the front door.

"Dean Seaborne! Open up in the name of the law!"

Ronan and Dean looked at each other as though they'd just locked eyes with Davy Jones. "What's going on?" Ronan asked.

Dean ran his hands through his hair. "This is a setup." He threw the hood back onto Jarret's head and shut him up in the closet. "Come on," he said, leading Ronan out of Rook's room. "We have to get rid of them. Can't let anyone find us like this." Ronan slammed the bedroom door behind him, muting Jarret's cries. The pounding on the front door persisted. "I'll answer it," Dean said.

He took a second to get in character and opened up the door. Arjent Ralian, his two elder sons, and a trio of palace guards were standing behind it. None of them looked very happy.

"What's the meaning of this?" Dean demanded. "What do you mean ordering me around in the name of the law?"

"Precisely what I said," Lord Ralian replied. "As minister of defense, I *am* the law on this island." He pushed past Dean into the apartment. His entourage followed. Dean tried to block their path, but it was no use.

"I don't remember saying you could come in."

"I don't remember asking. I'm looking for my son. He didn't come home last night. As his father, I am understandably concerned."

"What's that got to do with me?"

"He was last seen in the company of your friend Rook," said Junter.

"Seen either of them this morning?" Jin asked behind a wicked smile.

Ronan and Dean looked at each other like two explorers caught waist deep in quicksand. "Can't say that I have," Dean lied.

Arjent Ralian smiled knowingly. "Well. You don't mind if we have a look around, do you?" He nodded to the guards, who started opening doors and looking inside trunks.

"Actually, I do mind!" Dean protested.

The guards did not heed Dean's words. They went right on searching the apartment. "Is this how you treat your prince?" Ronan asked.

Lord Ralian stifled a laugh. "Still clinging to that, are we? My, but you are persistent."

"How dare you?" Dean asked, feigning the appropriate level of outrage. It was clear that the time for pretense was over, but he didn't know what else to do. "Get out of here now, all of you. If you're lucky, I won't tell the regent about this insult."

Dean stopped talking when Junter Ralian whipped off the cover to Sisto's cage. It was empty. Now Rook *and* the bird were missing. The day was hardly an hour old, and it had already gone from bad to worse.

"Hello?"

Waverly Kray knocked on the open door, and Dean winced. When he heard her voice, he knew the game was up. If she came in, there would be no way out. Not for him. Not anymore.

"Lady Kray?" Arjent Ralian said. "What are you doing here?"

She entered, cautious and confused. "I came to see the prince." Waverly crossed the room to Dean. "You were so upset last night, I wanted to make sure you were all right." She leaned in close to him and whispered. "What's the palace guard doing here?"

Dean's throat locked up. He had no words for her. Waverly was the first person he wanted to talk to that morning, but the last person he wanted to see at the moment.

"We're looking for my son," Arjent Ralian said, answering for Dean. "Jarret has gone missing. We have reason to believe your prince knows something about it."

Dean found his voice. "I don't know anything about—"

"Here!" Junter called out from Rook's room. "I found him!" Every head in the room turned toward the sound of Junter's voice. They rushed to Rook's room, where Jarret was getting free of his bonds.

"My son!" Arjent Ralian exclaimed, sprinting to his side.

"What is this?" Waverly asked, horrified.

Dean took her by the arm. "I know what this looks like, but you have to believe me. I had nothing to do with this."

"Liar!" Jarret shouted, once his brothers had removed his gag. "Don't listen to him, any of you. They're pirates!"

Waverly looked at Dean. "What?"

"Sound the alarm, quickly!" Jarret continued. "I caught his mate Rook snooping around the orchard last night after the banquet. I tried to stop him, but he overpowered me and I woke up a captive here. I heard them talking. They mean to signal their fellow buccaneers. We have to ready our defenses before it's too late."

"There's a ship on the horizon!" Jin called out from the window.

"What?" Dean said.

Everyone ran to the windows, Dean and Ronan included. Ronan snatched Jin's spyglass out of his hands and looked through it. After a few moments, he handed it over to Dean with a frown. "It's the *Maelstrom*. One-Eyed Jack himself."

"It can't be," Dean said, looking through the spyglass to see for himself. "How'd he get here so fast?"

Waverly gasped, and Dean realized what he had just said. He lowered the spyglass. She had tears welling up in her eyes.

"It's true?"

Dean was at a loss. He couldn't believe everything had fallen apart so fast. "I was going to tell you. I was. Please, you have to believe me."

Waverly put her hand to her chest and turned away. She looked like she might fall over. "I did believe you. I trusted you with everything. How could you do this?"

"I didn't do this, I—" The anguish in Waverly's eyes was unbearable for Dean. She could have run him through with a cutlass and it would have hurt less, but he deserved that. She didn't deserve the pain he'd caused her. "I was going to tell you."

"When?"

"Last night! Waverly, I swear it. This wasn't the plan. I wanted you to come with me when I left."

Waverly flinched. "You thought I'd come with you?"

"Yes! You said yourself you thought about running away. I thought this could be your chance. Our chance! To be free."

In a flash, Waverly's grief turned to fire. She slapped Dean hard across the face. "Yes, I thought about running away. My honor kept me here. Honor and duty! I stay true to the people I love. You're a pirate. You know nothing of honor."

"No! I'm not that kind of pirate."

"There's only one kind of pirate," Jarret Ralian cut in. He put a sympathetic hand on Waverly's shoulder. "Don't waste your tears on him, my lady. He's not worth it. He came here to steal our gold. Everything about this 'prince' has been a lie."

Dean's face fell. As much as he would have liked to, he could not argue with anything Jarret had said. All he could do was tell her he was sorry, but what was that worth? Apologies were just words. He hung his head in shame.

"Look at me," Waverly said. Dean raised his head as she wiped away her tears. "This will be the last time our eyes ever meet. I never want to see you again."

CHAPTER 30

JUSTICE IS SERVED

Iron manacles locked into place around Dean's wrists.

He hardly noticed.

He was thrown into a cell in the Tower of Justice. He didn't care. Dean went along without a hint of protest as the guards chained him and Ronan to opposite walls. By then, all the fight had gone out of him. He had been lost in a trance the whole shame-filled walk from the royal apartments to the top of the prison tower. Dean wasn't thinking about himself or what might happen next. That no longer mattered. All he could think of was Waverly and the unmistakable disgust in her eyes when she found out what he was.

Arjent Ralian had led Waverly away to inform her father of

his treachery and marshal the island's troops. She had left Dean a shell of himself as she walked out the door. He couldn't even muster the courage to call after her. Waverly had buried him with her words, just as he had buried her people with his actions. An invasion was coming. One he could have prevented if he'd been strong enough to tell the truth. That was the hardest part about all of this. It was his fault. There was no way around it. Waverly was right to turn her back on him, and he deserved to meet the end he had coming as a spy.

The cell door slammed shut and the palace guards left to help fend off the coming raid. The Ralian brothers stayed behind to gloat. "I told you I'd find out your secret," Jarret told Dean with a smile.

It wasn't until Dean saw the look on Jarret's privileged face that his anger settled in on something other than himself. He set his jaw and clenched his fists. "You did this."

"Of course," Jarret boasted. "Took a little while to get everything sorted, but I think it all came off rather well in the end. I knew exactly what to do once I heard your story. Your friend Rook was only too happy to tell it."

"Rook," Ronan spat. "Where is that mangy cur?"

"I can honestly say I don't care. I've no further use for him. Once he told me the truth about you, I let him go so he could signal your mates."

"You let him do that?"

"I needed him to," Jarret said.

Dean was baffled. *"Why?"*

Jarret held out his arms as if the answer were obvious. "I can't very well expose you as a traitor without evidence of treason, can I?" He pointed to the window in Dean's cell. "You should be thanking me. My father wanted you dead. I had a better idea." Jarret tapped his temple. "I realized that killing you wasn't my best option. It didn't do anything to enhance my own reputation. By destroying you in this fashion and raising the alarm about an attack, I become the hero." Jarret puffed up his chest proudly.

Dean looked out the tower window. "The hero." He shook his head. "You think you've won?"

"Remind me, which one of us is locked in a cell? I think it's safe to say I came out ahead."

"You have no idea what you've done," Ronan said.

"Spare me your threats." Jarret waved a hand, dismissing the warning. "We're perfectly safe from your friends here. My father has commanded island security ever since the real lost prince was taken. I know this island's defense capabilities inside and out. We can easily repel a single pirate ship."

"That may be, but you're not up against a single pirate ship."

Jarret squinted at Dean, looking for the first time as if he might not have all the answers. He said nothing.

"What are you talking about?" Jin asked.

Dean nodded toward the window in his cell. "If I were you,

I'd take another look outside. Your brother's not as smart as he thinks he is."

There was a brief, uncomfortable silence that was broken by Jin grabbing a key ring off the wall and nodding to Junter. "Come on."

"What are you doing?" asked Jarret. "Don't go in there."

Junter and Jin brushed past their younger brother. "They're chained to the wall, Jarret. I think we'll survive."

They unlocked the door to Dean's cell and looked out his window. A moment later, Jin leaned against the window frame to keep from falling over. "Then again, maybe we won't."

"What is it?" Jarret asked. "What's out there?"

Junter stepped aside with a grunt. "See for yourself."

Jarret hesitated, but curiosity eventually got the better of him. He inched into the cell, checking his arrogant swagger at the door. Dean stared him down the whole way, but Jarret purposely avoided his eyes en route to the window. When he saw nineteen pirate ships on the horizon, he turned as white as a ghost. Sweet victory had turned to bitter ashes in his mouth.

"Can your defenses repel that?" Dean asked. "I could have told you.... One-Eyed Jack wouldn't come after me with just one ship. You chose the wrong friends. Me, I don't have any."

"You reap what you sow," Ronan told the Ralians. "You've ruined everyone on this island. Not just the pair of us."

Jarret choked on his own breath and looked away without a

word. He staggered a step and sat down in a state of shock, not unlike the one Dean was stumbling around in a few moments earlier. Junter nudged him with his toe. "What now?" he asked. Jarret didn't answer. Junter prodded him again. "Well? You're the smart one. You said so enough times yourself. What do we do now?"

Jarret gave no reply. He was all but catatonic.

Jin knelt and shook his brother by the shoulders. "Come on, Jarret, this was your plan. What do we do?"

"Get off me!" Jarret said, pushing Jin back. "I need to think." He snapped out of his daze and got up onto his feet. Jarret paced the cell, running his hands through his hair and mumbling to himself. After a few quick laps around the room, he stopped and faced his brothers. "There's only one thing we can do. Flee."

"What?" Junter and Jin both exclaimed.

"You coward," Ronan said, his voice dripping with disdain.

"How long until they make land?" Jarret asked, ignoring Ronan.

Jin looked out the window. "Not long enough."

"Can we get out? On your fastest ship, can we make it?"

Jin motioned with his hand, gauging the speed of the pirate's approach. "If we leave now . . . *maybe*. We'd have to hurry."

"What about Father?" Junter asked.

The immediate reply was silence. After a moment, Jarret shook his head. "You heard Jin. There's no time. We have to leave now."

"Blow me down," Dean said. "I have known some blackhearted, lily-livered scum in my day, but you three win the pr—AHH!"

Dean was interrupted by a hard blow to the jaw, delivered by Junter. Ronan charged across the cell to help him, but his chains halted his progress halfway there. Junter drove a two-handed punch into Ronan's left kidney, dropping him where he stood.

Jin stepped up and kicked Dean in the stomach once, then twice more for good measure. "There. A little something to remember us by. You're lucky we don't have time to do you worse."

Dean looked up, wiping blood from his lip. "You'd better hope we don't meet again."

Jarret took the key ring from Jin and threw it out the window. "Don't worry. We won't." He and his brothers disappeared down the tower stairs as the sound of cannon fire filled the air.

CHAPTER 31

BITTER HARVEST

It took a few hours for the fighting outside to die down. Dean didn't watch the battle from his window. It was hard enough for him to stomach without taking in the action. Dean had been around long enough to know what to expect from a raid and didn't need to look outside.

First came the sound of cannon fire coming from the island toward the ships. That attack was met in kind by One-Eyed Jack shelling the island with an unyielding cannonade. Once the pirates arrived on gigs from the boats, Dean heard a chorus of muskets and flintlock pistols ring out. That went on for some time. There was fighting in the streets and people screaming as they were pulled from their homes. The clatter of steel cutlasses and the thunk of hatchets finding their mark was pervasive. Before the fighting was over, he knew people would use dirks, daggers, sticks, stones, and whatever else they got their hands on. Through it all, the outcome was never in doubt. Dean and Ronan spent the battle trapped in their cell, forced to listen. When silence fell at last, it was a mercy.

"I think it's over out there," Ronan said.

Dean nodded. "In here too."

"It doesn't look good for us, I'll grant you that." For what must have been the hundredth time, Ronan tugged on his chains to no avail. "What do you think's gonna happen?"

Dean leaned his head back to rest against the stone wall. He was miles away. "I've been thinking about that."

He didn't elaborate.

"Well?" Ronan pressed. "What'd you come up with?"

Dean's eyes snapped forward to look at Ronan. He took a deep breath and leaned forward, resting his elbows on his knees. "By now, One-Eyed Jack's on his way to the orchard, if he's not there already. There's gold left on those trees, but not enough. Not to suit his taste. Most of it went out with the harvest, and if he's looking to find enough treasure to fill nineteen ships, he's going to be disappointed. I don't have to tell you how he takes to disappointment. Odds are, he'll take his frustrations out on us."

"Aye." Ronan grimaced. "He finds us here, we're as good as dead."

"Unless . . ." Dean put up an index finger. "Unless he decides he's got bigger fish to fry. There's a chance he'll take what he can from the trees, rob the island for the rest, and realize he has to get out before the storm hits. If things go that way, he won't have time to sort out the two of us."

Ronan's face brightened. "I like the sound of that."

"But once he's gone, the people of this island will have all the time in the world. They'll want revenge, and they'll deserve it too. When the dust from this fight settles and the blood dries up, you can bet they won't forget about you and me."

Ronan's smile faded. "In which case, we're as good as dead."

"Exactly."

"So what you're saying is, it doesn't matter what happens. We're dead either way."

"Pretty much."

"Can you pick the locks on your shackles?"

"If I could reach them." Dean's hands were chained too far apart to get at the keyhole. "It's no use, Ronan. We're not getting out of here." Dean looked at the door to their cell. The Ralians hadn't locked it behind them when they left. It hung on its hinges, wide open, taunting Dean like a metaphor for his life. There had never been a time when he wasn't trapped somewhere he didn't want to be, with the way out just beyond his reach. It was always within sight, but a step too far away. From the looks of things, it always would be.

"What gives, Seaborne? You're supposed to be the optimistic one here."

Dean slumped further down against the wall. "Sorry, Ronan. You rubbed off on me."

Ronan let out a weary sigh. "I think so. Gentleman Jim did too, I can tell. Whatever happens, Dean, he was right to take you on. You're a good egg, sailor. You kept to the code."

Dean sat up with a puzzled look. "Ronan, we failed. Everything you and I tried to keep from happening happened. People are hurting out there, and we're next. We're going to die here."

"Looks that way," Ronan agreed. "It surely does. But if it comes to that, I'll step to the gallows with my conscience clear." Dean looked at Ronan as though the guards had locked up his brains in some other cell. "I will!" Ronan vowed. "If I have to. It's not an easy thing, trying to be a pirate and a good man at the same time. Gentleman Jim tried, and you saw where that got him. But even when things went bad, he never gave up walking that line. Right up to the end, he stayed true to what he thought was right. He'd have been proud of what you tried to do here. I am."

Dean took a minute with that. "Thanks." He didn't have much to feel good about at the moment, but he felt good about what Ronan had just said. Maybe it was because he had never thought of himself as being true to anything.

"Does this mean we're friends now?"

Ronan rattled his chains. "I'm here with you, aren't I?"

Dean laughed. "Not exactly your decision."

"I didn't say it was. And I'll tell you something else. I don't much care to stay either. There has to be something we can do."

Dean heard arguing in the hall outside. "Someone's coming up the steps."

He and Ronan listened quietly, wondering who was coming to get them. As the people outside got closer, their voices became clearer.

"I told you we should have started at the top and worked our way down," the first voice argued.

"That makes a lot of sense," the other shot back. "What if they'd been on the first floor? We'd have walked right past them and hiked up these stairs for nothing."

"They weren't on the first floor, were they? And we hiked up all these stairs anyway—at a snail's pace, thanks to you!"

"So what? You move about as fast as a fish floppin' on the beach does, anyway!"

Dean looked at Ronan. "Is that who I think it is?"

Ronan grinned. "None other. Kane! Marko! Up here!"

The bickering outside stopped abruptly. It was replaced by the sound of footsteps charging up the stairs. Moments later, the ever-sparring twins, Kane and Marko, burst through the door. "There you are!" Kane said. "Told you we should've started at the top," he added, giving his brother a shove.

"All right, all right," said Marko.

"I don't believe this," Ronan said. "What are you two doing here?"

"Looking for you," Kane replied. "Would've been here sooner if not for him."

"Belay that," Marko said, punching Kane in the shoulder. "We found 'em, didn't we?"

"Don't touch me." Kane punched Marko back, giving better than he got. As usual, they couldn't go two minutes without fighting. Both brothers were determined to get in the last shot. Things escalated and within seconds they were wrestling on the ground and trading blows.

"AVAST THERE!" Ronan thundered, loud enough to grind everything to a halt. He held up his hands, still locked in irons. "Forgetting something, are you?"

"Right," Kane said, freezing mid-punch.

"Sorry," Marko added, getting up. "Force of habit, you know."

"I do know! They should have called you two Kane and Abel!"

"Actually, I think that one spells his name different," Kane said. "You see, mine starts with a *K* and his ..." He trailed off when he saw the look on Ronan's face. "You're right. Not important."

"Is the rest of the crew here?" Dean asked before Ronan blew his top.

"Aye," Marko said. "The whole fleet is, not countin' the *Reckless*. One-Eyed Jack split our crew up onto different ships, but once we got here, they forgot all about us."

"The rest of the Pirate Youth's downstairs lootin' the castle. We came to find you two."

"Good men," Ronan said. "We need to pick the locks on these shackles. Can you find us something to do the job?"

Marko held up the key ring that Jarret had thrown away. "How about this? Found it outside on the ground. Thought it might come in handy."

Dean laughed out loud and sprang to his feet with a huge smile. "I never thought I'd say this, but you two are *brilliant*."

Kane and Marko beamed with pride. They unchained Dean and Ronan, and the four of them hurried down the steps.

"And you thought we were gonna die in there," Ronan chided Dean as they made their escape.

"We're not out of it yet," Dean replied. Before they left the tower, he stopped Ronan at the door. "When we get out there, I need you to talk to the crew. You were Gentleman Jim's first mate; they'll listen to you. We need to go to the orchard."

Ronan took a breath. He didn't like where Dean was going with this. "You can't stop him, Dean. The whole Black Fleet is here with him. What do you think you're going to do?"

"Whatever I can."

Ronan threw his head back and closed his eyes. "All right," he said. "Let's get the others."

One quick lap around the castle later, Dean was walking to the orchard with a crew of fifty at his back. Every member of the Pirate

Youth had dropped their loot where they stood and followed him without question. All it took was a word from Ronan. Dean was amazed at how quickly they all came together. He didn't have a plan, nor had he given the crew any incentive to rally behind him. There was nothing in it for any of them, but that didn't matter. All that mattered was that Dean needed their help, and Ronan had vouched for him. Never before had someone placed this kind of trust in him—certainly not someone who knew him. Having a friend was a new experience for Dean, but he knew one thing for sure. Friends like Ronan didn't grow on trees.

As they made their way to the orchard, Dean saw firsthand how One-Eyed Jack's pirates had laid waste to the island. Smoke filled the air as fires burned unchecked in the once peaceful villages. Blood stained the road, and people cowered in their homes as the wounded roamed the streets asking for help. Dean still hadn't worked out how to help any of them. He felt better walking in a group than he would have felt walking alone, but he didn't have enough pirates to challenge One-Eyed Jack. He didn't have enough by half. The Pirate Youth could maybe take on one ship of full-grown pirates. Maybe. What about the other eighteen? What did he plan to do about them? What did he plan to do, period?

Dean supposed he'd find out when he got there. Along the way, they passed through the poverty-ridden town, which had been all but destroyed by the battle. With a heavy heart, Dean stepped over the bodies of palace guardsmen on the way to the mill by the orchard. The islanders had made their last stand there, and One-Eyed Jack's forces had routed them. Dean prayed that he wouldn't find Waverly or her father among the fallen. He reached the golden orchard and found the iron trellis and false vineyard raised up high. A legion of pirates milled about in the fields before him. It was a loud, noisy scene. The badly injured were nursing their wounds and drowning their pain in rum. The ones who were just nicked were pretending to be worse off in order to shirk their duty and snare an extra pint of grog. All hands that were shipshape and seaworthy had been put to work in the orchard. Scurvy Gill was up on the ridge directing hundreds of pirates, but to what end, Dean couldn't tell. Gill didn't need that many men to pick the branches clean. There wasn't that much gold left.

The crowd of buccaneers in the field made way for Dean and the Pirate Youth as they passed. One-Eyed Jack's men should have blocked Dean's path to him, but they were too busy carousing to bother, or too badly wounded to care. When Dean cleared the mob, he saw One-Eyed Jack sitting on a large, comfy chair outside the mill.

One-Eyed Jack was feeding Sisto a cracker as Lunk brought him a cup of tea. Dean watched him take a sip and let out a satisfied "Ahh." He turned to Lunk with a smile. "One sugar. Just the way I like it. Thank you." The world's least likely waiter hobbled off, speechless. Dean was just as shocked as Lunk was. Never before had he heard One-Eyed Jack thank anyone for anything. Not unless he was being sarcastic. Dean had expected to find One-Eyed Jack in another one of his moods, but instead, he looked happy. What was going on here?

One-Eyed Jack caught a glimpse of Dean and sat up with a jolt. "Well, well! Prince Seaborne, as I live and breathe! Surprised to see me?" He motioned Dean forward. "I bet you're wondering how I got here so fast. After all, St. Diogenes is two days' journey from this place, and the bird only went out last night! I bet your little brain's tied up in knots trying to figure that one out."

Dean swallowed hard. One-Eyed Jack knew everything.

"Did you really think I was gonna just sit on my hands and wait for you? We followed that ship the *Tideturner* as far as we could before we lost sight of you in the Triangle. We were sailin' these waters for three days when Sisto finally showed up to lead us in. Now, what are you doing here with this pack of feral sea pups? First Mate Rook told me you were locked up in the tower."

Dean blinked. "He's first mate now?"

Rook stepped up behind One-Eyed Jack with his back as stiff as a board and his chin high in the air. "That's right. This is how the pirate king rewards his loyal hearties. If you played yer cards right, you coulda been one of 'em." He drew his index finger across his neck in an off-with-your-head motion. "Too late for that now. Don't try and take any credit for this business. I told him all about how you both went soft once we got here. How you stopped me from lettin' Sisto fly. I fixed you, though. Once I lined up the Ralian boys to take you out, I was free to act."

"You mean you knew One-Eyed Jack was close by, but you held off sending the bird just to save yourself a beating from me?" Ronan asked.

"That's no surprise," Dean said. "He's as much a coward as he is a rat."

Rook snorted out a laugh. "That's yer problem right there, Seaborne. You think yer so much better than me. Yer not. *At all.* Whaddaya call bein' a spy except a fancy name for a rat?"

"He's right," One-Eyed Jack said. "You used to be a good rat too. Unfortunately, somewhere along the line, you got it in your head that you were worth something." He drained his teacup and tossed it away, shaking his head. "What was it made you lose your way here? Rook says you took a fancy to some fair maiden. What was her name?"

"Waverly," Rook said.

"Ah yes, Waverly . . . Let's have a look. She in there?"

One-Eyed Jack snapped his fingers, and the men behind him pulled open the doors of the mill. Inside, along with several other prisoners, Dean saw Verrick, Arjent Ralian, the regent, and his daughter. Rook pulled Waverly out of the mill. "Get your hands off her!" Dean called out, taking a big step forward. Ronan held him back. He couldn't help her that way. Dean took a breath and thought through his options. There weren't many. He was relieved to see Waverly and her father unharmed, but he didn't expect that to last. She and the other prisoners were at the nonexistent mercy of One-Eyed Jack. Their lives dangled by a thread. Waverly looked at Dean, terrified, incensed, and unsure what to make of him. "Don't worry," he told her. "I'm going to get you out of this."

"You are?" One-Eyed Jack laughed. "Hah! If I were you, I'd be worrying about my own self." He got up and walked around Waverly and Rook, brandishing a pistol. "What should we do with her, you think? What can I do to remind you of your place?"

"No! Don't hurt her. Please!"

One-Eyed Jack shrugged. "Why shouldn't I?"

Dean breathed in quick, stilted puffs. He was at a loss for words, searching his mind for something to say. Desperate for anything he could do to make One-Eyed Jack stop. "What's the sense?" he asked. "You've already taken the island. Killing her won't make you any richer. If you've got business with me, let it stay with me. Leave her out of it."

One-Eyed Jack pressed the gun against Waverly's temple and eased back the hammer with his thumb. She closed her eyes, trembling. A tear ran down her cheek. One-Eyed Jack backed away and lowered the pistol. "I was going to do it to teach you a lesson, Seaborne. I started out the day very angry with you."

Dean and Waverly both shuddered and emptied their lungs. "What are you saying? You're not angry anymore?"

"No, I am," One-Eyed Jack said. "But standing in the shadow of this orchard cools my temper somewhat." He tapped the barrel of his pistol against Waverly's forehead. "Lucky for you, lassie. Your little friend over there's got nine lives, and you . . . you just might get to keep yours."

"Please," Dean said. "Enough blood's been spilled for one day. You don't have to hurt anyone else. There's gold left in those trees. Maybe it's not the haul you were hoping for, but it's something, and there's more in the palace. I can show you if you just leave them alone. There isn't much time. You have to get out of here before the storm returns and traps your fleet here for a year."

"I have to get out of here? Not *we*?" One-Eyed Jack turned to Scurvy Gill with an amused look on his face. "You hear that, Mr. Gill? I don't think Seaborne wants to come back with us!"

Standing at the edge of the orchard, Scurvy Gill spit on the ground. "Boy's gone native, has he? Wants to stay with his people?"

"Aye," One-Eyed Jack agreed. "I reckon that's it. A body spends a few days living in a palace, he's bound to develop a taste for it."

"That's not it," Dean said. "The only room they've got for me in the palace is a cell." Lightning struck in the distance where dark clouds were gathering. "I'm telling you the truth. The storm's coming back. You don't want to be on this side of the rain when it does."

"You don't have to tell me, boy. I know all about that storm."

One-Eyed Jack holstered his pistol and walked toward Dean. "Not to worry. Rook told me how things work here on the island. He says you know when the storm will break next year, just in case I want to come back." One-Eyed Jack scrunched up his lips. "Don't worry. I'm not going to make you tell me that. I don't have the patience for waiting. I waited thirteen long years to get back here as it is. I think that's quite enough."

One-Eyed Jack took Dean by the arm and led him up to the edge of the orchard. His choice of words shook Dean. "What do you mean back here?"

One-Eyed Jack nodded with a grin ten leagues wide. "Picked up on that, did you? About time. Aye, I've been here before, Seaborne. Years ago, back when I had two eyes. I swore that if I ever made it back, I'd be a little smarter about what I carted out of here. I'm taking more than the golden harvest this time around. Have a look."

Dean's head was flooded with questions as he walked ahead of One-Eyed Jack to the threshold of the orchard. When he saw what One-Eyed Jack was up to, his heart swirled around inside his chest like a ship being sucked down a whirlpool. An army of pirates, armed with shovels, was digging in the dirt and carefully pulling out roots.

"I've been dreaming about this since you were in diapers, boy. This time, I'm taking the trees."

CHAPTER 32

TRUE COLORS

Something inside Dean exploded.

When he saw One-Eyed Jack's men digging out the trees and loading them onto wagons, he didn't think, he just acted. Before he even knew what he was doing, Dean ran at One-Eyed Jack, trying to tackle him to the ground. He bounced back as if he'd smacked into the side of a ship. Dean recovered quickly and spun around with a kick. One-Eyed Jack saw the move coming a mile off and caught his leg easily. He held it under his arm, refusing to let go. Undeterred, Dean peppered his midsection with a flurry of punches, but they did no more damage than grass reeds whipping away at the trunk of an oak. One-Eyed Jack picked Dean up by the collar and held him a foot off the ground.

"We've got a live one here, haven't we?" He laughed. "What's gotten into you, boy? Don't lose your head now. That part comes later."

Dean reached forward and grabbed One-Eyed Jack's pistols from his gun belt. "You sure about that?" He took one in each hand and aimed them both at One-Eyed Jack's head. "These aren't much good at a distance, but at this range they work just fine." One-Eyed Jack froze. He set Dean down and backed away.

Ronan, Kane, and Marko drew cutlasses and moved in front of Waverly. The rest of the Pirate Youth formed a wall around the entrance to the mill, closing off access to the prisoners. It was a superficial show of strength, since less than half of them were armed. Meanwhile, the hundreds of pirates who were milling about in the fields took a sudden interest in Dean's conversation with their captain.

"What are we doing, Dean?" Ronan asked warily.

"What's it look like?" Dean replied.

"Looks to me like the baby shark has grown some teeth," One-Eyed Jack said. "Good for you, boy. Leastways, when this is over, you can say you gave it your all."

"It's over *now*," Dean said. "Tell your men to leave those trees alone."

"Or what, laddie?" Dean felt the tip of a knife prod his belly. Scurvy Gill appeared behind him. "Unless you wanna see me open up yer gut, you'll drop them pistols right quick."

Dean kicked himself for not checking his blind side. Thanks to that bit of carelessness, his little mutiny was over before it began. Not that he'd gone into the affair with any kind of plan. He had just acted on impulse. The gambit was doomed from the start. Dean lowered the pistols and handed them over to One-Eyed Jack.

"I should've just opened fire," he said.

One-Eyed Jack snickered as he took back his guns. "You don't have it in you." He spun Dean around and pushed him down the ridge. Dean tumbled to the bottom and landed in a puddle of mud. "That's why you're down there and I'm up here. Put him with the others."

"Yer not gonna kill 'im?" Rook asked.

One-Eyed Jack shook his head. "Let his new friends do it. That'll sting you worse, won't it, Seaborne? Getting strung up by the people you tried to save?" He waved a hand at the Pirate Youth. "Best put them all together. That's the side they picked. They're welcome to it."

"Aye," Scurvy Gill agreed. "Never did trust Gentleman Jim's brats. Better off without 'em. Ask me, you should do away with Seaborne, here and now, for raisin' a hand against ya."

One-Eyed Jack cast his eyes up at the heavens and tapped a finger on his chin. "That crossed my mind as well, Mr. Gill. However, it occurs to me that we wouldn't be standing here without him, now would we? Seems to me he honored our deal . . . in a roundabout way. Least I can do is pay him back in kind." One-Eyed Jack laughed as Dean was tied up and placed with the other prisoners. "Seaborne can have his freedom for as long as he lives. Never let it be said that I'm not a man of my word."

One-Eyed Jack and Scurvy Gill went off to inspect the crew's progress excavating the trees, leaving Dean alone with the captive Zenhalans. Dean felt their eyes bearing down on him like the tips of red-hot pokers. He knew they would like nothing better than to see him dead, but just in case there was any doubt, they cursed him, bumped him, and spit at him as he squirmed through the crowd, trying to get to Waverly.

"Are you all right?" he asked her.

She turned away. "Don't talk to me."

"I'm trying to help."

Waverly let out a scornful laugh. "A bit late for that!"

Dean found it hard to disagree with her.

"You want to help us?" Lord Kray asked. "Now? Where do you find the nerve to say something like that? You've ruined us! That orchard is the lifeblood of this island. Without it, our people will starve. Thanks to you, Zenhala is finished."

"And don't expect any thanks for your posturing here today," Arjent Ralian chimed in. "Cheap theatrics as far as I'm concerned. We can see through your lies easy enough."

Dean glared at Lord Ralian. "You're a fine one to talk about lies. You had your sons try to kill me!"

"My sons!" Arjent Ralian said. "Where are they? How did you escape the tower? I swear, if you've harmed them in any way—"

"They're gone!" Dean shouted. He turned to Waverly and her father. "It's true. The Ralians wanted me out of the way to clear a path to the throne. His sons tried to kill me during the trials. When that didn't work, they cut a deal with Rook. Jarret let him signal One-Eyed Jack, not me. I didn't bring them here!" Dean sneered at Lord Ralian, defiant. "Your boys confessed everything before they left. That's right, they ran out on you. Didn't think twice about it. Some family!"

"That's it, Dean, blame everyone but yourself!" Waverly exclaimed. "Don't you understand? Even if what you're saying is true, it doesn't matter. Not now! None of this could have happened without you. *You* are the cause of this."

Dean shut his mouth. She was right and he knew it. Dean had doomed Zenhala the same way he had doomed every ship he had ever spied on for One-Eyed Jack. There was no use pretending it wasn't his fault, or that he didn't have a choice. He did have a choice. He was going to make the right one too, but he waited too long. He wasn't strong enough. Like Waverly said, it didn't matter now. *What's done is done*, Dean thought. *You don't get points in life for good intentions.* There was nothing left for Dean to explain, and no way for him to fix things up with words. It was over.

Dean felt Verrick staring at him. "I believed you were the

prince," he said sadly. "I truly did." Dean fixed his eyes on the ground, unable to look Verrick in the eye. The old man was judging him and punishing himself at the same time. It was too painful to bear.

"I'm sorry, Verrick. I didn't want this."

"I convinced myself you were the one," Verrick said, not really listening. "I wanted the search to be over. I wanted to believe in you so badly."

"I never believed," Dean replied. "Until now."

How could I be so stupid?

Dean realized One-Eyed Jack had played him from the beginning. He had been to Zenhala before. He'd lost his eye stealing the golden harvest and the infant prince thirteen years ago. *What does that say about me?* Dean asked himself. As if the answer weren't obvious. It was all so clear to him now that it was too late to matter. Dean had grown up on board One-Eyed Jack's ships. He was thirteen years of age. His arm was branded with the mark of Aquos. Never in his wildest dreams had he ever imagined this was possible. One-Eyed Jack, being the ice-blooded scalawag that he was, had used him to destroy his own people. Dean was so busy thinking about what was in it for him that he had gone right along with the plan.

Rook found Dean in the crowd of prisoners. He couldn't resist gloating. "Finally figurin' it all out, are ya?" he asked Dean. "I'm so glad I get to see ya like this. One-Eyed Jack told me about his last trip here. I knew before we set sail on the *Tideturner*. The way you dragged yer feet on this job, I thought maybe you suspected, but no. You couldn't see the forest fer the trees." Rook cackled as he moved on to Ronan. "As fer you . . . you had me pegged. I might as well tell ya now. Was me that cut the rope on Gentleman Jim's raft. I set him adrift back when we was lost at sea, and not a moment too soon, neither." Rook pointed to Verrick. "Another day and that one woulda picked us up. He'd-a nursed ol' Jim right back to health, and then where would I be? No, I took care of him just in time!"

Ronan growled and lunged at Rook, but his hands were tied and his ankle was weak. Rook took a step back and Ronan fell flat on his face. "You're gonna pay for this, Rook. Mark me, and mark me well. You. Will. Pay."

Ronan struggled with his bonds like a man possessed, but things being what they were, Rook wasn't worried. "Don't seem likely," he laughed. "Look at ya, down in the dirt like that. Big, tough Ronan MacGuire. Pull yerself together, will ya? Try and go out like a gentleman."

Rook stepped on Ronan's ankle as he walked off, leaving him and Dean to contemplate their failures, which were magnificent in their scope. The hours passed slowly as Dean watched the pirates load Zenhala's trees onto carts and roll them down to the docks. His only hope was that they wouldn't be able to get them all out in time, but One-Eyed Jack would tolerate nothing less than a clean sweep of the orchard. He let his men know that every tree limb they left behind would cost them a limb of their own. As a result, his crew moved heaven and earth to excavate the trees. By the time the sun dipped low in the sky, and dark clouds began to gather, the golden grove was empty.

One-Eyed Jack stood with his hands on his hips, marveling at all he had accomplished. He turned around with a smile on his face and motioned to the vacant plot of land. "Not bad for a day's work!" He chuckled to himself as he approached Dean for a final farewell. "I'm joking, of course. There's more to it than that. Had to put you up all these years to get back here, didn't I?" He looked around, taking it all in one last time. "Zenhala. First time I saw this place, I figured I'd be coming back every year. Lord knows I tried, but I never got near the island again. Couldn't break through the storm. Wouldn't have been caught dead in these waters if not for you, Seaborne. I'm in your debt. In case you're curious, that's the reason why you're still breathing."

Dean looked daggers at One-Eyed Jack. That wasn't what he was curious about at all. "If you're done talking in circles, maybe you can finally tell me the truth. You say you owe me a debt; I say fine. Speak plain and shoot me straight for once. Am I the child from the legend? If I'm the lost prince, say so. Give me that much at least!"

"You're lucky I don't shoot you straight," One-Eyed Jack laughed, tapping the butt of a pistol on his belt. "Maybe next time. Until then, I hereby release you from my service. Fare thee well, Dean Seaborne!"

One-Eyed Jack brought the iron handle of his cutlass down on Dean's head.

That's when the lights went out.

When Dean came to, night had already fallen. There was a brief moment when he woke up that he thought everything was fine. It took all of one second for that to pass. Fresh memories swarmed his brain like angry wasps, and reality came crashing back in. He was in the courtyard outside the Aqualine Palace. Everyone was looking at him. The regent was there, as was Arjent Ralian, and a lot of angry people he didn't recognize. Dean's head was throbbing. Ronan and the Pirate Youth were with him too, and all of them were tied up like he was. Dean could hear Kane and Marko arguing about whose idea it had been to spring him and Ronan from their cell. That lasted until the palace guards knocked their heads together to shut them up. Every face in the crowd looked down on Dean with scorn except one. There was someone missing.

"Where's Waverly?" Dean asked.

All eyes turned to the regent.

"They took her," said Lord Kray in a quiet, broken voice. "They took her and the orchard. Your pirate friends struck this island like a hurricane. Again. I didn't think it possible, but they hurt us even worse than the last time they were here. We're left . . . *I'm* left with nothing."

"This can't be," Dean said. "What are you still doing here? We have to go after her!"

"He'll kill her if we do," the regent said.

"That's the whole point of taking hostages," Arjent Ralian added. "I would have expected you, being a pirate, to know that. Even if we thought he was bluffing, which we don't, he's beyond our reach. The storm has returned. Perhaps you noticed the fountains?"

Dean's head spun around, left and right. He hadn't noticed, but now that Lord Ralian had mentioned them, it was impossible not to. The dry fountains that lined the walls of the courtyard were all overflowing with water. The massive sculpture of winged horses in the center of the plaza was alive with dancing streams, straight from the ocean. Dean looked up at the castle. Water poured out from the mouths of gargoyles and cherubs at every tower window. It ran down the walls inside winding channels that led to additional fountains below. The waterworks made for a sight both awesome and terrible. The spectacle was a wonder to behold, but it also meant that the tempest that had kept One-Eyed Jack at bay for so many years had returned. The great storm of the Bermuda Triangle was back, and Dean was on the wrong side of it. "No! We have to save her."

"It's too late, Seaborne!" Arjent Ralian barked. "We couldn't mount a rescue now even if we wanted to."

"I want to!" Dean shouted. "You can't leave her with him. You can't give up!"

"You're the one who gave us up," Ralian stated, matter-of-factly. "Zenhala is dead, thanks to you. Lady Kray is lost, *thanks to you.*"

"What about your sons?" Dean accused Lord Ralian. "Don't forget them!"

"My sons . . ." Ralian gritted his teeth. "I forget nothing. But all I can do now is see that justice is served." He drew his sword and held it out. "The recommended sentence is death." He looked to the regent.

Lord Kray gave a nod. "Let justice be done."

"No!" Ronan shouted. "You can't do that."

Before Arjent Ralian got anywhere near Dean with his blade, Ronan broke free of his bonds. He grabbed Dean and pulled him away.

"What are you doing?" Dean asked.

"Just follow my lead," Ronan told him.

"You're wasting your time!" Arjent Ralian shouted as the palace guards unsheathed their swords. "You can't save him or yourself."

"Maybe not," Ronan said as the guards closed in on him and Dean. "But I can show you."

"What are you talking about?" asked the regent. "Show us what?"

"Who he is!" Ronan said, shaking Dean by the collar. "He's still got one more test to take, doesn't he? Don't you want to see if he passes?"

The courtyard fell silent.

"Where's the palace fountainhead?" Ronan asked.

Again, the crowd was silent. A voice called out the answer:

"Inside." It was Verrick. "Through those doors. The statue of the queen."

Ronan pulled Dean toward the steps of the palace. "Let me at it."

"Seize them!" ordered Lord Ralian. "SEIZE THEM!" His voice was wild. No one listened. The crowd parted as Dean and Ronan made their way into the palace. "What are you doing?" he shouted in disbelief. He raised his sword and went after them, but the regent blocked his path.

"Hold," said Lord Kray. "First, I would know the truth."

"No!" Ralian screamed. He looked as though he might explode, but the guards held him back as Ronan led Dean to the fountain.

The red marble statue of the queen and the infant prince was a unique fixture of the castle. Its crimson hue stood in stark contrast to the white stonework throughout the palace. The color served as a fitting reminder of the blood the queen had shed trying to save her son. Dean noticed the aquariums that lined the walls around it were filled with water and tropical fish. The storm outside had driven the sea and its inhabitants into the palace along with water for the fountains. He knelt down before the statue of the late queen. Now that Dean saw the fountain in full working order, he recognized its heartbreaking beauty. The water that ran down the queen's body to the bubbling pool at her feet started out as tears on her face. The queen was crying. The thought of a statue created in Waverly's memory made Dean want to cry with her.

Ronan took his arm and pressed the knife against his brand. "Trust me."

Dean felt the knife slice open his skin. It was just a tiny cut, but enough to draw blood. He held his arm out over the pool at the base of the fountain. His blood ran down to his wrist and dropped into the water, red as could be. At first, nothing happened. At least not as far as Dean could tell. Someone in the crowd saw the color before he did.

"Look!" they shouted.

A collective gasp overtook the room as the tears of the queen were transformed. Dean couldn't believe his eyes—or hers. Color swirled in the giant tanks of water on the walls, and Dean shook from head to toe as the room was cast in a cool shade of blue. He rose to his feet, stunned to find the people around him bending their knees.

"There you have it," Ronan said. "He's your prince."

Dean walked to the door in a fog. The fountains outside were all gushing brilliant blue water. The people in the courtyard didn't know what to think. He was their prince—their rightful king!—but he was also a pirate who had destroyed them. What were they supposed to do?

Dean knew what he had to do.

"I need a ship."

He ran back to the statue of the queen. "I need a ship," he said again. "I'm going after Waverly."

"The *Tideturner* is yours," Verrick said.

"It is not!" Arjent Ralian bellowed. "He has been sentenced to death."

"That was before," said Ronan. "He can pardon himself now."

"He'll get no such pardon from me." Ralian advanced with his sword once more, but this time the guards disarmed him and held him tight. "No! This is madness! He's ruined us. He's ruined everything!"

Ralian struggled to break free of the guards' grasp like a maniac, which was exactly what he was. His arrogant, unruffled facade had been shed like a second skin to reveal the madman beneath.

"Did his sons really try to kill you?" asked Verrick, eyeing him with a mix of pity and contempt.

"Every chance they got," Dean said. "But that doesn't matter right now. Only Waverly matters."

"Do you really think you can get her back?" asked Lord Kray.

"I'm going to get her back," Dean said. "Her and the orchard. There's an able-bodied crew tied up outside. All we need to do is cut them loose."

The regent looked at the Pirate Youth. "They'll follow you into the storm?"

"There's a boy on that ship who killed their captain," Ronan said. "They're not about to let that slide."

"It's time to square things, once and for all," Dean said. "We just have to make one stop on the way."

"A stop?" Ronan asked.

"That's right. I've got a plan."

CHAPTER 33

TURNING THE TIDE

A crew of fifty hit the waves on board the *Tideturner*, all of them members of the Pirate Youth. Verrick took the helm, with Ronan serving as first mate. Dean escorted the ship on his kiteboard, scouting ahead. The *Tideturner* raced across the water, riding the wind toward dark skies. Rough seas forced Dean back on board the ship, but the weather was the least of his worries. One-Eyed Jack was nowhere in sight.

Were they already too late?

"She's going to kill you," Ronan told Dean as he climbed back on board. "You know that, right?"

Dean looked out over the side and hauled in his kiteboard sail. "No. She understands me."

A mighty wave rocked the ship and almost knocked Dean back into the sea.

"The storm's just beginning," Verrick said, pointing at the inclement horizon. "Another day and the squall will be impossible to penetrate, but now . . ."—he bit his lip and gauged the wind—"we still have a chance. Provided these boys are fit to crew the ship."

"Fit to crew the ship?" Ronan repeated, incredulous.

Dean put a hand up to keep Ronan's temper in check. "Mark me, Verrick. The Pirate Youth are up to the task."

Verrick gripped the wheel as a bolt of lightning ran a jagged streak from the clouds to the water. "I hope so. Treacherous waters lie ahead."

"I've sailed them before," said Ronan. "It's not the water that worries me, but what lies beneath. Here there be monsters."

"I know," Dean said. He slapped the *Tideturner*'s gunwale. "Here too."

Thunder boomed as the *Tideturner* reached the edge of the storm, and Dean got a cold feeling in the pit of his stomach. It was so loud, it sounded like mountains splitting in half and crumbling into the ocean. The ship crossed an invisible line in the water, and the sun ran for cover, blown out of sight by a wind strong enough to strip flesh from bone. If this was what the storm was like when it was ramping up, Dean had no desire to see it at full strength. High seas pitched the ship up and down. Rain fell as if fired from tiny muskets. Waves pounded the hull like solid rock and immediately transformed into wild rivers that blanketed the deck. Through it all, the Pirate Youth scurried to and fro, manning their posts, holding the ship together. Ronan barked out orders just as he had done on board the *Reckless*. Despite the storm, and perhaps thanks in part to its furious winds, the *Tideturner* made excellent time. The ship forged ahead, gaining ground on One-Eyed Jack's Black Fleet. Verrick kept the wheel steady, clearly impressed with the crew.

"I told you," Dean said. "Cut this lot and they bleed saltwater."

Verrick shook his head. "They just don't have the good sense to be afraid. When you're young, you think you're invincible. Small wonder you're all willing to chase a whole fleet out here."

"It's not the fleet we want. There's just one ship we're after."

"*Maelstrom* ahoy!" shouted Kane from up atop the crow's nest.

Dean's head whipped around. He shot a spyglass to his eyes. "I've got them." The *Maelstrom* was still in the thick of the storm. From the looks of things, One-Eyed Jack had kept every tree from the pilfered orchard on board his ship. "I knew it! They're moving slow, carrying a heavy load. I knew he wouldn't trust a twig of that cargo to anyone else."

"What about the other ships?" Verrick asked.

Dean's eyes swept the horizon. One-Eyed Jack's fleet was clearing the mist and escaping to safety. He lowered the spyglass.

"No. They're all either gone or close to it."

"No escort?

"None to speak of. His fleet's too busy fleeing the storm to help him. Even if they weren't, I'll wager they spent every ounce of shot they had shelling the island. It's just him and us."

The winds howled. Verrick fought the wheel to keep it steady.

"You seem strangely confident, Your Grace. In this case, he is a first-rate English man-of-war—a hundred-and-ten-gun warship."

Dean raised an eyebrow. The *Your Grace*s were back now that he was the prince again. He had no desire for such honorifics, but he let it go. "It *was* a hundred-and-ten-gun ship, Verrick. Have a look." He handed over the spyglass. "A hundred trees on deck . . . how much do you think that weighs? He had to lighten his load somewhere."

Verrick peered through the eyehole and focused the lens. A moment later, he looked up from the glass as if he'd been given a gift. "The gun ports are all empty."

"With that much cargo, he had to cast off his artillery to stay afloat." A wave crashed down on the deck, and Dean grabbed hold of the rigging to keep his footing. "Especially in this weather! It'll just be our crew against his. Hand to hand, steel to steel. Ronan, is the boarding party ready?"

"Just about," Ronan called back.

"Tell them to hurry!"

"Maybe you want to tell them yourself?"

Dean looked at the crew gearing up for battle. They looked just as tough as they had the day they first met, when they had chased him through the streets of Bartleby Bay. He left them to their work. Dean looked through the spyglass again and set his sights on the *Maelstrom*. He saw One-Eyed Jack shouting orders at his men, and Scurvy Gill enforcing them. The pirate crew struggled to fight the storm on board the *Maelstrom*'s crowded deck. They were none too pleased to be caught in the Bermuda Triangle's fabled tempest. Unless Dean missed his guess, every man jack of them was scared stiff.

Good. We can use that.

Dean scanned the ship from stem to stern, but he didn't see Waverly anywhere. He had hoped to find her on deck, but it made sense that One-Eyed Jack would keep her stowed somewhere below. She had to be down there. One-Eyed Jack wouldn't part with his hostage any more than he would his coveted treasure.

The *Tideturner*, slender sloop that it was, sped onward through the storm like a shark chasing a whale. One-Eyed Jack's leviathan was less than one hundred feet away when Ronan walked up, holding a kiteboard and sail. "All set," he reported. "Now or never."

"Now for us, and never again for them," Dean replied. He clapped Verrick on the shoulder. "We'll leave you enough men to sail the ship home. Best get yourself out of here. Before conditions get any worse."

Verrick bristled at the thought of leaving. "I'm not going anywhere. I set all this in motion when I brought you to Zenhala. You'd best believe I'll see it through to the end."

"Don't be daft," Dean said. "You didn't set this in motion; One-Eyed Jack did. There's nothing more you can do out here. You can't fire on the *Maelstrom*. Suppose you sink *it*? Then what? You lose your trees again. We have to *take* that ship, Verrick. Make no mistake, this ends one of two ways." He pointed at their target. "We come back on board that vessel, or not at all."

Verrick grunted. "I don't like it. You're children going up against grown men. You saw what they did to the island. They're a cutthroat crew, hard as coffin nails."

"That may be," Dean said. "But hard men soften up once you scare them out of their pants."

"It's what we do," Ronan added. "We do it well."

Verrick looked at the crew with their face paint, skull masks, and kiteboard rigs. They had swords on their belts and clubs in their hands. A handful of them were staying behind to help crew the *Tideturner*. The rest were getting ready to fly. Dean buckled a sail harness around his waist as they closed in on the *Maelstrom*. "This is your prince talking now, Verrick. Go home. You've done your part."

A look of reluctant acquiescence came over Verrick's face, and he bowed his head toward Dean. "As you command, Your Grace."

Dean reached out to shake Verrick's hand. "I told you to call me Dean."

"Is that an order?"

"It is."

Verrick took Dean's hand in his and gave a hearty shake. "Godspeed, Dean."

Dean joined the other young raiders on the gunwales. "Are you ready, lads?" he shouted. The Pirate Youth gave a mighty cheer. Dean stuck his fingers in his mouth and blew out an earsplitting whistle. The snapdragon surfaced off the starboard bow and gave a high-pitched howl in reply.

Verrick backed up off the helm as the beast emerged from the water. He caught himself mid-step and stayed put to keep the wheel steady. "That one's going to take some getting used to!" he said. Dean smiled as the snapdragon raced alongside the ship. They were ready for battle. All of them.

Ronan shrugged at Dean. "I guess she does understand you."

Dean grinned a devil's grin. "Let's go to war."

CHAPTER 34

RIDERS ON THE STORM

Dean caught the wind in his sail and leapt out into the abyss. Ronan and the others followed, screaming loud enough to wake the dead. Dean figured some of them shouted to instill fear, while others worked to overcome it. For his part, he felt a strange sense of peace as he rode the storm into battle. A single-minded vision of what he had to do seized his brain, refusing to allow any thoughts that might distract from his mission.

He flew across the waves like a vengeful spirit, chasing down the wicked. He knew in the eyes of One-Eyed Jack's crew, that was exactly what he and his mates would look like. Every bloodstained hand on board the *Maelstrom* was a death-dealing snake, but under the dark stormy skies, in their skull masks and makeup, the Pirate Youth looked like a fate worse than death. They dive-bombed the deck, a wild pack of howling wraiths. The snapdragon looped around the ship, screaming with fury. One-Eyed Jack's men ran for cover.

So far, so good.

Dean hit the deck and drew a sword. It was a well-known fact that pirates—and all men of the sea, really—were superstitious creatures. Dean had counted on that, and the crew of the *Maelstrom* didn't disappoint. How could they? They were sailing in the Bermuda Triangle—waters that had been a cursed, stormy grave for more sailors than a man could count. They were under siege from a sea serpent and skull-faced raiders straight out of their worst nightmares. The Pirate Youth preyed on those fears as they ran around the *Maelstrom*, terrorizing its crew. It was the same scam that Gentleman Jim's boys had run for years now, but their secret was as safe as ever. Dean watched with pleasure as the toughest crew in the Black Fleet begged for mercy from children half their age.

"Ghosts!"

"Don't take me! Please!"

"I want me mum!"

Only Rook knew the truth of what was going on. "Stand and fight, ya cowards!" He stamped his feet, hollering at his new shipmates. "Stand and fight! They're not ghosts. It's just my old crew!"

The snapdragon whipped its tail into the side of the ship, and a row of splintered railing flew into Rook. When he picked himself up off the deck, he saw Dean and Ronan standing before him. For someone who had just been shouting about a lack of ghosts on deck, Rook sure looked like he'd seen one.

"How about you, Rook?" asked Ronan. "You going to stand and fight?"

When he saw the fire in Ronan's eyes, Rook backed away. The craven pirate ran scrambling up the rigging to the yardarms.

Dean threw Ronan a crooked grin. "Happy hunting."

As Ronan climbed after Rook, Dean went off in search of Waverly.

He ran across the ship, bobbing and weaving his way around dozens of one-sided skirmishes as the Pirate Youth overwhelmed the *Maelstrom*. Dean watched them execute surgical strikes with methodical, calculated moves that took away their opponents' advantages. The Pirate Youth were smaller and weaker, but smarter and faster. They worked their way across the ship, wielding clubs and blackjacks—items that served as great equalizers in any fight. As their prey cowered before the bogus, ghostly front they presented, the young pirates blindsided them and bound them up tight. They attacked in teams, and before One-Eyed Jack's men even knew what had hit them, the Pirate Youth moved on to the next target.

With the pirate crew occupied, Dean kept after his quarry.

He had his head on a swivel, searching out Waverly and One-Eyed Jack.

His first stop was the captain's cabin.

It was empty.

Dean moved to the brig.

Empty.

All around him, terrified pirates were fleeing artificial apparitions. Dean found a man hiding in a galley cupboard. "Got another one in here!" he shouted.

"No!" the man pleaded, closing himself back up in his hiding place.

The Pirate Youth kicked the doors in and dragged him out.

Dean continued his search, getting more and more worked up with every empty cabin he found.

Where is she?

Eventually, Dean came to the ship's magazine, which held all its powder and shot. The *Maelstrom*'s stores were very much depleted, but that hardly mattered. The ship had neither guns left to fire nor steady hands to man them.

Dean heard a pistol click behind him. He hit the deck.

The shot missed by a wide margin but found the next-best target. The musket ball ignited a half-full powder keg, and the resulting explosion was big enough to blow a hole in the roof. Dean cried out as a broadside of wooden shrapnel turned him into a pincushion. He had a good idea who was responsible—the one man on board who wouldn't be going down without a fight. When the smoke cleared, Dean looked over the burning embers of wood fragments and saw One-Eyed Jack. He tossed his gun away and drew a cutlass from his belt. "You don't know when to quit, do you, boy?"

Dean got up, racked with pain. He had covered himself in time to avoid serious injury, but there wasn't an inch of skin on his back without a splinter. He held out his blade, the tip pointed squarely at One-Eyed Jack. "The girl. I want her back."

One-Eyed Jack and Dean circled each other, stepping over flickering patches of fire. Rain poured in from overhead, beating down the flames, but not extinguishing them. "Making demands, are we, Seaborne?"

"Aye," he said. "That I am."

"Sorry. I already tossed her overboard."

Dean growled. "If that's true, you'll be going over next. There's a sea serpent out there licking its chops for you. I hear you're scared of them."

"You see me quaking?" One-Eyed Jack swung his sword at Dean, hard and fast. Dean got his cutlass up in time to block, and their blades clashed. "I saw that water snake you brought with you. You call that a sea serpent?" One-Eyed Jack pulled back and brought the sword around again, this time harder than before. Dean countered, but the blow knocked him back a few paces. One-Eyed Jack charged forward and went at Dean again. He turned the thrust aside, but One-Eyed Jack came right back with another blow. He gave no quarter. Dean would have been chopped into fish bait if One-Eyed Jack's attacks weren't so sloppy. They came in big sweeping motions that betrayed every move before he made it. Dean met his blade and deflected it every time, but crossing swords with One-Eyed Jack took its toll. Like a castle gate stopping a battering ram, sooner or later it had to give. Jack was too strong. He was bigger, meaner, and fought dirty to boot. Dean parried his latest advance, but One-Eyed Jack stomped on his foot and pushed. Dean fell back. One-Eyed Jack raised his sword high in the air like a black-hooded executioner. Dean thought he was dead, but he heard a mighty thunk, and One-Eyed Jack's hands flew forward without his blade. The killing blow had been halted by a wooden beam in the ceiling. One-Eyed Jack stumbled forward and stepped on the flat of Dean's sword, denying him the use of it. His own cutlass remained trapped in the ceiling behind him. Dean sprang up empty-handed as One-Eyed Jack went after him with his fists. Dean grabbed a loose board to block a punch, and One-Eyed Jack smashed right through it. Dean tossed the broken pieces away and kept moving.

"Stand still, boy. I promise I'll end you quick."

He swung a looping right hook that Dean ducked under easily, but it was a feint that left him open to an attack from the other side. The pirate grabbed Dean by the collar and held him fast. "I should have killed you years ago. This is what I get for being charitable."

Dean planted a foot on One-Eyed Jack's leg, swung the other on his chest, and ran up the man like a ramp. When he got to his face, he pushed off hard and flipped backward out of his grasp.

"Agh!" One-Eyed Jack bellowed. "Get back here!" He threw a knife at Dean, but missed. He threw another. That missed as well.

"You're rusty," Dean taunted. "Too many years of Scurvy Gill throwing knives for you." He grabbed One-Eyed Jack's sword from the ceiling and slipped in behind him. Dean slashed at One-Eyed Jack's back, drawing blood and cutting away his gun belt and knives. One-Eyed Jack spun around like lighting, catching Dean's face with the back of his fist. It was a reflex punch. Dean had no time to dodge it.

"These hands are all I need for you."

Dean staggered back into fire, and the heat of the flames made him jump. It came as such a painful shock that he dropped his sword. One-Eyed Jack chased Dean through the magazine, swiping at him with big meaty paws. Dean led him around the room, then back toward the flames that had singed his boots. Unarmed, he spun around toward One-Eyed Jack and dove between his legs as another explosion of powder, smaller this time, erupted in One-Eyed Jack's face.

One-Eyed Jack screamed in pain and rage. He turned around with a frenzied look and a face full of splinters. Dean climbed up broken beams to the top deck above.

"Where do you think you're going?"

Dean was halfway through the hole in the roof when One-Eyed Jack grabbed his leg. He tried to kick himself loose, but One-Eyed Jack wouldn't let go. He was pulling Dean back down when the ship rolled hard to starboard. A huge wave crashed in from the port side, and water flooded the empty gun ports, filling the magazine. Dean and One-Eyed Jack shot into the air atop a geyser of seawater. A moment later, they were deposited on the top deck. Dean saw One-Eyed Jack roll over and get up with a sword lodged in his shoulder. He must have landed on it. Another giant wave dropped an avalanche of water on them both. This time, when Dean wiped the seawater from his eyes, One-Eyed Jack was gone.

Gone?

Had he been thrown overboard?

The ship rolled hard on the waves, nearly capsizing. The *Maelstrom* rocked back and forth, threatening to sink before the battle ended. With half the crew tied up and the other half running away, there was no one to steer the ship. Dean looked out on the wild, lawless sea. He had to find Waverly, and prayed that One-Eyed Jack had been bluffing about throwing her off. As the boat tumbled this way and that, Dean scanned the deck. He saw Ronan and Rook near the stern of the *Maelstrom*. Rook's yellow-bellied nature was on full display as he continued to evade Ronan, moving in and out between the golden trees that were tied up all around. With his strength, Ronan could have knocked Rook out with one punch, but he had to get a hand on him first. Rook used his speed, taking advantage of Ronan's injury and losing him among the stolen trees.

The ship listed hard to port, stretching the lines that bound the trees together until they snapped. Thick ropes struck Ronan like bullwhips. He went flying back as if kicked by a mule. Rook stepped across the tangled lines of thick rope and stood over Ronan with a dagger. Dean shouted to the others, telling them to help Ronan, but the wind was too loud, and the bulk of the Pirate Youth were either busy with One-Eyed Jack's crew or had their hands full keeping themselves upright and on board. Rook raised his knife high in the air and was about to stab it down when the snapdragon reared up across from him and hissed. Rook backpedaled and got caught up in loose ropes from the trees.

Another wave hit. The ocean picked up a handful of white-blossomed trees and carried them off. Rook's legs flew out as he went sliding along with them. He grabbed the handle on a hatch and held on tight as the trees went overboard. They dangled over the water, pulling him down. He cried out for help, but the only one there was Ronan.

By the time Dean got there, Rook was gone.

"He begged me to save him," Ronan admitted, looking down into the bubbling darkness. He gave a slight shake of his head. Dean put a hand on Ronan's shoulder. Whatever else it might have been, it was justice too. No bones about it.

Ronan's eyes shot open. "Look out!"

He pushed Dean out of the way as One-Eyed Jack came charging in from behind with a head full of steam. He swung his cutlass right where Dean had been standing and hacked clean through the railing of the ship. One-Eyed Jack cracked Ronan in the face with the iron handle of his cutlass and sent him tumbling down below deck. Dean swung his sword, but One-Eyed Jack spun around to block it. Their blades clashed and held in place, each one of them trying to overpower the other. One-Eyed Jack looked down where the cluster of trees had sunk into the ocean. "I'm going to take that lost gold out of your hide," he growled.

One-Eyed Jack pushed hard, knocking Dean back a few steps. He moved in with a downward, diagonal strike. Dean put his head down and somersaulted under the blade, springing back up a few feet away. "Where's Waverly?" he demanded.

One-Eyed Jack chortled. "I told you. She's gone where you'll never see her again. Leastways, not till you follow her over the side."

"No!" Dean swung his sword, and the blades collided again. He pulled back, then darted forward with another attack. The clang of steel matching steel rang out over and over as Dean unloaded on One-Eyed Jack, trying to cut him down. One-Eyed Jack fought back against each strike, but each of his counterattacks hit with less ferocity than the last. The puncture wound in his shoulder had robbed him of his power.

Sisto flew in, pestering Dean as he fought, distracting him. One-Eyed Jack bashed Dean in the face with a vicious head butt. His arm might have been wounded and weak, but his head still hit like an anvil. Dean stumbled back, seeing stars. One-Eyed Jack was about to end him when something bounced off his forehead. Dean didn't see what it was or where it came from, but One-Eyed Jack floundered on the deck as more projectiles struck him. Dean covered up, thinking the rain had turned to hail, but he soon realized the pellets were hitting only One-Eyed Jack. Not only that, they were gold in color. Ronan and the Pirate Youth were pelting him with fruit from the golden trees.

"Stop! STOP!" One-Eyed Jack roared. "MY GOLD!"

"It was never yours!" Dean shouted, revitalized. He sliced through the air with a blow that nearly cut One-Eyed Jack in half. "*My life* was never yours!" Dean went on the offensive as his mates showered One-Eyed Jack with his ill-gotten loot. The extra hands had swung the odds in Dean's favor, and something inside him snapped. Dean's sword flew out and drew blood as tiny gold pellets the size of cherries bombarded One-Eyed Jack. "All my life you told me I was nobody. Worthless! And I was stupid enough to believe you." He slashed One-Eyed Jack's shoulder, causing his sword arm to drop low. "I bought what you were selling because I thought you were someone . . . some*thing* . . . to be feared. You're not!" Dean threw a kick into One-Eyed Jack's stomach as the remains of Zenhala's golden harvest flew at him in furious torrents. "You're nothing without your crew." He slashed One-Eyed Jack's forearm, causing his sword to fall from his hand. "Where are they now, Jack? Done! Beaten! *You're* beaten. We've got the numbers here."

One-Eyed Jack looked around and saw his men all tied up. As his victory slipped away, he snarled like a trapped animal and ran at Dean in a last-ditch effort to take him down. Dean spun around low, swept Jack's legs, and dropped him on his chin. One-Eyed Jack flipped over onto his back and froze when he felt the tip of Dean's blade poke his neck. The barrage of gold nuggets stopped. "You call yourself a king, but you're just another pirate. There's nothing special about you."

One-Eyed Jack craned his neck as far back from Dean's cutlass as it could go. "You think you're any different?" he sneered. "We're cut from the same cloth, you and me."

Dean shook his head. "You're wrong. I know the truth now."

"What truth?" One-Eyed Jack asked. "That you're the lost prince of Zenhala?" He tried and failed to keep from laughing. "Is that what you think?" The snickers grew into uncontrollable guffaws.

Dean blinked through the rain. One-Eyed Jack's laughter bothered him. "My blood turned the palace water blue."

"I don't care if it turned it green," One-Eyed Jack said, cackling. "You're no prince! You're a decoy!"

"What?"

"You're not a prince!" One-Eyed Jack said again. "The real prince died ages ago. Fever. You're just another sea-born orphan. I kept you around in case the Zenhalans ever caught up with me. Scurvy Gill branded your arm himself. You're a decoy, Seaborne! That's all!"

One-Eyed Jack roared with laughter. Even in his current predicament, the thought of Dean believing himself to be royalty delighted him no end. Dean's stomach went cold. He hated to admit it, but One-Eyed Jack's story held water. There was no one on earth who was worse equipped to care for a newborn baby than a fleet of pirates. The child One-Eyed Jack stole away probably didn't last more than a week on St. Diogenes, if he lasted even that long. That didn't explain the blue water in the palace fountains, although Dean began to have an inkling of how it might have happened. Something about the way One-Eyed Jack was laughing told Dean he was telling the truth. For once in his life, he was telling the truth.

"So be it. I didn't come here to be king. I came here for my freedom, and I'll have it." Dean raised his sword and stood poised to strike. "Before I do, I'll ask you one last time. Where is Waverly?"

One-Eyed Jack kept laughing. "Look behind you."

Dean's head whipped around. He looked across the deck of the ship and saw the girl he came to rescue caught in the clutches of the dirtiest dog on board. Scurvy Gill was standing at the edge of the boat with the barrel of a flintlock pressed against Waverly's cheek.

CHAPTER 35

THE BELLY OF THE BEAST

Ｗe was right about you to begin with," Scurvy Gill told Dean. "Too big fer yer britches, plain and simple. Maybe this'll cut ya down to size." He slid the pistol under Waverly's chin and cocked the hammer.

"No!" Dean shouted. Out of the corner of his eye, he saw Ronan take a step toward Scurvy Gill. "Nobody move!" he blurted out.

Ronan halted and Dean pulled his sword back from One-Eyed Jack's neck.

"Don't," Waverly warned. "Dean, don't you drop that sword!"

"Quiet, you!" Scurvy Gill ordered.

Dean threw his sword down and stepped away from One-

Eyed Jack. "There! I let him go. It's done. Your turn, Gill. Let her go."

Scurvy Gill loosened his grip on Waverly and backed off of her, but only far enough to reach a sack of gold lying at his feet. He snorted out a laugh as he tossed the bag into a lifeboat. "Who said I was gonna let her go?"

Waverly glared at Dean. "You see? I told you not to drop your sword!"

"Let's talk about this," Dean said, taking a cautious step toward him and Waverly. "What do you think's going to happen if you get in that boat? I'll tell you. The same thing that'll happen if you pull that trigger—you'll die. Look around. The ship's ours. You can't weather the storm without it. Hurt her and we'll take you apart piece by piece, but you let her go. . . . Let her go and we'll let you live." He looked at One-Eyed Jack. "That's the deal." Lightning struck the sea, close to the ship. The thunderclap that followed punctuated Dean's terms as the *Maelstrom* swayed on the sea. "I suggest you take it before the storm takes us all."

"That's the deal on the table, eh? Whaddaya say, Cap'n?" Scurvy Gill called out as One-Eyed Jack got up off the deck. "We gonna take the sea pup's deal?"

One-Eyed Jack straightened his collar with a look of indignant contempt for the young pirates around him. He was surrounded and outnumbered, but his pride wouldn't buckle. "I'd sooner take my chances on the waves." He looked at Dean's sword on the ground and shook his head with a condescending laugh. "That's two times you should have killed me when you had the chance. Dumb, boy. Stone dumb. Blow the man down, Mr. Gill! Let's see how tall this lot stands with Seaborne a head shorter."

Scurvy Gill turned his gun toward Dean and pulled the trigger.

"No!" Waverly shouted, pushing his hand up.

"Blast you, wench!" Scurvy Gill cursed as the musket ball flew harmlessly up to the sails. He swung the butt of the pistol around, trying to hit her. She dodged it, but wobbled, losing her balance.

"WAVERLY!" Dean shouted as she fell over the side.

He rushed to the gunwale in time to see Waverly regain her composure mid-fall and execute a perfect swan dive into the sea. A wave splashed Dean's face and he lost her. He called her name again but heard nothing in reply.

Scurvy Gill was directly to his left. Dean had every right to grab up his sword and run him through, but he grabbed a kiteboard and sail instead. The Pirate Youth converged on Gill and One-Eyed Jack, but Dean wasn't with them when they made their move. He was already jumping into the water after Waverly.

At first, he dropped like a stone. Then Dean's feet found the footholds in the board and he let out his sail. The wind pulled him into the night. He swirled around in the air as if caught in a tornado, and he wrestled with the crossbar to control his flight path. Lightning flashed, illuminating the angry sea. Dean saw nothing but the most fearsome storm imaginable. He thought he heard Waverly, but thunder drowned out her voice. He turned his board in the direction from where he thought it had come, struggling to ride winds that threatened to carry him to the moon. No matter which way he turned, his trajectory was predominantly skyward. Only with great effort was he able to angle his sail to bring himself back down to the surface of the water, but the moment he splashed down, the storm pulled him right back up. Lighting split the sky again, and Dean scanned the waters for Waverly.

There! He saw her flailing in the foamy surf, trying to stay above the waves.

"Hang on! I'm coming!"

But he was going the wrong way. He twisted his body in midair and swung his sail around to face the opposite direction. A gale took hold of him and yanked him back across the water, but the wind proved too wild. Going far too fast, Dean blew right by her.

Using every ounce of strength he had, Dean wrenched down on the crossbar, turning the sail to come around for another pass. Something heavy hit the water near Dean, and he saw that it was One-Eyed Jack and Scurvy Gill escaping from the *Maelstrom* in a gig. The Pirate Youth had run them off the boat.

Dean turned from the path of a twelve-foot tsunami before he got crushed under its weight, shifting his focus back to Waverly's position—and his own. He felt naked in the storm without a ship, literally hung out in the wind to twist. His eyes again swept the sea for Waverly. She showed up, coughing water, twenty feet off. Dean couldn't believe the currents had pulled her so far so fast. He turned his sail one last time, changing course. This time, as he closed in on Waverly, he ditched the sail to make sure he stopped where she was. He skidded up to her and slid off the board, catching a hand on a freshly vacated foothold. She grabbed on to the other foothold, relieved to have something buoyant to cling to, though not necessarily happy to see Dean. "What are you doing out here?" she shouted. "Are you crazy?"

"Isn't that obvious?" Dean replied.

Waverly lost her grip on the board, but Dean caught her and pulled her back on. She fought off his assistance and found the grip on her own. "Let go of me. I hate you!"

"Hate me later!"

"There won't be a later." She balled up her fist. "I'm going to hit you now."

"That's fine! Just keep your eyes peeled for the ship while you do it."

A wave shook Waverly, and she nearly lost her hold on the board again. She relaxed her fist and latched both hands onto the float. "I can't let go," she said, resigned to not hitting him.

"I know."

She looked around. "I can't see anything, either."

Dean nodded, a grim feeling of dread settling in. "I know."

Huge swells threw them across the water like floating wreckage. Dean held tight to the board, craning his neck to check all sides for the ship. He too saw nothing. He didn't say it, but he wondered if the *Maelstrom* was even still out there. It was impossible to tell. All was dark and murky. He could barely keep his eyes open in the rain, and the bounding sea rocked him without mercy, keeping him disoriented. The *Maelstrom* might have been right behind him, or it might have succumbed to the storm. He had no way of knowing. He prayed the ship was still afloat and that they would spot it before the storm carried them out of reach. As the reality of their situation sunk in, Dean regretted not taking to the water with more of a plan. He'd found Waverly, but he had not saved her by any means. How long before the storm separated, drowned, or dropped them somewhere ten miles off? As they bobbed along, helpless and exposed, Dean searched the dark horizon for the ship and his mind for answers.

What now?

One-Eyed Jack and Scurvy Gill came into view, struggling to stay afloat in the tempest. They were close, within range of a musket ball. As Dean's luck would have it, One-Eyed Jack had a shooter in hand. He looked daggers at Dean as he extended his arm and took aim. Dean was about to duck his head underwater so as not to give One-Eyed Jack a clear shot, when lightning flashed and a massive shadow loomed behind him. Dean trembled and reached for Waverly when he saw what it had come from.

A giant sea serpent rose from the deep—big as a whale and twice as long. Armored scales covered its hide like shields, and waves of sharp fins ran down its back like swords. One-Eyed Jack dropped his pistol into the water as the creature's snakelike body writhed in the air and looped around his tiny boat. "Now, that's what I call a sea serpent," Dean said.

One-Eyed Jack's face displayed the kind of terror reserved for men who knew their time had come. The beast opened its mouth wide, and One-Eyed Jack screamed as it dove down toward him. Dean shut his eyes and held tight to Waverly as a surge of water displaced by the diving monster pushed them away. When he opened his eyes, he saw only broken pieces of wood scattered across the sea where One-Eyed Jack had been. Lightning flashed again. The sea serpent was still there, sizing up its next meal.

Then the snapdragon surfaced. It shrieked at the massive sea serpent like a dachshund barking at a mastiff, but it made its voice heard. Dean didn't know if the snapdragon was vouching for him and Waverly or claiming them for itself. He didn't care, either. The answer came when the giant sea serpent departed and the snapdragon took Dean and Waverly on its back.

"Are you sure this is okay?" Waverly asked, grabbing hold of a dorsal fin.

"Relax," Dean replied. "Where's your sense of adventure?"

The snapdragon swam them to a ship at the edge of the storm. Someone threw down a line, and the pair of them latched on. As they were hauled on board, Dean recognized the *Tideturner* and Verrick at the helm. Finally free to relax without consequence, Dean flopped on the deck. He had not been this relieved to be out of the water since his involuntary shark tank expedition a week ago. *A week*, he thought. It felt like longer. Dean's head was swimming and his ears were waterlogged, but he heard Verrick give the order to heave to and flee the storm as fast as possible. It took until they reached clear skies for Dean's breathing to return to normal and his heart to dislodge from his throat. He looked over at Waverly, who was draped in a blanket and coming down from the same hypersensitive state of shock as he. Their eyes met as the *Tideturner* sailed back to Zenhala on the wings of a gentle breeze.

"Are you all right?" Dean asked her.

Waverly's only reply was a silent stare. She was still furious with him. Dean figured that if she was well enough to hold on to her anger, she was well enough to talk.

"Just so I'm clear, is the wedding back on now, or what?"

Waverly's whole body jolted. Her face was so full of rage it looked like white-hot lava might erupt from her eyes. "There isn't going to be a wedding. I hate you."

"You have a funny way of showing it. I mean, you did save

my life back there, after all. Almost got yourself drowned for your trouble."

Waverly scoffed. "Everyone makes mistakes."

"I'm glad you feel that way. I came after you, hoping you might forgive mine."

"There's no forgiving what you've done. Saving me doesn't change anything, Dean. Trusting you is the worst mistake I ever made. The orchard is lost. The island is doomed. You lied to me. You're a pirate, for God's sake!"

Verrick cleared his throat and leaned in to offer Waverly a spyglass. "Things aren't always what they seem, my lady."

Curious and confused, Waverly took the glass from Verrick. She got up and raised it to her eye. As she looked to the island, Dean kept his eyes on her. He knew what she would find in its sights. Beneath the light of the moon, the dancing water of the Aqualine Palace was visible in all its blue brilliance.

When Waverly put down the spyglass, she was startled to find Dean standing so close to her. He had crossed the deck to show her the cut in the sigil on his arm. She touched the mark that had turned the water blue.

"It can't be."

"*Maelstrom* ho!" someone called out from the crow's nest.

Dean snatched the spyglass from Waverly's hand. He focused the lens and breathed a sigh of relief when he saw the ship emerge from the fog behind them. It was headed back toward Zenhala with Ronan at the helm and the golden orchard intact. Dean flipped the glass over, handing it back to Waverly.

"I don't understand," she said. "Are you the prince or aren't you?"

Dean said nothing. She had asked the crucial question.

The answer was entirely up to him.

CHAPTER 36

NEW HORIZONS

"I can't believe you told her you weren't the prince!" Ronan complained.

A day had passed, and Dean and Ronan were back on board the *Tideturner*. It was early in the morning, and One-Eyed Jack's ship, the *Maelstrom*, was docked in Zenhala's main harbor alongside them. The work of bringing the trees back to the orchard and replanting them was under way. Everyone on the island not moving trees was fast asleep. The two boys were alone on the main deck, getting ready to put to sea.

"I had to tell her," Dean said.

"No. You didn't. The only people who knew the truth was our crew and One-Eyed Jack. The Pirate Youth wouldn't have said anything, and One-Eyed Jack's dead! Even if he hadn't been gobbled up by that sea serpent, no one would have trusted a word he said. Your blood turned the palace water blue. That's all anyone cared to know. You were in."

Dean couldn't argue with Ronan's logic. He was right. They could have gotten away with it. "It was a good trick. Wiping your blade with flowers from the golden trees before you cut my arm? That was quick thinking."

Ronan grunted. "Had to do something, didn't I? They were gonna have your head, and mine right after. Someone had to save our lives."

"I owe you for that, Ronan. That and more. You're a good friend."

"You're not so terrible yourself, but I'll be tarred and feathered if I understand you, mate. All you had to do was keep your mouth shut and you could have been king—a *real* pirate king!"

Dean shook his head. "No. It wouldn't have been real, because it wouldn't have been true. I'm done lying about who I am. I didn't come here chasing life in a castle. I came to earn my freedom. I told you I'd do whatever it took to get it."

"Aye, but to give up the greatest treasure in all the Caribbean!"

"Depends on how you look at it," Dean said. Waverly and her father appeared at the end of the dock. "Maybe I did, maybe I didn't."

Ronan saw what Dean was looking at and shook his head. "She could've been your queen. I'll give you two some time alone and see how Verrick's doing. Have a few more things to check before we head out to sea."

Ronan disappeared below deck, and Dean went to the gangplank to wait for Waverly and her father. When Dean had brought her and the orchard home safe the day before, Lord Kray had wanted to crown him king right there on the dock. By then, Dean had already told Waverly the truth. He wasted no time telling her father. It was a relief to do so. That night, completely unburdened, Dean slept the deepest sleep he'd ever slept. For the first time in his life, he relaxed. Truly relaxed. One-Eyed Jack was gone, and Dean's life as a spy was over. When he woke up that morning, dawn's light brought a new day and new horizons to pursue.

"You're really leaving," Waverly said when she reached the ship.

Dean turned up his palms. "I asked you here to see me off, didn't I? Verrick's given me the *Tideturner*. He said that when he told me it was mine, he meant it."

"But why so soon?" Waverly asked.

"The storm's only getting worse. If I wait too long, I won't be able to leave at all." Dean pointed out across the sea. Dark clouds swarmed the horizon, but they kept their distance and the sun shined down happily on Zenhala's colorful landscape.

"Why don't you stay here?" Lord Kray asked. "I understand your shipmates have all opted to stay. Why not you?"

"I just can't," said Dean. "I'm sorry."

"Stay for my coronation at least. It would hardly be worth celebrating if not for you."

"Father wants to give you a medal," Waverly added. "Zenhala would have been lost if not for your actions yesterday. We avoided disaster, thanks to your bravery."

Dean chuckled. "The only disaster you avoided was the one I brought here with me. Funny how no one seems to mind that now."

The regent, soon to be the king, smiled. "All's well that ends well."

Again, Dean could not argue. All had ended well. One-Eyed Jack's crew was locked up in the tower, and the Pirate Youth were retiring from piracy, making Zenhala their home. The golden harvest would be used to help the needy once again, and the island of Zenhala would finally have the king it deserved. The Ralian family's scheming had all been in vain. Neither Junter, Jin, nor Jarret would ever occupy the seat of power they coveted so greatly. As for their father, Dean saw him up on the *Maelstrom*, frantically searching the deck for his trees. He wouldn't find them.

"What's going to happen to him?" Dean asked.

Waverly's father sighed. "It's already happened. We have no proof of Arjent Ralian's crimes as you described them, but that is of little consequence. Even if we did, I can imagine no punishment more fitting than that which he has brought upon himself. Without his family trees, he is ruined. Without his sons, his line will end with him. The House of Ralian is finished."

Dean almost felt bad for Arjent Ralian. Then he thought about all the times he'd tried to have him killed.

"I wonder what happened to his sons," Waverly said. "Do you think they got out?"

Dean thought a moment before answering. The Ralian brothers had left before the Black Fleet invaded, like rats deserting a sinking ship. "They got out. I'd bet my boots on it. We haven't seen the last of them."

"What about us?" Waverly looked sad. "Have you and I seen the last of each other? Is this good-bye?"

"I'm afraid so," Dean said. "Unless . . ." He gave a shrug.

"Unless what?"

"You could come with us."

Dean's offer caught Waverly off guard. "Come with you where?"

Dean pointed. "Out there. Way out there. Anywhere."

"You want me to come with you?" Waverly asked again.

Dean nodded. "And you want to go."

Waverly looked to her father, no doubt worried what he must be thinking. "I was afraid this might happen," he said.

"Your Grace," Dean began, relieved to call someone else by

that name. "I told you I didn't know what to expect to find when I came here. That was the truth. But what I found on this island was worth far more than the gold in its trees. For the first time in my life, I have friends. People I care about who care about me. Your daughter is one of them. With your permission, I'd like to ask her to come with me when I leave."

"With my permission," Lord Kray repeated. "You've already asked her. I suppose this is the price of my crown? The lost prince giveth and the lost prince taketh away, is that it?"

"I'm not the lost prince," Dean said. "I'm nothing special. Just plain old Dean Seaborne."

Lord Kray shook his head. "You might not be a prince, but you're a special young man, no two ways about it. Only one soul in ten thousand would have given up this crown. You have great honor."

"It's new," Dean said. "Yesterday, I was going to ask her to run away with me." Lord Kray looked upset. "But that's not who I am anymore," Dean added, putting up his hands. "I'm done taking things from people. I'm asking if you'll let Waverly come with me."

Lord Kray's face took on a pained expression. Dean was well aware of the magnitude of his request, but he had to ask. Lord Kray looked at his daughter. She looked back with hopeful eyes. "Is this what you want?" he asked her. Waverly clasped his hands with a pleading expression. Before she could reply, Lord Kray turned away. "Oh, don't answer that. It's obvious you want to go more than anything. I can see that as plainly as everyone else here. The truth is, I've known for years."

A hatch on deck opened up, and Ronan emerged with Verrick.

"There you are," Verrick announced. "Stocked up with enough provisions for six months at sea. It's a fine ship, but I still say you need an extra hand or two to sail it."

"Not to worry, Captain Verrick," Lord Kray said drily. "Young Seaborne is recruiting new crew members now."

"Oh?" asked Verrick. He looked at Waverly and understood Lord Kray's meaning. "Oh. I see."

Lord Kray shook his head at Dean.

"You place me in an impossible position. On the one hand, how can I refuse the boy who saved my kingdom? On the other, how can I let my daughter go to sea with pirates?"

"Technically, I was more of a spy than I was a pirate," Dean said.

"That's true," Ronan piped up, eager to help. "Me and my crew, we were the pirates. But we never hurt anybody. Not if we could help it. Conning people out of their ships, that was our bread and butter. We were more like seafaring con artists than anything else. Our captain taught us to be honest thieves."

Lord Kray grumbled, his face stern and unamused. Waverly had her head in her hands. Dean glared at Ronan.

"I'll stop helping," Ronan said.

"That would be wonderful," Dean said. "Thank you."

"Thirteen years ago, pirates took a child away from this island," Lord Kray said. "Here it is, happening again."

"He is asking for your blessing," Verrick argued in Dean's favor.

Lord Kray shook his head. "She's my only daughter, Verrick. I can't allow her to leave this way."

Dean and Waverly shared a helpless moment, their hopes fading before their eyes.

Lord Kray put up a finger.

"Not without an escort."

Waverly and Dean's faces lit up at the possibility. Verrick understood perfectly. "Very good, my lord. If the lost prince is gone, my duty as a seeker is no more. I now owe my allegiance to the king and his daughter, the princess. Should you choose to let her go, it would be my privilege to serve the crown in defense of her life and honor."

Lord Kray closed his eyes and nodded reluctantly. "Very well, then. You have my blessing."

Waverly rushed to her father's side. "Truly, Father? Do you mean it?"

"I do," he replied. "You are free to go, by order of the king." He shrugged. "Well, a king soon enough." Waverly clutched her father tightly, and he opened his arms to do the same. "I know I can't keep you here forever, no matter how much I'd like to. I just hope you know that no matter how far you go in this world, you always have a home to come back to." He looked up at Dean. "And I expect you to bring her back, young man. For one month a year, at the very least."

Dean nodded. "You have my word."

"I hope so," said Lord Kray. "After all, this place is home to you too."

Dean smiled at that. A home. A true home for him, not someone he was pretending to be. "Thank you. I've always wanted that."

Waverly hugged her father again. "Thank you, Father."

Thunder rumbled in the distance. "I still don't see why we can't wait until the storm breaks before we leave," Ronan said. "I could use a vacation."

Dean wouldn't hear of it. "I've waited thirteen years for my life to begin. I can't wait another day, let alone ten months. Anyway, don't waste time thinking about those clouds out there, Ronan. Think about what's on the other side of them."

"And what might that be?"

"Every place you ever wanted to go but couldn't."

"What about sea serpents?" Lord Kray asked. "You're not concerned about them?"

"Not a problem," Dean said. "Snappy will look out for us."

"Snappy?" Waverly asked.

Dean banged a hand on the gunwale and whistled loudly.

"Snappy!" he called out. The snapdragon surfaced off the starboard bow. It let out a playful bark as it circled the ship. "What? I had to call her something, didn't I?" Dean took great pleasure in the stunned looks on everyone's faces.

"Take care of my daughter," Lord Kray told him, offering Dean his hand.

"I promise we'll stay out of trouble," Dean said. They shook on it.

Ronan put a hand on Dean's shoulder and spoke softly in his ear. "Thought you said your lying days were done."

Dean raised his right hand in a pledge. "On my honor as a gentleman," he said with a wink. He turned to Waverly. "Are you ready?"

Waverly shivered with delight as she stepped on board the ship. "Let's see. I haven't packed a thing or planned a step. I'm not at all dressed to travel. . . . Yes. I've been ready all my life. I can't believe this is really happening."

"Neither can I."

"Where are we going first?"

Dean's imagination called up an ocean of possibilities. For the first time ever, he was free to explore every last one. "We'll find out when we get there. It's a big world. Let's not keep it waiting."

ACKNOWLEDGMENTS

It has been a while since I have had the privilege of writing an acknowledgments page for a new novel. Three years, in fact. I have to admit, there were moments during that time when I wondered if I ever get to do it again. If you are reading this, know that I am more thankful than ever to be in this club of published authors. It is not something I take for granted. The feeling I get when I walk into a bookstore and find one of my books on a shelf remains as much a thrill to me today as it was the first time it happened. It has become something I need in my life, and I don't get to that place alone. I have lots of help.

The first person I want to thank is you—for reading. For keeping me in this club. I hope you enjoyed Dean's first adventure. There are more on the way.

I also want to thank Chris Richman for being the first person to believe in this story apart from myself, and for ultimately selling the book. Thanks are also owed to Greg Ferguson, who acquired the book for Egmont USA, and Jordan Hamessley, my editor. The opportunity to work with a talented, insightful editor such as Jordan is a gift, plain and simple. Her guidance and ability to read between the lines pushed me to get Dean's story right. The book you are currently holding would not be the same without her.

I also want to thank the entire Egmont team, including Andrea Cascardi, Margaret Coffee, Michelle Bayuk, Georgia Morrissey, and Joy Simpkins. I have said it many times before: I may have written the story, but they are the ones who make it a book. Working together with all of you and collaborating on Matt Armstrong's wonderful cover has been one of the highlights of my career.

Finally, I want to thank my family for always being there. My mom, my brother, my two boys, and my beautiful wife . . . together we make so much good stuff happen. I love you all.